MOONLIG

The chamber was .... that burned half-heartedly on the bedstand. Alexandre lay down beside her, his lips pressed to her neck as his hands caressed the mounds of loveliness that hardened beneath his touch. "Are you asleep?" Turning her ever so gently, he slipped her underdress off her shoulders and down her arms.

"Nay," she replied, shutting her eyes as he began to ease her dress down to the floor . . .

"You are as I imagined and more," he said, his breathing changed. He lay down beside her and drew the covers over them. "I will not hurt you," he whispered. "I am your husband."

"Nay," she whispered, turning her head to one side as his mouth traced a line of kisses.

"Trust me," he replied, stroking her tenderly. Trembling, she narrowed her lips and held her breath as he continued to kiss her, kisses that bespoke love and caring . . .

SUMMER EYES

"Joan Lancaster is a writer with a fresh new approach sure to have an impact on the historical romance market."

—Jenna Darcy, author of
The Very Best and *Heart of the Storm*

JOAN LANCASTER

SUMMER EYES

CHARTER BOOKS, NEW YORK

SUMMER EYES

A Charter Book / published by arrangement with
the author

PRINTING HISTORY
Charter edition / April 1988

ISBN: 1-55773-015-6

Charter Books are published by The Berkley Publishing Group,
200 Madison Avenue, New York, New York 10016.
The name "CHARTER" and the "C" logo are
trademarks belonging to Charter Communications, Inc.

PRINTED IN THE UNITED STATES OF AMERICA

10 9 8 7 6 5 4 3 2 1

For Dougal, Oho, ·Julie and Margaret

SUMMER EYES

1

———————◆———————

"I hate wheels!" Dominique Winburn moaned, her nose pressed against the small window of her father's buggy. She did not know for certain where the wheels would carry her that May morning in 1798. She only knew if they did not stop churning soon, she would scream.

" 'Tis not much farther now," Doctor Elton Winburn said, admiring the mass of topaz curls that cascaded over his daughter's shoulders. He had promised her a prize if she traveled with him to Bucks County that day. The trip would be neither business nor necessity, he had assured her. He would look at some land near a place called Walking Purchase, and they would stay the night at her cousin Jenny's in Newton.

The winter had left the rolling countryside above the Delaware River wet and clean. The smell of spring perfumed the air. Snowy white dogwoods sparkled in the sun while drifts of colorful, wild daffodils waved beside the road. Dominique begged to stop and pick flowers beside a duck pond that overflowed into a creek.

"Dewberry Farm is on this road," her father said, helping her down from her seat.

Dominique's eyes sparkled. A farm meant horses. Perhaps the prize was a long-awaited Arab?

1

"Nay, 'tis not a horse, child." Elton chuckled, reading his daughter's mind. "Don't we have enough of them yet? You have the elegant black mare from Virginia, then there's the chestnut stallion I call mine, but which in truth is yours."

"Father dearest," she crooned, standing atop a rock and gazing up at him on the road. "You know well my mare is no jumper and I'm overly fond of the hunt. You promised me a milk-white Arab when I was little and I've not forgotten." Her arms were laden with lilies and the hem of her gold-colored traveling dress was splattered with mud. She cupped a lily to his nose believing he played a game with her. "I shall ride him home by the shortest route," she said smartly. "But you should have warned me to wear my boots and habit."

"You shall have your Arab when you make me a grandfather and not before," Elton replied, stone-faced. "As for a gift horse this day, I regret 'tis not what I had in mind."

"Damn!" she fumed, tossing the flowers in the air and tramping off for the buggy. "You've tricked me for the last time, father. I would not have come had I known your *prize* would be another man."

"I'll have none of that sailor's talk you learned in Boston, miss!" he fired back, sorry she had found him out and stifling a snicker in spite of himself. He took out a handkerchief and mopped his brow, thinking he was getting old. "Now that you know, I expect you'll conduct yourself like a proper lady, do you hear?"

Receiving no reply, he stared at her back. Was it possible the girl really preferred horses to men? Ah, but she was young still, not yet the age of eight-and-ten. There was still hope. Not that there had been no suitors. Aye, there had been scores, and all had found themselves at a loss for words when she cleverly turned the conversation to horse breeding or, worse, conveniently riding off to leave her father to do the entertaining. Aye, there were those foolish enough to try and woo her on horseback, he recalled with a grin. But none who could ride as well or as fast as his Nikki.

He straightened his face and considered the caliber of men she had to pick from of late. "Come along, Nikki," he said kindly, turning her around. "Monsieur Chastain is not like the others, I promise."

"Must I ride farther cooped up in that hotbox, father?" she whimpered, thrusting out her lower lip in a pout.

He remembered her abhorrence of buggies and realized she had come a long way from their home in Germantown without a tantrum. " 'Tis just over the hill, child. We stand on Chastain land even now."

The doctor's buggy was black and plain with well-traveled wheels that transported the physician-surgeon over most of southeastern Pennsylvania. But the team in hand was far from plain. Two magnificent and perfectly matched bays from England kept up the pace now, superbly conditioned and handsomely harnessed in silver and black leather.

Elton looked first at his animals and then at his only child, nearly overwhelmed by pride. A masterpiece in symmetry, the girl was already more shapely than her mother had been at her age, if that were possible, since he considered his Adele a voluptuous beauty who still turned men's heads. Ah, but Nikki had more than good looks, the girl was unique in his way of thinking; a long-legged filly with asking eyes and a fiery temperament the likes of which he had never observed in another female. 'Twas unfortunate she was happier in a stable than in a parlor, but he had only himself to thank for that. It was he who had introduced her to the fleet-footed beasts. Now she would never be satisfied until she had a stud farm of her own nourished by the blood from the sultan's finest, if you please.

He shrugged, thankful he had seen to a proper education in Boston's finest school for females, even if she had spent her time enjoying the city instead of learning to be a lady. Strong of will and high-spirited like a racehorse, he concluded with a grin. But a thoroughbred could be gentled by the right master and he believed he had found just the man.

"You will like Alexandre Chastain," he began tactfully. "He's from Martinique and the South and has a promising career in medicine."

"My French is deplorable," she groaned, pressing her nose to the window and picturing Alexandre Chastain as another intellectual bore. Worse still, he was a Frenchman and most probably short. Another of her father's hideous choices for a husband, she decided, pressing her lips together in a grim line. If Alexandre Chastain was anything like the men of science she had met in Winburn House of late, she would refuse to set foot outside the damnable buggy. She would rather die of heatstroke than suffer a lovely afternoon wasted in listening to a deep discussion on blood-letting and leeches.

"Alexandre studied in Paris," Elton said.

"Aye, father"—she sneered—" 'tis certain Monsieur Chastain is related to Napoleon himself."

"He is."

There was no more said as the buggy's wheels whirred past long rows of blossoming fruit trees and freshly plowed fields. The horses raced by thick woods splashed with color, slowing to turn into a long poplar-lined drive that led to a stone carriage house where they came to a smooth stop.

Dominique looked out the window and sighted a handsome crane-necked phaeton. Perhaps the day would not be lost? A carriage that smart was bound to be drawn by fine horses. A huge stone barn overlooked moist green fields that stretched for miles and a brick walk bordered in young boxwood led to a long two-storied farmhouse, shuttered and roofed in black. Big friendly elms sheltered a stream that rushed through a springhouse.

Half a dozen hounds, gray grizzled and massively boned, ran up to greet the visitors. The bays held their heads high as if repelled by the hounds that smelled their hocks and the wheels of the unfamiliar buggy. They watched curiously as the shaggy beasts stood on hind legs to peer inside the little windows.

"It appears no one is home but the hounds," Dominique said wistfully, eyeing the dogs.

"Alexandre is here somewhere, 'tis certain," Elton said confidently, stepping down between the pack. A dinnerbell clanged near the house and cats by the dozen poured out of the barn. A man wearing nothing but leather breeches and wooden clogs emerged, his unbound hair like polished brass in the sunlight. Elton smiled broadly and hurried around the buggy to hand his daughter down.

"Elton, my friend, *bonjour*! Welcome to Dewberry Farm." Plainly embarrassed by his state of undress, the man hastily plucked a linen shirt from the branches of a young pin oak and slipped it over his nakedness.

"Alexandre!" Elton replied, tugging Dominique along by her sleeve. "I've brought my daughter to meet you."

Dominique lifted her chin and studied what she believed to be her father's prize. Pleased by his height and genuine masculinity, she was ill prepared for the show of lean hard limbs, skin-tight breeches, and bare chest. She dipped into a little curtsy and peeked through lowered lashes to hide her curiosity. She had made up her mind not to like Alexandre Chastain and she would not weaken now.

"Mademoiselle," Alexandre said, " 'tis indeed my pleasure at long last." His voice was deep and resonant, and his bow formal as he planted a kiss on her gloved hand. "Pray forgive my attire, or lack of it," he said humbly. "I did not expect you until midday."

" 'Tis noon, monsieur," she retorted, glancing at the sun and thinking him no gentleman but an oaf drenched in sweat and offensive barnyard odors. She guessed his age at thirty years, his warm brown eyes and boyish grin so engaging she found it necessary to tighten her lips.

Alexandre squinted and raised his hand against the light, or was it her reflection? Surely an angel of the Lord could not have been more radiant. Her hair shimmered in the sun's rays. Her eyes, bright and alive beneath arched brows reminded him of the rain forests of Martinique, and her lips revealed the slightest hint of a smile. "I was in the process of giving Jeanette a bath," he explained awkwardly, looking down at his soaked breeches and exposed legs.

"Jeanette?" Elton queried.

"*Oui*, doctor, the old girl tangled with a skunk this morning and I fear I've not yet rid her of the smell."

A tall, dripping-wet Irish wolfhound peered out of the barn and, seeing company, ran up to Dominque's skirts where she shook her coat vigorously.

"Jeanette!" Alexandre exclaimed too late.

Elton stepped back and eyed his Sunday breeches, now thoroughly sprinkled. Jeanette finished shaking and slid on her side through new grass, rolling on her back and moaning with relief. Dominique caught her father's eye and held her tongue, recalling his words of warning that morning.

"Mademoiselle, I am truly sorry," Alexandre said in earnest. "Jeanette dearly loves the ladies. Can you ever forgive her?"

Her face near crimson, Dominique glared at her father and held up her dripping skirts.

"Shame, Jeanette!" Alexandre scolded. "Look what you've done to the lady's dress. Now you must tell her you're sorry."

The shaggy bitch looked up into her master's face with black-rimmed eyes and apparent shame.

"I'm waiting," Alexandre urged firmly.

Jeanette sat up on her haunches and waved a paw and Dominique brought a hand to her mouth to suppress a giggle, a charming dimple beside her lips where none had been before.

Elton laughed heartily. "My daughter forgives the beast, Alexandre. Now, might we see the litter I've heard so much about these past weeks?"

"*Oui*, doctor, but first allow me to take you and your lovely daughter inside where my housekeeper will clean and dry her dress."

Dominique grabbed her father's arm and pressed her nails into the fabric of his sleeve. "The air from your hound's tail will dry my skirts, Monsieur Chastain 'Tis late and we stay the night at my cousin's in Newtown. Even now she awaits our arrival."

Elton lifted a bushy brow to cast a disapproving glance her way.

"*Oui*, I quite understand," Alexandre said, accepting her aloofness as a challenge. "Come, I'm eager to show off my pups." With a sweep of his hand he bid her to walk beside him, relishing the new feelings engulfing him that made him suddenly aware of being male. "Six survived and only one is not available," he said. "You will understand why when you see him."

Six shaggy pups frolicked on the lawn beside a fenced herb garden, their legs ungainly, their ears too big for their heads. Thinking them homely and wanting desperately to leave, Dominique wished to teach her father a lesson. She did not take kindly to his clever maneuvers to wed her to a man of medicine like himself and she would not sit still like some poor laboratory mouse waiting for the outcome of his experiment. Wedlock may be what most girls her age wanted but she was clearly not most girls. Her plans for the future did not include husbands or bawling brats and her father and his Frenchman would not stand in her way.

She observed her father evaluating the litter and scanned the grounds quickly for a horse. If she could borrow or steal a mount that could walk she would ride to her cousin Jenny's and leave her father behind with his foul-smelling friend.

At that moment one big-boned pup, taller and sturdier than

the rest, trotted away from the others and settled abruptly on her feet with a groan.

"Go away," she whispered, wriggling her slipper from beneath the pup's claws so as not to attract attention. "Go back to your master." Cocking his head, the pup yawned and curled his lip. "Go away, I tell you, pup," she said more firmly now. "Don't you understand good English?"

The pup began to bark, his voice high-pitched, his hair abristle. The pup's mother came running, followed by a larger hound and half-grown pup. Dominique swore beneath her breath and looked up to see the hound's master striding leisurely toward her behind the pack, returning her blameless look with a frown.

"I'm afraid Adam has found you out, mademoiselle," he chided. "Hounds are excellent judges of character. They know when one is not what she pretends."

How impudent and insulting! She gave him a scathing look as she stomped off toward the buggy in a huff.

"Mademoiselle!" he called. "I meant no offense, pray do not leave!"

"Go back to your hounds, monsieur," she cried sharply, walking briskly across the yard through a flock of peafowl and geese who parted raucously as she passed. But an aggressive gander blocked her path. "Shoo!" she screeched, sweeping up her damp velvet skirts in an attempt to march around the bird. But the gander refused to budge, and to her horror nipped at her heels. "Ohhh!" she squealed, turning to flee blindly through a freshly fertilized flowerbed.

Alexandre shouted something in French and peeled off his shirt to thwart the bird's attack, coming to Dominique's aid by sliding his arm about her waist and lifting her from the ground.

"Put me down!" she demanded, pressing her gloved hands to his bared chest. His eyes wandered over her face and drank in its dewy freshness. "Are you hurt?" he asked, ruffling his dark brows and holding her so close she felt the strength of him.

"I am not!" she choked, catching her breath and pushing him away.

Elton jogged across the yard. "What happened?" he asked, taking note of his daughter's expression and muddied slippers as Alexandre put her down.

"I shall wait for you in the buggy, father," she said, her voice uneven.

Alexandre watched as she tottered along the side of the house with the pup, Adam, at her heels.

"I must apologize for Nikki's mood this day, Alexandre," Elton said. " 'Tis none of your doing, believe me. She's angry with me and has been from the start. You see, I tricked her into coming here today."

"Tricked her, doctor?"

"Aye, my boy," Elton said with a twinkle in his eye. "Nikki can be difficult at times, like all females," he added in a fatherly tone. "You see, she had her mind set on getting a horse today."

Alexandre frowned. "Forgive me, Elton, but I don't see the point."

"Of course you don't, my boy. 'Tis a long story and one you should hear. My daughter has this dislike of buggies and coaches and the like, any manner of wheel or rudder that keeps her penned in for a spell. 'Tis a condition she's lived with since childhood."

Alexandre looked at Elton in puzzlement.

"I've thought long and well on it, my boy," Elton said, shaking his head. "I cannot place the cause. Too much freedom, some would say. 'Tis a fact the girl's spoiled, I don't deny it. I've given her too much, I suppose."

"The horse, Elton?"

"Aye, the horse," Elton nodded, drawing out his handkerchief to wipe his brow. "You see, Nikki is mad about horses and wants to raise the beasts. 'Tis all she talks about, really." He smiled, taking note of Alexandre's baffled expression. "Somehow, she got it into her head we came here to get a long-awaited Arab, milk white if you please." He chuckled.

Intrigued, but uncertain he understood any of it, Alexandre listened intently as the two doctors walked, trailed by panting hounds and mewing cats, past a hedge of hemlock.

"Which brings me to my daughter's fondness for hounds, my boy," Elton said, after a long explanation of his daughter's idiosyncrasies. "The girl dearly loves to ride and cannot get her fill, yet she has this unsatiable need to surround herself with hounds." The middle-aged doctor's face crinkled and he smiled broadly, fully aware his daughter was quite satisfied with one pet dog at home. "Much like yourself, eh?" he asked, stroking his graying beard.

Alexandre blinked in bemusement, for he had seen no indication of this great love of hounds in the girl.

"I see by your face you're confounded, my boy," Elton said, his hazel eyes twinkling as he circled the younger physician's shoulders with an arm. "Don't worry." He winked. "Nikki is riled now but she'll get over it. She always does." He took a gold watch from his frock-coat pocket and studied the time. " 'Tis my wish to purchase that big pup for her, Alexandre. The one you call Adam."

Alexandre looked at the teacher he had come to love and respect. 'Twas unthinkable to part with the hound that represented years of selective breeding. Adam was the foundation for a new line. The hound was irreplaceable.

"Name your price, my boy," Elton urged, stroking his beard. "I know the beast is valuable."

Alexandre smiled. Perhaps he had the solution to both their needs? "Elton, my friend," he said, taking the professor's arm and guiding him to a far corner of the yard, beyond earshot of Dominique. "I make the hound a gift to your beautiful daughter."

"Nay, my boy," Elton said, holding up his hand. "I did not come here to presume on our friendship. You are more than kind, but name your price. I know Adam is your best."

"*Oui*," Alexandre readily agreed, "but money must have no part in this. Pray hear me out."

They discussed the hound and the girl at length then, neither admitting to the other they had the same end in mind. Talking quietly on the other side of the house, they finally struck upon a bargain. In exchange for the hound, Alexandre would have the privilege of visiting Winburn House as often as deemed necessary.

"To study the hound's progress, of course," Elton said solemnly.

"To be sure," Alexandre agreed.

Further, the hound would be delivered in a fortnight by the hound's master himself, and the father would make certain his daughter did not stray far from home.

Unaware she was part of a gentlemen's agreement, Dominique sat on the cold step of her father's buggy and talked to the pup. " 'Tis no prize I see," she said sourly, turning up her nose and wiping her slippers in the grass. "Or do you prefer to be called Adam?" She narrowed her lips. " 'Tis a stupid name for a hound. If you were mine, your name would be Macbeth."

The pup looked at her through the matted hair over his eyes and leaned solidly against her velvets.

" 'Tis a fitting name for a handsome hound," she said. "Even if you're not Scotch."

The hound threw back his head and Dominique laughed merrily. She wanted to take the beast in her arms and clutch him to her breast, but she would not. Nay, she would not give Alexandre Chastain the satifaction of knowing she fancied the pup.

"The ill-mannered oaf!" she fumed, standing up to shake off the hard discomfort of the buggy's step. She had seen more than she wished of her father's "prize." The trip back to Germantown would be miserable and long and she would surely be made to suffer a lecture on ladylike behavior.

"Your master is a cad!" she announced to the pup that wagged his tail. "You agree, eh?" she teased, thinking the hound smarter than his master and sneaking a pat between his ears. "No gentleman expecting a lady would meet her bare-legged and bare-chested," she complained. She walked back and forth in the drive. "Did he think to impress me with his physique?" she asked the hound. Bending low, she whispered in the pup's floppy ear. "If you ask me, he's too pale for my liking and *he's* the one who needs a bath!" She stood erect and lifted her chin, feeling the heat of anger flood her cheeks. The nerve of him speaking to her in such a manner, then having the indecency to remove his shirt a second time! What did he take her for? Some sniveling milkmaid who never saw a man before? Perhaps if he combed his hair and put on clothes befitting a gentleman and a physician, his looks would improve. But he was sorely in need of manners.

Adam hung his head and her eye caught sight of her father rounding the house. She casually walked to the bays to stroke their noble heads.

The men came across the yard to join Dominique. "You must forgive us, Nikki," her father explained. "Alexandre and I have been discussing a curious malady we find fascinating. I fear we were forgetful of the time." Elton smiled slyly at Alexandre and shook his student's hand. " 'Twas kind of you to show us your pups, Alexandre."

"My pleasure," Alexandre smiled. "I regret you and your lovely daughter could not stay for tea. My housekeeper will be greatly disappointed." He approached Dominique with care. "Adieu, mademoiselle, my apologies again for my hounds and myself. It seems we're all out of manners this day. You must come again and meet my Percheron family."

Dominique's eyes grew wide, their gold flecks stirring feverishly against the muted green. Percherons on his miserable acreage and she had missed them! Alexandre grinned. "Emma, my mare, will foal any day now," he said. "But 'tis an event a fine lady such as yourself would have little interest in." He sniffed the air. "What a foul smell. I pray you did not have the misfortune of stepping in something." Her dislike of him intensified and she turned on her heel to step up into the buggy before he could assist.

"*Au revoir*." He smiled, waving as her father joined her on the seat and took up the reins.

The wheels bumped over the deep ruts on the road back to Newtown and Dominique slid down on the leathers of her father's buggy, certain she would soon be ill. The sun was setting behind the hills. She felt cheated of her prize, recalling Alexandre's words earlier. Could she have mistaken his meaning? No matter, she would not be seeing the smart aleck again.

"Nikki," her father said, speaking for the first time since they left Dewberry Farm, "I was most distressed with your behavior this day. I can only hope Monsieur Chastain understood."

"I'm sorry, father," she lied softly.

"I am your father and I understand your moods, my dear, but when Alexandre Chastain comes to sup in a fortnight, I expect you will make this day up to him and conduct yourself like the lady I know you to be."

Seething at the prospect of seeing Alexandre again, Dominique squirmed in her seat and thought she would retch, although she consoled herself with the plan to go riding early in the day and not return until the Frenchman had gone.

"And you will not embarrass me by going off on your horse, young lady. You will help your mother prepare for our guest and you will make me proud that you are my daughter."

"Aye, father," she responded, narrowing her lips and scheming a way to rid herself of her father's "prize" once and for all.

2

The fortnight passed all too slowly for Alexandre. Then, one glorious morning before dawn, he placed the hound, Adam, in a wicker basket and lifted him into a carriage by the light of the moon. "I shall return in two days' time," he told his housekeeper, Mrs. Yarborough. Then, thinking of the high-strung filly, Nikki, he added: "Perhaps sooner."

"Ye're givin' up yer hound fer that girl, I see," Mrs. Yarborough complained, shivering in the cool morning air and watching her master load the carriage. "Beats me how ye can do it, sir, after all yer hard work and lost sleep over them pups."

Alexandre looked at the stark white face and small blue eyes. He should not have to answer to a servant, but the woman had been like a mother to him for the past several years. "Just because you have served me faithfully these many years, 'tis no reason to nag me now," he scolded gently. "Pray keep your advice to yourself." He gave her a fond farewell squeeze on the arm and took the basket of food she held out to him.

Mrs. Yarborough set her heavy jaw and shook a stubby finger. "You know as well as I, Adam's the best ye ever fed on this farm, and there's none finer in the isles," she grumbled.

" 'Tis no loss, I tell you, woman," Alexandre chided with a grin. He felt his patience ebbing and examined the harness of the gray Hungarian. "I shall have my hound and the beautiful damsel in the bargain."

"Ye're a might sure if you ask me, sir. I wouldn't trust a lass who didn't see fit to come inside a gentleman's house like a proper lady."

Alexandre ran his hand over the leg of the lead gelding and spoke softly. "I have tried to explain why Mademoiselle Winburn did not sample your delicious tea that day, Mrs. Yarborough, just as I've tried to make you see my reason for parting with the hound." He sighed, certain his words were wasted on deaf ears. " 'Tis senseless to discuss it further. You'd best go in before you catch cold."

"Ye're desperate the way I see it!" the woman cried. She stood back and pulled a heavy shawl about her. "You'll lose yer heart and yer hound together, mark my words! Ye have no time to court a girl and ye know it well. What with yer studies and all these critters to care for. You'll be sorry, I tell ye. You'll be sorry. . . ."

Alexandre stepped up into the buggy seat and raised the whip over the Hungarians' heads and the carriage bolted out of the drive, thundered across the yard, and turned into the long lane on two wheels. Moments later the farmhouse had all but disappeared behind the trees, but Mrs. Yarborough's words still echoed in his ears. Of course the woman was wrong. He had Elton's hound, did he not? 'Twas a bargain between them. The hound in exchange for courting the girl. If she could not be swayed to his way of thinking after a reasonable amount of time, then her father would have a talk with her. But only after all other forms of gentle persuasion had failed. 'Twould be a most pleasurable task taming the shrew. Ah, but if he were fortunate enough to make Dominique Winburn Mrs. Alexandre Chastain, then what? How would he talk her into going to the South with him, and how would she take to hounds in her house and owls on her bedpost?

Adam cried out as if to mock Alexandre's delusions. Was he daft? No girl in her right mental capacity would leave the civilized North to travel to the untamed wilderness of the South! Certainly not a hard-headed and spoiled female who despised carriages and hated rudders. "Fool!" he said,

cracking the whip over the horses' heads to drive them onward
at a furious clip.

The four-wheeled conveyance, equipped with a dog compartment behind the seat, arrived at Winburn House by dark
and was met by servants carrying torches. Elton Winburn stood
at his front door and waited for his guest to come up the steps.

"So good of you to come, Alexandre," Elton said with a
broad smile. He shook his student's hand heartily. "You're
staying the night, of course?"

"I think not," Alexandre replied.

"Relax, my boy," Elton advised low. "Nikki is at home and
her mood is bright."

Alexandre tied a hasty bow around the pup's neck and
brushed the dust from his breeches. "After you, doctor." He
smiled.

Like its master, Winburn House was warm and hospitable.
Inside its door a leaded crystal fanlight reflected candleglow
from sconces set high on the light green walls. Shadows
danced all about, and the hardwood floors gleamed beneath a
long pine table banked with white tulips in a pewter bowl.

"Nikki!" Elton called up the staircase that curved above his
head. "Monsieur Chastain is here!" Smiling for his guest's
sake, Elton tried his best to appear calm. Where was the girl?
He had seen her just minutes ago. If she had gone off riding he
would have her hide! "Nikki!" he called again.

Alexandre's face paled.

"Wait here," Elton advised Alexandre. "I'll just go and find
my wife. The girl is most likely with her."

Alexandre straightened his cravat, then checked the shine on
his boots and the crease in his buff-colored breeches. The pup
squirmed in his arms as he heard a pleasant rustle of skirts that
make him look up. His breath caught in his throat as the most
beautiful creature he had ever seen stood smiling down at him.

"Monsieur Chastian," Dominique said sweetly. Dressed
beguilingly in palest pink and deepest green, she glided down
the stairs, and it wasn't until her slippered foot touched the
floor where he waited that he could breathe.

"So very pleased to see you again," she said sweetly,
offering her hand.

"Mademoiselle," he said, bending low to kiss her hand and
realizing his own were trembling.

"You have brought your hound?" she said with a curious look.

"For you," he replied with care.

Her eyes met his for a brief instant, then darted about in search of her father. "For me, monsieur? But . . . I don't understand."

"There you are, dearest," Elton said, rushing from the hallway. "Alexandre wants you to have the hound, Nikki. 'Tis your prize for taking the long trip in the buggy a fortnight ago."

"The . . . prize?" Nikki stammered.

"The hound is yours, dearest," Elton smiled. "Earned fairly."

Her carefully planned strategy temporarily interrupted, Nikki felt tears filling her eyes as she rushed to loop her arms about her father's neck. "You did not forget," she murmured. "Thank you, father dearest."

"Alexandre's the one you must thank, child," Elton said low, removing her arms and pulling out his handkerchief.

Dominique smiled, confident it was her father who had purchased the hound. "I shall love him forever," she said.

"Take the beast into the garden and allow him to stretch his legs," Elton said, blinking a tear from his eye. He diverted attention from his momentary weakness by wiping his brow as if sweating profusely, though the room was washed by a cool evening breeze. "Monsieur Chastain as well."

Taking the pup into her arms, Dominique clutched the beast to her breast and planted a kiss atop its head. "This way, Monsieur Chastain," she said politely.

Following obediently, Alexandre marveled at her thick hair and the way it danced about her waist as she moved. Their heels clicked pleasantly across the wide oak planks as they entered a breezeway, the air suddenly scented with roses.

"My mother's flowers," Dominique said gaily, setting the pup down and skipping down a grassy path between rows of thorny bushes. She called to the hound and hid behind a tree to catch her breath, her hair coming loose from the combs fixing it in place. Some strands fell over a well-arched brow. Alexandre thought her a Circe of the night, an enchantress who quite obviously had caught him in her spell.

"Macbeth!" She giggled, opening her pink embroidered jacket to reveal a velvet bow at her waist, its streamers aflight when she whirled beneath the trees. The ruffle of her lace-collared blouse caressed her neck innocently choked in coral and amethyst. "His name is Macbeth now," she announced. "Do you approve, monsieur?"

She was less than an arm's length away now and her lips reminded him of butterfly wings, fragile and upturned and exquisite. The dimple he recalled seeing earlier at the farm once again appeared.

"*Oui*," he replied, as though in a trance. He followed her onto a flagstoned terrace and watched her take a seat on an ivy-covered wall.

" 'Tis a determined hound." She laughed as the pup tugged relentlessly on her sash.

"Like her master," Alexandre replied. "Dominique," he began, finding it difficult to believe he had progressed to such intimacy. "From the first time I saw you . . . I knew I must see you again . . ."

"Must we speak of that awful day?" she said, lifting the hound into her lap and stroking its ear.

"Can you ever forgive me?" he asked humbly.

"There is nothing to forgive," she said convincingly. Had his looks improved or was it the fact that he wore clothes? Her eyes fell on the fit of his breeches as she placed a kiss behind the pup's ear.

"But there is, *chérie*," Alexandre insisted. "Pray allow me to explain."

"Your hounds . . ." she began on a serious note, changing the subject abruptly and giving him a serene smile. "Father tells me you're dedicated to establishing a new line. Is that not so?"

"*Oui*," he replied. "One day I shall produce the finest in all America. Bigger and sounder than their ancestors and free from disease."

She smiled seductively and leaned back to eye him in a better light, noticing his hands and the shape of his lips. "Your animals mean everything to you, don't they?" she asked without thinking.

"*Non*," he replied firmly. "My family is everything to me. Wife and children."

"But you have no wife," she said with care, "unless father made a mistake?"

"No mistake," he replied quickly. "I'm a free man and able to marry when I wish."

"And the South?" she responded, studying him through lowered lashes. "Will you return?"

"*Oui*," he replied emphatically. "I came north to study medicine. My roots are in Georgia."

"Georgia?" She sighed, making a little face and moving away. "That horrid place they call the dumping ground of humanity? 'Tis a land set aside for convicted murderers and vagrants, so I understand. Useless people who cannot support themselves. Why, pray tell, would anyone want to live there?"

"Forgive me, but Georgia is not unlike the Commonwealth of Pennsylvania," he said. " 'Tis a magnificent land with hills and mountains, rivers and seashore . . . golden isles. Plantations sprout like wild rice along the Savannah River, thanks to Mister Whitney and his cotton gin. Forests are thick with hardwoods and pine and our waters overflow with fish. There is all kinds of wildlife. I have seen eagles, bears, great panthers and giant tortoise, deer elk, buffalo, alligators . . . and—"

"Vipers?" she added scornfully. "Don't forget snakes, monsieur."

"But serpants are everywhere, *chérie*." He chuckled.

"Not in Germantown," she advised. She smoothed her skirts. " 'Tis clear you love this land named for an English king, monsieur. 'Tis only right you should return." She smiled. "As for me, I would not knowingly go where vipers live in abundance, for I loathe the things." She shivered in replusion. "No matter," she added smugly, "I have no plans to leave the North."

He felt suddenly ill as her message saturated the depths of his mind. He had never considered snakes. Georgia was full of them. At least five poisonous varieties he had personally observed.

"Why do you scowl so?" she asked, admiring a lilac bush and smelling its perfume.

Alexandre looked away and heard her skirts rustle across the flagstones, turning back in time to see her hair catch the starlight. "You would like Georgia," he said softly. " 'Tis a perfect place for horses."

"I shall breed my horses here in Penn's Woods, monsieur. A safe haven where one need not fear being scalped or attacked by savages, at least not in Philadelphia." She picked a sprig of lilac and stuffed it into her hair. "Might we talk of the civilized world now? Father tells me you come from Paris?"

"Martinique," he corrected, his voice barely audible. "The Paris of the West Indies."

Satisfied she had quelled any ideas of marriage he might have harbored, she sought to amuse herself further. "Napoleon, monsieur, did father tell me you are related?"

"Through marriage," he replied dejectedly. "Josephine and I are cousins. I had the honor of attending the lady's wild animals at Malmaison."

"Wild animals?" she parroted.

"*Oui*," he replied. "The lady dearly loves African beasts. Giraffes, lions, and the like. She keeps birds as well and has a keen interest in dogs."

"How very pleasant for her." She yawned. "Living in a palace with one's very own zoo. Pray tell me more about your cousin, monsieur. Is the lady as beautiful as they say?"

"More than a delight than a great beauty," he said, caressing her with his eyes. "Josephine is glamorous, yet naturally sweet, a quality you possess as well."

"You're most kind, monsieur, but I am not sweet. Might we go in now?"

"You are modest as well," he said, boldly taking her hand and placing it in the crook of his arm. He guessed her perfume was lily of the valley. How much older than her years she seemed, her height and manner deceptive. She could strip a man with her tongue when she felt the need. Ah, but she was so right, so very, very right.

They left the garden by way of a walk that wrapped itself around the trees. They strolled alongside the stone house to where torches burned brightly on either side of the front entrance. The flame's light illuminated their faces and Alexandre speculated on the children they would produce together. Blonds, he reasoned. Her coloring together with his would produce blonds. If only he could take her in his arms while they were yet alone. But an inner voice quelled his urge. He would wait.

The candlelight at the dinner table was most complimentary to Adele Winburn. She lay her napkin across the lap of her best silk dress and smiled brightly.

"Chicken, Alexandre? All Southerners like fowl, is that not so? Elton tells me you plan to return to your father's plantation soon. Tell me, is it safe? I've heard of Indian uprisings and other tales too horrible to recount."

"The Indians of the Southeast are a fair and peace-loving people, madame," he replied assuringly. "My family has learned to trust them over the years." His mind raced back in time to when he was small and his brother, Jacques, was kidnaped by Creeks and carried away in broad daylight. Alexandre had been hiding under the kitchen table.

"What tribes have you there?" Elton asked.

"Creeks or Musgogees," Alexandre replied. "The Chocktaw, Cherokee, and Chickasaw are in Alabama, Tennessee, and northern Georgia."

"Thank God we live in the North," Adele said. "I pray you will stay safe from harm when you leave us, Alexandre."

"Now, now, mother," Elton soothed. "There's no need to worry about Alexandre. Perhaps we can persuade him to stay on in Philadelphia?"

"You're most kind," Alexandre said, stealing a glance at Dominique. "But I must return to Georgia as soon as my studies are completed."

"Might we be excused, father?" Dominique asked. "I'm anxious to show Alexandre our Romeo."

"The two of you have not eaten a bite," Adele said, gazing at all the uneaten food. "Do you not wish dessert?"

"Please, mother," Dominique said, giving her father a look he understood.

"Be off with you," Elton said, "But take care the beast minds his manners." Knitting his brows in worry, he watched the young people leave. Had he made a mistake in trying to match them up? Nay, Alexandre was the best student he had ever encountered, the finest mind he had ever had the pleasure to observe, a gentleman who would make a good father and husband. The man who could give his daughter what she wanted. He pulled out his handkerchief and mused on the possibility of losing Nikki forever. There had to be a way to prevent Alexandre from leaving. There had to be.

Alexandre opened the stable's door and lifted a lantern high above his head. A big dog growled from the stalls that held the horses, his warning sounding sinister.

"Close the door quickly," Dominique said, stepping inside.

"But the dog is growling, *chérie*," he said. "He does not know me. Might we get acquainted first?"

"Surely you aren't afraid of dogs?" she said, looking him in the eye.

"I respect dogs I do not know," he said, dropping the wooden latch in place and stiffening as a huge dog came forth from the shadows into the lantern's light, padding across the dirt floor.

"Romeo," Dominique called sweetly. The beast responded by pushing its way between them.

"He's big enough to eat a man," Alexandre said hoarsely.

" 'Tis a wonder to me father did not warn you," she said. "Romeo's the biggest dog in Germantown—Philadelphia, perhaps. But don't fret, he won't bite unless I tell him to."

Alexandre raised his hands slowly. "How old?" he asked.

"Barely a year," came the proud reply.

"Good Lord, and already two hundred pounds!"

"More or less." Dominique giggled, sliding her hands over the mastiff's broad back. The dog eyed Alexandre and sniffed his breeches while protruding his teeth from beneath his lips.

"He smells Macbeth," he said, noting the dog's bone and large yellow eyes.

"The two will meet on the morrow," Dominique said. She went to where the horses stood and gave each one a good-night kiss. "What are you thinking?" she asked, lifting the lantern high and sweeping his face with its soft glow. She faced him and locked eyes with him over the flame.

"You don't like me very much?" he said, aware the mastiff held his ground. "Pray call off your dog."

Amused, she laughed aloud and stroked the beast's broad head, aware she held the upper hand. "You would not hurt Monsieur Chastain, would you, sweet Romeo?" she cooed. The dog's reply came back like thunder as it raised its head and barked. "I'll say good-bye now," she jeered. "The ride to Philadelphia is both wearisome and long and 'tis certain you are anxious to be on your way. There is a matter I would make clear before you go, though."

Beads of perspiration glistened on Alexandre's forehead, and his mouth went dry as his body tensed for what might come next. He swallowed hard, moving his eyes in acknowledgment.

Dominique laughed softly. "I don't know what my father

told you about me and I don't care, but let me assure you I'm not ready to be mated and when I am I shall do my own choosing."

Had it not been for the monstrous mastiff that stood ready to pounce at the slightest flinch, Alexandre would have dropped his jaw onto his chest. He shivered with the realization of Dominique's loathing, creasing his brow at having so misjudged her.

"You may turn around slowly now and let yourself out," she said coolly. "Tell my father whatever you like, then take your leave and be on your way quickly." She smiled and curtsied. "Farewell, Monsieur Chastain, farewell."

3

Lightning lit the bleak gray walls of the laboratory as rain streamed across the slanted roof windows. Thunder crashed and huge brass lanterns on iron hooks swayed to and fro above men's heads.

"Doctor Chastain, I believe this cadaver is yours, is it not?"

Students garbed simply in black frock coats, some with shirtsleeves rolled up, others with blood-splattered fronts, moved out of their instructor's way.

"*Oui*, Doctor," Alexandre replied.

"Then do something about it, man! Or do you intend to stand there and look at it all day?"

Alexandre picked up his scalpel and counted hours instead of bones, minutes instead of muscles. Days were drops of blood mixed with sweat and longing and nights were filled with fantasies that thwarted restful sleep. Work had become all but impossible for the young surgeon from the South now, his mere existence hinging on one burning desire: to see Dominique Winburn again.

The cadaver, a female past middle age, reminded him of his servantwoman, Mrs. Yarborough, and he recalled her words of warning. *That girl's put a hex on ye, sir. Ye've lost twenty pounds and yer hounds don't know ye.* Lightning flashed and thunder boomed so loudly, it could have been the end of the world. The end of *his* world. Unable to finish his grisly task, he set aside his knife and climbed the stairs that led to a small study loft, then he settled into a worn leather chair and closed his eyes. *Racemont* appeared in his scarlet-hued imaginings, his father's magnificent plantation shining like a jewel set in emerald green.

"Alexandre, my boy, wake up! 'Tis late and the storm is past. Wake up, doctor. Night comes early and I'm taking you home."

"Home?" Alexandre queried. He recognized the voice as Doctor Winburn's. Elton had pleaded with him to come to Germantown countless times since that night . . . the night Dominique had dashed his hopes. "*Non*," he muttered.

"I'll not take nay for an answer, my boy," Elton said firmly. "Come, for I'll not leave you be until you do."

Alexandre moaned and felt the elder man's hands on his shoulders. "Come home with me now, Alexandre," Elton said. "You fell asleep but the fresh air will awaken you. Come along now."

The fresh air did stir him. Alexandre breathed deeply and looked up into the sky as Elton's buggy moved toward Germantown. The storm had drifted out to sea and dark clouds had rolled back to reveal a scattering of stars. The road swirled with water and mud, the deep ruts forcing the bays to slow their pace.

"Winter is coming early this year, Alexandre. I can feel it in my bones." Elton shifted his weight in the buggy seat and drew a woolen blanket over his legs.

"*Oui*, I've made a thorough study of bones, doctor." Alexandre yawned.

Elton chuckled and watched his student's head sink slowly to his chest. "You've not heard a word I've spoken since we left Philadelphia, my boy. I diagnose your malady as love. You may speak frankly of your pain."

Alexandre sat up in the seat and rubbed his face with his hands. "A persistant ache in the vicinity of my heart, doctor," he said with a sigh. "Quite real, I assure you."

"Of that I have no doubt," Elton replied. "I tried to warn you it would not be simple, but then nothing worth the while ever is."

Alexandre frowned. "Perhaps I should have consulted Bonaparte as well."

Elton chuckled into his scarf and recalled what it was like to be young and in love. "My Nikki is like her mastiff, my boy. Her bark is worse than her bite. She has a distinct dislike of medical men, as you may well have discovered by now."

"And I thought it was only me."

"Nay, my boy, 'tis all men of science," Elton said. " 'Tis more distrust than dislike, I believe. 'Tis my fault. You see, 'twas I who carried home tales of incompetence in the field, and I who set the example. 'Tis a curse dedicating your life to medicine, Alexandre. The doctor's family suffers for it."

"I suppose 'tis too late to tell your daughter I'm a banker or a beekeeper?"

"Aye," Elton replied, raising a brow. " 'Tis most curious you've not been back to see your hound, my boy. Nikki can be a difficult adversary, but you must continue to persist. You must never give in to her."

"I've been busy, doctor. There is much to do before I return to Georgia, and so little time."

"Aye, I understand, Alexandre. Tell me, has your father's condition worsened?"

"The same, doctor. My brother, Jacques, writes that the stroke father suffered had aged him considerably."

"These things take time, Alexandre. 'Tis my experience that the patient who wants to get on with his life gets well. Aye, they are the lucky ones."

"I pray you're correct, doctor. My father is not one to remain idle, I assure you. Still, I would be relieved if I were there. He should have a physician close at hand."

"He could have none better than you, my boy," Elton said, stroking his beard. "You'll be leaving us soon then, eh?"

"In the spring," Alexandre said.

"And what about Nikki?"

"I have no answers, doctor. Your daughter possesses my heart and my hound, but there is little I can do. She despises me."

"Despises you?" Elton repeated incredulously. "Preposterous!" He pursed his lips. "Surely you jest?"

"I do not," Alexandre added sadly.

" 'Tis a battle of the sexes, my boy," Elton said. "Aye, you must be one step ahead of her. Tonight is the night. She'll listen to reason if you handle her rightly. 'Tis no coincidence we think alike."

Alexandre looked at Elton blankly.

"The girl's birth was planned, you see," he said with a shrug. "Vanity, some would call it. Mere calculation for a scientific mind as I saw it. You see, I wanted a son, a male heir to carry on my work in medicine." He smiled. "Then, too, there was my love of horses. Every man wants a manchild, Alexandre. You understand that, I know. I did not get mine, but the good Lord saw fit to send me a female who thinks like a male. Nikki should have been born a boy." He sighed. "If she had, she would own the finest stud farm this side of Ireland by now."

"Horses mean that much to her?"

"Horses are her passion, lad. The girl would have a herd if it were up to her." Elton eyed Alexandre. "Is is possible you might oblige her?"

"If your daughter were to marry me, I would give her so many she would need a slave to count them, doctor."

Elton's laughter boomed. "God, that would please me, my boy. I knew from the start you were the man for Nikki. Now we must convince her of it. Have faith, my boy. You and my Nikki were meant for one another, I know it. You will have sons, you'll see." He stroked his beard. "Tell me, my boy, you have spoken of your brother Jacques many times. Do you have other brothers as well?"

"Jacques is older than me by ten years," Alexandre began. "He has a son, Coosa. Coosa is a man now, about twenty-and-three, I would guess. Coosa and I are like brothers."

"Another male." Elton nodded in satisfaction. He tapped a finger to his lips and raised a brow. "Coosa . . . Coosa . . . 'tis a strange name. Tell me, is it French?"

"Creek." Alexandre smiled. "Coosa is half Indian."

Elton nearly dropped his straps and Alexandre looked straight ahead. " 'Twas a long time ago," Alexandre explained. "My brother, Jacques, was kidnapped by renegade Creeks while he was yet a boy. 'Twas not until many years later we discovered he was still alive. He returned to Racemont with a wife and son."

"The woman was Creek, I take it?"

"*Oui*, a girl of high breeding, a princess of the elite Wind Clan. Quite beautiful, as I recall."

"Forgive me for prying, Alexandre, but your story fascinates me. I've heard tales of kidnapings by savages before, but none quite like this. Did Jacques stay, then?"

"He did," Alexandre said. "Father was so happy to see him alive he saw to it that his grandson, Coosa, received an education worthy of a Chastain. Jacques's wife returned to her people and Coosa was sent off to Paris to study."

"And what life does Coosa lead today?" Elton queried.

"Coosa chose the life of his people," Alexandre said.

"Too bad," Elton said, allowing the horses to trot and finding himself caught up in the tale. "Did your father hold the Indians responsible?"

"Father is a wise and compassionate man, doctor. Few white men consider Indians as humans. Father does. He knew the Creeks were a civilized tribe and, as such blameless for the sins of others. Father became friends with the chiefs of the Musgogee and they saw to it the lawless were punished. 'Twas by way of the incident my father acquired lands and secured rights to hundreds of thousands of acres. 'Twas the beginning of his plantation. Perhaps now you understand why an operation of that size needs so many slaves to tend its fields. But don't fret yourself into a fever over my father's darkies. He treats them with kindness and understanding, I assure you. They are his family."

"Quite a family, I would say." Elton chuckled. "Still, I don't believe the good Lord meant men to be in bondage to one another. I hope to meet your father one day. But for now, I must ask you to save the spinning of this tale for Nikki until the knot is tied. Such matters can surely wait, don't you agree?"

"*Oui*." Alexandre nodded. He breathed a sigh of relief then, for he had purposely neglected decribing his brother Jacques in too much detail. Poor Jacques had been born a bastard. Ah, but the telling of that tale would have to wait.

"Does Alexandre have brothers or sisters, Nikki?"

"I don't know, mother."

"I doubt any brother could be more handsome or charming," Adele said. "Alexandre has everything a young girl could want in a husband. Intelligence, education, position."

"You forgot money, mother," Dominique added.

" 'Tis better to marry a man of means than a man of want," Adele replied knowingly.

Dominique took the English china from the cupboard and set the table. "I'm not looking for a husband, mother. Rich or poor."

"But Alexandre adores you, Nikki. Surely you've seen the look in his eyes?"

"I've seen nothing in Monsieur Chastain's eyes a good night's sleep would not cure," Dominique said smartly, facing her mother across the Sheraton table. She placed silver and brass candlesticks beside a centerpiece of copper chrysanthemums. "Pray believe me when I say I have no wish to marry now. And when I do, I will not choose a man of medicine."

Adele frowned indignantly. "And what does that mean, young lady? Your father is a doctor."

"Aye, he is," Dominique agreed. " 'Tis the life he chose for himself. The life you chose as well. Pray do not choose the same life for me. I have other plans."

"Aye, I know," her mother huffed. "Plans too vulgar for words. Who ever heard of a woman raising horses? 'Tis a profession designed specifically for men."

"All professions were designed specifically for men, mother. Just because I had the misfortune of being born female does not mean I must be a wife and mother. There are other things a woman can do."

Adele's face went blank.

"I wish to *breed* horses," Dominique said emphatically. " 'Tis a dream I've cherished since I was little. A dream father encourages."

"All little girls have dreams," Adele scoffed. "I myself wanted a pony once. But you're a woman now, dearest, made for having children and serving a good man. 'Tis time to think on these things. Husband, home, little ones." She frowned. "I pray you haven't told Doctor Chastain this."

"Monsieur Chastain and I have not discussed my future," Dominique replied softly. "I've not seen or spoken to him since—"

" 'Tis time you did," Elton said, holding open the front door for Alexandre. "Where is everyone? The horses need putting up and there's not a stableboy in sight."

"I'll attend to them, father," Dominique said, slipping into the foyer while her father kissed her mother's cheek. She watched as Alexandre bowed graciously before her mother, then sought to gather her wits about her. Why had he come back? She glanced in the mirror and pushed a long braid over one shoulder, fingering her dark flannel dress. She couldn't have looked worse had she been a scullery maid.

"Mademoiselle," Alexandre said, coming toward her from the dining chamber.

"I must see to the horses," she said, turning on her heel.

"You will stay put, miss," her father said, coming behind her to take her arm. "Pray set another place at the table, my dear. I insisted Alexandre come home with me and I look forward to the four of us sitting down together."

"Of course," she choked, half smiling, as her father placed a kiss atop her head. "Pray excuse me, Monsieur Chastain, while I go do my father's bidding." Spinning on her heels, she hurried off to the dining chamber and turned the key in the cupboard. 'Twas the first time she had seen the Frenchman in doctor's garb, black breeches, frock coat, white shirt, and hose. Clothing sickeningly familiar to her. He had lost weight and his face looked drawn; he had dark circles beneath his eyes.

"Forgive me, mademoiselle, but your father gave me no opportunity to say *non*," Alexandre said apologetically, following her into the dining chamber.

"Think nothing of it, monsieur, 'tis not unusual for father to bring home students. He sometimes carries home strays as well. Kits and kids and hares who need to mend a leg. My father is a kind man who believes every soul should have a family and a warm meal."

" 'Tis a good belief," Alexandre said, looking toward the stairs as a big dog barked and bounded down the steps, braking at his side to growl low and beat his tail on the tablecloth. "At least the beast seems glad to see me, or perhaps he's hungry?"

"Your coming awakened him from his nap, monsieur. Romeo was asleep on my bed."

"Fortunate fellow," he muttered, watching her cross the room. The dog followed and she bent low to pat his head, her braid falling over her shoulder to dangle before the huge dog's mouth. She teased the dog with the length of hair and the dog playfully nipped the air. Alexandre's eyes fell on the white column of her neck, and he tried to decide if she should wear emeralds to match her eyes, or rubies to match her spirit.

"I presume you came to see Macbeth?" she said, not looking his way.

Macbeth who? he wondered.

"May I show Monsieur Chastain our prize before supper, father?" she asked her father politely.

"Take all the time you need," came the reply.

Dominique looked at Alexandre blankly and led the way to a small room off the kitchen where a leggy wolfhound pup pawed his barricade. "What do you think monsieur?"

"Perhaps pearls would be best?" he murmured, lost in his reverie.

She frowned quizzically. "The hound, Monsieur Chastain? Do you find his progress acceptable?"

Embarrassed, Alexandre grinned and looked at the beast that stood with front paws on a low gate. "I cannot believe the size of him, mademoiselle. He's grown at least a foot!" Duly impressed, Alexandre reached out and patted the huge hound's head. "Might I step inside?"

"As you like, monsieur." She shrugged, folding her arms across her breasts and sighing deeply.

Alexandre lifted a long leg over the gate and the hound jumped up and placed his paws on his former master's shoulders.

"I have tried to break him of that awful habit," Dominique said. "'Tis something he did when he came to me."

"Oui." Alexandre laughed. "A trick he learned from his mother."

"He is happy now," she said softly, watching the dog close his eyes as Alexandre stroked his softly furred back.

"He knows I care for him," Alexandre said. "Animals sense love. They are more perceptive than humans in that regard."

Dominique lowered her lashes, watching him kneel and examine the hound's legs. Macbeth could not stand still and broke loose to romp about the room, jumping up to nuzzle his master again and again. Alexandre sat down on the floor and stretched out his long legs before him.

"Forgive me, mademoiselle, but I find I'm suddenly overtired."

Dominique leaned over the gate and smiled down at him, finding his words and the scene comical.

"You look amused," he said. "Do I look so ridiculous?"

"I was watching the hound," she replied icily. " 'Tis none of my affair what you do."

Not realizing he was staring, he scanned her perfect face, admiring the cheekbones, creamy-pink complexion, and glittering teeth. Her eyes sparkled with mischief. God, how he wanted her! His blood soared and he was glad the hound sat on his lap.

"*Chérie*," he began, "you must know how I feel . . ."

"You are ill, doctor?" she asked politely.

"*Non*," he responded, "I . . . I . . ."

"What?" she asked cynically.

God help him—he had forgotten his words, the speech he had rehearsed countless times. The condition of his heart and his burning desire drove him to the brink. "I . . . I . . ." Before he could say another word the hound reared up and banged his massive skull against Alexandre's jaw, knocking his head back and striking his temple on a large oaken bucket.

"Monsieur?" Dominique giggled, thinking the scene hilarious now. A grown man beneath a shaggy hound that straddled him like a lion. Hanging onto the gate she laughed with abandon until she recognized Alexandre's awkward position and turned quickly away in embarrassment.

"Ohhh," Alexandre moaned.

"Monsieur?" she queried softly, turning slowly to see him unmoving. "Alexandre?" she called, lifting her skirts and climbing over the gate. "Macbeth, you silly hound," she scolded, "what have you done?" Alexandre opened his eyes to a glimpse of shapely legs in white hose set off by wide ruffles. "Ohhh," he moaned again, this time more energetically. The overgrown pup lay atop the downed man's chest and looked up lovingly at his mistress, wagging his tail slowly.

"Get off him at once!" Dominique commanded. "Get up, I say!"

And so he did—springing to his feet and plowing through her skirts to topple her. "Ohhh," she wailed, tripping over Alexandre's legs and falling over him. The dog was a genius! Alexandre moaned slightly and felt the warmth of her breath, the pleasure of her body covering his.

"Monsieurrrrr . . ." she gasped, struggling to get up as Alexandre moaned again and she felt the heat of his lips.

He moaned softly, kissing her passionately and wrapping her in his arms. His lips slanted across hers and she experienced a

sensation of tingling, the hardness of his chest pressing against
her soft breasts and her legs against his as he trapped her in his
arms. "Monsieur," she choked, gasping for air and pushing
against his chest to free herself.

"Monsieur Chastain!" she breathed.

"*Chérie*, my love," Alexandre drawled.

Breaking loose from his hold, she freed her limbs and came
to her knees, yanking her skirts down. "You are no gentleman,
monsieur," she raged.

Alexandre rubbed his head and sat up. "*Chérie*, I beg you
to—"

"I am not your '*chérie*,'" she hissed, smoothing her hair
and turning from his half-closed eyes.

"Pray hear me out, Dominique," he pleaded hoarsely. "I'm
glad our lips met. Now you know how I feel."

"I know nothing, Monsieur Chastain," she gasped, her
voice uneven. "And I wish to hear nothing more from you."

He stood beside her and braced an arm against the doorjamb
above her head, looking down into her face and speaking
quietly. "I return to Georgia in the spring with a new wife," he
said evenly. "A fine lady who loves horses and hounds as I do,
a ravishing adventuress who will be my helpmate and ride at
my side, an intelligent and vibrant woman who will bear my
children and share my life until 'tis spent."

Bent on sending him away, she refused to meet his eyes. His
heartfelt speech meant nothing to her and she would not allow
him to affect her plans. " 'Tis my wish to see you happy with
this wife of whom you speak, Monsieur Chastain. A woman
would have to love a man overmuch to travel to such a
godforsaken place as Georgia."

"Love comes when two people share their lives, no matter
where it happens to be," he advised. "I'll not press for your
answer now, but pray do me the honor of considering my
proposal overnight."

"There is no need," she said quickly. "I am not interested in
marriage and I have no intention of leaving the North. I have
tried to make that clear, monsieur. Pray let me pass now."

Their eyes met and he thought he saw a tear clinging to her
lashes. Gripped by a terrible sense of loss and helplessness, he
stepped aside and attempted to help her over the gate. But she
pushed his hands away and unhooked the latch capably.

"Good-bye," she said in a whisper as she slipped through the gate and put her lightning stride between them.

" 'Tis not good-bye," he said to the hound that looked up and yawned, whining curiously at the man whose eyes burned wetly.

The grass glistened in the morning sun, winter's wind sending its first frosty breath across the fields of Germantown. Dominique mounted Thor, her father's big Irish stallion, her hair catching the wind. She had a lot of thinking to do and her best headwork was accomplished on horseback as she breathed in the fresh clean scent of the woods and experienced the fantastic flying sensation only riding could give. Her father did not think she could handle his spirited stud from Erin, but when she sat on the chestnut's back she transcended the world somehow. Her father said she would rather ride than eat. Of course he was right.

Closing her eyes, she saw Alexandre's face, pathetic, his eyes on the verge of tears. Could a man really suffer for want of a woman? Her father had said Alexandre had known the pangs of Hades because of her and she had thought it humorous at the time. Now she was not so certain. Nay, she felt nothing for Alexandre Chastain, yet she could not forget that brief moment when he encircled her in his arms and their lips had touched . . .

"Damn him!" she exclaimed, opening her eyes to the light and narrowing her lips into a pout. How dare he interfere in her life! Spurring the stallion's side, she drove the beast across the fields to the edge of the wood, past fallen trees and down a steep ravine. A stream frothed cold and clear at her feet. Why couldn't she get Alexandre out of her mind? Water splashed on her leg and she hated him for complicating her plans. She guided Thor along the stream and up an incline. A good ride would put Alexandre Chastain out of her mind. Aye, that's all she needed. A good ride.

Thor jumped a downed fence that marked her grandfather's estate and the walls of the old homestead rose naked behind a circle of mulberry trees. With a sting of her quirt she guided Thor across a stretch of grass and slowed to look back. Glancing over her shoulder, she saw a horse and rider crossing her father's cornfield on the other side of the ravine. "It cannot be!" she whispered, recognizing the black mare as her own.

Alexandre waved, his mount splashing through an icy creek and thundering toward her.

"*Chérie!*" Alexandre called. "Wait up, please!"

He looked stronger on horseback somehow, the browns and tans of his breeches and jacket blending with the burnished gold of his hair, now lighter in the morning sun.

"Wait for me, *chérie!*" he called again. "Pray hear me out!"

His face carried a worrisome frown and Dominique's hands trembled on the reins. Dear God, she did not want to see him! Did not want to look in those eyes, sad with loneliness and denial. Starved eyes! What could she do? Where could she go to hide from the questions she knew would come?

"Go back!" she screamed. "I wish to ride alone!" Flicking her quirt to her stud's side, she vowed she would not look at Alexandre. She cared less for his misery and she could not bear to hear him beg! Thor obliged her wishes by stretching his legs to the full. The mare's lungs heaved behind her and she imagined she felt Alexandre's breath on her back. Let him come. She smiled. The mare could *never* catch Thor. Leaning forward in the saddle she thrilled to the chase, hooves flying, hearts pounding, earth rushing beneath her skirts.

"I love you!" Alexandre called on the wind.

But Dominique heard nothing save the pounding hooves. Bent on outdistancing the mare and showing Alexandre Chastain who was in command, she stung Thor over and over with her quirt until the stallion reached out in ever longer strides, his hooves leaving the leaf-covered ground as he raced at breakneck speed. Entering a grove of trees, Dominique lay down to hug her steed's neck, her hair exploding in a sunburst over her moss-green velvets. Then she saw the wall. The old stone wall her father used to lift her onto when she was little and they went riding together. The wall that made her sick just looking at it. The wall her father said was too high for *any* horse alive to jump! "God help me," she whispered as she tried to turn the stallion. But Thor paid no heed. Dominique pulled on the reins and bit her lip until she tasted blood. The stones were larger now and Thor was headed straight for the wall, running his heart out for her. Perhaps the stallion could make it? Wasn't he a born jumper? Aye! With God's help they could fly over the wall and land safely on the other side. She would show Alexandre how to ride a horse. "Please God," she said, narrowing her lips and readying herself for the jump, closing her eyes tight as horse and rider left the earth together.

"Will she live?" Alexandre asked.

"Only God knows, my boy. Her injuries are more serious than the broken bone you discovered. I've sent my manservant for Doctor McLaurin, the Scotsman who specializes in craniology. 'Tis a blessing he's in Philadelphia and not Edinburgh."

"But his patients seldom live, you told me so yourself, Elton," Adele said, trying to control herself. "And if they do, they may as well be—"

"Don't say it! Don't even think it!" Elton took out his handkerchief to blot his eyes.

"Tell me she won't die," Adele sobbed.

"Our girl's in good hands, my dear," Elton soothed, taking his wife's arm gently and leading her from the darkened bedchamber. "We must have faith now." He spoke low to Alexandre as they passed the foot of the heavily draped bed. "Take over, my boy. Watch her closely and call me if there is any change."

Alexandre nodded, his face ashen, his eyes red. He went to take Dominique's pulse and found the beat considerably slowed. She slept abnormally now, her complexion near the color of the bandages that practically encased the top of her head. He studied the face he adored, the badly bruised skin and eye swollen shut. Her right arm was broken above the wrist and lay in a makeshift cast across her abdomen. Her most serious wound was to the head, a gash so deep he had found it necessary to cut her hair to close it.

'Twas his fault it had happened. If only he had not gone after her. If only she had not fled! If she died it would be his doing and he would have to live with it forever. He closed his eyes, finding it difficult to accept the possibility, gazing out the window and recalling how it had happened. "Dear God, forgive me," he whispered.

Doctor Winburn came into the room with Mrs. Yarborough. "Alexandre, see who is here. 'Tis your womanservant come to assist."

Alexandre looked at Mrs. Yarborough blankly and then at Elton. "I will not leave her," he said firmly. "She is my patient."

"Three days have passed, my boy," Elton said. "You've not slept once. Mrs. Yarborough and I can manage until the Scotsman comes. Pray let us take your place."

Alexandre's voice wavered, his words barely discernible. " 'Tis my fault your daughter lies there like a sleeping princess. 'Tis my fault for it all. Pray do not make me leave."

"Leave 'im ta me, sir," Mrs. Yarborough said. "I'll look after 'im like always." Removing her wet cloak, the servant-woman began to tidy up the room. Elton sighed, sinking into an overstuffed chair beside his daughter's bed and staring into the fire. The door opened slightly and a huge dog padded across the rug, dropping with a thud at the elder doctor's feet to rest his giant head on a twisted paw. With a whine that sounded like a distressed moan, the dog raised a dark brow and looked mournfully at the bed.

"The beast loves her, too," Elton said, choking back a sob. "And there's another one downstairs that paws at his gate for her kisses."

Alexandre's eyes were heavy in their sockets, his body numb from the round-the-clock vigil. Mrs. Yarborough stood proudly behind her master and pitied him, eyeing the pale form on the bed and thinking 'twas all for the best. She would have her master back now. He would return to his farm and his animals where he belonged and there would be no more talk of marriage.

The wind had no rest as well that night. It howled around the house till dawn, then went rushing to meet the sun, licking its icy tongue across the already frozen fields and creeks of Penn's Woods. It was snowing hard when Doctor McLaurin arrived in a sleigh from Philadelphia. The Scotsman came directly to Dominique's bedchamber and nodded at the two doctors who stood grimly at the foot of the patient's bed. Mrs. Yarborough helped McLaurin out of his greatcoat and he wasted no time opening his bag.

"How long has she been like this, gentlemen?" the bewhiskered Scotsman asked, his long narrow face red from the cold.

"Nearly four days now, doctor," Elton replied.

"Your man told me how it happened; nevertheless I would like to hear it from you," he said in a thick brogue.

Alexandre quickly recounted the facts of the accident and explained how he and Elton had lifted Dominique into a haywagon and transported her to the house. McLaurin examined the broken arm and asked questions about the patient's past history.

"She's always been a healthy girl," Elton said, wiping a tear from his eye.

McLaurin carefully removed the bandages from Dominique's head. "The man who did this knows his business," he said, pleased to find the wound closed and clean.

"Doctor Chastain's work," Elton offered.

" 'Tis sewn so fine I would have believed a woman plied the needle," McLaurin said. " 'Tis apparent you're a surgeon, sir."

Alexandre nodded.

"The skull does not appear to be cracked," McLaurin said, "but there is little doubt the brain suffered a damaging blow." Dominique lay in a deep stupor and could not be roused. McLaurin guessed there had been some cerebral bleeding. " 'Tis serious, doctors. I needn't tell you that." McLaurin snapped his bag shut. "You have done exactly as I would have, gentlemen. Now we must wait."

"Is there nothing more we can do for her?" Elton inquired.

"Keep her head slightly elevated," McLaurin said. "No stimulants and cool applications to the face and neck. Continue to keep the room dark." McLaurin shook his head. "We don't know what damage might have been done to the spine, gentlemen. We can only pray she awakens from this. Some do not."

Alexandre closed his eyes and lowered his head, dropping a hand to stroke the velvet of Romeo's ear.

"We must face the possibilities, of course," McLaurin continued. "After this many days one can only conclude—"

A soft moan came from the bed and all heads turned at once. Romeo trotted quickly to his mistress's side, nuzzling her hand and whining curiously. Alexandre stood motionless, his heart dormant, his tongue whispering a prayer.

"Her eyes, doctors!" Alexandre whispered.

Dominique's eyes opened to the firelight that shone through the drapes of her bed.

"Nikki, dearest . . . Nikki!" Elton knelt beside the bed, his eyes filling with tears. "Tell me you know your father, Nikki. Pray take my hand."

Looking bewildered and confused, Dominique closed her eyes.

" 'Tis a good sign, doctors." McLaurin smiled, stepping forward to take the patient's pulse.

Alexandre slipped silently from the chamber, Mrs. Yarborough at his heels.

It was later that evening when Dominique woke again. She brought a hand to her face and touched her brow, looking curiously at her father who hovered over her.

"You were hurt, Nikki. Thrown from your horse. Do you remember?"

Dominique's eyes roamed the room until they found Alexandre's face in the shadows. "Thor?" she cried, a terrible aching in her throat and eyes, her head throbbing until she became aware of the pain. "Thor?"

"Sleep, Nikki," her father said, stroking her brow. "Sleep and forget."

November went by like a sleepless night. Rain came and thawed the earth and then turned to snow. By Thanksgiving the fields were blanketed in solid white and the wind howled with the cold, frosting the windows of Winburn House.

Dominique lay in her bed and recalled the virgin beauty of the woods she loved, pulling the quilts to her chin and dreaming of a fast ride in the snow. But riding was over for her now. Life and its dreams were suddenly spent. The fire was going out and she looked steadily into its dying embers. She was a year older now, but what of it? The future held little for a girl who could not leave her bed. She tried to wriggle her toes but could not find the strength. "God help me," she whispered, her lashes wet with tears as the door opened.

Her father and Alexandre walked into the room.

"Nikki, my child, did I waken you? Forgive me for not coming home sooner my dearest. The roads are hazardous and Thomas had to fetch me with the sleigh."

She looked into her father's eyes, ashamed for the deed that had caused his stallion's end. He looked older now and she was suddenly aware of how much she loved him. "Oh, father, can you ever forgive me?"

" 'Twas an accident, my child."

"I'm so sorry."

"Nikki, dearest, don't cry. I'm helpless when a woman

weeps. You must think no more of it. *You're* alive and that's all
that matters."

"It matters that I'm forever bound to this bed!"

"Forever is a long time, dearest," he said kindly. "It will
take time, but you will be your old self again, you'll see." He
took out a clean handkerchief and wiped her cheeks. "There's
someone who would see you now, my child. A man of science
who knows more than your father."

"You're the doctor I saw before," she told McLaurin,
thinking him an ugly man: his long face was framed in wiry
hair, and his skin was red and discolored from the long ride in
an open sleigh.

"Your heartbeat is steady, lass," he replied, taking note of
her trembling hand.

She narrowed her lips and drew back her hand. "I don't trust
doctors."

"Neither do I," McLaurin replied, passing a lighted candle
before her eyes and sitting beside her on the bed.

She met his gaze boldly and opened her eyes wide for the
candle's light. McLaurin asked to see the wound and Mrs. Yarborough came quickly to unwrap it. "The wound has healed as
expected, doctors," McLaurin said, satisfied. "You're a lucky
lass, miss." He smiled. Her father gave a sigh of relief and
smiled broadly. McLaurin thought a moment, then spoke to
Elton and Alexandre. "Might I have a word with you, gentlemen?"

Elton's face was apprehensive and he and Alexandre
followed the Scotsman out of the chamber to the hall.

"Your daughter's most fortunate, Doctor Winburn."

"Thank God for that," Elton replied.

"Aye, for a girl to be in a coma all that time and recover, one
must believe in divine intervention. We can only pray her legs
and mind have not been affected."

"What do you mean, doctor?" Elton asked, his face pale.

"I understand the lass is quite the horsewoman," McLaurin
said, casting a glance at Mrs. Yarborough.

"Aye," Elton replied with an impatient frown.

"Explain yourself, doctor," Alexandre pressed, his face
concerned.

"You are the girl's bethrothed, I take it, doctor?"

"Why do you ask?" Elton queried.

The Scotsman glanced again at Mrs. Yarborough, then back at Alexandre.

"You may speak freely, doctor," Alexandre advised. "Mrs. Yarborough is more than a servant to me. The woman is my nurse and can be trusted."

McLaurin shrugged. "The brain is a complicated mass of which we know little," he said, shaking his head. "*Very* little indeed. Some patients who suffer a blow, such as the one your daughter experienced, never recover."

"But she has recovered!" Alexandre interrupted.

"I pray she has," McLaurin said. "However, we must prepare ourselves in the event that the young lady does not return to normalcy. There's the chance her legs will never serve her again. If that be the case, she won't ever walk, much less sit a horse."

Alexandre stared at McLaurin and Mrs. Yarborough brought a hand to her mouth, stifling a little sob.

"Only time will tell, doctors. I must go now. Pray write me of the outcome. I'm most interested in the case."

Mrs. Yarborough rushed down the dimly lit hall and quickly descended the stairs to the foyer. Alexandre stepped in front of the Scotsman, his eyes wild. "What haven't you told us, McLaurin? I would hear the worst now!"

"You love the lass, don't you, lad?"

"*Oui*, I do," Alexandre replied honestly. "I plan to make her my wife, if she'll have me."

McLaurin's face went white. "I would think long and well on such a serious step, doctor. The lass may never be the lass you once knew."

"Pray tell me why, doctor?" Alexandre pressed, his tone primed with anger.

Mrs. Yarborough listened at the bottom of the stairs, hidden from view.

"Aye, doctor, we're men of science like yourself. Pray tell us the truth," Elton said calmly.

"Believe me when I say my prognosis is based entirely on similar cases, doctors, each being different, of course."

"Get on with it," Elton said tersely.

"Your daughter could develop a multitude of symptoms, the least of which is melancholia, lapse of memory . . . er . . . hallucination . . ."

"Is that the end of it?" Alexandre asked.

"She'll experience head and neck pain for some time, as one might expect," McLaurin said, hesitating. "But you must not despair when she displays fits of temper such as you've never seen before."

" 'Tis apparent you don't know my daughter." Elton sighed.

" 'Tis my judgment she's an independent lass, and quite determined to have her way," McLaurin continued, "but that's in her favor. I speak now of a total change in personality, so severe a change as to affect her mind."

Mrs. Yarborough stepped back into the shadows of the foyer and clutched the cross that hung around her neck.

"I'm sorry, doctors, but you must consider all these possibilities and more."

"What *more* could there possibly be, man?" Elton queried, his face drained of color.

"If she were *my* daughter, I would never allow her to marry."

"Not allow her to marry?" Elton's eyes blazed. "Just a bloody minute, McLaurin, you're going too far!"

" 'Tis not my way to interfere in private lives, doctor. I'm a medical man like yourself, please remember that. I can tell you only what I've seen and prepare you for the worst. The girl should never have children."

Elton turned away, feeling sickened by the thought. "Poor Nikki," he whispered.

"Thank God the lady is *not* your daughter, McLaurin!" Alexandre said, moving aside. "For I fully intend to make her my wife. And God willing, we'll have children."

The Scotsman set his jaw and descended the stairs to the foyer where Mrs. Yarborough was waiting to open the front door for the departing physician. He stood with his back to the cold and faced Alexandre, voicing a final thought before going to the waiting sleigh. " 'Tis your decision, Chastain. Forgive me for saying so, but you're too close to the patient to see the facts. Good day, doctors."

Mrs. Yarborough closed the door and leaned her weight against it as she watched a dejected Doctor Winburn climb the stairs.

"You must never speak of Mademoiselle Winburn's condition, do I make myself clear, Mrs. Yarborough? *No* word of it must ever leave this house!" Alexandre said low.

Mrs. Yarborough nodded and dropped her gaze, dipping into

a half curtsy as the bottle of sedatives thumped against her knee. She patted the bottle in the folds of her skirt where she kept it stored for safekeeping. Aye, she understood all right. She understood perfectly. The master was too involved with the girl to face facts. But *she* knew what was best for Dominique, even if he didn't! Leave Miss Winburn to her. She smiled. She would take care of her, just as she'd cared for the doctor's pups. She knew the right dose of poison to give a hound in pain, and she knew it corresponded with the right dose for a lass. *She* was the only one in the house who was thinking clearly now. Aye, she understood. Miss Winburn would sleep the rest of her life away, if it was left up to her.

4

Elton Winburn sat at his desk in the library of Winburn House and studied a progress report on his daughter's illness. Began as a means to pass the time and keep Alexandre awake during the all-night vigils, the detailed notes now filled half a journal, ending with the notation THE SCOTSMAN WAS WRONG!

Leaning back in his chair, Elton gazed out the window at the fields coated with fresh snow. He would give his life to see Nikki ride again. He thought then of the grandchildren he would never have. A man who relied more on common sense than medical know-how when it came to difficult decisions, Elton knew his daughter's recovery was delayed for some irksome reason. Nikki *had* changed. McLaurin had said she would. The girl slept entirely too much and had lost her will to live. Not like Nikki. Not like her at all. Closing the journal, he grasped the arms of his chair and pushed himself up. Something was amiss.

" 'Tis not my wish to hurt you, Miss Nikki, but it will take hours to get these tangles out, you must sit still." Nancy, the maid, worked diligently at the rat's nest in Dominique's hair. "I won't take your torture, Nancy. Leave me be!" Dominique cried, hurling the silver brush across the room.

"Is the toilette over?" Elton queried, sticking his head inside the door.

"Aye!" Dominique shrieked, frightening the dogs that rose hunchbacked beside her bed to pad hastily across the Chinese rugs with their tails tucked between their legs.

Nancy burst into tears.

" 'Tis not like you to treat a servant this way," Elton said softly. " 'Tis not Nancy's fault your hair is knotted."

" 'Tis *his* fault!" Dominique wailed. "Look at me! Look at my hair!" Watching the dogs go, she slipped down in her bed and pulled the covers over her head.

"Tell Nancy you're sorry, Nikki," Elton advised, consoling the maid with a nod of his head and a warm wink.

"I'm sorry for myself," Dominique muttered beneath the covers.

"I know," he replied.

"Nay, you do not!" she cried, throwing the covers aside. "You don't have to lie here and watch the light come and go, wait for the night and pray for sleep!"

"You'll get used to it, dearest."

She removed her hands from her face slowly and stared at him.

"Doctor McLaurin was right, or so it seems," he said.

"*Right*?"

"Aye. His prognosis suggested a problem with your legs." He walked to the window to watch the snow drifting down from the trees. "I didn't believe him at the time, but I was wrong."

"What else did he say?" she asked, her lips tightening.

"That you would continue to improve, time being the key, of course." He saw her atop her horse then, sitting astride at the edge of the woods, bold and beautiful in the sunlight as the wind captured her hair and sent it aflutter. More than three months had elapsed since the accident, and he wanted more than ever for her to marry Alexandre. He listened to her sniff and wished he could take back the words. "There are worse things," he said, facing her. " 'Tis not like you'll have to give up riding. I'll have a buggy designed especially for you, with fine imported upholstery and seats to help you sit erect. You could ride to town and—"

"You know well I *despise* wheels!" she screamed, her voice breaking. She fell to one side and beat her fist into the pillows, envisioning herself being carried about like a lame dog. "Damn that doctor!" She broke into tears.

"You could prove him wrong," he said, pulling his handkerchief out and wiping his eyes. "You must make up your mind to pick up your life where it left off. You can do it, Nikki. My girl can do anything she wants."

Dominique buried her face in the pillows and listened to him walk away. Elton closed the door behind him and sighed deeply. All he could do now was wait.

Dominique pushed the soaked pillows from her face and looked out the window at the falling snow. If only she could go back to that day. If only Alexandre hadn't chased her! If only he had stayed away! She thought of wheels and litters and buggies and boxes. There would be no more offers of marriage now. So final. So damnably final! She tried to move her toes and lifted the quilts to look at her legs. Anger formed a knot in her chest and she vowed to prove the Scotsman wrong. She *would* walk and she *would* ride again. She could do anything and she would do this! She *would*!

Several weeks later Dominique leaned on Alexandre for support. He slid his arm about her waist and held her hand. Ten steps. Just ten little steps. If only she could! Alexandre's voice was kind and encouraging. "Come, *chérie*."

"I'm afraid," she whispered, reaching out and nearly losing her balance.

"Don't be," he said reassuringly, "I'm here and I'll not let you fall."

Why was he so good? Was this her punishment for treating him so badly? Could he love her still? She repeated to herself over and over that she wasn't afraid, then she glided with only the slightest wavering into Alexandre's arms.

"Marvelous!" he said, holding her close and lowering her onto the green velvet cushions of the windowseat. A full moon rose over the trees, spectacularly large and yellow as it lit the snowclad garden below.

" 'Tis a moment I'll remember forever," she said softly, watching the moon.

"Do you believe in predestination, *chérie?*"

"Do you?" she replied.

"A Creek told me once that we were set on a course at the time of conception and there is little we can do to alter our journey."

"If I believed that I would be lying in that bed and feeling sorry for myself now."

"Oftentimes we are taught in mysterious ways."

"What do you mean, Alexandre?"

"That life is precious . . . that it is only lent to us for a brief time." He smiled, holding her gaze and studying her eyes. Once cool and clear, like a forest pool, they now lacked sparkle. He thought of opiates and dismissed it at once from his mind.

" 'Twas my fault I fell, Alexandre," she said, lowering her lashes in shame. "I alone am responsible."

"*Chérie*," he began, taking her hand in his.

"Pray say nothing more," she said. "I'm tired and I want to go to sleep."

Lifting her in his arms, he carried her across the room to her bed. "I rode that morning to tell you I loved you, *chérie*. I love you now even more."

But Dominique did not hear him, her eyes closed tight and her thoughts already adrift in sleep. Alexandre laid her down gently, placing a kiss atop her head and covering her lovingly.

The moon rose full and pale over Penn's Woods, the heavens above open and filled with stars. Bells swung gently against the Percherons' great bodies, their powerful muscles rippling in the moonlight.

Dominique sank down on the furs, enjoying the crisp night air and the warmth of Alexandre's body next to hers. He tucked a beaver throw around her legs and made certain she was warm. Looking up at him, she thought him exceedingly kind and good. The man who had saved her life. A man to whom she owed much. She looked at him in a different light then, studying his handsome features, the strong jaw and creased cheeks; wanting to touch his face.

"Why do you stare, *chérie*?"

"I have never been this close to a man before. 'Tis strange. I know so little of men."

"I will teach you all you need to know."

"Perhaps I don't wish to learn," she muttered, thinking he presumed too much. She secured her gray fox bonnet. "Perhaps 'tis not *meant* to be?"

"We are back to that." He chuckled.

" 'Tis you who first told me," she said, narrowing her lips. "When will my journey begin and where will I go?"

"If I told you, you would be angry with me." He reached beneath the furs to take her hand.

"I think I know," she said softly. "But I cannot accept it. I long for something else . . . something I want so badly I don't know what it is."

He set aside the reins and tilted her face toward his.

"Marry me," he said low.

"I would make you unhappy, Alexandre. I was not meant to be a wife. To keep house and bear children."

"I have no need for a housekeeper, *chérie*. As for children, we have plenty of time."

"I could never be a doctor's wife," she explained. "Sick people make me ill!"

"I promise never to bring a sick person home, *chérie*." He kissed the tip of her nose.

"Nay," she protested. "I have plans of my own. I want what women cannot have. What *ladies* do not want."

"I will give you anything and everything, *chérie*. Just tell me what it is you want."

"That is what you say now," she scoffed. "But once I was your wife, things would be different."

"I need you."

"You need a wife, Alexandre. I am not—"

He leaned over and fastened his lips over hers in a long, lingering kiss.

"Please, I cannot give up my freedom," she breathed, pushing him away.

His chuckle was deep and warm.

"Don't laugh. You don't understand, Alexandre."

"Ah, but I do, *chérie*."

"You see nothing wrong with a woman breeding horses?"

"Nothing whatever. When we get to Georgia we'll begin importing at once. The best blood of Europe will be at your disposal."

She looked into his eyes and saw the love they held for her. "I'll *not* leave Penn's Woods," she said evenly, thinking that would change his mind.

He drew her close and kissed her deeply. When she had recovered he held her close. "I'll never force you to do anything you don't wish to do, my love. 'Tis my earnest desire to make you happy beyond all your expectations."

"It doesn't matter that I don't love you?" she said, not realizing her words had cut his heart like a dagger.

"It matters, *chérie*." He smoothed her hair, stung by the pain of rejection. "The love I hold for you will suffice for now."

She pulled away and tried to look beyond his eyes, to see inside his soul. "And if I wish to leave, Alexandre? Would you hold me?"

He thought how empty life would be without her, knowing full well he would probably die if she left him. "*Non*," he replied, the word shattering his being.

"Then I'll marry you!" she said smartly.

He looked at her for a long time, stunned, then drew her close and wrapped her within his embrace. "My love!" he whispered, overcome with emotion.

The runners glided through the snow and sang then, the moon smiling overhead. Dominique closed her eyes and shivered in the crisp night air. What had she done? Had she finally agreed to marry a man she did not love? Oh, God, what would it be like married to a Southerner? A foreigner! What possible excitement could there be for Mrs. Alexandre Chastain? The trees swayed over her head and whispered their reply. It was a blessing she did not hear.

Spring returned to Penn's Woods and the trees were once more in leaf, the sun having warmed the frozen fields and melted the snow. Meadows turned a lush green, creeks flooded into the roaring Delaware, and blossoms dotted the woods. A new litter of hounds was born on Dewberry Farm and Emma, the Percheron, delivered her second foal.

"A gentleman to see ye, sir," Mrs. Yarborough called up the stairs to her master's bedchamber.

Alexandre dressed quickly in leather breeches and flannel shirt, stepping lively down the narrow twisting stairs to the kitchen. "Who is it, Mrs. Yarborough?"

The servant woman slid a tin of muffins into the hot ashes of the fireplace. "Says he's darn near kin, sir. Someone from the islands, or so he says. A dark man, near brown as an African, I'd say. Name's Jules somethin' or tother."

Alexandre's stomach turned to bile. Jules Cocteau from

Martinique? A quick glance out the window revealed the visitor was indeed dark. Black hair, beard, and suntanned skin. Could it be Jules? His cousin? His mind swirled. Jules was older than him by six years and *no* friend. Unpleasant memories crept through his brain. Memories long buried. Jules was the son of Uncle Baudoin, who had helped raise him. Baudoin was a man up in years now, perhaps ill?

"Alexandre, Alexandre Chastain! I would have known you anywhere, monsieur."

It *was* Jules. How long had it been? The last time he had seen him Jules was nothing but a boy. A big, hateful boy. Worse, he'd heard stories that cast his cousin in a bad light.

"Jules Cocteau. Forgive me, monsier, it has been a long time," he offered, smothering his distaste.

"A lifetime, my friend." The tall man dressed in island whites walked briskly toward Alexandre from the stable, his dark face carrying the same strange smirk Alexandre remembered. There was bad blood between them and Alexandre had not forgotten. Stiffening, Alexandre flinched as Jules embraced him.

"I bring news from Martinique, my friend. May we go inside? The ride from Philadelphia was long and quite dusty."

"But of course," Alexandre said, "come inside." He felt ashamed for his lack of manners. Perhaps Jules had changed? It *had* been a long time. "You will be staying the night, monsieur?"

"You are most kind, Alexandre. Several days, if 'tis no inconvenience. I come to Philadelphia on business. Then there is your wedding, *oui*?"

"*Oui*," Alexandre replied, knowing full well Jules had not been invited. "Tell me, monsieur, how did you leave your father?"

They entered the house and settled in the library. Mrs. Yarborough brought cakes and brandy.

"My father is an old man, Alexandre. Old beyond his years. He lives in the past, I fear."

Alexandre frowned. "What is wrong? Some malady I can help with, perhaps? Baudoin is not much older than my father."

"Father is his own physician, my friend. He will see no other. I might inquire as to your father's health?"

"As well as can be expected, monsieur. Father suffered a

stroke some time back, but he is well under the circumstances.''

"And your plantation in Georgia, Alexandre? I have heard wondrous tales of *Racemont*. Is it true the lands are a hundred times greater than your father's *Madiana*?''

" 'Tis true.''

Jules smiled. "And your brother, Jacques? Is he still a slave?''

"I never think of Jacques as a slave, monsieur. No man is chained on Chastain lands. Jacques may leave whenever he wishes.''

"You left, did you not, Alexandre?'' Jules had hatred in his eyes. "I understand you are a physician. Soon to become the bridegroom, eh? I can't wait to see your bride. 'Tis certain she's beautiful.''

Alexandre had to turn away. The last thing he wanted was mad Jules at his wedding. Why had he come? Now of all times! But knowing he must remain polite to a cousin, he fought to control his impatience. After all, Jules was blood and hopefully harmless. "I doubt you'll be seeing my fiancée before the wedding, monsieur. 'Tis less than a fortnight away.''

"Must I wait until then to see a pretty face, my friend?'' He chuckled. "I've been traveling for a long time and I yearn for the company of a female.'' He laughed. "Does your betrothed have a sister, perhaps? Or do you know where I might find, er . . . accommodations?''

"Philadelphia has whatever amusement a man could want, monsieur,'' Alexandre said, fighting down his disgust. "Trenton is just across the river. Other than the houses of ill-repute there, I'm at a loss as to where to send you.''

Jules smirked. "True to one woman, eh? 'Tis what I would have expected.''

Alexandre felt the need for a drink and poured himself a brandy. He had nothing more to say to this ghost from the past. He lit his pipe and settled in his chair.

"Perhaps you would like to accompany me to some houses, Alexandre?'' Jules continued. "If I know you, 'tis what you need. What you've needed for a *long* time.''

Alexandre sipped his brandy, swallowing down his dislike. He would offer his cousin the basic amenities and no more. "You may stay at Dewberry Farm while you're in Philadelphia, monsieur. Mrs. Yarborough will prepare a room for you and are free to come and go as you please. Now, if you'll excuse me, I must see to my animals."

"My thanks, *old* friend," Jules mocked, raising his glass. "I'll be leaving soon after the wedding. Father could not come and sent me in his place. His wedding gift will be delivered to the bride's house."

Alexandre stopped short of the door, the latch cold in his hand. "I'll write Baudoin our thanks with my wish for his improved health. 'Tis most unfortunate he could not come."

Then they parted. Jules with a familiar self-satisfied smile curling his generous mouth, Alexandre drawing his brows together in a worrisome frown. Alexandre did not enjoy unwelcome guests in his house, and in the days that followed he would find himself striking off the days until Jules departed.

Gnarled branches groped toward a cloudless sky, the queen of vines circling above the woman's head to form chandeliers of ivory, amethyst, and delicate pink. Adele Winburn marveled at the beauty of the Japanese wisteria. It would make a perfect backdrop for her daughter's wedding.

She picked up a basket filled with blue iris and hurried along the garden path, her skirts of peacock blue in contrast to the heavy-headed white peonies. Elton saw her from where he stood. "Adele, dearest!"

Adele saw her husband coming toward her in the company of a dark-complexioned stranger, the man's beard and tricorn hiding his face.

"Adele!" Elton puffed, half running to catch her. "We have a guest from the islands, dearest. Monsieur Cocteau, all the way from Martinique!"

"Madame Winburn, how very beautiful you are. I mistook you for the bride." Jules removed his tricorn and bowed low.

"You're very kind, monsieur Cocteau," Adele replied politely. "How good of you to come to our daughter's wedding."

"I come in place of my father who is ill, madame."

Adele thought him ruggedly handsome in champagne and brown. His pock-marked skin was colored a deep copper from the Caribbean sun. "Cocteau? Aye, I recall the name. Your father, Baudoin, is Alexandre's uncle."

"Yes, madame. Alexandre lived with my family when we were children."

"I see." Adele smiled, although there was something about the islander she did not like. "Pray forgive me, monsieur. I was on my way to the house. 'Tis certain my daughter needs me."

"Monsieur Cocteau will be staying with us after the ceremony, dearest," Elton said.

"But of course, monsieur. I will see to your rooms. Pray excuse me for now."

They watched her follow the path to the house, standing together aside a sculptured fountain covered with clematis.

"I don't wish to be a burden, doctor. 'Twas my intention to return to Philadelphia after the wedding. My vessel is docked there."

"Nonsense, monsieur, you're part of our family now. My wife and I wouldn't hear of you returning to the city when we have room here." He smiled. "Our kitchen overflows with food!"

They laughed and struck up a conversation about marriage, their voices carrying high above the twisting wisteria vine to the open window of the bride's chamber.

Dominique sat before her mirror dressed in a silk under-dress, its low-cut neckline bordered in lace, her rising breasts moist with tears. Surrounded by flowers, gifts, and dogs, she sat staring at herself in a feverish state. A tiny herd of china horses, imported from France, galloped across her lace-skirted dressing table. The horses were a gift, having arrived only moments before, exquisitely wrapped in white silk and silver ribbons. A single white rose was tucked beneath the bow; a card was signed simply ALEXANDRE.

"Mrs. Alexandre Michel de la Ramée Chastain," Domini-que whispered, studying her reflection in the glass. Her voice was strained from hours of crying, her eyes swollen and red. How could she marry a man she did not love and allow him to make love to her? In just a few short hours she could be with child!

The clock struck twelve; the ceremony was set for one.

"Nikki, you're not dressed!" Adele Winburn entered the room.

"Oh, mother," Dominique sobbed, "I can't marry him!"

"Dearest," her mother said compassionately, hugging her and taking her hand. "Of course you can."

"Nay, mother," she sobbed, "tonight . . . when he . . . when we . . ."

Adele smiled. "You must not think on it, darling. Tonight will be perfect. The most perfect night in your life, I'm certain. Alexandre's a wonderful man. Kind . . . sensitive. He'll make you happy, I promise."

Dominique tried to stop crying but only succeeded in choking. Her mother picked up her silver brush to arrange her hair in a lovely topknot surrounded with a wreath of white violets.

"I don't love Alexandre," Dominique sobbed. "Perhaps I never will."

"Alexandre has enough love for you both, dearest," Adele consoled her, giving her a hug. "Trust him. Love grows as you grow." Adele helped Dominique into her wedding dress. Tailored from fabric as light and soft as rose petals, the gown had been designed by Josephine Bonaparte's own couturier in Paris, made to order for the bride and shipped in time for the wedding. Adele fastened the tiny covered buttons that climbed her daughter's back, the high neck of the gown caressing the bride's lovely neck, now trailing with wisps of hair.

"You're a vision, my dear!" Adele beamed. "Alexandre will be speechless." A tear escaped her eye and she handed her daughter a bouquet of pink and white hyacinth, set off with queen's lace and lily of the valley. It was all wrapped in satin and tied in bows with long streamers.

Dominique viewed herself in the mirror with skepticism. The lace-scalloped bodice of her gown swept tenderly over her breasts, her small waist accented by a satin sash that flowed into a full skirt adorned with hand-sewn flowers. White was for purity and virginity and she was both. But she was cheating Alexandre.

The dogs whined and she bent down to stroke their heads and give them a farewell kiss. "I cannot, mother! Tell Alexandre I'm ill—the fever, the plague, anything!" Sobbing, she tossed her bouquet on the dressing table and stumbled to the bed. In the last few months she had strengthened her legs so she could walk, albeit awkwardly. Her prognosis was good. Her father had pronounced her cured, and able one day to glide across the room once again.

"What's this?" her father asked, coming into the room and closing the door behind him. "I heard you crying outside."

Dominique sobbed into the pillows. "Pray don't make me marry him, father. 'Tis wrong!"

Elton sat beside her on the bed. "You can love anyone who is good to you, my dear. Alexandre will take care of you, cherish you."

"But I don't want to marry, father. Please, I beg you, tell Alexandre something."

He thought then of Alexandre and what it would do to him if Dominique did not go through with the ceremony; of dying and leaving her alone in the world. "Alexandre needs you, dearest. The poor boy saved your life, remember? He helped you regain your strength so you could walk. You *must* marry him. 'Tis the least you can do." He took out his handkerchief and wiped her eyes and helped her up.

"And what if I find myself with child tomorrow?" she asked. "I don't want to be fat and ugly."

Elton chuckled. "You could never be fat and ugly, dearest." He took her in his arms and held her tightly while her mother smoothed her hair. "You're marrying the best physician I've ever had the good fortune to know, dearest. Alexandre has a brilliant career ahead of him. He'll make you proud one day."

"I never wanted to be a doctor's wife," she sobbed.

"And what of Alexandre? Have you no feelings, child? What do you suppose it would do to him if you backed out now?"

Dominique looked at him steadily, drying her tears as her mother stretched out the train on her gown.

"Your father knows what's best for you," he advised. "The North needs surgeons and doctors and we're most fortunate to have found such a man as Alexandre Chastain. Marry him, Nikki. Marry him and after the ceremony I'll give you both a surprise that will make you forget your tears!"

Her eyes brightened and her sobs lessened.

"Come," he said, straightening his waistcoat and taking her arm. "The groom awaits."

The bride's veil cascaded behind her as she descended the curving staircase on her father's arm. The balustrades were graced with stephanotis, with baskets of white tulips banking the foyer. A carefully orchestrated mix of flowering trees and plants lined the path to the garden.

Jules Cocteau feasted his dark eyes on the bride as she came into view: desire stabbed him sharply in the loins. A woman-child held her father's arm and came toward him on the flower-strewn path. Young, innocent, untouched. She had a slight limp but he'd heard she was recovering from a nasty fall. Other than that, she was a flawless beauty. What would it be like to take such a woman? To take the woman Alexandre Chastain chose for his own?

The bridegroom took his place beside the bride and held her hand. Jules edged closer, envying the weak Chastain who had no stomach for hunting or taunting beasts. They were exchanging vows. A woman's body lay beneath those yards of silk and lace, a full and delicious meal waiting to be devoured by a man. If only he could be that man. If only . . .

The pastor pronounced them man and wife and the bridegroom lifted the bride's veil and kissed her. Jules watched their lips touch, noting how the bride pulled away. Alexandre said something in French and held Dominique close.

It was done! Alexandre took her hand and guided her to where her father and mother waited. Elton shook the bridegroom's hand. "Congratulations, my son," he choked out. "Are you happy at last?"

"Pray don't wake me, monsieur. I fear I'm dreaming."

"Look at your bride and tell me she is not real, my boy." Elton beamed. " 'Tis no dream you married."

Alexandre drew Dominique's hand to his lips and gazed deeply into her teary eyes.

"Now then, I have a present for you," Elton said, dipping into his frock-coat pocket and withdrawing a ribbon with a key dangling at its end. "Your key to happiness, my children."

"A house?" Dominique asked.

"Nay, not *just* a house, dearest. *The* house you've wanted since you were a litle girl. The house with the lake and the swans and room for a hundred horses."

"*Winwood!*" she exclaimed, her eyes wide. "You purchased Winwood for us. Oh, father, I love you!" she squealed. "Now Alexandre can forget about the South! We shall live in Winwood and raise horses!"

Alexandre felt his heart lurch, his blood slow as his plans to return to Georgia shattered. He had hoped to find a way to coax his bride to go south with him after the honeymoon. Now there seemed little chance of it. With a fine house and a farm on which to raise her horses, what hope did he have of ever leaving Pennsylvania?

"Enjoy your wedding day, children," Elton said. " 'Tis the most memorable day of your life."

"Congratulations," Jules said, stepping forward from the crowd of well-wishers and looking directly at Dominique. "Would someone be kind enough to introduce me to the bride?"

Alexandre flexed his jaw, frowning deeply, his perfect day further crumbling. "Dominique, may I introduce my cousin Jules Cocteau, the son of Uncle Baudoin, the man *you* invited to our wedding."

Dominique took note of her husband's tone and expression, trying hard to play the wife. "I'm most pleased to meet you, Monsieur Cocteau." She curtsied. "Alexandre has told me much of Martinique and his father's plantation, Madiana."

"There are no flowers so fair as you in the islands, dear lady." Jules smiled, kissing her hand. "You must come to Martinique one day."

She withdrew her hand with a little frown, feeling inexplicably uneasy. She smiled. "I would very much enjoy meeting your father, monsieur, and visiting your island."

Jules's smirk lifted one corner of his mouth. "I'll look forward to that day with great anticipation, madame."

Alexandre held Dominique's hand tightly and handed her over to her father. "Forgive me, *chérie*," he said low. "It has been a long and trying day. If you'll excuse me I'll see to our carriage."

Dominique looked at him as he moved away into the crowd. Surely they were not leaving so soon? Jules was staring at her. She attempted to make excuses for Alexandre.

" 'Tis my sincere wish we shall meet again, Monsieur Cocteau."

"I'm quite certain we will, dear lady," Jules replied, bowing low as she left on her father's arm to mingle with the guests.

"Friendly fellow," Elton said, smiling at his friends and neighbors. Dominique's cousin, Jenny, came and hugged her. "Toss the bouquet to me," she whispered. " 'Tis my turn to marry."

Dominique kissed Jenny and stood on tiptoe to try and locate Alexandre in the crowd.

"Everything you need is at Winwood, dearest," her father

said. "Your mother and Jenny have been quite thorough as you will see."

"My horses and dogs?" she queried.

"I'll send them out to you on the morrow," he replied. "You have no need of them this night."

"Then 'tis good-bye," she said, near tears.

"Your mother and I are only an hour's ride away, child. 'Tis not good-bye, Nikki. Only good-day."

Alexandre returned and Elton drew him aside. "Take care of her, my son. She's a woman but a child in many ways. I can tell you she's frightened."

Alexandre nodded and shook Elton's hand. Then he took Dominique's hand and ran with her to the waiting curricle, handling her up as friends and neighbors shouted and tossed rice.

The red wedding carriage was upholstered in black leather and the spoked wheels were decorated with sprigs of white lilies and bows, and the two white horses drawing the dazzling vehicle had their forelocks plaited with flowers and their bridles tied in white streamers.

Alexandre picked up the reins and jerked them so roughly the conveyence bolted into the lane, nearly unseating the bride.

"Must we be in such a hurry?" Dominique asked, aware he raced the horses. "We've sufficient time before dark."

The chill of his tight-lipped response cooled the air between them considerably. Dominique clung to her seat, shivering at thoughts of what might lay ahead. Thank goodness the carriage was open.

She breathed in great gulps of air, looking up into the sky and regretting her marriage to him. "I cannot wait to see Winwood," she ventured after a long while.

"I can," he replied with a lift of his chin.

"I have loved it for as long as I can remember," she said.

"Then you should understand my feelings for Racemont," he replied low.

"'Tis different," she said, glad they were talking again. "Winwood is ours."

"*Yours!*" he corrected. "I have no need for another house. I have a farm and a great plantation awaits me in Georgia."

"But father gave Winwood to both of us," she moaned. "Now you can stay in Pennsylvania and become a partner in father's practice."

He sighed, flexing the muscle in his jaw and cracking the whip above the horses' heads. " 'Twas my intention to take you to Dewberry Farm for our honeymoon."

"You know well I hate wheels," she said smartly. "Your farm is far and already I feel ill."

"We would have spent the night at the Eagle's Nest in Philadelphia. Reservations have been made for some time."

"Winwood will be better, Alexandre. 'Tis close to my parents and I'm certain you'll like the house."

The remainder of the journey was suffered in silence. When Dominique was certain she could bear it no longer, she sighted a lake in the distance, a long curving body of water gleaming like a mirror beside the road. The land sloped upward from the water to form a rise behind a thick wood. A lane bordered with old elms curled through the woods.

Alexandre drove the horses at a furious pace and it seemed only moments passed before they were racing up the drive.

"There it is! There behind the trees, Alexandre. Winwood!"

He caught a glimpse of the roof and chimneys, then slowed the horses' mad gallop to a trot. Dominique held onto her seat and breathed deeply.

" 'Tis most impressive, don't you agree?" The carriage came to a halt before an ivy-covered bank set with stone steps. Ruthe, and her husband, Thomas, the estate's caretakers, introduced themselves to the new husband and fondly greeted their mistress. Then Alexandre jumped down and offered his hand to his bride.

"I don't want your help," she said softly so the servants would not hear, pushing his hands away and leaving the curricle on her own. " 'Tis clear I am a wife now," she huffed, "but do not count me your mate!"

" 'Tis fitting that I carry you over the threshold," he said, attempting to take her arm.

"I'm no longer an invalid," she replied. "I shall walk into *my* house, thank you."

Before she could get away his arm came about her waist and she found herself glaring through scattered tresses. He took the steps with ease as she struggled to be free, and they crossed the threshold.

"*Your* house, madame!" He set her down gently on the rug before the parlor's fireplace.

A full-length portrait of Dominique hung above the mantle.

Alexandre stared at the girl on the canvas. Dressed in gold the way he would always remember her, she stood in a wood beside a white horse, Macbeth and Romeo at her side. She was the golden goddess he had fallen in love with at first sight, in all her regal splendor.

"Another gift from your father, I see," he said. He read the inscription on the plaque at the bottom of the painting. "*Lady of the hounds*," he said low, excusing himself and leaving her alone. She watched him cross the carpet, then heard him talking to the servants in the entrance hall, instructing them to take the carriage and leave for the night.

"There is no need for you to stay." He was saying. "My wife and I plan to retire early. You may return after noon on the morrow."

Inflamed that he would be so bold as to dismiss *her* help, Dominique strode into the entrance hall, but forced herself to remain calm. "What if *I* have a need of them?" she said stonily. "We've not eaten."

"A cold supper has been prepared for us, *chérie*." Alexandre drew her aside. "Do you wish Ruthe to help you undress now—prepare a bath, perhaps?"

"Nay!" she retorted, her temper flaring beyond its boiling point. "I wish to see to my house first! To see it all!"

"Then look, madame," he replied with a smile. "I'll just see Ruthe and Thomas off and join you in a moment."

Mouth agape, she watched him go, then she fumed in silence. Now was her chance to get away. But where? There were no horses except the ones that drew the carriage. If only she could hide. The house was big enough. The door closed and she heard the clatter of hooves in the drive. She ran to the windows in time to see the carriage turning around and driving away. Plainly irritated now, she snatched a lighted candle and climbed the main staircase to the second floor, dragging her train up the Persian carpet that swirled beneath her feet.

The master chamber was a suite of three rooms tastefully decorated in shades of pumpkin and purple and banked with flowers. A sheer gown of French design, with matching peignoir, was laid out across the mammoth bed; its canopy was draped in purple satin. She would be damned if she would display herself in something so flimsy for him! Gathering up the clothes, she dropped them behind a bowl of white lilacs.

Hurrying now, she struggled with the buttons at the back of

her gown as she walked through the rooms, discovering a white marble bath with a giant copper tub. An adjoining sitting room was furnished with a chaise longue covered in French lilac fabric, an oriental writing desk, and a round table skirted in white cotton arrayed with lilies and morning glories.

Returning to the bedchamber, Dominique stood before the fireplace and listened for footfalls. Birds sang their evening song outside the windows, the house seemingly empty except for herself. She went to the bed, piled high with little wedding pillows, and yanked back the satin quilt before diving in and covering herself with its bulk. She would feign a dizzy spell, she decided. The trip *had* made her ill, so it would not be a lie.

She heard whistling and lay very still, listening to footsteps approaching the bedchamber from the hall to where she lay.

"Some Madeira, my love?" Alexandre asked, coming to stand beside the bed. "Will you join me in a nightcap before your portrait?"

Pushing back the covers, she exposed one eye and pretended to be awakened from sleep. "Is that you, Alexandre?" she muttered softly. "I'm very tired and wish to sleep."

"Did I hear you rightly, madame?" he asked incredulously. " 'Tis our wedding night! Surely you want to drink to our happiness?"

"I do not!" she replied, turning over.

He peeled back the covers slowly then. First the quilt and then the satin sheet, taking her arm ever so gently.

"Pray let me be, monsieur!" she wailed. "Can't you see I'm weary?"

"You would miss our wedding night, *chérie?* Come now, I find that difficult to believe."

"I'm not dressed," she moaned.

"You look very much dressed to me, my love," he drawled, catching sight of the breasts that swelled above the decolletage of her underdress.

"Give back my covers!" she moaned. "I'm cold!"

"If you would prefer," he said, staring, "we can go to bed instead." He grinned, undoing his cravat and removing his jacket. "I could keep you warm."

"Very well!" she cried, sitting up and sliding out of the bed with the quilt wrapped about her. " 'Tis too cold to sleep here. I'll go downstairs and sit before the fire. Perhaps then you'll leave me be."

"You *are* cold," he said, concerned, feeling her hands and helping her with the quilt. He slid his arm about her waist and helped her to the door. "Come, *chérie*, I'll light a fire for you."

He helped her down the stairs to the parlor and guided her to the French settee covered with Italian brocade of palest peach. "Someone went to a great deal of trouble to make us comfortable here," he said. " 'Tis a shame to disappoint them. Don't you agree?"

"Light the fire, damn you!" she muttered beneath her breath, thinking it would take his mind off the bedchamber.

"Did you say something, *chérie*?" he asked.

"Aye," she replied. "The rooms need warmth. I can feel the cold."

"I feel quite warm, my love." He grinned, laying a large log on the crackling fire. "I've waited a long time for this night. *Your* house or ours, I intend to enjoy it." He placed a pink crystal goblet in her hand and filled it with wine. "To us, *chérie*—may we celebrate life together for a long while, *wherever* it may be."

She looked at the wine and smelled its bouquet. Her father prescribed Madeira for his patients who could not sleep. Good for the nerves, he said. If she could fall asleep perhaps he would leave her be? Screwing up her face, she gulped the dark liquid and held out her glass for a refill.

"More?" he queried.

"Aye." She smiled, settling back against the cushions.

The flames caught the log and its tongues licked the wood hungrily. Alexandre poured the wine with care, filling her glass only partway. "Sip it this time, *chérie*. 'Tis strong stuff when you're not used to it."

"But I *am* used to it," she lied. Deflecting his attention, she asked, "Pray tell me what you think of the artist's work?"

"I think him a most fortunate fellow." His eyes never left her. " 'Tis really quite good, but I must confess I'm already spoiled. Owning the original, I have no need for copies."

"Owning?!" she emptied her glass and tossed it into the fire, drawing her legs under her and giving him a black look.

" 'Tis merely a figure of speech, my love," he said calmly. "Most women wish to be possessed by a man. I keep forgetting you are different."

"Different indeed!" she fumed.

"I believe you misunderstand, *chérie*." Coming to sit beside her, he looked into her eyes. "A man considers his wife his property. You must not blame me for wanting you all to myself. 'Tis my way."

His gaze made her suddenly aware of the heat and she threw off the quilt. " 'Tis so blasted hot in here!"

"*Oui*, I feel it as well." Sliding his arm about her, he moved closer. " 'Tis a natural thing between lovers."

"I'm tired." She yawned, moving away. "May I go to my chambers now, my husband? I'll be a good wife and ask permission."

"I'll go with you." He smiled.

"But the fire," she said, moving back. "You'd best look after it. There's no need for you to help me up. I'll see you in the morning. Good night." Picking up the quilt, she tossed it over her shoulder and crossed the room, nearly tripping on the trailing ends.

"I'll help you up," he insisted.

"Well, make up your mind! First you want to go downstairs, then up. I've changed my mind," she said smugly. "I'm staying here."

Her nerves were frazzled, but Alexandre seemed to understand.

She glanced about the room. " 'Tis truly large," she said, narrowing her lips. "Larger than your Racemont, perhaps?"

His arms enfolded her and he stroked her face with his hand. "No house I have seen is larger than my father's, *chérie*." His body was so close she felt the strength of his thighs, his body's heat. He kissed her neck, while his fingers deftly released her hair from its pins.

"I take it you have seen all the houses in the North?" she said, her eyes near closing.

"All that I wish to see." His lips teased the lobe of her ear as his fingers carefully undid the back of her underdress and the quilt slid to the floor. "My father's house is the grandest of them all." He kissed her along her hairline. "Built for the most beauteous of mistresses."

All this talk of houses was making her sleepy. Who cared? She would never see his damnable Racemont! His lips teased hers lightly, ever so lightly, parting, teasing. She felt herself wanting to tease in return.

"We must light some candles," she said, regaining her senses by force of will. " 'Tis so dark in here I can barely see."

"I can feel you," he replied patiently. He came behind her and captured her about the waist, drawing her close and sliding his palms over her abdomen to cup her breasts.

She closed her eyes for an instant and sighed. But with one final effort she spun around to face him. "I wish to see the stables." Already her resolve was slipping away.

"Now . . . before . . ." Unable to say more, his kiss swept her breath away, his hands holding her fast.

"Nay," she mumbled. But he would not release her, his kiss so passionate she became light-headed. Their tongues met and it sent ripples across her scalp, her limbs suddenly weak. "Alexandre . . ."

"*Oui*," he replied as his lips found the hollow of her neck and blazed a trail of kisses there.

She held her head back, feeling helpless in his arms. Her breathing came in pants.

"You are mine," he whispered low, "*my* property . . . *my* wife!" His hands brought her head to his and his fingers explored the waves and curls of her tresses.

"Don't fool yourself," she said, touching the wings of his fine, soft hair, swept into a neatly-tied queue at the back of his head. She giggled; the perfume of the flowers and the smell of burning wood suddenly overpowered her.

Alexandre caught her before she fell and cradled her in his well-muscled arms. "You've had too much wine, *chérie*." He smiled, gazing into her eyes as he carried her to the stairs. The crewel hem of her underdress drifted above her calves, her hair brushing the ballustrade as he began to climb.

He strode across the carpet and deposited her with care upon the massive bed.

"Goodnight," she whispered, snuggling into the pillows as he covered her with a fur throw.

He removed his snowy-white shirt and stood looking down at her. "Are you warm enough?" Sitting beside her, he undid his breeches.

"Aye," she moaned, not looking as he pulled off his boots. The chamber was dark save for a candle that burned half-heartedly on the bedstand. Alexandre lay down beside her, his lips pressed to her neck as his hands caressed the mounds of loveliness that hardened beneath his touch. "Are you asleep?"

Turning her ever so gently, he slipped her underdress over her shoulders and down her arms, pooling the silk fabric onto a nearby chair.

"Nay," she replied, shutting her eyes as he next eased the dress down over her midriff, thighs, and long slim legs to rustle to the floor.

"You are as I imagined and more," he said, his breathing changed. He lay down beside her and drew the covers over them. "I will not hurt you," he whispered, kissing her breasts in turn and concentrating on the peaks that responded beneath his lips. "I am your husband."

Her hands held his head close and she trembled in his arms. His hair fell from its ties, blending with the gold of hers on the pillows, as he eased closer. He stopped to stare at the face he found so bewitching. "I love you," he said, holding her so tight her breasts were pressed beneath the hardness of his chest. "I shall love you forever."

Dominique looked into his eyes and believed him, parting her lips as his tongue circled hers, then darted little flicks here and there to set her senses afire.

"Nay," she whispered, turning her head to one side as his mouth traced the ivory ridge of her breast and slid gently down her ribs.

"Trust me," he replied, stroking her tenderly and parting her thighs. Entering her with care, he searched her face for some sign that she wanted him as well. Trembling, she narrowed her lips and held her breath as Alexandre kissed her in a way that bespoke love and caring. She pulled him close and spread her hands across his back, crying with the pain that made her his wife.

5

───────────◆───────────

Dominique's eyes flew open. She lay in Alexandre's embrace, listening to the pounding of his heart, his arms wrapped tightly beneath her breasts, his lips pressed against the nape of her neck. He mumbled in his sleep and drew her closer, a smile lighting his face. How often had he made love to her? Once, twice, three times? How could she face him? Pretend she did not enjoy his kisses, his tender touch? Their mouths had met countless times; her lips were still sensitive. An uninvited smile coaxed the dimple beside her mouth. He *had* made her happy. Aye, very happy.

She looked beyond the bed to the windows draped in pumpkin velvet caught up with bows. The moon was up and high above the house. Suddenly she wished to see the lake and the swans in the moonlight. Moving a leg, she was caught instantly and held in a grip that tightened like a boa about her waist. Alexandre moved against her, his hand rising on one breast, his leg slipping between hers, his lips searing the arch of her back. Raising one knee, she gently pushed him away with her heel. "Nay," she whispered.

"*Chérie* . . ." he moaned.

"Pray forgive me, Alexandre. 'Twas the wine. I cannot—"

"Stay!" he replied, his tone final. Rising up on one elbow,

64

he turned her face to his and forced her to look at him. "We are married, *chérie*—man and wife!"

"Aye, I know, but I should never have—"

"Never?" he rasped. "*Ma chérie.*" He frowned, drawing her into the shelter of his body to kiss the tear that rolled down her cheek. He pushed back the wisps of hair that lay against her temples. "You welcomed me as I prayed you would. Gave yourself freely, as I did to you." His kiss came as a respite from guilt and she clung to him. Covering her, his fingers reawakened the pink halos of her young breasts, caressing the satin curves of her loveliness in wonder and appreciation. "You are marvelous in design, my wife."

She entwined her fingers in the golden hanks of his hair and brought his mouth to hers once more. His kiss was deep and sensuous, leaving her quivering. Fitting her to him, he rewarded her with a more demanding caress this time, his hand tracing the silky curves from her ribs to her inner thighs. "*Mine!*" he whispered. His touch was startlingly intimate, causing her to moan and draw up her knees. Trembling, she turned her face from him.

"I love you, *chérie*," he said, conviction in his voice.

She held her breath and allowed him to stroke her, digging her nails into his back as he moved over her.

Bang Bang Bang! Someone was knocking on the door downstairs!

Alexandre froze, listening, not breathing. *Not* now! Not on his wedding night. Surely no man would disturb a doctor on his wedding night. Perhaps if they made no move the visitor would go away?

There it was again. Louder and more insistant.

"Don't go down there, Alexandre," Dominique whispered.

Squeezing her, Alexandre kissed her gently and pulled himself slowly from her warmth. "I'm coming!" he shouted. "I hear you!" He pulled on his breeches and ran down the stairs to peer through the frosted glass panels on either side of the door. He could make out the figure of a man holding a lantern. "Who is there?" he called.

" 'Tis I, Jules Cocteau! With a message of great urgency from Doctor Winburn!"

"*Mon Dieu!*" Alexandre gasped, unlocking the door quickly.

"There has been a fire!" Jules breathed. "Many are burned,

children have broken limbs. Elton begs your assistance at once!"

"But my wife . . . I've released the servants and dare not leave her alone."

"There's no one here but yourselves, my friend?" Jules asked. "Not a kitchen maid or a stableboy?"

Alexandre shook his head, considering his choices, realizing Jules was the only one. "*No* one, monsieur."

"Then you must go! 'Tis your duty as a doctor. I'll stay until you return."

Alexandre felt more than discomfort; his insides oozed with fear. "My wife is most precious to me, monsieur. If anything happened . . ."

"Of course she is, my friend," Jules agreed. "You need have no fear for her safety, Alexandre. Please hurry."

"Horses?" Alexandre exclaimed. "The only one we have is in the pasture."

"Take mine, of course!" Jules insisted. "He's fast and eager to please."

Alexandre ran to the stairs and looked up to see Dominique wrapped in a purple quilt. "*Chérie*! There's been a fire and your father needs my help. Monsieur Cocteau will stay until I return." He hurried up and answered her questions as he hastily pulled on his boots. "Try and sleep and don't worry. I'll be back before you know it." Shoving an arm into the sleeve of his shirt, he kissed her good-bye. "Forgive me, my love. I'll make it up to you, I promise."

"I understand, Alexandre," she replied, helping him with his coat. "Pray take care." She watched him run down the stairs to the hallway and stop to converse with Jules.

"Jules . . ." Alexandre said, his face grave.

"Save your words, my friend. Your wife is in good hands."

Dissatisfied, Alexandre made no reply. Jules opened the front door and watched Alexandre mount his gelding and wheel away, his ear hearing the closing of the bedchamber door upstairs. He walked from the hall to the parlor and stood before Dominique's portrait, looking up to study each line and curve. Beauty the likes of which he had beheld only once before. Brows arched above thick lashes, eyes the color no man could forget, the look in them haunting his every breath. He took a candle from a sconce on the wall and lit the wick, holding it close to the canvas. Lips the color of flamingos' wings were exquisite and full. He absorbed the luscious length of her, fancying her naked, breasts atremble, legs open wide to reveal the precious haven he dreamed of possessing. A rare piece. One he may never get his hands on again. He smiled, congratulating himself on starting the fire. She would bless him for what he had. *Oui*, she may scream and claw at first, but few had been pleasured by such a man as he. He knew that well.

Returning to the grand staircase, Jules placed a boot on its first scarlet step, listening and waiting. Did she sleep? He thought he heard a cough, or was it a sob? Uncertain, he listened to the drumming in his ears, his excitement at taking a fresh bride fueling his lust. Another step. He felt the warmth of her skin beneath him, the soft and flawless skin, finer than silk. Another step and he smelled her hair, clean and fragrant, the spun gold that was piled high beneath the wedding veil only hours before, surrounded by tiny violets. So innocent, completely and totally innocent.

He was at the top of the stairs now, listening . . . waiting . . . She *was* sobbing. He was certain of it now; it was louder and more pronounced. He must take care. She could easily be taken if he was clever. No one would know. No one would come. The time was ripe. Blood throbbed impatiently in his manhood, pulsating with desire. He reached the bedchamber door and turned the knob.

"Alexandre? Is that you?"

He moved steadily toward the voice and held his hands out before him.

"Alexandre?" she coughed, her sobs high-pitched and uncertain. He could see her form in the moonlight, the pale covers accentuating her white skin.

"Pray say something, Alexandre," she choked, her throat aching from crying, her voice tinged with fear.

Jules breathed in the fragrance of lilac and roses and reached out to take her hand.

"You are back so soon?" she whispered.

Jules came down on her like a bird of prey, clapping his hand over her mouth and stunning her with the suddenness of his attack. Her eyes strained in the darkness, unblinking and fearful.

"Don't scream and you'll thank me for what I have for you, sweet Nikki."

Her head was forced back, her screams smothered beneath

his open palm. Aware that her life was in jeopardy, her hands beat against his arms, attempting to loosen his hold. But she could not. In another ploy, she twisted her head sharply and bit him in the hand.

"Bitch!" he swore, slapping her face and knocking her back on the bed. "Fight and scream if you wish, dear sweet Nikki. Howl like the curs your husband coddles, for no one will hear! Your husband thoughtfully removed the servants, remember?" His laugh was that of a madman. He pinned her wrists above her head and his mouth swarmed over hers, his manhood released and pressing on her belly.

"God, nay!" she screamed, kicking and thrashing until her legs were bruised and cut by his boots. Finally exhausted, she choked and cried together, gulping air. "Please," she begged, "please!"

"That's better," he grinned. "Now then, let's have a look, eh?" Gripping the quilt that rode above her thighs, he ripped it away and stared.

Seizing her chance, Dominique flew at his face with her fingers, scratching, jabbing, gouging, digging his flesh until her nails bulged with his skin. She must mark him for the beast he was. If he killed her, Alexandre would know.

"Take care, bitch!" he warned, slapping her with heavy hands. "I'd hate to break that lovely neck just yet." Grinning, he balled his hand into a fist and waved it above her head.

Tasting blood, choking for air, Dominique felt him grab her knees and pry them apart. "Nay, I beg thee!" she cried.

"Begging now, eh?" he laughed. "Keep it up, sweet Nikki, 'tis what I expect. 'Twill be soon enough now, I promise." Shifting his weight, he slid over her and forced entry.

"Help!" she cried, her hands pushing against his shoulders. His fist struck her hard in the jaw and she saw lights, then felt a terrible ache in her neck as she slumped back and her stomach heaved, a soft ringing filling her ears.

When Dominique awoke she lay limp and beaten beneath the weight of the man from the islands, his pock-marked face lost in her tousled hair, a wetness seeping from deep within her.

" 'Tis regrettable I was not in time to break virgin soil," Jules breathed. "Nevertheless, the ewe was still fresh and most pleasurable." Laughing heartily, he rolled off and sunk his teeth into the ripe tip of a delicious mound, biting until she screamed. "I see you are none the worse for wear." He grinned. "I would have you again but I fear I must be going. Thank Alexandre for me, will you?"

Night raised her murky skirts and allowed the peach and blue gown of dawn to descend above the rider who made his way west from Germantown. Alexandre's hands burned on the reins, the skin of his fingers raw and blistered beneath bandages applied in haste. His pain was dulled by thoughts of the bride who awaited him. He had witnessed the horrors of fire and tended the family of eight survivors. Still, he concentrated on a private need: to return as quickly as possible to his mate.

The gelding he had borrowed from Jules turned between the stone pillars of Winwood and galloped down the drive beneath the elms, spurred on by the rider's heel. The house looked deserted, dark and lonely above the lake where swans floated still as death.

Jumping down from his horse, he ran up the steps and threw open the front door, bounding through the hallway to the staircase. "*Chérie*, I'm home!" he called. Climbing the stairs so fast he was out of breath by the time he reached the master chamber, he hurried across the room.

"*Chérie*," he said softly, relieved she was asleep. "*Chérie*," he whispered, removing the covers from her face and taking her into his arms. It was dark, but he sensed something was wrong. Reaching for the candle on the bedstand, he lit the wick and held it above her head. "*Mon Dieu*!" he gasped, unable to believe his eyes. Her face was bruised and swollen, one eye closed completely, a break in the center of her quivering lip. "Jules!" he growled. The man was still mad. . . . The memories of Jules's arrogance and abusive ways surfaced until he had to choke them down.

Shaking in his arms, Dominique wished to affirm the name but could not speak. She coughed and sobbed, turning her face from his in shame.

"Tell me what happened, *chérie*? Did Monsieur Cocteau do this to you? Tell me quickly, for I must know!"

Her eyes were fearful and he drew her close for a long moment. Dominique trembled in his arms, her words barely a whisper. "Take me away," she sobbed. "Anywhere, even to Georgia."

* * *

Swans moved effortlessly on the mirrored lake below Winwood, while bees droned in the garden beneath the windows of the master chamber.

"It would be unthinkable to take your wife on a journey such as you describe at this time, Doctor Chastain. I'll be no party to moving her. She is weak and if the bleeding continues it is highly likely she will miscarry."

"Nothing is more important than my wife's life, Doctor Henninger," Alexandre replied. "I'll wait, of course."

"I commend your decision, doctor. I can tell you your father-in-law will be relieved. He wants his first grandchild very much. He wants you to stay in Philadelphia more than you know. I understand you've been invited to join the masters at the College of Physicians here."

"*Oui*, doctor, but I've declined."

Doctor Henninger frowned. "You'd best forget the South, doctor. With a sickly wife and a babe on the way, you cannot consider such a wilderness as Georgia."

"You're most kind, doctor, but there is more to consider."

"I don't know the whole story, true, but take that girl from civilization and you'll lose her *and* the babe. Take heed, doctor, take heed."

Alexandre walked the doctor to the door and bid him good day, then climbed the stairs to his wife's bedchamber. What had become of his plans to return to the South? What had become of the girl he married? He shrugged. Dominique had changed since the night of the fire. What exactly had happened? Would he ever know? Dominique had been in a state of catatonia for weeks afterward, never speaking, rarely moving. She had acted half alive. Two months had passed. He thought he would go mad. Jules Cocteau! A scoundrel never changed his colors. Yet Alexandre had known Jules was unstable . . . volatile.

Ah! If he fretted much more, he'd go insane. It was best to forget. Not forgive. Someday he would parcel out his punishment to Jules. Alexandre would wait however long he needed for a sign of vulnerability, then strike.

"*Chérie*," he said, entering his wife's bedchamber and trying to ignore the flame that burned his stomach.

"What did Doctor Henninger say, Alexandre?"

"That you are doing well, my love." He smiled.

"I've become a burden to you, Alexandre. You must release me from my vows."

"Hush, little mother," he whispered, wanting to touch her cheek but unable to for the pain gripping him. He rubbed his hand on his thigh nervously. "I don't wish to hear such nonsense. Soon you'll be up and about. The babe is the important one now, *chérie*. A child from our union of love. Your health must be guarded above all else." He had all he could do to hold himself together. Swallowing hard, he smiled at her and sank down beside the bed.

"I wish to go riding," she said softly. "I miss the horses."

"You'll be riding soon enough, my love. Sleep now."

Dominique listened with closed eyes as he crossed the room and closed the door. Tears wet her cheeks. She felt restless—how she needed to feel the sun on her face, to feel the power of a horse beneath her! Swinging her legs over the side of the bed, she gripped the posts as blackness engulfed her, yellow specks lighting her closed eyes. Shaking the nausea off, she stood and began walking toward the door. The stairs were straight ahead and the need to see the garden and breathe fresh air urged her on. Moving slowly, she found the balustrade and felt its coolness beneath her moist hands. Her thoughts flushed to the unborn babe. She did not want it because it belonged to the beast. Clinging tightly to the rail, she thought of Alexandre and the unhappiness she had caused him, the misery the child would bring them both. She did not hear Ruthe calling to her as she sank to her knees and rolled over and over again to the bottom of the stairs.

Dominique woke to the sharp clatter of a horse's hooves followed by shouts of alarm. "Doctor Chastain, sir. Thank God we caught you in time!"

"Where is she, Thomas?"

"We carried her upstairs, sir."

God, what terrible sin had he committed to deserve this? Alexandre took the stairs two at a time, prayers for his wife's and unborn child's lives on his lips.

Dominique felt cool hands on her belly. She turned her head to watch Alexandre press his ear close to listen for heartbeats, his breath warm on her skin. Tears filled her eyes and forced her to blink. Why was life so difficult? She had only wanted to feel the warmth of the sun and to run with Macbeth and Romeo. If only she could get away. To ride far away . . .

"Pray don't scold me, Alexandre. 'Twas not my idea to be with child so soon." She forced a smile and did not mention the pain.

Alexandre frowned, pleased she sounded like the Dominique of old. "Don't fret, *chérie*. The time will pass and you'll be your old self again. 'Tis soon for both of us to be parents, but God has his plans."

Plans! She did not believe in plans. She had had her own plans once. "I warned you I'd make no fit wife," she sobbed.

"After the babe comes I'll take you away, *chérie*. Away from this place that makes you unhappy."

Memories of her wedding night washed over her; the drive beneath the trees, Alexandre carrying her over the threshold, the wine . . . "God forgive me, I don't want this child," she sobbed.

He wanted to cry with her then. To cry away the hurt they had both suffered since that night. "Come spring we'll journey south *chérie*. You'll have a much grander house than Winwood and all the horses your heart desires." Lovingly, he wiped the tears from her eyes. "Forgive me, *cherie*. Forgive me for ever leaving you alone."

Another harsh Pennsylvania winter descended. Snow blanketed the gardens of Winwood and the elms sighed their discontent. The lake became a frozen sheet and the swans were nowhere to be seen. The house was cold even though smoke curled constantly from four chimneys and fires blazed in the fireplaces.

Dominique screamed into her pillow, her heels feeling the heat from the fire that blazed before her bed. Alexandre knelt beside her. "You must let me help you, *chérie*. I'm your husband—a physician!"

"Don't touch me!" she panted between pains, her upturned palms grasping the head of her bed.

"Your father may not arrive in time, *chérie*. I *must* examine you! 'Tis my right as your husband, my duty as a doctor."

"Rights! Duty!" she wailed. She almost wished to hurt him, to lash out and strike him so that he would feel the pain that made her bear down like a bitch in whelp. But he was not at fault. He only wanted to help because he loved her. She could not blame him for the pain. She screamed again, smothering her mouth into the pillow as Alexandre's hands pulled down her bedclothes and propped her up with Mrs. Yarborough's help.

"*Chérie, you* must help now. Push out the babe."

"Aye! Push, Nikki," a kind voice said. "Push, my daughter, and have it done with."

Her father's voice! Her darling wonderful father!

"Nikki, sweet Nikki, 'tis almost over now. Push the babe into the world and then you can sleep."

If only she could! If only she could have it done with and sleep for the rest of her life! Oh God, how she wanted it over. Pushing was unbearable! She screamed.

"Help the babe, *chérie*," Alexandre coaxed, holding her hand. Pulling his knuckles into her mouth, she touched the hair on his hand with her lips, biting into the bone with her teeth. Oh, God, she must be dying! She bit down hard and Alexandre brushed back her wet hair, later kissing her brow and wrapping her in warm blankets heated by the fire.

" 'Tis a girl!" came the joyous pronouncement. "A fine fat girl with the looks of her mother." Elton wiped his eyes with a big handkerchief and thanked the Lord.

Tears streaked Alexandre's cheeks. The past year had been hell but now it was over! Perhaps now he and his wife could be happy? A new babe, wrinkled and wet, had come into the world, an innocent who needed parents and love.

"Hair changes in time, my boy," Elton said. "A dark head of hair now means nothing. She looks like you, I'd say. I can see it in her eyes. Aye, she's a Chastain all right."

A *Chastain*? His mother had been fair, as was his father. His grandparents were both fair and dark. It *was* possible. He *had* made love to Dominique several times on their wedding night. He examined the babe, counting fingers and toes. "She appears to be healthy," he said, placing his finger in its tiny hand.

"Aye, that she does, my son. And feel that grip!"

Alexandre felt pride then. Who was to question God's plan? The babe was from his wife and their union of love. Why not accept it? The grandfather gently picked up the infant and placed it beneath the covers with its mother.

"A babe should be with its mother first, I believe. See how content it is now, Alexandre. Nikki smiles in her sleep. She'll make a good mother, you'll see. Praise God, my son, you're a father!"

* * *

The Arab, El'Ramir, arched his head and lifted his tail elegantly, intelligence visible in his black eyes. Dominique laughed gaily and kissed her father's cheek, mounting the milk-white stallion with a stableboy's help.

"But another stallion, Elton?" Alexandre said in disbelief. "Forgive me if I cannot comprehend your thinking."

" 'Tis a promise I made a long time ago, Alexandre. Look at her! She's missed her riding, I can tell you. Now she has something to keep her occupied. Horses are her love, my boy, her true love!"

Alexandre thought on the words and shook his head, squinting in the bright sunlight. "*Oui*, Elton, but she has the child now."

"She's but a child herself, my boy. I realize that too late perhaps. The girl was not ready for marriage, much less motherhood." Elton hung his head. "I blame myself for her unhappiness, my boy."

Alexandre observed his wife numbly. "The blame is mine, doctor. I regret I've been unable to make her happy."

"Ah, but you can, Alexandre," Elton said reassuringly, laying his arm about his shoulder. "You're what she needs now. Aye, I know she's not been well and you've had to play the physician more than the husband. But things are going to change, my boy. Nikki's herself again, I know it!"

Alexandre wished with all his heart that Elton spoke the truth. He admired the woman executing perfect circles beneath the spreading elms, her beauty striking against a cloudless sky. Dressed in green velvet, she guided the white Arab artfully, performing as if a sultan looked on. Turning away, he could not watch. He took long strides toward the kennels. The hounds at least would be glad to see him. The babe was three months old now and his wife had still not called him to her bed.

He looked up to see Dominique wheel her horse and boldly cut him off, her eyes flashing as she drew rein and looked down on him. Reaching out an arm, he stepped back and seized the Arab's head, Dominique's quirt striking his cheek as he did so. His expression was one of bemusement as she applied the quirt to her horse and rode off in a frenzied gallop, the white and green of horse and rider a speck that traveled past the lake to the woods.

"Ride out after her, my boy!" Elton had seen what had taken place.

"You do not understand, Elton," he replied. "Your daughter and I . . ."

"I understand more than you think, my boy," Elton advised. "Go after her, I tell you. Nikki loves you. She just doesn't know it."

If he were only correct, Alexandre mused.

"Hurry, man, go after her, and quickly!"

Breaking into a run, Alexandre ran to the stable and mounted a palomino mare, giving the beast its head and covering the distance to the lake at full tilt. A freshly disturbed trail cut sharply through the woods, black earth overturned by flying hooves, and he took up the chase.

"Damn him!" Dominique swore, riding her gift horse into the ground. "Damn him!" Free at last, she was determined to forget her husband. Forget the damnable bed and house with its stifling walls and crying babe. She breathed deeply of the air and looked up into the sky. *This* was what she wanted, heaven, earth, a steed of purest blood. The ride cooled her mood and the sun warmed her back. Why had she ever married? But she knew the answer: To please her father! And now she had a child. She thought of the strange little creature who made odd sounds and turned night into day, cuddling warmly at her breast, sucking and smiling strangely. She had seen her father in the infant's eyes, herself as well, but Alexandre? Her thoughts whirled and she dug her heel into the Arab's flanks, hearing hoofbeats from another horse. Alexandre! Why in God's name couldn't he leave her alone?

"*Chérie!*" he called.

The babe! Perhaps something was wrong with the babe? She reined in her horse and called over her shoulder in a loud voice: "Is there something wrong with the babe?"

"The child is fine!" he returned, coming up alongside. "May I join you or must you ride alone?" His gold hair shone even in the half light of these woods. He wore no coat, the laces of his white linen shirt untied like a stableboy's, his mushroom-colored breeches tight against his thighs to reveal a man she had near forgotten. She would not admit she loved the creases in his cheeks or the smooth skin and velvet-brown eyes that bespoke such tender love. "There's plenty of space for two," she countered, lifting her chin and spurring on her steed.

"I'll just follow along then," he replied.

Her nod seemed enough as she rode into the sunlight, off the beaten path and into a field of swaying grass. "We should stay on the trail," he warned, trying to keep up with her.

"Ride where you wish!" she shot back. "I didn't ask you to come."

" 'Tis uneven ground, a place where rodents dig holes!" He watched as her Arab seemingly left the earth, his hooves never touching ground. Dominique's hair was bound in a heavy knot that caressed the nape of her neck; the place he longed to kiss. Yellow strands strayed about her head, tangling with the wind. The mare tried to keep up the pace but the stallion had been sired by lightning. Suddenly the palomino cried out and broke her stride, going down on one front leg as Alexandre plunged head first over her neck.

A sharp pain stabbed his shinbone and his senses reeled for countless moments. When he opened his eyes he could see the mare grazing nearby and the sun blazing in a cavernous sky. He moved his head, surprised to discover his neck was not broken. A pity. He frowned. A broken neck would have solved all his problems. He heard the thunder of pounding hooves and lifted his head slightly to see his wife approaching.

"Alexandre?" Dominique called, riding up to him and sliding from her saddle, she hurried to his side in a swish of skirts. "Don't play games, Alexandre Chastain," she cried, scanning his body. "You forget I am a doctor's daughter."

Forcing his facial muscles to relax, Alexandre held back a moan, the ache in his head allowing him to forget his leg momentarily.

"Alexandre?" she said in a concerned tone, bending down to examine him. Her cool hands ran over his chest and ribs and pulled his shirt from his breeches. She loosened his belt. "Pray nothing is broken," she muttered, sliding her hands over his loins. Alexandre bit his lip to keep from screaming as she squeezed his knee and moved his leg. "Ouch!" he said at last, flinching at the tenderness of the bone.

"I would say 'tis broken," she announced. Was it rain or tear that splashed onto his cheek? He looked up into the sky and saw no clouds. God help him, could she possibly care?

"Be thankful 'tis only your leg," she said. "Speak to me, Alexandre. Open your eyes."

He fluttered his lashes and rolled his eyes back, moaning deeply.

"You could have been killed," she scolded, resting her cheek against his face. Her lips nuzzled his cheek and it was not difficult for him to feign delirium. "You shouldn't have followed me," she said. "I'm sorry I struck you back there, but you made me angry. I know I've been no wife to you, but that does not mean—"

"What?" he queried, pulling her down to him. Her hair fell like a golden curtain about their heads and their lips met in a searing kiss. Dominique tried to pull away, but to no avail.

"Don't leave me, love," he said hoarsely. "I live, I breathe, I want!"

She jerked her head back and smiled because he was alive, taking his face in her hands and covering it with little kisses.

"Forgive me, my husband," she said, taking him in her arms and falling back with him into the deep grass, the green of her habit melding with the vibrant color that surrounded them.

"My love," he said, opening the front of her habit. "When I look at you I cannot believe my eyes." His mouth found a bare breast and tasted its trembling tip. His fingers caught her hair and pulled so he could fasten his lips over hers, to meet her tongue with his. Her eyes were moist as he explored her flat belly and marveled at how quickly her figure had returned. He awakened a desire in her she thought was dead, a desire she refused to accept.

"I want you," he rasped. "You are my wife and my patience has been tried." He drew her hand to his, the pain in his leg so intense he seemed driven by it. He brushed the hair from her face and waited for her reply.

"I cannot," she said softly, trying to see his face in the sun's glare. "Pray leave me be!"

"I am your husband, *chérie*! The man who loves you! Strike me, curse me, but heaven above don't send me away!" His voice broke and he drew her close, his tears wetting her hair.

She looked up then and studied his features, the kind, warm eyes and sensitive mouth.

"We were joined together in holy matrimony before God, remember? You took an oath to be my wife." He held her close and loved her the way a man should love a woman, kissing her face and neck, adoring her perfection. "I shall love you for as long as we both shall live," he whispered, "and afterward."

She listened to his words and trembled in his arms until the sun disappeared and the gold-streaked sky turned purple and pink.

"We'd best be getting back now," he said at last, rising and wincing at the pain.

"Alexandre, your leg?"

His face was white and he had sunk back against her.

"I'll fetch Thomas and we'll bring you back in a cart."

"*Non*," he said. "Pray help me to my horse before your father sends the hounds for us."

"But you cannot ride!" she moaned.

"Your concern overwhelms me, my love, but your husband is not mortally wounded. I will be fine."

"Poor darling," she said, helping him mount the mare and suffering with him as he sagged in the saddle. "You go first this time," she said, pulling herself up on El'Ramir and smiling back at him. "I'll follow you home."

Alexandre lay on the sofa in the parlor of Winwood and counted the plaster swans on the ceiling.

" 'Tis broken, my boy," Elton said. "You'll not be doctoring for a while." The elder doctor's eyes sparkled as he winked at his son-in-law. "You were out there long enough to see all two hundred fifty acres." He chuckled. "From the look of things you accomplished what you set out to do?"

Alexandre grimaced with pain. "It would seem so, doctor."

"My granddaughter survived as well," Elton said. "The little one suckles at her mother's breast like it was her last meal." Laughing aloud expressed his heartfelt merriment, the robust laughter filling the house.

Dominique awoke to the sound of her father's voice and felt surrounded with radiant warmth, her body wrapped tightly in her husband's arms. "Desiree?" she queried softly.

"Asleep in her cradle," came the reply. " 'Tis late. You slept well into the night."

Closing her eyes, she enjoyed the nearness of his strong body, remembering what he had said earlier that day.

"I need you," he said, pressing urgently against her.

Turning in his arms, she slipped a hand about his neck and parted her lips, cuddling close. The memories of the last time she'd been this way with a man now faded as she enjoyed surrender.

" 'Tis bliss," he said. "God let it forever be thus." Their bodies came together and her breasts felt full with the milk of motherhood. His fingers traced the mountains and valleys of her body and caressed her belly as she twisted and turned in his arms. Her nipples brushed his chest and he bent down to kiss and drink of her warmth. "Pray let me love you," he pleaded, kissing her deeply and delving into the velvet of her mouth.

"I'm afraid," she whispered.

"You must never fear me," he said, his lips leaving moist kisses as his hands gently parted her thighs. "You must trust me."

She held her breath until she felt the wonderful strength of him and he moaned in her ear. "I love you."

Dear God, she needed him as well. But was it love? A longing rushed through her, and she surprised herself by giving in to it completely.

6

Spanish moss hung from the trees along the Savannah River, the morning air thick and eerie in the fog. Dominique trembled and her husband wrapped a light shawl about her shoulders.

"Is it the fog or Georgia that sets you atrembling, *chérie*?"

"A bit of both," she replied, looking around the landscape. " 'Tis strange. The land, the trees, the air."

"The air is better where we are bound, *chérie*. We travel north toward the mountains in a day or two, and in the high altitude there are no mosquitos." He looked down into her green eyes fringed with soot-black lashes.

"But snakes, Alexandre?"

"I promise to kill the first serpent that crosses your path, milady." He grinned.

"If I don't die first," she moaned.

"Look there!" he exclaimed, pointing between the land and their ship. "Gators!"

Dominique's eyes filled with excitement. "All I see is logs," she said, grabbing his coattails and holding him fast.

"Logs that could chew off a man's leg," he said, folding her in his arms. He pointed to a high bluff nearly hidden in the fog. "Savannah, my love. We're almost home."

The *New Hope* was met by a crowd that struggled to see who

and what was on board. Dominique looked down into a sea of straw hats, bandannas, planters, and tricorns. Skins of many colors caught her eye: Black, beige, brown, and tan. Some Africans wore scanty coverings, while others had clad themselves in an abundance of clothes.

"Stay close, *chérie*," Alexandre said firmly, taking his wife's hand. "My brother Jacques should be somewhere milling about."

A young man, bare-headed and dressed modestly in black, shouted to them warmly and rushed up the gangplank. "Welcome to Savannah, Doctor and Mrs. Chastain," he smiled, handing Alexandre a letter of introduction. "Francois Chastain asks that you accompany me to his house here in Savannah. Preparations have been made to receive you and your servants."

"Myron Smith," Alexandre read. "Teacher and reader of the law."

Dominique descended the gangplank on Alexandre's arm, but before her foot could touch Southern soil he swooped her up into his arms and loaded her aboard a waiting carriage.

"Forgive me, *chérie*, but the animals are still aboard. You understand, of course."

"Of course," she replied. He had explained they would be separated once ashore and that she must be prepared to abide with the misery of wheels for a time. "Please hurry," she whispered as he placed her babe in her arms.

"Mr. Smith will go with you," he said. "I'll catch up as soon as possible." He kissed her cheek and disappeared into the crowd before she knew it. Fog drifted into the open door of the coach like smoke from Hades and Mrs. Yarborough heaved herself up to take her place beside her mistress. Myron Smith settled himself into the opposite seat and gave the order to leave. With a crack of the whip they were off, over slippery cobblestones and up a steep hill to the city of Savannah.

Chastain House sat on a square with huge magnolia trees on either side of the stairways that led to the front door. A dark girl named Mocha handed Dominique a large lemony-smelling bloom and curtsied, dropping her gaze to the ground. Dominique thanked the girl and looked over the house that bore her married name. Constructed of tabby with shuttered dormers and steeply pitched roof, it looked small in comparison to Winburn House.

"I'm sorry for not meetin' your carriage, honey," a woman said, coming down the stairs. "We've been expectin' you for weeks and I was sleepy this mornin'."

Dominique held out her hand to the woman gowned elegantly in persimmon silk and wearing black coral about her neck. She was about her mother's age, Dominique guessed, attractive and brunette, with eyes that appeared to be violet. Her ample figure was most appealing.

"Catharine Ross, honey," the woman said. "Cat, to my friends. And you're the fair-haired sweetheart Alexandre married." She smiled. "Welcome to Savannah, darlin'."

Dominique curtsied and Cat embraced her.

"The third cottage down the square's mine," Cat said. "The blue one with the white picket fence and the carriage house in back. Now then, where's that handsome boy you married?"

"Alexandre's seeing to the animals," Dominique replied. "He'll be along soon."

"I'm certain of that." Cat smiled. "Alexandre wouldn't leave you waitin' long if he's smart, and I know he's more than that." She laughed and showed Dominique into the house, taking her to the second floor where she excused herself.

"What right has she to call the doctor *boy*?" Mrs. Yarborough whispered when Cat was gone. "Who is she, anyway?"

"I'm certain we'll find out soon enough," Dominique replied.

The morning passed slowly and Dominique freshened herself from the long voyage and changed into a lighter dress, returning to the downstairs to chat with Cat. Dark-skinned girls garbed in blue-and-white-striped muslin and frilled caps served tea and cakes while Cat's eyes appraised the new Mrs. Chastain.

"You're not to concern yourself with nothin' while you're here in Savannah, ya hear, honey? We'll have a late supper when your husband gets back and all you'll do is make yourself gorgeous for the menfolk."

"Who are you expecting besides Alexandre and Mr. Smith?" Dominique asked.

"Captain Cooper from the *New Hope*, and a gentleman I met recently here in Savannah. A dashing young planter." She smiled. "I thought Alexandre might hire him as his overseer. Racemont needs one, you know."

"I thought Alexandre's brother Jacques was the plantation's overseer," Dominique said.

Cat raised a brow and sipped her tea thoughtfully. "Has your husband told you about his half-brother Jacques?"

"Only that he would be meeting us here," Dominique replied.

"Then you have much to learn about." Cat smiled. "Much indeed."

Before Dominique could query further, the conversation turned to servants. It was decided that Mocha would sleep in Mrs. Yarborough's room on a pallet beside the baby's cradle. The shy black girl took an immediate liking to the infant and Dominique felt an implicit confidence in her. Alexandre arrived in the late afternoon in time for his wife's bath.

" 'Tis what every man should come home to," he said, leaning over the screen beside the tub and reaching down to caress a full breast.

"Alexandre!" Dominique cried. "You startled me."

"You saw the hand was white," he chuckled, lifting a lock that floated beside a creamy shoulder and admiring her with husbandly pride.

"I did not think on the color of the skin," she shot back. "I thought myself alone."

"We are," he smiled. " 'Tis a pity I'm so exhausted."

She flicked a finger and sprinkled his face with suds. "Is that all you think about?"

"Would you rather I called upon the Cat?"

She glared back at him.

"I see you've met the purring widow with the appropriate name?" he teased.

"She came as a surprise," she replied softly. "You should have told me."

"My father's friend, not mine. She's been around a long time. I had no way of knowing she'd be in Savannah. I've not seen her in years."

"I don't think she likes me," she replied, sponging the soap off her arms.

"Pay her no heed, *chérie*. She's been the only woman in father's life for a long time and she fancies herself mistress of Racemont."

"Perhaps she will be?"

"*Non*, I know my father better than that." He offered his

hand. "Come, my pale beauty. Supper is about to be served and the smell of cornbread is driving me mad!"

She snatched up a towel to cover herself.

"After supper we shall have our dessert here." He grinned, filling his eyes with the image of her stepping from the tub. She fled behind a screen but not before he saw the dimples in her luscious derriere. " 'Tis the first time I've viewed you from this angle," he said. "I fear I've missed a most magnificent sight."

"Remember the cornbread," she said as he followed her behind the screen and removed her towel.

"I missed you," he said, bending to kiss the pink tip of a breast and pulling her close.

"Cornbread," she said, "you must not ruin your appetite."

"Nothing could be more appetizing than the ripe fruit I see before me now," he breathed.

"I thought you were exhausted." she giggled.

A loud knock came at the door. "Your presence is requested in the dinin' chamber, Doctor and Mrs. Chastain," a young female voice drawled.

Alexandre paid no attention and turned his wife to kiss the hollow of her back, sliding his hands over her hips. "One kiss to last me through the evening," he said as his lips caressed her shoulder.

"Your presence is requested for supper," the voice repeated.

"Remind me to have her chained and gagged after we eat," Alexandre said, kissing his wife deeply.

Supper was sumptuous. Tureens of crab stew in sherry and cream, cold shrimp, red snapper and catfish, and black-eyed peas and cornbread. Alexandre poured his wife a glass of Madeira and admired the French creation she wore, sheer pink with knife-pleated sleeves and delicate lace that draped her hands. Her hair was arranged in a swirl of curls that dangled languorously over one shoulder, and the necklace Alexandre had given her showed off her swelling breasts.

"Rememeber our dessert," he whispered in her ear.

Four elderly slaves stood in the corners of the room, white-haired and dressed to the teeth in velvet breeches and waistcoats, their frilled shirts and hose white as virgin snow.

"Your gems!" Cat exclaimed. "Haven't I seen them before?" She stared at the shafts of light that were reflected by Dominique's raviere, her eyes reduced to slits.

"A gift from my husband." Dominique smiled. "They belonged to his mother."

Cat made no attempt to hide her envy. " 'Tis most gratifying to be a Chastain." she purred. "Pray tell me how it feels?"

Dominique looked at her blankly, uncertain of her meaning. "No different than it feels to be a Winburn," she replied modestly. " 'Tis the man, not his name, that makes the difference."

Alexandre smiled to himself and Myron Smith cleared his throat.

"I've never seen your father looking better," Myron said to Alexandre. "He and Jacques wanted to be here to welcome you but neither could leave the plantation."

"You saw my father recently, Mr. Smith?"

"A fortnight ago, sir. The servants were polishing the silver and the house was being cleaned from the cellar up." He turned to Dominique. "I understand you attended school in Boston, Mrs. Chastain?"

"Aye," she replied. "Boston is most cultural."

"Nothing like this godforsaken hole," he replied. "Georgia is backward, as you will soon find out. They don't know culture from a cow! I regret to say you'll see many wild animals and Indians in Savannah, my dear. We have nothing but illiterates and thieves here, not to mention blacks and foreigners. 'Tis a fact we're subject to attack any moment from the sea, and our streets are mud-encased. Pray forgive me if I cannot fathom why a lady of your background would leave Philadelphia to come here."

Dominique looked at Alexandre.

"My wife came with me," Alexandre put down his fork. "Tell me, Myron, do you know my father well?"

"I met Francois when he arranged for the education of his slaves," he replied uneasily, loading his plate with food. "A most generous and unique gesture, I thought, although I understand he has gone overboard to the point of schooling savages."

"*Indians*," Alexandre corrected. "Father believes learning is as necessary as the light of day. 'Tis a pity some men never see the light no matter how long they study."

"Ignorance is beyond belief in Georgia," Myron said.

" 'Tis up to us to change that, Myron. I see no reason why the South cannot be like the North. Better even."

"There's need for men of your caliber here, Alexandre," Captain Cooper commented. "Perhaps you would consider practicing in Savannah. We have no doctors yet."

"I regret I cannot, captain," Alexandre said. "I've waited a long time to come home."

"Where is your gentleman friend, Cat?" Dominique asked. "Was he detained perhaps?"

Cat smiled. "I was aware of a previous engagement. You'll meet him another time."

"I shall look forward to it." Dominique smiled.

"Someone I know?" Alexandre queried, hearing for the first time about the wayward guest.

"Nay, Alexandre. Some planter I met at the inn a week or so ago. An eager young man who seeks employment on a large plantation such as your father's. No one you know," she assured him.

"Will you be going to Racemont with us?" Alexandre asked Myron Smith.

"Not this trip, monsieur. I'm tutoring the children of an English family until they sail for New England."

"Too bad," Alexandre said, silently blessing the English family and he pushed back his chair.

"Colonel Hawkins is in Georgia," Captain Cooper told Alexandre. "There's talk of unrest among the Indians and some of us believe it will lead to war."

"War against the Indians or war against the whites?" Alexandre asked.

Dominique drained her goblet and listened to every word while a slave refilled her glass.

"Bloodshed one way or the other!" Captain Cooper said. "The settlers press the red man west. Colonel Hawkins believes war is inevitable."

Alexandre looked at his wife's pale complexion and reached across the table to envelop her hand. "We can talk of this another time," he said. "I'll be glad to discuss the facts when you and Colonel Hawkins visit Racemont."

The conversation took on a lighter tone then. Still, Dominique was certain she'd heard the words *massacre, murder,* and *savages*. Dishes rattled and her ears buzzed, the room suddenly short of air, the sickening odor of food making her ill. Why *had* she left Philadelphia and civilization? Myron Smith was right, but now it was too late. She was in another world, a place where red men roamed free, where snakes and ferocious beasts abounded. Feeling sick in the pit of her stomach, she realized she'd made a terrible mistake. She had to return to Philadelphia. . . .

"My wife and I thank you for your kindness," Alexandre said. He stood beside his wife, helping Dominique from her chair. "It's been a long day and I fear my wife is overtired." He kissed Cat's hand, waited until everyone had left the room, then took his wife into his arms. "The babe is tucked in for the night, *chérie*. Come, 'tis time for bed." His voice was kind and she went with him to the stairs, her thoughts filled with visions of warring red men and crawling vipers, howling beasts and death by war.

It was two hours later when the Swiss clock on the mantelpiece struck twelve. "I'll be a failure as your wife, Alexandre. 'Tis certain Cat Ross is more qualified to be mistress of Racemont than I."

"You'll be all I expect you to be," Alexandre replied. He lay staring at the oaken beams over their heads. "The epitome of beauty, womanhood, and charm. I ask nothing more."

"But a house *larger* than this, Alexandre! Dozens of servants. Surely I cannot—"

He held a finger to her lips and raised himself up on one arm. "I'll never ask you to be more than you can be," he said. "You have taken our guest's words too seriously."

"If you mean the talk of war and bloodshed, aye, I did," she retorted. "Not so much for myself as the babe!"

"Such talk is greatly exaggerated, *chérie*. I know the Indians as well as anyone. They're not the savages you think they are."

"But they will fight for what is rightfully theirs, will they not?"

"There's no danger, I tell you," he assured her. He took her hand in his and kissed it lovingly. "Do you really believe I would bring you here if there were?"

"Why not?" she replied. "You *love* Georgia!"

"I love you more," he said. "Georgia is new and wild, *oui*, but so are the lands south of Pennsylvania. 'Tis up to us to make friends of the Indians."

"*You* make friends with them!" she said smugly. "I want no part of your savages!"

"As you wish," he said. "We'll be home soon and that's all that matters."

"I'll soon tire of playing mistress to a house," she advised.

"You will have your horses," he said. " 'Tis not my intent to press you into duties you don't enjoy."

She placed a kiss on his cheek impulsively.

"My love." He pulled her to him. "What was that for?"

"For being so good to me," she replied simply.

"For no other reason?"

" 'Tis late," she said, suddenly sorry she had kissed him. Her feelings were engulfed by a surge of uneasiness and confusion. "I am tired," she said, turning on her side to close her eyes.

"Do not be afraid," he said, kissing her neck where it was bared. He moved over her and whispered in her ear. "I love you, my wife. You must believe what I say and think of nothing else."

He got out of bed and went to the window. A young city slumbered outside and he lifted the drapes to study the simplicity of the square. Lamplight twinkled and the air smelled of magnolia. He looked at his slumbering wife. Would she ever find peace from the past? His jaw pulsated, the painful memory of their wedding night haunting him. *Was* Jules Cocteau the sire of the babe? The jagged truth tore at him. They had never spoken of what had happened that night. His wife couldn't talk about it but he had not forgotten. A dark pock-marked face leered from the darkness and laughed at him. "God help me find him," he prayed, falling to his knees. "Deliver Jules Cocteau into my hands!"

Sun splashed through the crotch of a giant oak whose thick vines camouflaged an eagle's flight as the entourage of horses and wagons thundered by. Dark forests of pine stretched as far as the eye could see, their brown needles carpeting the road to the mountains. Savannah and the sea lay sixteen days behind, the road to Racemont stretching endlessly in front of them.

The passenger dressed in dove gray wiped her forehead with a lace handkerchief and pushed back the moist wisps of topaz hair that escaped from her pleated bonnet. God, how she hated wheels! Another day of travel and she would be climbing the walls of the carriage. Dominique lifted the skirts of her linen traveling dress above her knees and looked up suddenly. The light had suddenly disappeared.

"Carolina parakeets!" Cat said. "Frightened by something, I'd guess. They are here by the thousands."

Dominique stared out the window and saw a mountain lion leap atop a large rock. "Dear God, how does one live in the company of wild beasts?"

"You'll manage, honey." Cat laughed. "You've nothin' to fear with a house full of males to protect you."

Doninique fanned her face nervously. "Why can't I ride with Alexandre?"

Cat laughed again. "Because you are Mrs. Alexandre Michel de la Ramée Chastain, honey. The mistress of Racemont and daughter-in-law of François Chastain. A lady of your class travels in the safety and comfort of a fine coach, drawn by the purest blood, of course."

"You make me sound like a pompous queen!" Doninique objected. "I'll not pretend to be something I'm not. I don't wish to ride in this black box and if I could find my Arab I'd soon be out of it!"

"Then do it!" Cat urged. "We'll soon be at a way station and you can don your best habit and demand your horse. No one will stop you. Least of all Alexandre."

"Why do you say that?"

"I know him. Aye, he's dependable like a good wind and gentle as a summer breeze when it comes to you or his animals. Try him—you'll see I'm right."

Dominique smiled and looked out the window to see her husband wheel his horse and trot alongside her carriage, then signal the driver to stop.

"I know you're weary, *chérie*," he said, looking down at her face in the coach's window. "Can you and Mrs. Ross make it to the next stop, another hour or so uphill?"

Dominique wanted to cry out, but smiled instead. "Aye." She nodded assuringly, watching him as he backed his stallion to allow her carriage to pass.

"We may as well put the time to good use," Cat drawled. "Let's talk about men."

"The only man I know is Alexandre, and you know more about him and his family than I do. Pray tell me what his father and brother are like?"

"François is a man of great wealth and charm," she began.

"A gentle man, like your husband. Good to his friends and respected by all who know him."

"You're in love with him, aren't you?"

Taken aback, Cat blushed and removed her hat. " 'Tis a straightforward question, honey. Aye, I guess I am. I've known François a long time, since he landed in Savannah and needed a scout to take him into Indian territory. My husband, Morgan, was a woodsman and friend of the Creek Indians. He knew the territory from Savannah to Knoxville like most men know the way to their outhouses. Morgan introduced François to the chiefs of the five tribes and helped him secure land rights." Cat's expression changed, her tone bitter. "Morgan was in Choctaw country when he got wounded and died. I was with child . . ."

"Forgive me for prying, Cat. 'Tis a bad habit of mine."

" 'Tis in the past," Cat said, gazing out the window to conceal her face. "François invited me to come to Racemont after that. The house was only a sketch then but he said he needed a housekeeper. When I declined he gave me a house with slaves in Savannah." She sighed deeply. "Since then we've become very close."

"I see." Dominique lowered her eyes and fumbled with her babe's bonnet.

"You're wondering if we're lovers?"

Dominique's face paled.

"The answer is nay. François is in love with someone else."

"I'm sorry."

Cat laughed. "Alexandre's mother," she whispered softly. "Margo's still very much alive in François's mind."

"Does Alexandre know this?"

"He's been away a long time, honey. Alexandre knows little of his father's life. Now then, tell me *your* story. How did you meet Alexandre?"

" 'Tis quite dull," Dominique said.

"Tell me anyway," Cat insisted. "I'd enjoy a tale of romance since there's none in my life."

"I can't believe that, Cat. Surely there are men in Savannah who seek a wife. Forgive me—'tis none of my business."

"We're friends now." Cat laughed. "Aye, there are men in Savannah. All hungry for a woman's body and a bed mate to keep them warm. I'd have none of them."

"What of the planter? The gentleman from the islands who didn't come for supper?"

Cat's eyes lit up and her lips parted in a smile. "He seems to have disappeared. Gone back to that island he came from, no doubt." She laughed. "Forget him! Pray tell me about Alexandre. I wish to hear all of it."

Dominique leaned back and dipped her handkerchief between her breasts where she felt stickiest, and giggled. Then she recounted the tale as Desiree slept peacefully in her lap. Cat's shrill laughter at the humorous climaxes carried to the ears of the men and accompanying entourage of female help, who rode in a separate carriage. Inside, Mrs. Yarborough, Nancy, and Ruthe glanced at each other in curiosity.

The long inn was two-storied and built of logs to accommo-date twenty overnight guests. Dominique wrinkled up her nose as Nancy fastened her rose-colored habit. "Impractical," Dominique snapped, brushing her hair over her shoulders until it cascaded down her back and danced on the tapestried bench were she sat. " 'Tis for a ride on the park on Sunday, not a dusty trail in Georgia!"

" 'Tis the only one I can find," Nancy said. "Should I twist up your hair and pin it out of your face for the ride?"

"Do it quickly, Nancy. I must be gone from here before my husband sees."

"May I say the carriage is the place for a fine lady such as you, Miss Nikki? What will the master's father think when you arrive dirty and tired, like a farmer's wife?" Ruthe ventured.

"I don't care!" Dominique said. "I *despise* wheels and I'll not ride another mile in that cursed coach!"

Ruthe said no more and Nancy pinned Dominique's golden tresses in place while her mistress fanned herself.

"I've never been so hot!" Dominique complained. "Why in God's name did I ever leave Germantown to come here?" She jumped up to look out the window at the goings-on below, spotting Alexandre in the crowd of men. Her husband's golden hair fluttered in the breeze as he stood atop a wagon and instructed a group of slaves, his legs tapered in beige breeches and tan leather boots. 'Twas her husband down there, she reminded herself, the man whose name she bore, the *reason* she'd came to this land of never-ending trees.

"Forgive the intrusion, Madame Chastain," a deep voice drawled behind her.

Startled, Dominique whirled around to face a tall dark-skinned man in the doorway, impeccably dressed in white shirt and yellow breeches. He held a planter's hat over his heart and bowed low.

"Jacques Chastain, your servant, ma'am. Welcome to Georgia." Handsome by any woman's standards, the nostrils in his straight nose flared, his black hair was tightly coiled, and the look in his eyes was most engaging. Jacques stepped forward and took her hand.

"Alexandre's brother?"

"We have the same sire, ma'am." His smile revealed good teeth in perfect alignment. "And you are Dominique, perfection in the form of a woman."

She curtsied and smiled into his face, noting the little lines that fanned around his eyes when he smiled back.

"My brother requests your presence in the dining hall, little sister." He bowed again and let her pass, showing her down the hall to where her husband waited. Alexandre's face was lit with a grin when he saw them approaching, and his hand reached out for hers.

"What do you think of him, eh?" Alexandre asked. "Frightening-looking devil, isn't he? Wonderful tan, though, don't you agree?"

She laughed and Jacques gave his white half-brother a glare as they clasped hands and broke into a husky roar. Dominique tried to slip past them, but Alexandre stopped her.

"You look fetching, *chérie*," he said escorting her into the dining hall. "But why the velvet habit?"

"I told you I wish to ride the remainder of the way on my Arab," she said. "I request your permission, of course."

His brow creased with concern. He played the husband well. "We've several hours of daylight left, madame. You're in Creek territory now and you'll ride where you're told, where you're safest. In the coach with your babe!" His words were clearly stated and he gave her chair an extra push for emphasis as he seated her.

"Will we arrive before dark?" she asked sweetly, smiling at Jacques.

"We'll have enough light to bed the hounds," Jacques replied.

They broke bread and the brothers talked of times past, of family and friends, old slaves and future crops. Dominique listened until she was weary of men's talk, finding herself lost when they conversed in French. She ate cold turtle soup and bread smeared with honey, excusing herself when platters of bass were served. She hurried outdoors to where the slaves and servants gathered about the horses.

"Saddle my Arab and bring him to me at once," she told Thomas. "Release Macbeth and Romeo as well."

Ruthe's husband Thomas had known her since she was a babe, and it was clear he did not approve. But obeying obediently, he passed her order to a husky black who set off in a run for the stallion. Nancy joined her mistress with a bemused face.

"The babe, Nancy? Is she sleeping?"

"Like a puppy, Miss Nikki. Mrs. Yarborough watches over her like a hawk and Ruthe is watching Mrs. Yarborough."

Dominique laughed and mounted El'Ramir with Thomas's help. As she climbed into the saddle she spied Alexandre and Jacques walk out the inn's door.

"A woman of such magnificence together with a steed of noble breeding brings tears to my eyes," Jacques said, breaking his stride.

" 'Tis a woman bent on killing herself!" Alexandre said. "A wife who *deliberately* disobeys her husband."

"Don't be hard on her, Alexandre. The way is well protected by my Creek brothers. I for one will enjoy her company. Your strong-willed wife can ride between us."

"If she has her way she will lead!" Alexandre said. "You don't know this girl I've chosen as my mate."

"I can see she has spirit and I approve," Jacques said. "Come, let us ride with her and make tracks before the light is gone."

Dominique's proud figure graced the Arab's back. She refused to meet her husband's gaze.

"You may ride between my brother and your husband," Alexandre told Dominique. He looked up at her and couldn't resist a grin. "Unless you have the need to fly." He did not think she accepted his jest seriously, not until she smiled back and he saw the dimple indent her cheek.

"Thank you, my lord," she replied, touching her heel to the Arab and taking off like an arrow. She shook out her reins and gave El'Ramir his head, her skirts blooming in a cloud of red dust.

"*Chérie!*" Alexandre yelled, seeing Jacques mount his bay gelding in a swoop and ride out to catch the Arab.

The sun was no longer bright, its heat instead a rosy blush on Dominique's nose and forehead. She looked back and saw nothing but pines and road and sky. Alone at last, she wondered where everyone was. The forest grew darker with every pound of Ramir's hooves and the road swept upward abruptly. She slowed her steed to a walk, the dogs lagging behind her, panting and halting abruptly when El'Ramir flicked his ears and raised his head and tail in alarm.

"What is it?" she asked her mount, as if she expected a reply. All ears pricked up in anticipation.

Then from a clearing a rider appeared, naked except for a breechcloth and red cloak draped over one shoulder. The man seemed unsurprised by Dominique's presence and cast her a proud, defiant look. Gold crowned his head and flashed brilliantly from a well-muscled bronzed chest and upper arms. His full head of hair was hung with plumes of black and white. Cold chills rippled up Dominique's spine and she squared her shoulders to indicate a fearlessness she did not entirely feel. But then Romeo and Macbeth suddenly became animated and lunged forward, barking furiously.

By the time Dominique had gotten the dogs under control, the strkingly handsome rider had vanished.

Alexandre's eyes darkened and he dug his heels into the sides of his stallion. It was not like him to run a horse uphill but there seemed good reason now. His wife had disappeared! If anything had happened he would never forgive himself. Hands tense on the reins, his fingers tingled with fear as he watched the excited pack of hounds round a bend. Perhaps Jacques had caught up with Dominique and they had reached the plantation's gates? Perhaps Ramir had stumbled and his wife lay dead on the road? Perhaps his brother and his wife were resting in some leafy glade, laughing because they had outridden him?

A whippoorwill called out his evening song, its incessant message a plague to his ears. If he got his wife in his sight again he would not allow her to stray beyond Racemont's gates! His mount crested the hill from where Alexandre spied two horses in the distance. "Thank God," he whispered, spurring his steed to a trot. Relief swelled inside his chest and his breath escaped in long draughts.

"Alexandre!" Jacques called. "What took you so long? We've been worried."

Alexandre cleared his throat and dismounted, walking in long strides to reach his wife's side. "If you *ever* do that again . . ."

"What?" Dominique asked innocently.

He swept her off her feet and held her so tightly her breath escaped in a gasp.

"Pray forgive me, my husband," she said, realizing for the first time that his conviction she was his property had grown. "I only felt the need to—"

"*Fly*?" Jacques chuckled.

"*Oui*! She should have been born an eagle!" Alexandre moaned.

"*Non*, an Arab perhaps?" Jacques chuckled.

"Better a man!" Dominique interjected.

"Such a waste God would not allow!" Jacques exclaimed. "You were fortunate to find such a woman, my brother. You will never be bored with matrimony."

Alexandre held his wife close and smoothed the topaz tresses that covered her back. "We'd best be on our way. The gates of home stand yonder."

"I promise to follow this time," Dominique said softly as he lifted her into her saddle and made certain the girth was tight.

"I want you before me!" he replied with a frown. "With your loveliness in view." He gave her hand a squeeze and mounted his peppered stallion.

"Look!" Jacques called out. " 'Tis Benjamin Hawkins."

A man in buckskins raised his hand in greeting as he approached, straddling a pony like the one she had seen the Indian riding.

"Benjamin!" Alexandre called, galloping out to meet the Indian agent and clasp hands with him. They spoke in the tongue of the Creek and Jacques related the story of his kidnaping as a boy, assuring her the Indians in the area were friendly. Alexandre introduced his wife to Benjamin Hawkins, their exchange of words cut short due to his eagerness to be home before dark.

"Every wagon train should have a scout that looks like you,

Mrs. Chastain, ma'am," Ben said. "She's quite a beauty, Alexandre."

Alexandre's grin made Dominique blush. Reins snapped as the horses took off, her husband in the lead. Dominique rode between Alexandre and Jacques as her eyes searched for some sign of a plantation. Then the foliage changed. Among planted trees of cherry, black walnut, and peach, tall hardwoods of sycamore, hickory and chestnut, the road became a drive bordered by stones and flowers and vines growing beside a three-railed fence.

"Are we there?" Dominique asked.

Alexandre's face glowed with excitement. " 'Tis your new home, *chérie. Oui*, we're here at last!"

Chills swept through her as she looked to see a rock mountain beyond the trees. Gray and barren, awesome and lonely, it resembled some forgotten altar to the gods.

"The *gray egg*," Alexandre told her. " 'Tis a holy place to the Indian. So sacred, women are forbidden there."

Macbeth and Romeo chased a flock of ducks and geese and the birds hissed and quacked before the horses, peafowl darting behind stands of bamboo.

"Why?" Dominique queried.

"Indian law," he replied. "They have their reasons."

Romeo nipped the tail of a proud bird and forced the gander to fold his wings and run for cover while a pack of hounds bayed in the distance. Alexandre shouted commands in French and Dominique could hardly believe her eyes as dozens of hounds began to swirl through the trees, pouring between hedges and onto the road, barking and baying their alarm.

"Father's hounds!" Alexandre cried, then called to the dogs. "Tilda, Waldo, Milton, Schooner! 'Tis your master! Don't you know me?"

The dogs seemed to quiet when Alexandre spoke French to them, circling and wagging their tails. Mangificent Spanish gates, constructed of black iron bars with polished brass handles, opened onto a broad avenue of sand.

"Racemont plantation, Madame Chastain," Alexandre announced.

Dominique let out a little gasp, suspense mounting as her Arab cantered beneath a roof of stately oaks. Out in the open again, a house appeared pink and golden in the sunset, a mansion of such proportions Dominique could do nothing but gape. Multiple chimneys and a coral roof over hanging balconies, slender white columns behind sculptured trees, created a picture the likes of which she had never seen. Formal gardens in half moons, diamonds, and squares formed a tapestry of color as the entourage swarmed into the compound, led by the hounds. Peacocks strutted amid boxwood and roses as the horses came to a stop before an island of pink azaleas.

Dominique looked up at the great hall and black boys came running with torches to light the way. Alexandre drew his wife down atop a hitching block and Dominique caught sight of the windows above them twinkling with candles. A tall double door topped by a magnificent fanlight opened and a man looked over the balustrade. He smiled warmly.

"Alexandre!" the man called.

Alexandre kissed his wife and dashed across the courtyard paved with granite setes, leaping up the twin stairs to the main veranda.

"Alexandre, my son, you have returned!" Tears filled the old man's eyes and slaves poured from the bowels of the house to have a look at the new mistress. Jacques introduced Dominique in English and French and panting hounds pushed against her skirts, begging to be petted.

"Pray come up and join us, my wife!" Alexandre called, coming down the stairs with his arms outstretched.

Dominique went with him to the veranda, the hounds Romeo and Macbeth close on their heels. François Chastain held out his hand.

"Welcome to Racemont, my daughter! 'Tis truly spring after so long and cold a winter!"

Tall and handsome with a smile like Alexandre's and the same strong countenance Jacques bore, the elder Chastain leaned on an ivory-headed cane.

" 'Tis honored I am, monsieur." Dominique smiled. " 'Tis my wish to be as your natural daughter." Tears blurred her vision as the two men ushered her inside the great hall.

" 'Tis yours, *chérie*," Alexandre said. "The house I promised."

7

Chimes from all sizes of clocks set around the mansion gonged at once. Romeo yawned beside Dominique's bed in the sumptuous master bedroom, stretching and looking sleepy-eyed at his mistress. Dominique slid her hand across the sheets to discover Alexandre was gone. Disappointed, she listened to the pink china clock on the mantle chime seven, the aroma of coffee, cinnamon, and bacon filling the air. She wrapped her arms about Alexandre's pillow and closed her eyes, only then realizing she was quite naked. Someone tapped lightly on the door and she opened her eyes, seeing several feathers, brown, white, and black, lying on the Persian rug.

"Morning, Miss Nikki, did you sleep well?"

"Nancy, where is Doctor Chastain?"

"In the dining chamber with his father, Miss Nikki. Mrs. Ross and Mr. Jacques, as well. The cook waits breakfast for you."

Embarrassed at having disrupted the household's schedule, Dominique quickly directed Nancy to prepare her toilette. Two young girls tiptoed into the room carrying buckets of steaming water, eyes wide at the sight of their golden-haired mistress and her several trunks from which spilled gem-colored gowns.

Dominique watched them go. "Good God, Nancy, they're only children!"

"They're slaves, Miss Nikki. It's the only life they know. They're lucky to be house slaves, Marie says."

"Who is Marie?" Dominique asked, stepping into the hot tub and holding her breath.

"Cook and housekeeper, Miss Nikki. Big and black she is, too. Mr. Jacques and Doctor Chastain call her Mère."

Dominique muttered and pursed her lips, scrubbing herself with the magnolia-scented soap until her skin was pink. "Lay out my white dress while I dry myself, Nancy."

"But you've not had a proper bath, miss. 'Tis I who should be doing the bathing!"

"You said yourself my family awaits, Nancy. Hand me my chemise and slippers. You can brush my hair while I dress."

Nancy tried to arrange her mistress's hair while Dominique wrestled into a garden dress of white muslin sewn with forget-me-nots and tied with green ribbons. "Leave my hair, Nancy!"

"But, miss, 'tis hot outside. You'll want it swept off your neck."

"There's no time for more, Nancy. I have no patience this morning." Wriggling into white slippers, Dominique tied their long ribbons about her ankles.

"How lovely you look, *chérie*." Alexandre stood tall in the doorway, dressed in ivory breeches and royal-blue waistcoat, his silk shirt revealing the golden hair she'd nestled against only hours before. Grinning like a schoolboy, he filled his eyes with the vision of her. "Come, join us!" he said, taking her hand. "I want to introduce you to Oliver."

"Oliver?" she queried.

"*Oui*. I want you two to be friends."

"Is Oliver a horse or a dog?"

"Neither, my love. Oliver is a bird. No ordinary bird, mind you."

"I can't wait to meet him," she giggled. "I love birds."

"And Oliver loves ladies, *chérie*. Come." Chuckling, he watched her slip past him and out the door, hurrying down the hall while he beamed with husbandly pride.

François and Jacques rose from the table.

"Come, sit here beside me, Nikki," François said. "The sight of you 'tis more welcome than food."

" 'Tis pleasant to hear my nickname." She smiled. "How did you know?"

"Your father wrote me some time ago, my dear. To congratulate me on the rearing of my son. 'Tis I who wish to congratulate him now." He smiled. "You are everything he said you were."

Dominique blushed, lowering her lashes. "You're most kind, monsieur."

"Thank you for my grandchild," he said. "My life is full again."

Cat looked on with a forced smile, seated between François and Jacques. The vibrant fabric of her silken gown fitted tightly over her bust and fell to full sleeves veiled in white gauze and tacked with silken camelias. The woman caressed François with her eyes and turned her attention to Dominique. "Tell me, Nikki, did you sleep well?"

Dominique nodded, blushing at her sleepless night due to an owl in her room.

Thankfully, Cat changed the subject. "Where is Colonel Hawkins, Alexandre? Is he not joining us for this welcome feast?"

"Ben rides north in search of runaways, Cat. I wanted to join him but unfortunately I could not."

"There's plenty of time for that, my brother," Jacques said. "Today's agenda is already full for you and your lady."

The swinging doors to the kitchen opened and a huge woman dressed in black, her apron and bandana a spotless white, pushed through. "Now that you all's here, the bacon's cold and the eggs is too! So you's gonna have to wait till I fries up a fresh batch." Wide as an ox, Marie flashed her eyes in warning should anyone challenge her.

"Thank you for waiting for me, Marie," Dominique said. "I'm sorry for the inconvenience. It won't happen again."

Marie stopped short of the doors and smiled. "You's welcome darlin'! Wish mo' people 'round here was to 'preciate what old Mère does. *You* knows what side yo' biscuit's buttered on."

Laughing heartily, the men enjoyed Marie's insult.

"Is she a slave?" Dominique asked once Marie was gone.

"Freed long ago, child. Marie will never leave Racemont if it's up to me. She raised my boys for me. She's quite a woman." François smiled.

Alexandre agreed. "The best cook this side of Paris, too."

"I wish to meet *all* the servants, to know each one by name," Dominique said, looking at Jacques.

"What you ask is impossible, *chérie*. We have hundreds of darkies here." Alexandre laughed.

" 'Tis possible, Alexandre," François contradicted. "Your mother knew them all by name on Martinique. There was little she didn't know about them. And we had more there than here."

Jacques smiled at Dominique. "We've arranged a tour for you, little sister. My brother wants to show you off. But I think it's best to keep you away from the village for now."

"Why?" Dominique asked.

"Because there is sickness there, *chérie*," Alexandre said. "Sickness on a plantation this size spreads rapidly. You understand, of course."

"Of course." She nodded.

"Your mounts stand ready, then," Jacques announced. "I shall accompany you wherever you wish to go. Much has changed since Alexandre was here last."

They talked of changes while the table was spread by elderly house slaves dressed in black. Platters of ham and all manner of eggs were laid before them. There was hominy and red-eye gravy, hotbreads filled with apples and cinnamon. Little girls carried blue crockery pitchers of milk together with baskets of fruits, jams, jellies, and biscuits.

Alexandre drank black coffee and excused himself. "Forgive me. I cannot think of food when there is sickness among our people."

"Don't go, Alex, honey. They're not gonna die. Not yet anyway. Sit, enjoy your food with your family and me," Cat whispered.

"I have my duty, Mrs. Ross," he replied, standing to leave. Jacques followed suit and trailed his half-brother into the kitchen.

"It seems I'm left with all this food and the company of two beautiful ladies." François soothed. "Shall we make Mère happy by stuffing ourselves?"

"I don't wish to anger my host or the cook," Dominique began, "but may I accompany my husband?"

"Not now," François soothed. "Mère is slow to anger, and I know better at my age, but there will be numerous opportunities to accompany Alexandre. You have a lifetime ahead of you here at Racemont. I would like to know you. First, we must drop the formalities. Pray call me François."

Dominique agreed and he squeezed her hand affectionately. She could not help but think how much he resembled Alexandre. He was handsome still, his features enough to stir a woman of any age, the lines in his face adding depth to his charm. It was not difficult to see why Cat loved him.

"Alexandre says you ride exceedingly well," François said. " 'Tis a necessary attribute for a plantation mistress. My Margo was an excellent horsewoman as well. I can see her now, galloping full tilt, the wind blowing her hair wildly around her head . . ." His voice faded and his face grew sad for a moment. " 'Tis a fine Arab you brought with you."

"Aye," she replied, realizing the sight of food was repulsing her. She fidgeted in her chair. "Ramir was a gift from my father. He has superior breeding and will sire many a fine foal."

"Alexandre has told me of your plans to bring blood here from Europe. 'Tis a fine idea. Good horses are needed in the South. Georgia has the perfect climate for them. Indians may present a problem. Though . . ." His words trailed off. "However, that has never stopped a Chastain before."

Nauseated now, Dominique stood slowly and prepared to make a quick and graceful exit. "Pray excuse me, Fran—" Her vision blurred and she reached out for his chair. François grabbed her before she fell.

"Help him, you idiots!" Cat commanded as the servants crowded together in the corner and stared at their mistress.

Marie burst through the doors. "Someone sick? Give dat po' chile some air, peoples!"

Cat called for the smelling salts and a peacock fan but Dominique did not hear. She was unconscious on the floor.

Dominique lay on her green bed, so green it reminded her of a field in Germantown where she had once sprawled out. She listened to the lilting notes of a red-crested finch and recalled that day. 'Twas over a year ago, when Desiree was a new babe. She could see Alexandre on his tawny mount, the ties of his shirt blowing in the wind, the brown velvet of his eyes searching.

"Swooning the first thing in the morning, honey? Tsk, tsk.

That can only mean one thing, I'd say." Cat leaned forward in her chair and smiled. "You'd best stay in bed till the doctor comes, ya hear? You've given us all a good scare." Cat rose to close the drapes and Dominique wished she would go away. She was tired and sleepy and didn't want to talk. She thought of Ramir as she drifted back to sleep to ride across a pink desert on her mount.

"*Chérie*, my love, are you awake?" Alexandre's voice was filled with concern.

"Alexandre, you are back?"

"Jacques and I have been gone most of the morning, *chérie*. 'Tis twilight now. I sent a message with Saul, but you were not awake to receive it."

"But I just ate breakfast."

"I'm told you ate nothing, *chérie*. The spell you suffered cannot go unheeded. Describe how you felt."

"All that food made me ill, 'tis all," she said. "A mere peculiarity. How are your other patients?"

"Alive, thanks to the conjure doctor. But 'tis you I'm concerned with. Pray let me examine you."

"What on earth for?"

Nancy drew the drapes about the bed and left the room. Alexandre pulled back the covers and stroked his wife's neck and shoulders, turning her gently. "Any pain?" he asked, his lips touching the curve of her spine.

" 'Tis a foolish examination if you ask me, doctor! I'm healthy and fit, I tell you, and I wish to see this great plantation I'm mistress of! Pray call for my mount."

"You're staying in bed, madame," he said firmly. "Now stick out your tongue, or must I call for someone to hold you?" His hands glided down her sides and over her hips, drawn to her swollen breasts, where she cried out slightly. "Do I sense some soreness here?" he asked, his hands still on her breasts.

"Aye." She frowned. "A little tender, I would say," she whispered, clasping his hand and looking up at him.

"Intriguing," he said seriously, lifting her chemise. "I believe I know what the problem is." Stripping her, he reached down and pulled off his boots, tossing them aside and slipping out of his breeches. " 'Tis most serious, Mrs. Chastain," he said, sliding in the bed beside her. "You'll have need of a physician constantly now."

"What is it?" she begged.

"Hmm, let me see. Off your food, more ravishing than ever, swollen breasts . . ."

"Alexandre!" she pleaded.

" 'Tis unfortunate there is no cure," he replied.

Her lips trembled. "No cure?"

" 'Tis possible I'm mistaken, but you have all the classic symptoms. To be positive I would have to examine you more closely."

"Examine me where?" She pulled the covers to her chin and threw a pillow at him. "I'd like to see you try!"

"Shhh," he cautioned. "You don't want the whole household to know, do you? Lie still, please, and close your eyes."

"I'll do no such thing!" she snapped, attempting to get out of bed. Grabbing her, he held her hand, pulling her back and drawing her fingers to his lips. "Congratulations are in order for both of us, love," he whispered. "As the sire of our unborn child I . . ."

She didn't hear the rest, the word *child* stinging her like a handful of pelted pebbles. "*Child*?" she breathed. "You're certain?"

"*Oui*," he replied. "You're as pregnant as our finest mare. I must say I'm proud."

"Pregnant! But Desiree is not yet two years!" she cried. "My breasts still carry the milk of motherhood! Dear doctor, say you're wrong! Tell me you've made a mistake!"

Coming to her, he held her close while she shivered in his arms, and spoke softly. "I'd stake my reputation as a physician on it, *chérie*. You're indeed with child."

"Nay! I can't be! I won't have it! I simply won't have it, I tell you. I won't!" She began to cry, twisting away and sobbing and panting like a doe felled by hounds, her tears choking her.

"Hush and listen to me, my wife. I cannot lie to you. You're truly in a delicate condition and I am deliriously happy! 'Tis *our* child, love, yours and mine together. *Our* child, *chérie*. You must not be afraid. I'm the sire and I take full responsibility. I shall deliver it with pride."

"With *pride*?" she sobbed. "With pride!" Dear God, didn't he know what he'd done? Just when she was feeling fit and able to ride! Just when she was looking forward to being his wife and mistress of his house! Now she would grow fat and ugly again and be unable to do the things she wanted. God! she wailed silently. It wasn't fair!

"*Chérie*, are you all right?"

The look she gave him was so sad he could have cried. Instead, he wiped away her tears and wrapped her in his embrace, whispering words of love and devotion, kissing her head and hair with gratitude and adoration, covering her face and neck, breasts and stomach with little kisses.

"I kiss our son for you, love," he whispered.

The night was still save for the solo of a lonely whippoorwill backed by a chorus of katydids, crickets, and frogs. Dressed in lemon ice chiffon, her shoulders wrapped in a light meringue fichu, Cat Ross tucked a rose between her breasts and smiled seductively at François Chastain.

"I love it here, François. This haven of peace and contentment you carved from the wilderness." She placed her hand in the crook of his arm. "I find myself not wanting to leave," she added with a note of sadness.

They walked in the rose garden beneath old magnolias.

"I've offered you my house time and again, Cat, but you've seen fit to reside in Savannah away from me."

"I'll not share your house unless I am your wife."

"Dearest Cat. My house is your home. I meant nothing immoral when I invited you to live here."

"Of course not, François." She smiled. "That's just it, don't you see? You're *too* moral. You can't see the need I have for you. The need I had long before my husband died."

"Your husband was my friend, my dear. I could not forget that then and I cannot forget it now."

"Morgan is dead!" she retorted. "So is Margo!" She wanted to scream, to slap his face. She removed her hand and backed away. "Dead, François! Do you realize what that means? You are free to marry! The church allows it. God blesses it, society smiles on it. We can be wed, you and I." her tone was sharp, clear, desperate. She threw her arms around his neck, causing him to drop his ivory-headed cane.

"You're young, Cat. I am old. Unable to fulfill a husband's obligations. I'm twice your age." His voice was patient and understanding. *Fatherly*. "Forgive me, Cat, my heart lies buried on the isle of Martinique with my wife; my manly yearning as well."

She kissed his mouth and brought his face to hers, pressing against him.

"Forgive me, please," he whispered. "I'm worthless to you."

"You feel *nothing*?"

"Endearment," he replied. "I'll not deceive you, my dear. 'Tis neither love nor passion."

She stepped back and leaned against a clump of myrtle, her chagrin piqued.

" 'Twas not my intention to hurt you now or ever, Cat. Please believe that. You're an old and dear friend, one I'd give my life for without question. Pray seek a younger man. One who will make you happy in all ways." He came to her and grazed steadily into her eyes. "Don't be angry, dearest, 'twas a fine evening I had planned for us." Reaching into his waistcoat pocket he retrieved something and held out his hand. "I wished to give you these at dinner, but decided to wait until we were alone. They are little compensation for the unhappiness I have caused all these years."

Stones glittered in his extended palm, reflecting starlight and beckoning to be touched.

"Diamonds!" she exclaimed. "You give me diamonds because you love me!"

"Teardrops seem appropriate now, though totally meaningless when conceived."

She caressed the gems with her fingertips, then lifted them before her reddened eyes, smiling as they swung back and forth like tiny pendulums. Her hopes rose anew. "You love me, François, I know it!"

"You are precious to me," he agreed. "You welcomed my son and his bride to Savannah as Margo would have done. For that I love you, *oui*." He steadied himself with his cane and kissed her forehead.

"If I were your wife, I would make you love me," she said. "The rest would not matter!"

"It would matter a gret deal." He sighed. "I *know* you, dearest. Pray accept what I have said this night. I broke my vows once, never again."

"Vows!" she mocked, suddenly wanting to throw the baubles in his saintly face, thinking better of it when she remembered their worth. She forced herself to stay calm. "I respect your wife's memory, of course," she said kindly, lowering her eyes to hide her true feelings.

"The stones belonged to no other, if that is what you think," he said. "Alexandre chose them for me. They were designed for you by Philadelphia's finest jeweler and have been a long time in coming."

"Then they are more than for my services to Alexandre and his bride?" she enthused. "You *do* care, François, admit it now!"

"*Oui*," he whispered. "I've cared all these many years. But not in the way you think. Not the way a man cares for a woman. You are my *responsibility*, Catharine. I promised Morgan I'd watch over you and take care of you."

Cut to the quick, Cat held her tongue as tears stung her eyes.

"I would ask a favor of you now, Cat. Something that may be to your benefit as well as my own."

She refused to look at him.

"There is a man in Savannah, a young unattached Frenchman by the name of Jules Cocteau."

Cat's ears pricked. "What must I do to serve you and this man? A *trick*, perhaps?"

"I've hurt you tonight and I do not blame you for hating me. Pray hear me out. Hopefully the hurt will pass in time."

"*Hate* you?" She laughed. "Have I not begged for your name time and time again? Loved you over my husband?"

"Perhaps I can right myself now," he said kindly. "This man is in need of a good and understanding woman. These facts have been confided to me through correspondence with his father, Baudoin Cocteau, my half-brother."

"How old is Monsieur Cocteau?"

"Several years older than Alexandre. A man of the world, so I understand, but ready to settle down with the right woman. I wish to help Jules find a position befitting a gentleman, to afford him my hospitality. Do you grasp my thinking?"

"I am not without sense, François."

"I wish to offer Jules the position of overseer of this plantation, if he will take it. 'Tis my plan to bring him here in time for the Jubilee celebration, the time when all past deeds are forgiven."

"Does Jules need your forgiveness?"

" 'Tis rather complicated. Alexandre and Jules are old enemies. Some childhood difference over the persecution of animals. Some trouble with local authority . . . but Jules is my blood. And much time, healing, and maturing has taken place . . . I hope."

François' goodness and sanctity fairly sickened her. She fitted the earrings to her ears. "How do they look?" she asked. "Do they sparkle sufficiently? Do you think Monsieur Cocteau will consider me for his mate? His bedmate?"

"Dearest Cat, can't we forget our differences? I thought—"

"What?" she snapped. "You could not have considered my pride or my needs? What then? Surely you couldn't have dreamed I fancied being bedded by you. What *did* you think? Pray tell me, for 'tis not clear. Am I matchmaker or whore to your new overseer? Put your wishes in writing, old friend. I leave before dawn. Pray have my coach ready!"

Mourning doves called softly from the giant post oak in the courtyard as her husband lifted Dominique into her saddle, her habit of emerald green blending with the foliage of magnolia, camelia, and gardenia.

"If we hurry we might see a herd of white-tails grazing beyond the river, *chérie*." Alexandre made certain his wife was comfortable, then mounted his stallion. "Are you certain you're up to riding this morning?"

"Quite certain." She smiled. Her coifed and netted head was held high as her white Arab cantered about the circular drive so he could take the lead.

"Stay with me," he said, knowing his words were wasted.

She shook her reins and gave him a sweet smile, taking off in a gallop. Alexandre could not be angry with her this morning, for the knowledge of his seed growing inside her was overwhelming. It would be a son, blond and handsome with a good head on his shoulders and his mother's looks. Aglow with pride, Alexandre watched Dominique ride before him, her gathered tresses bouncing off her neck, her slender waist turning into the most tempting hips and buttocks any man had ever gazed upon.

"Magnificent!" Dominique shouted, pointing to nearby Stone Mountain, that which the Indians called the "gray egg." It loomed ahead.

"*Oui!*" he returned, still admiring her figure. Horseback was not the place to converse with a woman who rode like a man. Dust blew in his face and he urged his mount forward, soon finding himself neck and neck with her Arab. "Thou art radiant, milady." He grinned, holding out his hand. "I truly adore thee."

Her breasts tingled and she felt a newfound joy in being with him then. "Thank you, my lord." She smiled back. "Thou art most kind."

"Motherhood becomes you," he said.

He blew her a kiss and spurred his stallion into a trot, riding on the inner side of the trace to escape the dust their hooves churned up. Feeling no need to outdistance him now, the Arab fell behind and they rode in silence for what seemed hours over old Indian trails. Crossing streams and granite outcroppings, they galloped away from the rock mountain until they reached a high place where Alexandre pointed to a pastoral scene. A large herd of white-tail deer grazed peacefully on the other side of the Yellow River.

" 'Tis times like these I feel privileged to be alive," Alexandre said. "Behold Jehovah's creatures." Helping her down, he brought her hand to his lips and kissed it tenderly. "These are some of the things I've longed to share with you, my wife. We are most fortunate to abide in Eden." He led her to where the rocks slanted upward and returned to remove a blanket from his saddle. "We shall rest here, little mother, delighting in our future, our horses, our hounds, our sons."

"And if 'tis another female?" she suggested.

"One accepts God's gifts with gratitude," he said simply. "I adore little girls." He leaned back against the rocks unaware they were being observed from a thicket of birch trees on the river's banks. "Now then, I have a surprise for you." Taking her hands in his, he pulled her into his lap and wrapped his arms tightly beneath her tender breasts. The horses grazed before them and blocked all but the immediate scenery, and their human audience as well.

"In the fall there will be a celebration at Racemont. A day of rest for those who serve us so loyally. The Jubilee is a time when all past wrongdoing is forgotten and all manner of things are prepared. The darkies dress in their finest and we recall the day the halls of Racemont were completed. There will be dancing and singing and—"

"Dancing?" she repeated, pushing his hands away.

Hooves rumbled in the distance.

"The deer leave us," he said, pulling her up with him.

"Forgive me, Alexandre," she said. " 'Tis I who made them go."

His lips covered hers and, feeling desire well up in her, she looped her arms about his neck, and savored the warm press of his lips.

"I can forgive you anything, love," he said. "You're my enchantress, my beloved, my life. Come, lay with me." He smoothed out the blanket on the sandy soil at the base of the silvery rocks and helped her down with him.

"If this be paradise, 'tis more than I deserve," she said. Their lips met again and he kissed her passionately.

"Forgive me for not wanting another child, Alexandre," she whispered. " 'Tis wrong, I know, but . . ."

He pulled her into his embrace and assured her he understood. He began opening the buttons of her habit just as a deadly rattle from the rocks behind her head awakened his senses.

"Don't move!" he breathed, holding her face rigid in his hands. His eyes reflected the terror he felt as he spotted the head of a coiled pit viper, its persistant rattle a prelude to death. Dominique screamed and Alexandre rolled over her, grimacing as the snake's deadly fangs struck below his left shoulder. Recoiling in pain, he felt a thousand heated needles shoot through his arm.

"Alexandre!" Dominique cried, rolling with him in the sand, her worst fears a stark reality as poison spread through his body. "Tell me what to do!" she cried. "Please tell me what to do!"

"My bag," he said. "Hurry."

Running to his stallion, she returned with the medical kit he always carried.

"You must help me, *chérie*. We don't have much time."

Finding Alexandre's scapel, she made a cross cut over the fang marks and released a surge of dark blood that streamed to his elbow.

"Ride for help," he said. His speech was already impaired by nausea and dizziness. Finding a bandage in his kit, Dominique made a tourniquet and tied it tightly about his upper arm. He was on the verge of slipping into unconsciousness. The arm was already swollen and discolored. Ramir whinnied and snorted, the dull thuds of approaching hooves a song to her ears.

"Dear God!" she cried, looking up. The savage she had seen that first day on the road sat atop his piebald pony with an arrow notched to his bow.

"Nay!" Dominique threw herself over Alexandre and screamed as the arrow left the bow. When she looked again she saw the snake's twisting carcass pinned to the earth. "Alexandre!" Dominique shook her husband violently as the Creek slid from his mount.

"Thank God," Alexandre mumbled, a smile lighting his face as he recognized the bare and bronzed legs of the man who straddled him. Dominique stood by breathlessly as the lean, lithe man in breechcloth and moccasins knelt to tear the tourniquet from her husband's arm and made a slash with his knife near the elbow, bleeding the new incision with his mouth and spitting out poisoned blood.

"Will he die?" Dominique asked, biting into the bone of her ring finger. But there was no time for talk. The Indian moved fast, lifting Alexandre over his shoulder and heaving him onto his horse before leaping up behind and riding for the river. Who was this savage her husband obviously trusted? Trembling like a sapling in the wind, Dominique prayed for her husband's life.

Driving rain beat against the jalousies and streamed between the twelve pillars of Racemont to wet the long galleries and transform its steps into waterfalls cascading into the gardens. Dominique pressed her face against the master chamber's outer door, the cool glass causing her head to ache.

"Hot tea, missy? Ain't gonna help dat babe none fo' yo' to starve yo'self." Marie tried to comfort her mistress as her master lay senseless on his bed. "Jacques done rode fo' dah conjure doctah. Been gone a long time, too. Yo' is too young 'n' purty to be a widow-lady, missy. Please eat fo' ole Mère now. I loves dah doctah same as yo'!"

Dominique watched a red bird land on the gallery and turned to look into Marie's eyes, seeing the black woman's face twisted in sorrow.

"Ain't neveh been no boy like mastah Alex, missy. I raised em from a lil chile, I did. He's like mah own." Marie started to weep and Dominique went to embrace her, laying her head on the woman's shoulder and sobbing.

Mrs. Yarborough wept silently in the corner, her rosary slipping through clenched fists while her lips moved in silent prayer. François Chastain prayed as well.

"He is a healer of men, Lord, kind and compassionate and

eager to eliminate pain. A father to one child with another
growing inside his young wife's womb. A staunch believer
who worships purely and fears you, Lord. Pray grant him his
life and limb. Take my life, Lord, for I am old and willing to
join my beloved wife." His prayer finished, François Chastain
sat motionless and listened to the rain, recalling a day long
past. Images of Martinique formed in his mind. High country
and trees laden with ferns, sparkling raindrops beneath the
sun's midday rays. François smelled the jungle and breathed
deeply, looking hard until he saw the whiteness of Madiana,
the manor house he had built with the sweat of four hundred
slaves.

Rain trickled down the windowpanes with a gentle sound
that soothed him. He was in a small room draped in white,
drawn against the heat of the day. The fragrance of flowers
filled the air, mixed with blood and odors of childbearing. A
candle flickered at a woman's bedside, bathing her coffee-
colored skin in lovely shadows, her black hair wet like a thick
mat pillowing her tear-stained face.

"He is *your* son and you cannot deny him!" she said. "He is
a Chastain." Her face was young and delicately boned, her
dark eyes slanted and defiant.

"He is a bastard and my wife must never know." François'
hands held hers to keep her from striking him.

"Your precious wife!" she spat. "If she is so pure of heart
and so *magnifique* a woman, why did you bed me?"

"Because she could not give me a child. Because I wished to
have a son." Releasing her hands, he walked to the window to
stare at Mount Pelé.

"I don't believe there have not been other bastards," she
said.

François turned to face her. "Watch your tongue, woman!
You have been the *only* one I have bedded beside my wife."
He returned to her bedside and spoke more gently, laying his
hand on her hair. "Tomorrow you will move into my house,
never to toil in the fields again. My son will be cared for as if
he were white and provisions made for him in my will. I shall
not desert him or you, but I will not allow you to hurt Madame
Margo."

"What will his name be?"

François tried to soothe her and kissed her hand. "His name

will be Jacques and he will be educated in France as a
Chastain."

"He is not white like you."

François looked at the newborn babe and thought him strong
and handsome. "He is neither black nor white."

But there *had* been another son. Five years later, François'
wife Margo had given birth to Alexandre. Margo had died soon
after that. But not before she'd made François promise to leave
Martinique, and to call their son Alexandre. François had left
his sons with his dear friend, Baudoin Cocteau, and sailed to
America to begin a new life. Baudoin had a son of his own and
the three boys would be raised together for a time. Until
François could build a house and return to the islands for his
boys.

There was a deathlike silence in the room, save for the
labored breathing of Alexandre and the drumming rain.
François lifted his head from his hands to see Alexandre stir,
calling out for Dominique.

Dominique came through the doors and hurried to her
husband's side, wiping his brow with a cool cloth and sponging
his arm. She repacked the dressing with wet leaves and studied
the handsome face that was now pale and gaunt. Mrs.
Yarborough wandered over to the bed.

"The good die young," the servantwoman said. "God needs
men like the doctor in heaven."

"Take your beads and go to the babe!" Dominique said.
"She needs you, I do not."

Mrs. Yarborough looked as if a knife had been plunged into
her heart.

"The doctor is needed here on earth!" Dominique added.
"God gave him a talent for healing and seed to carry on his fine
qualities." Wrapping her arms around Alexandre, Dominique
held him close and closed her eyes. Too frightened to sleep,
she recalled that awful moment when her husband was felled.
He would have given his life for hers! Dear God, let him live
and she'd be a better wife. She would obey and do what her
husband asked. She *could* change. It would be difficult, but she
would! Her mind raced. She would familiarize herself with the
plantation and make friends with everyone. She must find and
thank the Indian for what he had done to save her husband's
life, but she did not even know the heathen's name. She
recalled the red man's face and felt his gaze wandering over

her, touching her, caressing her. She was tired. So very, very tired.

When Dominique awoke the conjure doctor was chanting in the courtyard below. The black man stood over a boiling pot on the granite setes and shook a viper's tail at the sky. The rattling sound made Dominique think of the snake and she ran to the gallery to look down on the African.

"Go tell him he may practice voodoo in his house but not in front of mine!" Dominique commanded Marie.

"I'll tell him," Marie replied.

When the racket had ceased, Dominique thought she saw a horse with a plumed rider standing beyond the lake.

"*Chérie*," Alexandre called.

"Aye," she replied, running to his side.

"*Ma chérie*," he repeated in a whisper.

"Thank you, God," Dominique whispered, unable to hold back her tears as Alexandre reached out to touch her hair with his good hand. His eyes queried hers. "My arm . . . is it still there?"

"Of course," she replied, placing her hand in his. "The Indian bled the poison from your arm and the limb is intact. The fever has dulled your senses."

She kissed his hand and removed the poultice the Indian had made for Alexandre for his shoulder. The swelling had diminished and the limb was cooler. She replaced the poultice with a new one and talked softly to her husband.

"You live because of the red man," she said. "I will find him and thank him for us. Do you know his name?"

"Moon," Alexandre said. " 'Twas the man called The Rising Moon."

The Savannah night was perfect: the moon brilliant and the stars twinkling against a heaven of sapphire blue. Cat Ross heard the clatter of hooves outside her house and was glad she had invited Myron Smith to dinner. A lady could never be too careful, especially when entertaining a second man she did not trust.

Cat parted the lace curtains and watched as the dark man stepped from his landau, catching a glimpse of his face as he paid the driver. Rushing to the French directoire mirror in the hallway, she assured herself her hair was exquisitely coiffed and her high-waisted gown of rose-colored silk, with a tunic of gray ecru net, was stunning, even though it was very nearly transparent.

"Show him in," she told her maid, Lila, smoothing her cheeks and refusing to believe the poor light told the truth about the lines around her eyes and mouth. "Monsieur Cocteau." Cat smiled graciously.

"Madame Cat," he replied, kissing her hand. His full lips disappeared as white teeth flashed in a bewhiskered and suntanned face.

The other dinner guest entered the hallway from the parlor.

"Monsieur Cocteau, Myron Smith of Savannah and Boston," Myron said, introducing himself.

Cat walked between the two men to the sitting room and felt Jules's blue eyes lingering overlong on the swell of her breasts. "François Chastain requests that you make his house your own while in Savannah, monsieur." Cat admired Jules's manliness and tight-fitting breeches set off by a lavendar waistcoat and ivory satin cravat in marked contrast to his dark complexion.

"What do you think of Savannah, Monsieur Cocteau?" Myron asked.

Jules eyed Cat up and down. "A pesthole!" he replied. "But the view from here is most pleasing."

"Shall we dine?" Cat suggested, putting down her faceted crystal glass.

Light conversation followed at the beautifully laid table. Cat felt uncomfortable and tried not to tremble. Jules's eyes strained to see beyond the layers of her gown, his hand brushing against her whenever possible. Myron dominated the evening with talk of his ancestors who founded Plymouth in the year 1620.

Jules ignored Myron and stared at Cat through six dishes of seafood and a drink of port in the parlor. Cat fidgeted in her gown, the bud of a gardenia tumbling from her fringed forehead and falling to the floor. Jules reached down to retrieve the flower, Cat's hand touching his.

"Get rid of that little bastard before I drub him!" Jules said hoarsely. Cat's face paled and she pulled herself upright in her chair.

"Your posey, madame." Jules grinned. " 'Tis wilted."

"So am I, monsieur," she returned. "Forgive me, but do you think—"

"You wish to retire? Of course, madame. I quite understand.

Mr. Smith and I will take our leave at once. Won't we, Mr. Smith?'' Rising to his feet, he handed Myron his tricorn and books. "I shall follow as soon as I have used the facilities of the house.''

"Forgive me, Myron," Cat said. "But I do feel rather tired.''

"But we've not yet begun to discuss the business of men," Myron protested.

"Another time," Jules replied, ushering Myron to the door and closing it before he could say another word.

Cat leaned back against the door and felt her heart thump wildly.

"Pray show me the way, madame." Jules smiled.

"My maid?''

"Dismiss her," Jules said firmly.

They climbed the stairs together and Cat called to Lila, telling her to go home for the night. She gripped the banister with moist fingers and placed one foot after another on the steps as if in a dream, wondering why she had obeyed Jules like a lowly servant. Surely she knew what he was about!

Once upstairs, Jules followed Cat inside her chamber and closed the door, removing his waistcoat and shirt and revealing a chest of curling hair. "Come now, Cat," he said. "You're not afraid, are you? Must I aid you in disrobing?''

Shocked and pleased by his audacity, Cat did not question his motives, but hungered with desire. Jules came to her and embraced her, kissing her passionately.

"I hardly know you," she breathed.

" 'Tis better with a stranger," he said, heaving her over his shoulder and carrying her to the bed. "The unknown adds its own element. The discovery will be doubly great.''

Lying on her back, Cat gripped the bedposts and shook with anticipation. "I'll scream if you hurt me.''

"You shall not have cause." He laughed. "You may only gaze tonight." Removing his breeches slowly, Jules stood proudly before her. "Allow me to introduce myself properly, madame, for you knew me before by another name. I'm known in Martinique as the stud. Speak of me and all will become hushed. For I am much in demand.''

Cat clamped her eyes tight and pressed them hard with her fingers. Jules laughed deeply, cupping her breasts and releasing an incredible softness that swirled gently upward between them, nuzzling her like the velvety soft nose of a friendly colt.

"You torture me!" she said softly, opening her eyes to an incredible sight. There he stood, like no other man Cat had ever gazed upon, a smirk on his face and his manhood before him. The most well-endowed male she had ever seen.

"You are not screaming?" He chuckled. "Can you not imagine the pleasure I could give you . . . sinking into the depths of your crimson haven?"

A gasp escaped Cat's lips and he took her hand and pulled her from the bed, lifting her gown over her head.

"Now you may touch," he said. "Clasp it and feel its strength, its breadth and width, its length!" Drawing her hands to him, Jules laughed when she pulled away, grinning as he forced her to touch him, amused when she caressed him and bent to kiss . . .

"You'll hunger for more, of that I have no doubt." He grinned. "I leave you now."

"Pray stay the night," she whispered.

Joining her on the bed, Jules parted her legs. "How long have you known François Chastain?" he asked, his fingers touching her intimately.

"A long time," she sighed, closing her eyes.

"And his sons, the black and the white? How much do you know of them?"

"Since they were children," she replied, placing a kiss on his shoulder.

"And Racemont? Can you draw me plans of its floors, its chambers, its many doors?" Jules' hands traveled to her breasts, his tongue tasting her nipples.

"Aye," she gasped.

"You will obey my every command if you wish to be pleasured beyond your wildest dreams, madame. Roll over!" he commanded. Proceeding to tease her, he traced a path from her buttocks to her neck.

"Please," she begged.

"I want news of a fair-haired girl called Nikki," he said. Cat's sighs were deep and her head rolled back.

"Do you know her?" he demanded.

"Aye," she sighed. "She is mistress of Racemont."

"You will tell me more," he replied. "Is that not so, Madame Cat?"

"Aye," she moaned, twisting and arching before him. "Whatever you say."

Cat had offered herself to this erratic, but handsome, Frenchman to please her Racemont master who had made it clear a relationship could never receive the blessing of the Church. Now she found herself delighting in the physical feast this rapacious man gave her each time they met. And she would do all she could, short of harming the mistress of Racemont, to keep him.

8

———————◆◆◆———————

Skirts of cerise silk swept over the uneven cobblestones of the Savannah riverfront. Clad in a long wine-colored cloak, fresh gardenias in her hair, Cat's earrings sparkled in the moonlight as she paused before the barque, wetting her lips and taking a deep breath before quickly boarding the vessel.

"You're late, Madame Cat," Jules said, lounging on his bunk, his long tanned physique bare, his eyes lazy from drink.

"A gentleman calls upon a lady at her house," Cat said.

"But ours is not the usual relationship between gentleman and lady." He chuckled. "You came because you have a need, is that not so?" Coming to his feet, he grabbed her cloak and yanked it off, breaking the garment's clasp and forcing her beneath him on the bunk. "Don't trouble yourself to strip, my feline. I prefer to take you in my own time, discarding your finery as I see fit." His tongue stabbed between her lips and his hands tore her gown from her shoulders to her waist. "That's better!" he rasped. "You may fondle your stud before he pleasures you." Forcing her hands to him, he watched her eyes grow wide as her mouth gaped in wonder. He ripped away her underclothes and mounted her with a powerful thrust.

"God!" she cried out.

"*Oui*, I am your god!" he cried, taking her hair in his fists

119

and drawing her mouth to his, bruising her lips in a savage kiss that left her lip broken and bleeding. "Tell me 'tis so, tell me!"

"Aye," she moaned, prepared to tell him anything.

"Would you have more?" he asked. "For I've much more to give." He laughed.

Her eyes scanned the scars on his face and his turgidity trailed across her thighs as he released her. His eyes glistened like rare gems, a quality that left her weak and helpless.

"You are afraid!" He laughed, flaunting his manhood and giving her the back of his hand. Stunned into fear, she cowered before him.

"You'll comply to my wishes, Madame Cat! I would have you in all manner of ways until you purr." His laugh was like a maniac's and he struck her again. " 'Tis more than you bargained for, eh?" Entering her from behind, he caused her to cry out, filling his hands with her breasts and boring deep until she fell against a wall. He took her ankles in his hands and yanked her up, penetrating her from above until his satisfaction erupted.

"No more! Stop please, I beg you!"

" 'Tis not over yet," he said. "You're indeed fortunate." Yanking her to her feet, he dragged her across the room and collapsed with her upon the bunk. "Ride!" he commanded. "Ride as you have never galloped upon a steed. Sit your mount until you can ride no more!"

"Nay!" she cried, begging him to release her. "I cannot!"

"Ride!" he growled, tightening his grip and applying pressure to her bones.

"Please," she begged. " 'Tis Dominique you want, not I. The mistress of *Racemont* is the one who enjoys the ride so much!"

His eyes changed and he cocked his head like a hound that heard the hunter's horn. "Dominique, you say? Might she be the one they call Nikki?"

"The same!" she squealed. " 'Tis her you want, not I!"

"Sit erect in your saddle and take your steed's head," he ordered. "Post!"

Performing as best she could, Cat grimaced and suffered the burn and sting of torn flesh, her face wet with tears.

"Tell me you've never ridden such a steed before, puss," he laughed. " 'Tis true, no man has more than I!" His merriment shook her and she gasped.

"Now you may dismount," he said. "I mean to have you another way." Casting her to the floor, he stood over her. "Come," he said. "Lift your tail and back up to your tom."

Crawling to his feet, her buttocks bathed in beams of moonlight as it streamed through the porthole, she cried and whimpered. "Pray enter my abode," she said.

"And so I shall," he drawled, coming down on her and spreading her wide to accommodate himself. Her moans were a source of his pleasure. "Purr, my black and white kitten, roll and lick and scratch the way you promised." Laughing, he plunged deep and withdrew, taking her breasts in his hands and pulling her to him to pull her up to the bunk. "Nikki!" he moaned, closing his eyes as he kissed her, reaching a fiery climax. "My Nikki!" The cabin was bright as dawn when he glimpsed her black hair and, pushing her away, went to the basin to retch.

The sunset turned pink, then coral and lavender blue, flowing upward into clouds of purple and gray before it escaped over the calm sea. The clock in Cat's bedchamber chimed six and she stirred in her bed, a sharp burning sensation between her thighs reminding her instantly of her night aboard the barque. Moaning, she pulled a pillow to her face and held it tight, recalling Jules and the bittersweet hours she had spent with him. Such pain . . . and such pleasure.

Lila knocked and opened the door. "Monsieur Cocteau," she announced.

Before Cat could reply, Jules pushed the girl aside and entered her room, boldly handsome in island whites, his strange smirk less pronounced than the night before.

"The day grows old," he drawled, "yet I find you in bed, puss. The vapors, perhaps?"

"Who invited you here?" she asked, dismissing her servant and trembling as he came to sit beside her on the bed.

"Shall I take you again, my scratching she-cat? For I am ready as you can see." Unlacing his breeches, he bid her to behold.

"Go to the stables!" she snapped, turning her head in disgust. "Only a mare could accommodate the likes of you!"

"I have known many mares in my lifetime!" He chuckled. " 'Tis quite a sight, eh? Look! I'm in complete control, as you can see. Stroke it if you dare."

Covering her eyes with her hands, she pressed hard until she saw red.

"Go on!" he said, drawing closer and taking hold of her hand.

When he touched her lips she lay back and moaned softly. He pressed her breasts lightly, stroking upwards.

"If I were healed, you could torture me forever," she whispered.

"*Torture*?" He smirked. " 'Twas tears of satisfaction I felt upon my chest last night. The cat I took was sorely in need!" He strode across the chamber and barred the door, returning to remove his breeches and boots quickly. "Some women pray a lifetime for such a sight," he said. "I fear I spoiled you."

"Not now!" she said, pulling the covers to her neck.

"You want your tom, don't you?" he asked, drawing back the covers and untying the sash of her blue satin wrapper. " 'Twill smart a bit, but I've never been guilty of wasting a ripe piece." He laughed.

Her mewlings were muffled by his beard then, her arms slowly coming about his neck as her body shook with anticipation.

When Jules was finished he lit a fresh candle and placed it beside the bed. "Now that you've received partial payment for the information you will provide me, let's get down to business."

Cat moaned deeply and lay upon her back atop stacked pillows, her bruised and aching limbs atremble. She watched him as he washed and dried himself, laughing as he tossed aside the towel.

"You cats are all alike," he said, pulling on his breeches and boots and returning to the bed. "You enjoy being tossed about by a man. 'Tis in you."

Not wanting to disagree and rile him needlessly, Cat smiled and showed him the bruise below her eye.

"Chastain might feel sorry for you, but I won't," he said. "You came to me last night, remember? I didn't come to you! You knew what manner of man I was. I'll not make excuses."

"I'm not askin' for pity, honey. It's just that you're so rough sometimes."

"Get used to it!" he said, twisting her hair. He brought his mouth to hers and flicked his tongue in and out. "We want the same things, you and I. We shall have our revenge together on the Chastains and 'twill be sweeter than before."

"I don't understand," she said, drawing his hand to her breast.

"I mean I've had the pleasure of riding with Madame Chastain in the past." He laughed. "Or should I say we rode together?"

"I don't believe you!" Her mouth was agape.

"You don't believe I've lain between those long silken legs?" He chuckled. "That the same pleasure you have known was hers first?" Aware she was in need of further proof, he went on. " 'Twas a night I shan't ever forget," he said with a smirk. "I was a guest in her father's house when visions of the beautiful lady's loveliness interrupted my dreams. She was a bride then, virgin and pure, with her groom on her wedding night. There was a fire and the villagers needed a physician. I rode for Alexandre and the good doctor left his young wife in my safekeeping."

"If I were Alexandre I'd kill you!" Cat said.

Jules glared at her. "Alexandre hasn't the stomach for killing!" he sneered. "Besides, I doubt he knows."

"You sicken me," Cat said, turning away. "If I were not so sore and weak I'd have you thrashed and thrown into the streets without delay!"

"After I broke you in so professionally, sweet puss?" he mocked. "I think not. Together we can have our pleasures . . . and possibly the Chastain fortune. After all, Chastain abandoned you and you are not what you once were," he said; that she was ten years beyond his age was not lost on him. He kissed her deeply until she responded by wrapping her arms around his neck to pull him closer.

"I can show you even greater heights," he said. "Tricks you have never tried or imagined possible."

Thinking him mad, Cat reached for the silver tea service and poured herself a cup. "François has told me of your appointment," she said. "The position of overseer is yours on the day of Jubilee."

Her words echoed in the recesses of Jules's mind as he wondered if Alexandre knew of his wife's ravaging.

"I know nothing of what happened between you and Alexandre when you were boys," Cat said. "Only that François owed your father a debt and wishes it paid before he dies." She sipped her tea and pulled her legs beneath her with a grimace.

"Tell me, my wounded puss," Jules said. "Does Alexandre know of this appointment?"

"Nay," she said. "François wants it to be a surprise."

"A surprise it will be," Jules smirked.

Cat's eyes became violet slits as she puzzled over the man whom she had chosen to please at François's pleading. Ah, but now it was she who was enamored. After saving herself for years for a man who would not return her love, now she at least had a lover, hot and passionate.

But what had she gotten herself into? she mused. If this Jules was as mad as she suspected, she would have to find a way to get away from him . . . Then again, she would have to see.

Dominique stood at the window and watched peach-hued birds snatch mulberries from a tree; a bluebird offered a grasshopper to its nestling's beak. Paradise complete with serpent, she mused. Paradise indeed! 'Twas only months now since she had arrived in this wilderness called Georgia. How she wished she had never come!

Lifting her chin, she felt resentment against Alexandre for getting her with child again. "Forgive me," she whispered, for her husband was good and kind and she was indeed fortunate to have him. He could have died like Mrs. Yarborough said he would, but the witch had been wrong. What more did the woman want? She had complete control of Desiree, and a slave of her own to do her bidding, together with a fine chamber on the floor with the family.

Thinking her thoughts unkind and selfish, Dominique grabbed her shawl and set out on a walk about the hall, beginning with the four parlors and ballroom complete with Viennese chandeliers and twin marble fireplaces. The library was next and she ventured by its walls of books on medicine, horticulture, zoology, and canines.

Careful not to disturb anything, Dominique left the library and went on to the music room where she met the gaze of Margo Chastain in a portrait over the fireplace. "I have done my best to be a good wife," she said softly. "I do not enjoy being mistress of a house!"

Closing the doors behind her, she left the music room to run to the place she liked best. The conservatory smelled heavenly.

Climbing vines twisted high above her head and she breathed in the fragrance of lilies, velvet moss, and sweet black earth. Parrots called and flew on wings of green and scarlet and blue as she wandered along a tiny brook.

The door opened behind her and she took no notice, her husband's footfalls lost on the grass as he treaded toward her and encircled her waist with his arms.

"Alexandre! You startled me! I had no notion you were here."

"I came in search of you," he said, kissing her tenderly on the brow. His fingers parted the sheer fichu that crossed beneath her breasts.

"Someone will see!" she said.

"Let them see," he said. "I've lain in that bed for over a fortnight and now that we're alone . . ."

"Nay, we cannot."

"Why?" he asked, pulling her along to a place where stacks of pots covered a bench, a low stone wall hiding a soft mound of pinestraw.

"My prayers for your health were answered, Alexandre," she said, "Have you thanked God?"

"I have." He swept back the tiny curls from her face and pressed her against a wall of vines. "Your beauty terrifies me at times, *chérie*. I cannot help being afraid I cannot hold you."

"I'm not a hothouse flower," she said, slipping away from him and going to smell a tuberose. "Although sometimes I think I am, hidden away behind walls and unable to feel the sun." She wanted to tell him she was unhappy and longed to go to Penn's Woods but she could not speak the words.

He took her hand and drew her close to him, smoothing down her gown of turquoise blue striped with scarlet.

"I dreamed of our babe in my delirium," he said. " 'Twas a boy."

" 'Tis my goal to make you happy," she said. "But the babe may well be female."

"Your love alone would make me happy."

"You have lost weight," she said quickly. "I can always tell by your hands."

He did not tell her that he could not feel her touch on his hand, the burden of his duties as a surgeon a terrible worry.

"Let's go on a jaunt," she suggested cheerfully. "You

promised to show me your pet tortoise, George, remember? I long for a ride and Ramir mourns for a good gallop!"

"I'll not have happen what happened before," he said. "Stay home."

"Stay home?" she asked incredulously. "Would you have me trapped like the flowers in this garden? I would have my freedom!"

"I see you haven't changed." His tone was bitter. "I'll have your carriage made ready."

"Carriage?" She laughed, her green eyes sparkling because she knew she would have her way. She took his hand and ran with him to the doors. "You surely jest!"

Nancy helped her mistress into a scarlet riding dress with satin lapels and buttons and a light capelet over the shoulders. Wrapping Dominique's long hair in red cords, Nancy tied double rosettes into the looped plaits, then stepped back to look.

"Tie it tighter," Dominique said. "I may be gone the remainder of the day and I don't want it coming undone." She stood before the coral-and-shell-encrusted mirror from Martinique and turned around and around, pleased with the way her red leather boots looked below her skirts.

"Your carriage awaits," Mrs. Yarborough announced, sticking her head inside the door. "The good doctor sent me to fetch you."

"Tell my husband I'm coming," Dominique replied, keeping her eyes to herself as the servantwoman watched her every move. "The child is yours for the day. Please see to her."

Mrs. Yarborough broke into a brisk curtsy and moved silently down the hall. The poor child may as well not have a mother, she told herself. All well and good. She could raise a babe. She'd done it with the hounds and a child was no different.

Outside, Jacques opened the door of a carriage for the mistress.

"No wheels for me!" Dominique said. "I want my Arab. I sent word to have him made ready."

Alexandre joined them, his face pale.

"You mustn't be angry, my husband," Dominique cajoled, giving Alexandre a sweet smile. "I can see nothing of your lands from inside that horrid box!"

A boy named Saul came toward them leading the Arab.

"But Marie packed a basket of food for us and placed it inside the coach! You cannot carry such a meal on horseback!"

"We'll eat berries like the Indians," she replied. "Pray don't ask me to ride behind closed doors again, Alexandre," she begged. "Not after that frightful trip from Savannah!"

Jacques smiled and helped Dominique mount El'Ramir, placing the reins in her hands. Alexandre frowned.

"See if you can confine yourself to the paths of Racemont," Alexandre said helplessly. Mounting his stallion with the silvery mane, he engaged the Arab in a canter, waiting for the release of the hounds.

"Macbeth, Romeo, Felice!" Dominique called. "Come see me!" Running together, the dogs obeyed her call and ran to the Arab's heels.

The plantation was at work that morning. Smoke curled from the cookhouse chimney and women hustled between buildings behind the great hall. The hounds ran around the outside kitchen and sniffed the air, the lingering aroma of barbequed pork sweet in their nostrils. The horses broke into a walk and Alexandre explained the boundaries of his father's vast lands.

"As far as the gray egg to the south, and the mighty Chattahoochee to the north and west—"

"Who owns the Mountain of Stone?"

"The Indians. Father has tried to negotiate to buy it, but without success. The Creek *mico* won't listen. The rock marks tribal lands, hallowed ground for the five civilized tribes of the Southeast."

"*Mico*?"

"Chief or king. In this case, Coosa Tustennuggee himself. The man called—"

"Rising Moon," she offered. She remembered the Indian who had saved Alexandre's life: his bronzed skin with its copper cast, his figure half naked and astride a painted mount. "I cannot blame him," she said softly. "Why does your father have need of such a thing?"

"'Tis a symbol of strength to him. The roots of this plantation come from that mount. An ancient place known by every man who has ever ridden across these lands. There will be highways here one day. Great roads around the mountain.

Georgia is central to the South and all roads must cross here sooner or later. Besides, every man wants to own a mountain.''

"Like a woman?" she asked, the curve of her mouth taunting him.

"In a way." He smiled. " 'Tis difficult to explain."

They rode to the slave village and past the empty overseer's house. Alexandre pointed out the cabins and stables the slaves used, their privies and blacksmith's shack lost in the dust stirred by their horses. His horse cut through dense trees and slowed to a stop in the woods, reined in before a log house flanked by old magnolias and honeysuckle vines.

A tall, white-haired slave ran toward them on the path. "Massa Alex, Massa Alex! Wait up, it's me, ole Gray!''

Alexandre's face beamed as he recognized a friend from the past. "Mr. Gray, how are you? I haven't seen you in years."

The old negro limped painfully, stopping for breath, his lined face twisted. "Massa Alex, sir. 'Tis so good to see you!"

Alexandre introduced his wife and Mr. Gray bowed as best he could.

"Your foot, Mr. Gray, what happened?"

"Chopped it wif a hoe, Massa Alex. Chopped it real good the mornin' of the Sabbath."

"Yesterday?" Alexandre asked. He slipped down from his horse and kneeled to unwrap the foot, swollen and bloodied, and encased in rags and twine. Examining it quickly, Alexandre went to his wife's horse and spoke low. "I'll be here for some time," he said. "Leave the hounds and return to the house."

"I'll stay and help," she said, trying to dismount.

"*Non.* The wound is infected," he said. "There's nothing you can do. Pray listen to me and follow the trail back to the road. Don't cause me further worry, I beg you."

"Of course," she replied, wheeling her mount and knowing full well she would not go home. She had been dying to go exploring on her own. Now was her chance to climb the mountain!

Thunder growled, dark clouds raced across the sky, and long fingers of a sudden wind tugged at Dominique's hair. A flock of prize merino sheep pounded across the fields, allowing the Arab's rider to pass unhampered.

"Good," Dominique said, caring little about the path she

took and giving her mount free rein. They galloped past clumps of berry bushes and young Georgia oaks. Dominique turned her face fully into the wind, her skirts flapping wildly about her boots as the Arab covered miles of ground.

Stone Mountain rose up like a friendly ancient ghost, tear-stained, sightless, and shrouded in a mist that seemed joined to the threatening sky. Rising Moon watched Dominique atop her pale horse, her scarlet capelet waving in the air, the golden bonnet of her hair shimmering in the light. Coosa watched the bright figure come closer, flying to the roots of the mountain like a swift arrow from a warrior's bow. Following close, the dark rider took care to keep to the trees, his black eyes straining to see more of the creamy white skin and pink lips he could not forget.

A spatter of rain fell on Dominique's head, a shaft of lightning jagged the sky, now veiled in smoky green; thunder crashed instantaneously with the light. Wind swirled clods of earth, stones, and timber helplessly upward toward the mountain.

El'Ramir reared, his nostrils and mouth open, his ears flat against his head. "Hold!" Dominique said, clutching the reins tightly with one hand, her other stroking the soft mane of hair. The Arab danced, sensing the Indian's presence as he moved haltingly over the slippery granite behind them. The pony's eyes bulged, his pink-speckled nose down to avoid the pelting hail. Dominique caught sight of a rider through the trees, his feathered head and naked body looking vulnerable amid spitting sand and falling leaves. Let it be Rising Moon! she prayed, not a renegade Indian out for a woman's blood. In a flash of lightning, she watched the piebald pony come closer, the rider's hair wrapped about his face. Nudging her Arab with her knee, she held fast to her seat and lay down in his sopping mane. "Faster," she told the horse as he trod over a slippery stretch of rock and lost his footing, going down.

Coosa's mount jumped over fallen trees and stepped through debris, fighting updrafts and driving rain mixed with hail. The Indian's black eyes searched for the Arab, seeing it go down, the scarlet capelet blowing in the wind. He urged his pony forward.

He found her beyond a granite ledge. Her mount hovered over her, looking lost. Tying down both their mounts, Coosa scampered back to the beautiful unconscious woman and dragged her toward pillars of rock below the mountain's face. The powerful wind the Spanish called *tornado* blew with a force that uprooted trees, threatening man and beast as he pressed himself against Dominique and touching his lips to her hair. Hail came from heaven like fire from the white man's hell and Coosa closed his eyes and embraced Dominique tightly, her safety in his hands.

When Dominique woke she was aware of a weight that held her down, a dark scarred face with black hair and eyes near hers. She tried to scream, the sound muffled by the Indian's wet hair.

"Coosa Tustennuggee, chief of the Wind Clan, your husband's nephew and friend to the Chastains!" Coosa explained to quiet her alarm. But the howl of the wind and the roar of the storm cast his words away like meaningless grains of sand.

"Nay!" she screamed, struggling to be free of him, kicking and shoving until she wrenched her hands loose to scratch his face.

"She-wolf!" he exclaimed in French.

"Alexandre!" she screamed.

"Alexandre is not here!" Coosa responded. "We are alone!"

Her vision blurred and she was back at *Winwood*. Alone, helpless under the weight of Jules Cocteau! "Help me!" she screamed, terrified no one could hear, twisting and biting until the Creek seized her wrists and pinnd her down. His breathing was heavy and his thick hair felt like a beard, the tattoos on his face now crystalizing as pock-marks. Her mouth opened to scream and Coosa covered it with his hand.

"Coosa will not harm you," he said.

Fighting him, she struck upward with her chin. A scarlet crack appeared in his lip.

"Help!" she cried, still thrashing like a trapped wolf. "Someone help me, please!"

Excited beyond the point of no return, Coosa's groin ached and his manhood throbbed as he rode high on her thighs, shaking with the lust he had carried for months for the woman who was finally beneath him. "Dom-ma-nique." He struggled to voice her name and watched the alarm in her eyes grow.

* * *

Mrs. Yarborough sat upright in her chair, jarred by the screams of her mistress. Taking a glass from a tray, she stirred the powders into hot milk and held it to Dominique's lips. "Drink," she urged. "You've had a close call and the doctor wants you to have this."

Dominique opened her eyes and pushed the glass away, clutching the velvet hangings around her head and calling for Alexandre.

" 'Tis only sleeping powders," Mrs. Yarborough said, "a harmless mixture prepared by the good doctor himself."

"Where is my husband?" Dominique demanded.

"He won't be coming," Mrs. Yarborough explained. "He's with that old man, the darky who's takin' the fits. Lockjaw, your husband says, a bad case, too."

Dominique looked at her and tried to understand, recalling a black man limping toward her in a fog. She remembered riding toward the mountain, saw it rising before her . . . felt the rain pelt her face. "There was a storm," she said, "thunder and . . ." She frowned, seeing the whirlwind again. "A tornado! Ramir?" she whispered. "My horse fell!"

"The doctor says not to worry. Your Arab's safe in the stable. 'Tis a terrible night. The streams are overflowing and the river is roaring so loudly you can hear it from here. Lightning struck the giant oak and hail destroyed the cotton and Indigo . . ."

Mrs. Yarborough went on with her talking and Dominique closed her eyes. Was it possible that what she remembered of the Indian was true, or was it only a horrible nightmare? Her hands fingered the cotton nightdress she wore, sliding down over her breasts to her belly, between her thighs where she expected to find some telltale evidence of the savage's attack. But there was none.

"Who brought me here?" she asked.

" 'Twas Mr. Jacques who found you," Mrs. Yarborough replied. "Your husband and 'im were out lookin' for hours."

Jules Cocteau's face leered at Dominique from the other side of the darkness and she covered her eyes with her hands.

"*Chérie*, are you awake?"

She felt Alexandre's lips on her neck as he whispered words of love and lifted his eyes upward in prayer.

"Send me home, Alexandre," she said softly. "I was not meant to come here and I have no wish to hurt you again."

"We'll discuss it in the morning," Alexandre replied, his voice near breaking. "You must sleep now." Wiping a tear from his unshaven face, he stood tall, his eyes burning from long hours of vigilance. "I've instructed Mrs. Yarborough to stay with you until I return. Good night."

The door closed and Dominique began to shake, a sense of fear and guilt gripping her. If the Indian violated her it was *her* fault and not her husband's. She hid her face in the pillows and felt a bandage wrapped about her head.

"Bring me my mirror!" she cried.

"The good doctor attended to your head," Mrs. Yarborough said. " 'Twas a nasty cut you had from falling off that horse."

"Leave this chamber at once!" Dominique wailed.

"I think not, madame," Mrs. Yarborough replied tersely. " 'Tis the good doctor who ordered me to watch you this night, and I'll not be disobeying his orders. You're to stay put, do you hear? There'll be no runnin' off so long as I'm in charge!"

Water streaked down the rock mount's face to the earth like tears from God, each droplet shed in love. Coosa Tustennuggee looked down on the realm of the white man from atop the gray egg and squinted into the flame of the sunrise, pools of water reflecting his bronzed body, gold bracelets, crimson girdle, and scalplock. The earth was green and gold and white like the woman, the forest the color of her eyes, the sun's rays a match for her hair, the morning mist her shoulders and breasts. He had to have the white woman one way or the other. He did not know how, but he vowed to try.

The haze lifted and Coosa turned his mount for the descent. If he were a white man he could go to her and make his plight known. Ah, but he was only part white. He sighted an antelope and notched an arrow to his bow, returning it to his quiver as the buck disappeared into the mist. A bald eagle soared overhead and he decided it was a good omen. His mother's people had worshiped on the mountain before the white man came, when the wilderness swarmed with bison and bear, stags and wolf, cougar and fierce mountain lions. Now, the wildlife grew sparser every day, slaughtered by the Georgians and foreigners who came to divide the land, the land that rightfully belonged to his people.

Lifting his hand to his eyes Coosa surveyed the Chastain domain at the foot of the mountain, planning his route to the north and clenching his fist against the cultured fields of Racemont, the plantation where part of his heart lingered. In time the whites would have it all, he believed. His people were being driven from this place where God had seen fit to build an altar. The white eyes would prosper and the five tribes would break up and go away. Where would it end? How much would the greedy whites take before they would be satisfied? Coosa's head ached with the weight of his thoughts and he longed to fight back. But what could one man do? A hundred? The Indian must unite and go to the white man's chief for answers. Perhaps the man they called Thomas Jefferson would help?

The pure white Arab stood motionless beside the gray egg, his finely drawn head and size identical to the wild horses of the Yemen in biblical times. He could have been standing at the foot of an Egyptian pyramid, his breed, remaining remarkably unscathed by the centuries. Alexandre stared in admiration, glad he had found the beast his wife loved.

"Let me have a look at that leg," he said, approaching the Arab with care, taking hold of his bridle and tethering him to a lone pine. Snorting, the beast pricked his ears and neighed at the approach of another horse.

"Ho, Alex-an-dre!" Coosa called.

"Coosa, my friend!"

The two men embraced and the Indian took his uncle's hand and placed it over his heart, repeating the words of Creek brotherhood. Alexandre eyed the strong and healthy youth whose hair was bound in a long braid, his thick topknot decorated with eagle feathers. What a healthy specimen of manhood his nephew was, he mused.

"The white one is swift like the wind, *mon ami*."

"*Oui*," Alexandre replied. "A fine beast in any man's language. El'Ramir belongs to my wife, Madame Chastain."

"The woman with the sunlit hair?"

Alexandre smiled and they spoke of horses.

"You wish to trade?" Coosa asked, drawing attention to the bruised leg the Arab favored.

"*Non*! My wife would throw me to the wolves!" Alexandre chuckled. "She has great plans for El'Ramir. He's the first of many. Even now we await mares from across the sea."

Coosa frowned. "The matching of horses is not women's work."

"Oui," Alexandre agreed, "but Madame is not like other women. She wishes to establish a stud farm here in Georgia, the likes of which one sees only in Europe."

Coosa's eyes grew large as he recalled the wise man of the Bible who had stabled thousands of horses, King Solomon. "For war?" he asked.

"For the Georgians." Alexandre laughed. "To upgrade Southern mounts. To make them faster and more fiery— courageous like yourself."

Coosa smiled. "Why would your wife need such swift beasts? Women have no need of horses. Females don't ride into battle."

"My woman fancies herself a man at times, Coosa. 'Tis difficult for you to understand, I know." Alexandre laughed. "Dominique is not like other women."

Dom-ma-nique! Coosa repeated the name again in his mind, observing the white horse and her husband and thinking of her. Her name reminded him of soft drumbeats from a friendly village on a warm summer's night. "Coosa does not know if he should be happy or sad for you, Alexandre. You don't sound pleased with your wife."

"Ah, but I am, my friend! She pleases me greatly. *Oui*, Dominique is foolhardy and disobedient at times. Like yesterday, when she rode into a storm that became a whirlwind that played havoc with our fields . . ."

"Is she well?" Coosa asked anxiously. He had left the white woman at the gates of Racemont when the storm had nearly died, and sent a brave to inform the household of her location.

"Oui," Alexandre replied. "She is home now and it will be a while before she rides off again, if it is up to me. Thank your people for having located her. Madame carries my child, Coosa," he said proudly. "She will not be active long."

The seed had been planted! Pangs of resentment stabbed at Coosa and he vaulted onto his horse and wheeled the pony about. "Coòsa rides north to his people, Alex-an-dre. Perhaps we shall meet again before the great hunt?"

"Wait!" Alexandre said. "My father and I request your presence at our Jubilee celebration in the autumn. Not many moons from now."

Coosa thought of the fair-haired beauty and the flat belly that would soon swell with child. He did not wish to attend a white man's celebration, but he could not insult his father's brother. "Coosa will come," he said. "Until the fall!"

Alexandre watched the Creek's dust and thought Coosa peculiar. Were not all red men strange? Wiping his brow, he recalled that Coosa was only half red, part of him white like himself. By rights a Chastain! He frowned, mounting his stallion and preparing to leave with his wife's horse. *Non*, Coosa was no ignorant Indian by any means. They had attended school together and played together; the same missionary had taught them French. Coosa had traveled to London and Paris and New York, and served as ambassador of peace for the five civilized tribes. He was chosen to be the Creek's *mico*.

9

Squirrels scampered up the walls of Racemont and Dominique listened to the scatter of rodents' feet above her, seeing her husband's eyes, hurt and saddened. Easing out of bed slowly, she stood and stretched, feeling her babe move inside her womb. Her time was not far away. How long would it be before she was with child again? *Damn*! Was she no different to him than the bitches in the kennel?

No maid came to help her dress and she went to the armoire to choose a suitable habit for a woman without a waist. Pulling down a heavy brown cotton sack with long fitted sleeves and square neckline bordered in apricot satin, she held it up to herself. Where was everyone? The house was unusually quiet. She brushed her hair and pushed it back in waves that showed off her lovely cheekbones. Would she be a mother forever? She had wasted precious time having two babies but soon she could start anew!

The heels of her Spanish boots carried her out of the room to the staircase that circled to the halls below.

"How beautiful you look this morning, little sister," Jacques said warmly. "Your husband asked me to look after you in his absence." His smile was devastating and his manner gallant as he bowed and held his tricorn over his heart.

"Thank you, Jacques," she replied, descending the stairs. "Pray where is Alexandre? For that matter, where is Nancy and everyone else?"

"I alone am here to serve you," he returned. "Your house servants are gone to the village to prepare for the Jubilee. Only Mrs. Ross remains. She is asleep in her room. Alexandre and Mrs. Yarborough are in his cabin with a young patient."

"And Desiree?"

"With Mocha and Mère. The child is well looked after, don't worry. You should be resting. Doctor's orders."

"What manner of illness has this patient my husband attends?" she asked, ignoring his last remark.

"Seems a boy ran and fell on a sharp trunk and cut his leg to the bone. Alexandre's having a time of it closing the wound, but he'll manage, I know it."

"Take me there!" she demanded. "Perhaps I can help."

"I cannot," he said. "I have explicit instructions to keep you here at all costs."

"Do as I say or I shall go and have my horse saddled myself."

"Forgive me, but I cannot." He followed her out the door and down the steps. "Why not take a stroll in the garden? The roses are still in bloom and we'd best enjoy them before the frost." His casual ignoring of her demand riled her and she flung back her reply.

"I'm mistress here, I believe. Since when does my husband's darky brother tell me where I can and cannot go?" Lifting her chin, she marched across the granite setes and smacked her quirt restlessly in her palm.

" 'Tis true, of course," he said, following her. "I'm merely a servant who does white men's bidding. My instructions are clear nonetheless. I'm to stay with you every minute you're not in your chamber."

"Instructions be damned!" she retorted, threatening him with a wave of her quirt and heading toward the stables.

"My brother's concern for you is genuine, madame. You're most dear to him, I assure you."

"For what purpose, I wonder?" she muttered, thinking he married her to give him children. A shower of leaves drifted down between them and he caught hold of her arm.

"Over a hundred slaves keep the trees pruned for your

pleasure, madame. Father takes great pride in his gardens. They were patterned after the ones in France."

"Unhand me at once!" she demanded. " 'Tis horses I'm interested in, not gardens. I want my mount!"

"Let me show you the summerhouse," he went on, guiding her down a brick walk. "I doubt you've ever been there."

"You're awfully bold for a—"

"*Slave?*" He frowned. He broke off a sprig of fuchsia from a late-blooming myrtle and handed it to her. "What do you think of our mountain?"

" 'Tis as hard-headed and dark as you," she snapped, looking toward the granite mass that loomed up eerily out of a flat landscape. " 'Tis what I see every morning and every night."

"You must climb it one day," he said, taking her arm again. "Women are forbidden, but the men who made the law had never heard of you."

"I shall!" she said, her face filled with color.

"Tell me about the North," he requested. "Is it so different from here?"

"As different as black and white," she replied without thinking. "Forgive me," she said, her temper calming. "I meant . . ."

"I know what you meant. 'Twas a good comparison. One I live with daily."

"But you're François Chastain's son and Alexandre's brother. Why are you not free?"

"Free enough," he replied. "In some ways, better off than you."

"Then we're alike?"

"In some ways. Different in others. Your future is assured. Mine is not."

She kicked her boots through the leaves and looked down. "Your son, the Creek king . . ."

"My *only* son."

"Would he ever want to live in Racemont?"

"Men want different things at different times for different reasons, little sister. Perhaps one day Coosa will live in a house like Racemont."

She laughed.

"Why do you laugh? Is it because you think of Coosa as a savage?"

"Isn't he?" Her eyes grew wide.

"My son could have lived here once. 'Tis the house of his blood grandfather. Coosa is rightfully a Chastain. He chose his mother's people instead."

"But he is not—"

"*Civilized?*"

"A suitable word."

"You're correct if living in a grand house and using the weak to serve you is civilized, madame. My son Coosa is not like the whites you know. He is neither barbaric nor cruel, he is human. 'Tis my belief that white men are savages."

"I cannot argue with you," she replied. "Still, some white men are good, as you well know."

"What a pity men must be judged by the color of their skin instead of their hearts. There is good and bad in all men, I believe. I cannot take the blame for white or black—I'm a mixture of both."

She laughed and changed the subject. "Is there another Creek who rides a piebald stallion and looks like your son?"

"*Non!* Creeks have little use for horses. They are tillers of the earth and planters like myself. Coosa is the only Creek I know who rides such a horse."

A tiny pain crept over her shoulders and down her spine. "Do we have cause to fear the Indians in these parts?"

"Not the Creeks. The Cherokee or Chocktaw, perhaps. Indians are people who think as individually as whites do. Some are troublemakers and others love peace. The five tribes of the South are civilized, to use your English word. 'Tis the whites I fear, the good Georgians and the Alabamans. The greedy take lands unjustly, stolen without a word of apology to the Indian. The Creeks live under the guidance of a good and just *mico*. 'Tis difficult to estimate how long Coosa can prevent bloodshed. There is talk of war and I believe it will come in our lifetime. Forgive me, I've said too much. Alexandre will be angry."

"Because you speak the truth? 'Tis something I've always known, I think. 'Tis better to bring these things out into the light."

"You must not leave Racemont," he said. "Alexandre believes you are not happy. He's in fear of your returning to the North and taking his son with you."

"Pray tell me how?" she asked. "I am not permitted to ride my horse!"

"I would never hold you prisoner, madame. I will only interfere when I know you will harm yourself or others. Please consider my words when you are alone."

"I shall," she said. "Alexandre needs a wife for his hall and a mother for his children. I see that now after speaking with you. I'm also glad we talked about the Indians. I wish to learn all I can of them."

"You are wise as well as beautiful," he said. "You can learn more from Coosa."

"Will he be at the Jubilee?"

"*Oui*, there is a horserace that day, which gave rise to the hall's name. Coosa will race Alexandre around the mountain."

"Jacques. Who brought me home the day of the tornado? Was it you?"

"*Non*. A Creek brave came to the hall and told us where you could be located . . . after the storm. We found you at the plantation gates. Though Alexandre hasn't been told, I know it was my son Coosa who carried you there. The brave and I talked after you had been retrieved."

There was stunned silence as Dominique absorbed the story of her safe return home.

"I shall thank Coosa properly when I see him," she said. "I've made a bad start here and I'd like to begin anew. My husband is always busy with patients or his hounds. You said yourself there are hundreds of slaves who need his care. Could you teach me about running a plantation?"

Jacques smiled. "Your skin is white but you would make a good squaw."

"Nay! Squaws don't get their way and squaws do what their husbands command of them!"

Barking hounds interrupted and Dominique looked up to see a cloud of dust, the rumble of hooves suddenly louder. Alexandre's stallion thundered down the broad avenue of sand, the child, Desiree, seated before him in the saddle. Mrs. Yarborough followed in a gig with Nancy and Ruthe, Mocha and Marie, and Macbeth and Romeo raced behind the wheels. A pack of hounds swept across the courtyard and Jacques protected his mistress from the dogs by standing in front of her.

"Mama!" Desiree squealed as Alexandre handed her down

from the saddle. Dominique welcomed her daughter into her skirts and held her close. "The boy?" she asked Alexandre.

"Fine." He smiled, wrapping his arm about her shoulders and greeting her with a kiss. "Stitched and bound and sleeping soundly when we left. We saved the leg, I think. I'll know for certain in several days."

"No doubt the family weeps with joy," Jacques said.

"You should have taken me with you," Dominique said. "Perhaps I could have helped."

"You, my pregnant wife, are to stay close to home and take care of yourself and nothing more!" he replied flatly. "I have Mrs. Yarborough to help with my medical duties. The woman has the stomach for blood and you don't."

Marie came running across the courtyard.

"Where's my supper, Mère?" Alexandre asked her. "I could eat a horse!"

"On dah fire, Doctah Alex! Roast 'n' taters 'n' chicken 'n' dumplin's!" Alexandre caught Marie's skirts from behind, slapping her wide rump like the behind of a well-behaved mare after a long ride. "How could I survive without you, Mère? Without you I guess I would starve."

Marie laughed and Mrs. Yarborough grumbled.

"Forgive me, Mrs. Yarborough, *dearest* Mrs. Yarborough," Alexandre said. "If it sounded like I've forgotten you, I have not. You gave me the best care a man could receive from a woman." He squeezed her hand. "I won't forget it."

The predawn sky shone white above the land, moonlight fading into streaks of day. In bed, Alexandre felt the flutter of his unborn babe against his back and crept away from his wife's warm body, tucking a quilt beneath her chin and smiling in satisfaction at the beauty he considered his alone.

Twenty years had passed since his last Jubilee at Racemont. Was it possible? There had been many Jubilee celebrations, but this one would be special. May all paths lead to Racemont, he said silently, vowing to do his part to fill its halls with the laughter of babes as well as ensuring the safety of all creatures who made their home on Chastain land.

Oliver the owl blinked an eye and hooted softly from the footpost of the giant bed, rustling his wings in preparation for his morning flight.

"Come, my feathered friend," Alexandre said low, stroking

the bird's head and slipping into his breeches. "You must take your leave from the gallery this morning, lest you disturb the mistress." He carried the snowy bird on his hand to the gallery and talked to it. "Invite all your friends to the Jubilee, my friend. There will be sunflower seeds for everyone and a chunk of pork for you!" Bracing himself for the huge bird's flight, Alexandre turned his head as Oliver's great wings flapped and the bird lifted into the sky.

"I thought perhaps I would find you here, Alexandre," François said.

"Father, you shouldn't be outside without a wrap—you'll get a chill."

"I couldn't sleep, my son. Cat and I talked well into the night."

"What about, father?"

"The past and the furture, the present as well."

"You're making yourself ill over that woman, father. Mrs. Ross is not your responsibility."

"Do you remember when I brought you here, Alexandre?"

"*Oui*, father, I do."

"Much has changed since then, my son. The house is larger, lonelier. There were no gardens in those days, now there are hundreds of acres of flowers, a hundred in roses alone! Many souls helped build these walls, my son. Cat Ross and her husband, Morgan, to name two."

"'Twas *your* plan, father, *your* concept! You designed Racemont sailing from Martinique to the Floridas."

François went on as though he did not hear a word Alexandre had said. "More than a dozen lives were lost because of my plan, my son. For what purpose? Greed . . . vanity?"

"You told me you built this house for my mother."

"Before you were born I was unfaithful to your mother, Alexandre. Margo forgave me, but I never forgave myself."

"Come, father, I'll help you to your room."

"*Non*! We must talk about your brother Jacques."

"What about him?"

"Jacques is a Chastain and I have never denied it. He is as much my blood as you are. Still, he is different. You are from the woman I took as wife, the woman I loved with all my heart, the woman I shall continue to love until my dying breath."

François looked at the mountain. "Do you remember the day the Indians took Jacques?"

"I'll never forget it."

"That day was part of my punishment, Alexandre. I know that now. I searched for your brother for months and he was nowhere to be found. 'Twas like the red clay swallowed him up, like he never existed! I told myself I would never see Jacques again."

"But you did see him again, father. Jacques came back."

"*Oui*, Jacques came back because he is a Chastain, a tiller of the soil, a planter. You, my son, have a higher calling. You are like Margo, the healer, the protector of God's creatures." He stared at the mountain, a living thing that watched men in their errors. "Jacques will have his freedom now. His papers are signed and sealed on my desk. There's nothing to do but deliver them."

"I'm pleased, father," Alexandre lied. "Will you tell him today at the celebration?"

"We shall celebrate the Jubilee as we have in the past, my son. All hurts and grievances will be forgotten, as in the Bible. You will light the bonfire and we Chastains will celebrate eight-and-twenty years at the foot of that mountain. Your nephew Coosa will be here and who knows who else, eh?"

"Will you be riding in the carriage with Dominique?" Alexandre asked.

"You and your darling wife must attend the festivities together. I shall stay here with Cat."

"But the Jubilee won't be the same without you, father!"

"Pray do as I ask, my son. I have attended many Jubilees in my time. 'Tis my experience the darkies enjoy themselves more than us. 'Tis their holiday more than ours—let them enjoy it without the old master for once."

It was not yet eight when Alexandre rode home from the slave village with a whistle on his lips, feeling the satisfaction a surgeon feels when his patient's flesh heals and the danger passes. The boy he had stitched days before would walk without a limp. More importantly, the slave would live. Giving his stallion a good pat, he rode into the courtyard and spied Benjamin Hawkins on his horse.

"Benjamin!" Dismounting, Alexandre went to his old

friend and Indian agent. " 'Tis good to see you, Ben. You're just in time for our Jubilee."

"I cannot stay, Alexandre. I have a packet here from Mr. Smith in Savannah. 'Tis from Paris, with the seal of Bonaparte himself."

Alexandre took the bundle and lifted the crested seal.

"Good news?"

"*Oui*, 'tis what I've been waiting for. A shipment of mares!"

"Where did I get the notion you bred hounds?"

"A pair of valuable and rare hounds also travel with the mares. One of them will make a fine mate for my wife's mastiff." He smiled. "You won't tell her, will you? I mean it to be a surprise."

"Not I, my friend. I've business over Athens way. Seems the Georgians have been poaching bass again. Why aren't whites ever satisfied? The more they get the more they want, it seems. Oh, I'll settle it, but they'll just continue doing it. Jefferson wants peace between the Indian and the white man but he'll not get it in these parts. Georgians are too greedy."

"Georgians, Tennesseans, Alabamans, Carolinians! Greed is not only here, my friend. 'Tis universal! I, like you, am convinced the whites cannot live in harmony with the Indian. Too bad, too—the red man could teach us much about this land and how to protect it."

"War is just a matter of time, Alexandre."

"Stupid fools! If they waited, the Indian would be wiped out from disease. It has taken most of them over the years. There is only a small percentage left as compared to what the Spanish found when they stepped ashore."

"Aye, the white man is truly blood guilty."

" 'Tis my belief it will always be so." Alexandre shrugged. They parted company beside the cookhouse and Alexandre ran to the twin stairways that led to the front door.

"Good morning," Dominique called from above.

"*Chérie*, what is wrong?"

"Must something be wrong for your wife to greet you when you come home from work?"

"I am not accustomed to it." He grinned. "Are you quite certain you're not ill?"

"Quite!" She laughed. "How is the boy?"

"I'm completely satisfied with his progress."

"Good, then we'll be attending the Jubilee together?"

"I am afraid not, my love. The morning is filled with duties for me. Three bitches are in heat and matings must be supervised. We dare not put it off." He did not tell her he was going to see a mare that had arrived the night before from Savannah. "Thomas and Saul will accompany you to the village. The festivities won't begin until noon. You'll ride in your carriage, agreed?" He squeezed her hand and brought her fingers to his lips.

Their eyes met and she smiled. "Agreed."

"No tricks," he warned, slipping his arm about her waist and pulling her along with him. He stopped in the middle of the foyer and kissed her tenderly. "I've no need of further tragedies, little mother. I ask your wifely obedience this day. I'll have your promise on it."

"You must catch me first," she giggled, running down the hall.

The piebald stallion snorted and shifted its weight as the carriage thundered by. Coosa Tustennuggee waited patiently for the horse that followed the wheels, an entourage of swirling, yelping hounds at its heels.

"Stay back," he said in Creek, leaving the company of his braves and galloping out into the open.

The white Arab came into view, the classic face of its rider's unequaled beauty causing Coosa to suck in his breath. Dominique sat erect in her saddle, her anguish obvious as the Indian blocked her way and his mount danced on the path. The hounds broke apart and circled the intruder, barking and snapping their teeth.

"Macbeth, Felice, Romeo!" Dominique called. "Leave him be!"

"Lady of the hounds," Coosa said, lifting his brows to resemble eagle's feathers. "Coosa is most grateful."

The long scratches, from the corners of his eyes to the flaps of his turban, creased and Dominique forced herself to look at the disfiguring tattoos, refusing to flinch.

"Must I go through the brush or will you move aside, Coosa—or is it Rising Moon?" Facing him with the cool dignity of a warring queen, she held her head high.

"Savage will do for now." Coosa scowled. He made a sign for his braves to go on without him. "The Great Spirit wills we should meet again," he said in a deep voice. "May I say your radiance is surpassed only by the new sun?"

"Save your flattery for your squaw," she bristled. "Now move aside, I'm on my way to meet my husband."

"Coosa has no squaw." He grinned, moving his mount to one side. "Coose is bound to no one."

His reply was pensive, this thorough perusal of her sending beads of perspiration over her neck and breast.

"Coosa will escort you to the Jubilee," he said courteously, wheeling his horse and bowing like a lordly knight.

She rushed by him like the wind, thinking it curious he wore no shirt beneath this doeskin jerkin. Dressed in Indian fashion, his chest and arms were adorned with gold. A scarlet mantle, hung with tiny bells, was draped over one shoulder, and his long legs were garbed in mushroom breeches and leggings. She breathed deeply to steady her nerves, her hands growing moist as her stomach knotted and chills rippled down her back. He stared at her the whole time. How bold the red devil was! What would Alexandre say when she arrived in the tow of a savage? They trotted on in deafening silence toward the site of the Jubilee, her racing pulse causing her to feel light-headed.

The tension was relieved when she heard hooves clopping across the clay toward her, a cloud of red dust nearly enveloping Alexandre as he rode to join them.

"Alexandre!" she shouted, her breath a short gasp. She prayed her face would not betray her anguish.

"I thought I told you to ride in the coach, madame!" Alexandre said.

"I ride with a friend." She smiled.

The peppered stallion thundered to a halt beside her and Alexandre made a sign of greeting to Coosa. " 'Tis a welcome sight to see you with my wife, my brother!"

"Coosa serves you well," Dominique said. "Pray don't be angry."

"You mistake concern for anger, my stubborn mate!" Alexandre replied. "I should have expected this! The hair on my head is turning white because of you, and still you do as you please! What husband would expect his wife to come riding into his midst accompanied by a fierce warrior of the Wind Clan?"

"Warrior?" she choked.

"*Oui, chére*, you choose your company well." He winked at Coosa.

"I didn't know," she whispered as he dismounted and drew her down before him.

Alexandre bid a servant to take the horse. " 'Tis good you brought your braves, Coosa. Might I engage you in a race around the mountain?"

"*Oui*, my brother." Coosa slid from his horse and smiled broadly. "No doubt Minooca will prove to be the swifter."

Alexandre laughed and made fun of Coosa's pony, placing an arm about the Creek's neck and walking with the red man to the fire where a boar's carcass on a spit dripped fat.

"Men!" Dominique sputtered, cursing the two of them beneath her breath and hiding her disgust. She joined the womenfolk and Desiree squealed with delight when she saw her mother.

"Handsome devil, isn't he, Miss Nikki?" Nancy said. "The red man, I mean. A body would never know he was red if it wasn't for his clothing. He's no darker than most men who work out in the sun. Look at those broad shoulders and the size of him. He towers over the good doctor!"

Pretending not to hear, Dominique began feeding her child.

"Do you think he likes white women?" Nancy asked.

"I'd expect he does, Nancy. All Indians like white meat, so I'm told."

Nancy looked at her mistress blankly.

"If you value your hair I'd stay away from him. He's a savage, you know. They treat their women worse than dogs, in case you're interested. They eat them for stew!"

Nancy gasped and clutched her throat.

"Stay with the child," Dominique said, leaving to mingle with the crowd. Impressed with the vast array of foods, she inspected the breads and pastries laid out on a long table, keeping her eye on her husband and the Creek. Platters of venison, wild turkey, and hams pleased her eyes. Crocks of spicy fruits and vegetables displayed on tree trunks were set among bright gourds and dried flowers.

Marie cornered her mistress and shook a wooden spoon beneath her nose. "Yo' hungry, chile? What dah mastah say when he seed yo' ridin' in on dat white horse wit dat big red man on yo' tail?"

"I'll have a slice of your pecan pie, Mère."

"Fo' dah noon meal?" Marie frowned. "Oh, no, yo' don't, chile. Yo' wait right over dah in dat clearin' while ole Mère gets yo' a plate o' barbequed pork dat'll melt in yo' mouth! Wild rice 'n' biscuits, too. Go on now, go on wit yo'."

Dominique giggled and followed Marie's pointing finger to a path that led to a clearing in a grove of walnut trees. She sat on a crudely carved bench beneath a silvery beech tree and leaned against its cool trunk.

"I would have believed you an apparition had I not feasted my eyes on you before," Coosa said. "Your beauty lights the wood!"

Dominique jumped at the deep voice she placed instantly. "Why do you follow me?"

Coosa stepped out from behind a towering oak and crossed his arms on his bare chest. " 'Tis not difficult for a savage to follow a white woman's scent, Dom-ma-nique."

Had she ever *heard* her name before? Her senses were swept by waves of excitement that she could not dispel. "Did you think me a phantom when you found me in the storm?" she returned. "When you held me down?"

He knelt before her and placed his hand over his heart. "Coosa's only intention that day was to protect his friend's wife," he replied. "Coosa did not touch you in the way you think."

"Your lips were near mine!" she said. "Your wet hair on my face . . . your hands holding me down!"

"Coosa held you fast to protect you from the wind," he said. "Coosa has pledged his life to you, Dom-ma-nique. Coosa knows you are Alexandre's woman."

"If you tell the truth, then why did you leave?"

Wanting to comfort her in the fold of his arms, he stood and kept his distance. "Coosa did not leave you, Dom-ma-nique. Coosa took you to your family as soon as possible. You were frightened and Coosa did not know why. There was fear in your eyes."

His expression was soft and kind and sincere like her husband's, his features strong and noble, his manner relaxed. She felt suddenly faint and the woods whirled around her, a loud buzzing like a swarm of bees filling her head.

When Dominique opened her eyes saw Coosa's face close to hers, his eyes piercing as he gazed into her own.

"When do you expect the child?" he asked.

" 'Tis not known for certain," she murmured.

" 'Tis sooner than you know," he replied in his melodious voice. " 'Tis good for Alexandre. A man needs his seed to carry on. Little children are part of the Great Spirit's plan."

"Plans!" she fumed, pushing his hands away. She propped herself up against the beech tree's trunk next to the bench and queried him. "Who are you besides chief of your tribe? A prophet?"

Coosa laughed. "*Non*! Coosa learned about your god from the wise men, so called because they were white." He shrugged. "We savages have our men of wisdom, too, and our women!"

Why did his presence taunt her, his smile and accent so charming she grew weaker by the moment?

"The red man's god is much like yours, Dom-ma-nique. He derives pleasure when we are obedient and displeasure when we disobey."

"I care nothing for heathen gods, Coosa! Pray help me up."

"*Chérie! Mon Dieu*, what happened?" Alexandre hurried toward his wife with Marie, his expression aghast when he saw her sitting on the ground.

Coosa held her up. "Your wife rested on Mother Earth, 'tis all, Alexandre."

Alexandre frowned. "Does my son still stir? Do you wish me to take you to the hall? You should have told me you were not well. I'll accompany you home at once!"

Drumbeats began, joined by melodic wood flutes and a chorus of voices. "The festivities begin," Coosa said.

"Aye, would you have me miss them, my husband? Pray go with Coosa and have your race. Marie has a plate for me. I'm famished!"

"Are you certain? I'd feel better if you would let me see you to your carriage. Better still, to your chambers."

She took Alexandre's hand and leaned against him, smiling sweetly. "Mère will stay with me, my doting husband. Go! I hear Oliver hooting and 'tis certain he is hungry. Go and have your race. I'll be fine."

"Stay with her and see she gets plenty to eat, Mère." He frowned, kissing his wife's forehead and taking her hands in his. "Come, Coosa, let us ride around the mount. Perhaps my wife will stay put now and be content to watch!"

Coosa laughed and bowed. "*Adieu*, lady of the hounds."

"Lady of the hounds!" Dominique mumbled, watching the men depart and feeling her legs go numb. What business was it of his when she delivered? First he frightened her to death's door and then he asked about her condition! Damn! Why did she tremble so when the Creek spoke? Why could she not take her eyes from him and why did she love to hear him speak her name? 'Twas her condition, of course. Everyone knew a woman's feelings changed when she was with child.

Marie pushed a plate overflowing with food into her mistress's hand. "What dat red man been tellin' yo', chile? Watch out fo' him now! Dat Coosaman done charmed lady peacocks outta dem peach trees!"

Dominique laughed. "Don't worry, Mère. I don't take savages seriously. Coosa even less."

"Oh, yo' can trus' Coosa, chile," Marie said frankly. "When Coosa was no mor'n a babe, he done won dah hearts of us all, he did. Even dah boss love dat lil Indian! Mastah Chastain calls dat holy man from dat French isle of his tah come teach Coosa 'bout dah white world. Dem priests say dat Coosaman brighter dan mos' white childrens. Dat lil Indian reads 'n' writes when he was jus' four!"

"You know a lot about Coosa, Mère."

"Course I does, chile! Dat Coosaman eat in mah kitchen jus' like dah res' of dem men! Lil Alex, Jacques, and Coosa. Dem all my boys once. You gonna bless dah good doctah with a manchile, huh?"

Dominique pushed her plate into Marie's hand and slid her hands over her belly. The drumbeats increased in tempo and the chanting of the slaves rose to the smoky sky. Alexandre came and joined them. Still panting from his loss of the race to Coosa, but he noticed Dominique was absorbed elsewhere. "May I have this dance, *chérie*? I trust you know the Nigerian jig?" he said, lowering his head in an exaggerated bow.

Dominique giggled and Marie clapped her hands over her head. "Yas sah, Doctah Alex! Dance with yo' gorgeous wife 'n' show off dah woman dat carries yo' babe. Goin' tah be a manchile!"

10

Alexandre danced with Dominique on the sandy earth beneath some old magnolias while pipes hummed and drums beat a rhythmic, exotic tune. Women in colorful ruffled skirts and indigo bandanas whirled and clapped hands while the men and children stomped feet and chanted. The celebrators circled their master and mistress and raised their voices to fill the autumn sky with revelry.

Alexandre held his wife's hands in his and spoke with his eyes, conveying words of love that longed for her reply. Listening with her heart, Dominique turned and moved as he bid her, touching, knowing, savoring his love for her until she ached with it.

When the dance was done, Alexandre led Dominique to a place of honor, seating her in a comfortable chair made specially for the occasion. Children of all ages gathered around them.

"I want you to see how it feels to handle a manchild, my wife," Alexandre smiled. "Try this one for size." Lifting a plump and frightened brown babe from his mother's arms, he placed it gently in his wife's lap. "His name is Moses." He smiled. "Pray hold him and tell me what you think."

Looking at the child and then at her husband, Dominique narrowed her lips.

"Turn him around and see for yourself what you'll have to contend with soon," he said.

Tears wet Dominique's lashes as the babe stuck out his lips and tears streamed down his fat cheeks, his luminous black eyes shining as he reached out for his mother.

"Don't cry," Dominique said, holding the boy close and soothing away his fears with little kisses. "Oh, how I wish you were mine," she cooed, "for 'tis a cherub you are! I pray our son will be exactly like him, Alexandre," she said, looking up at her husband. "For you."

Alexandre sat on the arm of her chair and whispered in her ear. "You're a madonna, my love. Would that I could keep you this way always."

"Heaven forbid!" she retorted, glaring at him and holding the babe close to reassure him her scowl was not meant for him.

"Stay where you are and don't move, *chérie*," Alexandre said. "I have a surprise for you." Taking off in a run, he left her as she looked at the mother of Moses.

"You like Moses?" the woman queried softly, pointing first to Dominique, then to her child.

"I love him!" Dominique breathed. "May he come and play with my son when he arrives?" She pointed to her swollen belly and leaned into the chair to take the strain off her back.

"*Oui*, missus," the woman replied enthusiastically, nodding.

"You have a husband?" Dominique said slowly.

"Hus-band?" the woman repeated.

Dominique pointed to Jacques. "Husband? Man—you have a man like Jacques?"

Jacques realized she was pointing to him and heard the word *husband*. He frowned deeply. The tall, thin servant girl looked approvingly at Jacques and came quickly to her feet, smiling.

"What did you tell her?" Jacques asked, trying to get away before the woman could tackle and knock him to the ground.

"I simply asked if she had a man like you," Dominique replied, watching as the crowd continued their singing and dancing as Jacques stepped back from the woman's firm grasp of his arm.

"Ho, father! What is this?" Coosa halooed, breaking

through the crowd with his braves behind him. "*Amour* in the afternoon?"

Moses squealed for his mother and Jacques broke free from the woman at last. "I'm a married man!" he growled. "*Taken!*" Scolding her in her own tongue, Jacques plucked Moses from Dominique's lap and placed him between his mother's bare thighs where she sat on a hill of sand. "Behold my son, Coosa Tustennuggee, king of the Creeks!"

Every eye was directed then to Coosa. Embarrassed, Coosa looked down.

"Coosa is yet a free man," Jacques advised, directing his words at the mother of Moses. "Coosa has no wife, no woman to do his bidding. Speak to him of your need!"

Coosa paled, his look now mixed with anger, the plumes of his headpiece trembling threateningly. "When the time comes, Coosa will choose a woman," he said low, causing the child's mother to shudder and the child to cry. Standing over the woman, Coosa crossed his arms and cast Dominique a look that lingered long enough for Jacques to decipher it.

Before he could react, someone cried: "Look! Doctor Alex!"

Dominique looked and saw Alexandre leading a lovely gray mare decked out in Bedouin trappings, her bridle tassled in red, her mane and tail as blue as a Pennsylvania winter's sky.

"For you, *chérie*." He grinned, handing Dominique the reins. "Her name is Jacqueline—she's French."

Dominique started, her mouth agape.

"'Tis my gift to you and Ramir on your first Jubilee at Racemont. Do you like her?"

"*Like* her?" Dominique managed, trying not to cry. She reached for his hand. "Alexandre," she choked. "She's too elegant for words!"

"*Oui*, her granddam was Percheron, her sire Arab. She'll carry you comfortably over the plantation. You need a larger horse for the fields and she jumps exceedingly well." Leading the mare closer, Alexandre held the beast while his wife nuzzled its pink nose and cooed.

"You're truly blue!" she said. "Has Ramir seen you?"

"He's smelled her," Alexandre replied. "His cries of desire are drowned only by the chanting and drums. You'll not be riding El'Ramir as often in the future, *chérie*. He will soon have a harem to keep him occupied."

"The horses have arrived at last?" she asked, making an effort to stand.

"Some of them," Alexandre returned, helping her from her chair. "The rest are stabled in Savannah for now. Jacques leaves momentarily to bring them home. Jacqueline is worn from her long journey here. I'm afraid we rushed her a bit, for you."

"Are they a healthy lot?" she asked, looking up into his eyes and stroking the mare's forehead.

"Marred and knotted a bit, 'tis all. But their wounds and stiff joints will soon leave them when they head north to Racemont. My men in Savannah will see to their cuts and scrapes, have no fear."

"I can't wait to see them!" she said, catching her breath as a pain gripped her back.

"_Chérie_? What is it? You're not well, I can see it in your face. Come, let me take you to the hall at once."

Breathing deeply, she knew he would allow her no say in the matter. She held onto his hand. "Thomas will take me back," she said. "You must ride to the rock with Coosa, remember? Pray forgive me for upsetting your day. I regret I can't go with you, but my heart is with you, my husband."

Alexandre held her close and she slid her arm about his back as they walked together toward the carriage.

"Pray allow me to sit a while and watch the race. I can ride Ramir home later, after I've rested."

"_Non_! Pray don't rile me to anger, my wife! You'll ride in your carriage if I have to set you in it and bar the doors!"

Not fooled by his tone, Dominique knew nothing and no one could incite him to violence.

Walking slowly to the coach she worried that Alexandre had seen the way Coosa had looked at her, praying he had not.

"The race be hanged!" Alexandre grumbled, lifting her into his arms when they came to a fallen tree across their path.

"But 'tis your duty as master to see to the enjoyment of everyone, Alexandre. You told me so yourself. Surely you'll not fail your father in his absense. François expects you to win the race. So do I!" She gave him a little hug as he set her down. "You know Jacques will not race Coosa. 'Tis _you_ who must ride against the Indian and win! 'Tis the most important event of the day!"

"Guard her well, Thomas," he said to the manservant as

they reached the coach. "This jewel carries my son. See that she goes straight to the hall and stays inside."

Dominique looked at him and smiled. "Please, my lord. Just a few minutes more. Until you ride over the hill yonder . . ."

"Go and fetch your wife, Thomas! Have her sit with the mistress until I'm out of sight!"

"Aye." Thomas nodded, wondering how he'd accomplish his mission if his mistress sought to do otherwise.

"I'm much obliged," Dominique said sweetly, placing her hand on Alexandre's cheek and stroking upward.

"You may dally a while longer, my tempting wife," he said, taking her hand and drawing it to his lips. "But return to the hall in short order. Do you understand? You must rest for what is left of this day. I'll join you when the race is done."

"Pray win for me," she whispered, placing a kiss on his cheek. "I feel fit, really I do."

Alexandre frowned, taking her face in his hands and kissing her tenderly. "If we didn't have a field full of company I'd carry you off into the wood, wench, for I'm sorely tempted."

"Alexandre!" she scolded. "I must return to my chambers as my master bids. A good wife always obeys her husband." She giggled.

"You're as predictable as the wind." He laughed. "If I didn't keep the French lady under wraps, you'd no doubt be trotting around the mountain right now!"

"Off with you." She giggled, leaning back in the carriage's seat to ease the pain in her back. "After your son arrives you'll see little of me. You'll do well to catch me and get me with child again! I mean to circle that rock mount many times before I'm too old to ride."

"Jackie will serve you well. Come spring, you may ride to the mountain—with your husband, of course."

"Of course," she said, sliding her fingers from his as he stepped back. He gave her a boyish grin, before disappearing into the trees where his stallion was tethered. As he left she thought him a kind, patient man who surrendered too easily to her wants, spoiling her the way her father had spoiled her.

She saw the stallions meet on a high green knoll fringed with cedars and low brush. Someone held up a flag and then she heard a shot, her heart beating faster as she watched the horses cloud the air with dust in their race along the high hills.

"I feel fine now, Thomas." She smiled brightly.

The manservant's face turned red, his head shaking as he opened his mouth to speak. "Nay, mistress, don't ask me, I pray."

"Ask you what, Thomas?" She giggled. "Go and enjoy the wrestling match. Find your wife and forget about me."

"My wife is accompanying you to the hall, mistress. Just as the good doctor ordered. I'm going to fetch her now."

"Aye," she replied, "I shall see who catches the greased pigs and meet you here when the event is ended." She climbed down with the servant's help and remembered that her father-in-law was alone with Cat at the hall. Perhaps precious words were being exchanged? "Go now, Thomas," she said. "We must do our master's bidding."

Shaking his head, Thomas skulked away, looking back to make certain Dominique was still behind him. She would not disobey her husband, Dominique told herself. She would return to the hall, but not in the carriage, and not yet. She must lose Thomas and Ruthe. Then she would mount her Arab and make a quiet exit. There was no point ruining the day for anyone but herself.

Jacques ordered the hounds rounded up and locked in a pen Alexandre had erected for them behind the physician's cabin. Macbeth was the last to be caught and the first to take up howling, pacing like a panther searching for a way out.

Dominique said good-bye to Jacques and then went to watch the greased pigs set loose. Saul took off after them, followed by Mocha and Colena. Saul ran faster than the others and jumped over logs and stumps with ease as the cloven-footed beasts headed toward the river. Drums beat wildly and merrymakers shouted as they were caught up in the event. Now was the time to leave, Dominique decided. Making her way down a deep ravine, she walked along its bottom and waded across a stream to the bank where Ramir was tethered.

The Arab's eyes brightened at her approach and Dominique looked from side to side, making certain they were unobserved. Quickly, she undid the stallion's reins, leading him down a path that led to the trace. "Come, my love," she said, clicking her tongue and making her way through the trees. "Be a good boy and follow me to where I can climb up and sit upon your back. Thank goodness you're saddled."

Snorting his reply, the horse followed her like a dog as they made their way past a break in the woods and she could mount him from a large rock.

A dog barked and Dominique craned her neck to see Macbeth racing toward them. "Macbeth!" she called, her heart skipping a beat as she looked over her shoulder expecting to see Alexandre carrying a big stick. "How did you escape?" she asked, knowing well the hound had jumped the fence. "Good dog." She giggled, beaming with happiness because he had come to join her.

Ramir walked swiftly, breaking into an easy trot when the trace turned into a twisting road. Dominique looked back to watch the growing space between the celebration and herself, breathing easier now that she'd made her exit quietly. Bees buzzed around her mount, birds called out from the wood, and a fat rabbit zigzagged into a clump of wildflowers. Dominique began humming a tune and Macbeth wagged his tail at the sound of her voice, the notes turning into a lilting song that echoed off a nearby bluff.

"I wonder what my babe will be—two moons more and all will see . . ." Giggling at the silly rhyme, Dominique patted her belly and spoke to her unborn child, wondering if Alexandre had beaten the savage in the race. What right had Coosa to ask her such a personal question as when she would deliver? But the Indian had seemed so kind . . . so very kind.

Then a thought burst into her mind, enraging her.

"Heathen!" she cried. Dressed in fine feathers and thinking himself white! Did he really think she had believed his story about the tornado? Saved her from the storm, bah! Her heart beat faster and a strange gnawing began in her breast. But didn't she owe the heathen her life? Nay! She owed him nothing, save a knife in the back for ravishment!

Smoky gray streaked the afternoon sky as dark clouds billowed overhead and a western wind chilled the air. Dominique shivered as Ramir's hooves clopped through drifts of leaves. The halls of Racemont looked abandoned as she approached. No servants ran out to meet their mistress and no stableboys took her mount. She looked up at the shadowy, slender columns of the house, grimacing as she dismounted and clutched her belly. Dear God, not yet. Not so soon!

She leaned against her mount's flanks and felt pain spread

through her back and legs. Her mother had told her women suffered the pain of birth because of Eve. Now 'twas her time. Fear gripped her as she clasped her belly when another pain ripped through her, then looked toward the gallery hoping to see a friendly face. She wanted to remove the saddle from her horse's back and take him to the paddock. Ramir whinnied as she began her task, and Macbeth wagged his tail and followed as she made her way across the granite setes.

"You're the lucky ones, my handsome boys" she said, nearly stumbling with the pain that stabbed her. "No foals or pups to carry and a harem of mares and bitches to come home to." She reached the carriage house and leaned back against its cool brick wall to rest. Macbeth growled and barked, but the warning came too late. A hand snaked out of the darkness to cover Dominique's mouth.

"Dearest Nikki," an amused voice rasped.

Suddenly numb, Dominique twisted desperately to free herself from the intruder's iron grip.

" 'Tis I, Jules Cocteau! Your lover come back to claim you! Though I must admit I never thought we would meet so conveniently." His smirk made her heart lurch, a tourniquet of fear cutting off her breath. "Alexandre will kill you," she choked.

Jules laughed, his dark bearded face appearing from the shadows. "Alexandre Chastain? *Non!*" He laughed, slamming his fist into the wooden door beside her. " 'Tis a mortal sin to jab the eyes of a full-grown treefrog! How could such a softling bring harm to me?" The sound of his laughter made her ill. She prayed fervently someone would hear him.

"Your husband's a weakling, madame. A mama's boy who wipes the snoots of kits and mends pigeons' wings!" Macbeth snarled and moved toward him.

"Nay!" Dominique cried, the sound of her voice echoing inside her head as she sagged to the ground.

"Out of my way, cur!" Jules said, kicking at the dog who snapped his jaws at Jules's leg.

"Be gone before I kick your teeth in!" Jules backed slowly, perusing the tools spread out on a carpenter's bench, reaching out for a leatherpunch just as the hound sunk his teeth into his arm. "*Non!*" he cried. Powerful jaws ripped into flesh and Jules screamed as the hound secured his grip. "Bastard!" Struck in the chest with the leatherpunch, the beast let go and yelped. "Bite me, will you?" The injured hound circled, striking again as Jules caught it in the head, his sharp tool jabbing like a knife. Macbeth howled in pain, but redoubled his attack. He leaped on Jules's chest, snarling, lunging for his throat.

"Ahhh!" Jules yelled, grabbing the hound's collar and twisting until the beast's eyes bulged and blood trickled from its mouth. Bone cracked and Macbeth's feet thrashed in the air.

"Die!" Jules tightened his grip and gouged the punch upward into the hound's chest. Macbeth let out a yelp, gasping and gurgling as he shook, then stiffened. The hound fell and Jules panted as saliva dropped from his lips, his curses stifled as he kicked the gray carcass from between his legs.

El'Ramir whinnied and danced, breaking away in a flurry of hooves, his frenzy fired by the violence in the air. Dominique moaned and opened her eyes, staring at the still body of her beloved hound, so near she could touch the bloodied coat.

"Macbeth!" she cried out.

"Damnable beast tried to kill me!" Jules said, rolling up his sleeve to examine his arm.

Dominique pulled herself up and began crawling away.

"No you don't!" Jules growled, covering his wound.

"Alexandre and Jacques will be looking for me," she said.

"Tell me more of your lies!" Jules said, bending to grab hold of her arms and jerk her up. He thrust her hands behind her and roped them together with twine he found hanging on the wall. "I planned well for this day. 'Tis a celebration, remember? We shall not be disturbed."

"You killed my hound!" she spat.

"*Oui*, and I shall kill you as well if you don't do as I command!" He held her wrists painfully, catching her at the back of her neck and squeezing until she gasped for air. "Come, my sweet, let me look you over. It has been a long time."

"Please," she begged, knowing she could never fight him in her condition. "I am with child and—"

"I see!" he said, crushing her against himself. "I've not forgotten our lovefest, my captive bride, or should I call you *mère*?" His face reflected disgust. "So you carry his brat, what of it? I've had fat wenches before. 'Tis no different. I'll take you from behind if you like."

"Let me go!" she screamed, thinking she would die if he touched her again.

"When I've finished with you." He chuckled. "Before I'm through, you shall be begging for more."

"Madman!" She spat in his face. "Alexandre said you were mad!"

"Bitch!" He caught her chin in his fist and kissed her so hard he split her lip. "Up with you," he said, pushing her up the steps to the hayloft. "We have some lovemaking to catch up on. This time you'll bless me, I promise." In the hayloft, he loosened her habit and rolled her over, exposing her full breasts and delighting in the way their tender tips trembled. "Let me taste the honey you have there," he said, lowering his mouth to her breasts and tasting each rosy peak. "Nikki," he whispered, "dear sweet Nikki."

"Nay!" she cried as his lips swept over her neck to her ear. His hands tore at her habit and she felt the cool air on her legs. How could it be happening again? She fought furiously to be free and felt the pain of labor knifing her back.

"Nikki," Jules moaned, rolling atop her and holding her down. His hands worked with the front of his breeches and she screamed again and again for help, hearing the soft hoot of Oliver overhead as she sank her teeth into Jules's shoulder.

"Bitch!" he howled, slapping her and stripping her to the waist. "I'll make you pay for that!" Muttery curses, tore off her underclothes in a single stroke, casting them aside and pressing his knees between her thighs.

"The babe is coming!" she sobbed. "Dear God, don't touch me!"

" 'Twill move aside," Jules said. "You'll soon be blessing me."

"Kill me," she begged, feeling the hot imprint of his hand on her face.

"Not yet, my sweet," Jules said, sweeping back her hair. "Feel me now! What I have saved for you all this time."

The owl Oliver hooted on the roof and Dominique could not believe the world went on. Stars shining in the sky and the moon rising in the heavens. Jules's hands forced her legs wide and she knew her time had come. Reality was beginning to fade as she heard a soft thud and a long moan. Jules's body fell to the side like a bag of sand.

"*Swine!* Dirty, filthy, stinking swine! Vermin crawling the earth in the body of a man!"

Dominique heard the voice of her father-in-law and tried to move, but an intense pain pierced her. She moaned.

"Dominique, my child, are you hurt? Where are you injured?"

"Father . . ." Hot tears flooded her cheeks in a torrent and she grew hysterical, shaking and sobbing so hard she was unable to form words.

"There, there, my child, don't cry. I do believe I've split the devil's skull with my cane. You're alive, child! You're alive! My son will be here any minute." Pulling her up, François helped Dominique stand, then wrapped her in his woolen cloak.

"Macbeth," she sobbed, glancing at her hound and remembering him as a pup, his wet brown eyes pleading her to take him home. Her courageous friend was gone forever.

"Leave the scum to the dogs!" François spat, stepping over Jules as Dominique stiffened in pain and collapsed in his arms. François struggled to hold her up as to her horror she saw a groping Jules taking a pitchfork from the wall.

"Do me in, will you?" Jules said, crashing the fork down and grazing François's arm. The prongs sent blood spurting through François's sleeve and twanged as they hit the stone floor. François caught himself and swung his ivory-headed cane like a mallet, his face caught in agonized pain as death choked the blood from his heart.

"Father!" Dominique smothered a scream and stared in disbelief as her father-in-law slumped to the floor, his mouth twisting in the dust. His heart had failed him.

"God, nay!" she sobbed, terror cresting in her.

"God does my work for me." Jules grinned, pulling her along with him though not before opening her cloak to gape. " 'Twas fate, sweet Nikki. The old man was past his time. Make certain you know I had no part in it. He tried to kill me first and received his reward."

Dominique's eyes glazed over and she stared at the lifeless form at her feet.

"To the hall, mistress!" Jules commanded. " 'Twill be dark soon and I wish to study your beauty while 'tis still light. Your flesh in its private glories." He laughed heartily, making her walk before him to the house. The sun was sinking behind the gray mount in a glorious blaze when he grabbed hold of her hair and kissed her. "When your husband comes you'll tell him I never touched his father, if you wish him to live the night. For I would just as soon see him dead as his sire!"

"Lead the way to your chambers and no tricks!" Jules warned. If she lived to bear her child she would never be the same, she knew. But could she survive Jules taking her again? Yet there was still hope. She was alive and Alexandre would come as soon as he discovered her gone! Would he go to the carriage house? Pain held her in a vise and she stumbled. God forgive her, but she wanted Jules Cocteau dead! If only someone—anyone—would kill him!

They climbed the steps to the gallery and moved behind the jalousies between the end pillars. Dominique seized her last chance. If she could jump . . .

"Perhaps later." Jules chuckled, as he held fast to her arm. "When your husband wants no part of you!" He laughed.

They reached the French doors on the gallery and stepped inside. Pushing Dominique onto the bed, Jules walked aimlessly about, unbuttoning his breeches and discarding his boots. "Kiss an old friend," he said, yanking Dominique's head up by a fistful of hair. His eyes glinted with repulsive, mortifying evil.

"I spit on you!" she cried.

"You'll kiss it in the end, you'll see!" His laugh was fiendish as he went to the armoire to throw open its doors, spying something in a drawer. "What have we here? Surely this cannot belong to your husband?"

A French flintlock lay beneath Alexandre's shirts, its steel-gray barrel never heated by a ball.

"Your husband keeps weapons of destruction? The good doctor of Racemont? I cannot believe it! 'Tis primed and loaded for bear!"

Shivering and sobbing on the quilts, Dominique watched Jules finger the pistol's carved butt. She fought to stay conscious, to warn her husband if Alexandre should answer her prayer and appear.

"I have hated Alexandre Chastain for as long as I can remember!" Jules growled. "At last I'll have my revenge, and you shall help me." Returning to the bed, Jules tapped the cold bore of the pistol lightly against Dominique's temple and whispered into her ear, "After you have known the elevation of the gods!"

Alexandre rode uneasily back from the mountain. The savage, as his wife called Coosa, had beaten him easily in the race. His thoughts had not been on winning. Why had he allowed Dominique to talk him into it? The time for her confinement had come and he was relieved. No more horses or wild rides until after his son was born. Then, a simple stroll would have to suffice.

On dismounting before the carriage house, Alexandre heard a shot ring out from the house, followed at once by a woman's screams.

By the time he reached the steps to the gallery he was out of breath. He took the steps by threes, hearing voices overhead, a slap, a muffled cry.

"Spoil my pleasure, will you?" a man cried out, then rumbled out more threats. Alexandre by then had identified the voice: his mad cousin, Jules Cocteau.

Panic gripping him, Alexandre braced himself and crashed through the bolted door, tackling Jules in one motion from behind. The two men toppled the giant armoire and landed on the floor. Jules's face went ashen when he saw his assailant, his eyes alive with rage.

"So, you've come to claim your wife?" Jules cried.

"Where is she, you depraved worm?" Alexandre cried.

Jules was attempting to reply when Alexandre wrapped his fingers around his neck, pressing his thumbs against Jules's windpipe. Alexandre heard a moan behind him and relaxed his hold, glancing over his shoulder and catching sight of Dominique on the bed. "*Chérie!* What has he done to you?"

Tears dimmed Dominique's eyes as she looked at him, his gaze sweeping over her as she stiffened in pain. Bruised and bare, she lay tied to the bedposts, a silk scarf stuffed in her mouth. Her eyes cried out in warning, but too late. The butt of the flintlock came down like a hammer on the side of Alexandre's skull. Blood trickled slowly down Alexandre's cheek, his fingers running red as he dropped to his knees.

"Weakling!" Jules taunted.

Dominique choked and twisted and strained with pain, her cries unheeded as waves of nausea swept over her and her head fell back. Alexandre struggled to his feet and was moving toward his wife when Jules struck him again.

Regaining his footing, Alexandre lunged, striking Jules in the jaw with all his might. A trickle of blood oozed from the corner of Jules's mouth.

"I'll kill you!" Alexandre bellowed, anger blurring his vision as he choked Jules again. Jules sputtered and gasped as fresh strength surged into Alexandre's hands. "Die, for touching her!" he cried. "Die, so I may cut you into little pieces and feed you to the hounds!"

" 'Tis enough, Alexandre!" Jacques burst into the room and pried Alexandre's hands from Jules's neck, his eyes filled with pity. "Stop," he said. "Unhand him now—killing's too good for him."

Jules gurgled as blood and saliva ran from his mouth.

"Relax, man," Jacques told Alexandre. "Your wife lives and Mrs. Ross needs you. She's been shot."

Alexandre frowned quizzically, tasting the salinity of blood and looking into his brother's face. "*Chérie*," he whispered, before the room grew dim and he slipped to the floor.

Few souls slept that night, the eventide rent by weeping and intermittent screams. Drums throbbed like broken hearts and the hounds howled for the dead. Jules had been locked securely in the root cellar and Jacques had ridden to the mountain to be alone with his thoughts.

Alexandre stood silently on the darkened gallery and listened to the drums of his father's people, the creatures of the night chorusing in concert. Staggering, he grabbed hold of the gallery rail as his head reeled with the events of the day. His father was dead, the finality of the truth made him weep. Then there was Mrs. Ross, the woman his father had planned to marry. Cat's wound was minor, but now she was his responsibility.

Dominique moaned on the bed behind him and he flew to her side, his face a mask of foreboding as Mrs. Yarborough prepared her for the delivery of his child.

"Let me die," Dominique moaned, her eyes closed. Alexandre wiped the sweat from her brow and kissed her cheek as she suffered another hopeless contraction.

"I'm going to help you," he said, nodding to Mrs. Yarborough. "Our child is coming and you're going to be fine." He kissed her hair and set about his task, the hours that followed the most painful he would ever know. Dominique's labor was pitiful, hopeless, and try as he might, his instruments proved useless in delivering the babe. Mrs. Yarborough's prayers were both repetitious and never-ending as Marie and Mocha kept a vigil outside their mistress's door. Jacques paced the floor and Romeo curled up in a corner to whine. Death had evaded Dominique for some reason, her wandering mind voicing her belief she was being punished for not wanting her child.

The pain ceased. Strong arms encircled her, warm lips fastened upon hers, a voice comforted as she rode to the mountain. "Summer eyes," the voice whispered. Gold-encircled arms drew her down from her mount as she found the contentment she had always sought. A life of freedom and everlasting love.

"*Chérie?*" a voice called to her, a light hovering in the distance, bright as the sun, white as a star. "*Chérie!*"

Rising toward the warmth of the light, Dominique felt like she was floating higher and higher, until she almost entered the light.

Alexandre's face was grim with despair, his brow beaded with sweat, his hands trembling. Placing his ear to his wife's belly, he listened to the fetal heartbeat and prayed for guidance. To perform a Ceasarean would be a death warrant. To allow his wife to continue in a hopeless labor, the same. He asked forgiveness for what he must do, wanting to comfort Dominique but knowing there was no time.

11

November was young, roses blooming in the gardens of Racemont, white and purple wildflowers mingling with yellow daisies at the foot of Stone Mountain. The sweetgum tree dropped its fruit reluctantly and squirrels and other rodents readied for the winter ahead. Days were warm and sunny with cool crisp nights overseen by a proud gold moon.

A fortnight had passed since the fateful Jubilee celebration had ended in tragedy and Racemont plantation struggled to return to normalcy. The horses and hounds arrived from Savannah and blacks and whites labored together from dawn till dusk settling the horses into their new quarters. When the task was finally finished, Mrs. Ross's carriage was prepared for its trip back to Savannah.

"We shall miss you, Ruthe. Seems unfair you should be the one suffering for somethin' the mistress did. But who could tell her anything? Not even the good doctor himself, I say. Whatever he asks of her, she ups and does the opposite!" Mrs. Yarborough was her usual self as she watched the cookhouse fire stoked with twelve-foot staves of wood.

"The mistress says she'll have me and my man back in no time at all, Mrs. Yarborough," Ruthe replied. "A trip to the sea this time of year is welcome. 'Twill be cold this winter in the shadow of that mountain.'' Ruthe tried to be cheerful as she watched Mrs. Ross's carriage loaded from the cookhouse door.

"The mistress has told me many times how she loves you, Ruthe,'' Nancy sniffed. " 'Tis none of her doing. She meant no harm to any of us that fateful day.''

Mrs. Yarborough huffed and fanned her face at the remark. "Well, she near got herself killed with the old master. Not countin' the wee babe the good doctor wanted so!'' Her lips curled and she watched Desiree through the glass of the door's window.

"Is it true the child was a boy, Mrs. Yarborough?'' Colena asked shyly. "Did you see him?''

"I cannot speak of it, child!'' Mrs. Yarborough barked back. "I couldn't bear to look at his precious face. 'Tis too horrible to recall.''

Colena said she was sorry in a whisper and went on washing greens in a wooden bowl, watching Mrs. Yarborough cross herself and say a quick prayer for all to hear.

"You do the master an injustice by discussing the subject, Mrs. Yarborough. Pray let the child's soul rest in peace.'' Ruthe walked to the door and went outside to watch Desiree play with a yellow kitten.

Mrs. Yarborough's eyes narrowed and she followed Ruthe. "Aye, the child's dead and dead the master is as well. Dead and nearly buried! The poor man'll never be the same thanks to her! He's in a world between sanity and madness. I swear, the woman is a witch!''

Ruthe turned slowly to stare at Mrs. Yarborough and Marie left her hams hanging in the chimney to join them.

"Yo' don' call mah mistress no witch, ya hear! Not dat innocent chile! Don' yo' have no feelins, woman! She done loss her baby, her little precious manchile lies out there in pieces like a torn-up rabbit. But dat ain't nuff fo' yo', is it, ole woman?'' Marie pursed her lips and with a deliberate push sent Mrs. Yarborough against a stone wall. "Yo' want tah see her suffer dah heat o' hell, 'cause yo' is dah witch yo' is!'' Slipping a paring knife from her apron pocket, Marie held the blade just near enough to Mrs. Yarborough's throat. "Now yo' hear dis, ole woman! Yo' keep yo' mouth off o' dat chile or yo' and me is goin' tah fight! An' Mère done fight clean!''

Mrs. Yarborough jerked her head back and began to sputter. Fearful of uttering a sound, she sank down to her knees. Marie swiftly returned the knife to her apron, returning to the cookhouse to continue her hock stringing inside the chimney.

"How long will you be gone, Ruthe?" Nancy queried softly, clearing the air with an attempt at civil conversation.

"I don't know, Nancy. We're to open the master's house in Savannah and keep it ready."

"All for that woman!" Mrs. Yarborough hissed, clasping her throat and standing erect. "How can you bear to ride in the same coach with the harlot?"

"Mrs. Yarborough," Ruthe said. "I don't judge my employers or their friends and I believe it wise for you to do the same."

"Will you and your man be serving Mrs. Ross in Savannah?" Nancy asked Ruthe."

"We serve Doctor Chastain," Ruthe said softly. "We'll do whatever he asks of us."

"Seems to me our mistress should be the one leaving here." Nancy shrugged. " 'Twas she who lost a babe. She cries most of the time and I cannot help but share the blame she shoulders. One of us should have been there when she needed help." Nancy broke into tears.

"And how were we to know a madman was on the loose, pray tell?" Mrs. Yarborough scowled. "I knew Jules Cocteau was evil the first time I set eyes on him. But who would have dreamed he'd show up in Georgia?"

"Is my husband well?" Dominique asked. Dressed in a warm nightdress and a white shawl thrown about her shoulders, she propped herself up in her bed.

"As well as can be expected, considering all that has happened," Jacques replied. "My concern is with you now."

"I'm fit as ever," she said, turning away. "I understand Saul sleeps in Alexandre's room. Have you found a suitable manservant for the doctor?" Her eyes were red and swollen, her hair knotted against her head, her beauty masked by a long ordeal.

"The man is here, madame. I purchased his papers when in Savannah. 'Twas difficult to find an educated black, but I believe you will be satisfied with my choice."

"I would know of the woman, Kish," she said. "The mother of Moses. Is she installed in her quarters inside the hall?"

"As you requested, madame. Kish and her little son have a room near the kitchen."

"Good." She sighed, closing her eyes and resting her head on the pillow. "I'll see your man now."

When she opened her eyes she saw a black man with a heavy beard flecked with white and a thick head of hair. He had whiskers that reminded her of walrus tusks, pointed and streaked white. The black man's eyes were bright.

"Moses, madame, your humble servant." He blowed low.

"Moses?"

"*Oui*, madame. My master named me from the good book. If you do not approve you may call me Socrates or Plato, perhaps Voltaire?"

She smiled. "Where did you receive your education, Moses?"

"My previous master was a ship's captain, madame. But he had a house in Boston and I was privileged to accompany him to Europe twice."

Dominique looked at Jacques who stood waiting at the door. "You have done well, Jacques. He's exactly what the doctor needs. Have him outfitted and see to his quarters."

Jacques smiled warmly.

December was cold and dreary. The rains came and stayed and the sun was not seen for weeks. Skies hung low and the red clay turned into rivers of mud. Fires roared in the fireplaces of Racemont and its young mistress pondered her life as Mrs. Alexandre Chastain.

She felt betrayed. What had wedlock brought her but tears and heartache, a disaster from the beginning! But what of Desiree? Surely her darling daughter was compensation enough for the unhappiness and pain she had known? Or was the child the offspring of the devil himself? God, if she dwelled on it she would go mad! She recalled the recent loss of her unborn son and began to shake. She must go away, but where? She was a prisoner in her own house, Mrs. Yarborough watching her every move!

Stepping from her bed, she went to the windows and tucked her fur robe about her legs as she sat in a big chair, pulling a lacy shawl about her shoulders and watching the rain beat furiously against the panes. How she longed to climb atop

Ramir and ride. Ride until her troubles disappeared! She would lose her mind if she stayed in bed much longer.

"Perhaps if you got dressed and came downstairs you would feel better, Miss Nikki?" Nancy said upon entering the room. "I could arrange your hair in a new way. You have not worn it up for a long time. We could walk to the conservatory. The amaryllis are in bloom—hibiscus and poinsettia, too. You could wear your pink velvet . . . 'twould do you good to be dressed elegantly again."

"You're most kind, Nancy. You're the only one who cares."

"The good doctor cares, Miss Nikki. So do Marie and Ruthe. Others, too, if the truth be known." Nancy lifted the entrapped hair from beneath her mistress's white shawl, stroking it fondly.

"I know how my husband thinks, Nancy. He despises me. Pray leave me alone."

Nancy left quietly, shaking her head, and Dominique donned the gown Nancy had laid out for her, the pink velvet trimmed in lace with a blue fox capelet and hem. It felt good to wear a gown again, but she wanted no part of the matching stockings or shoes.

She was brushing the knots out of her hair when Nancy opened the door and peeked inside. "Miss Nikki, you're dressed! Why didn't you call?"

"I dressed myself and my hair is free of knots, Nancy." Dominique looked at her maid by way of her shell-encrusted mirror.

"But your blue slippers and the lovely pink stockings that go with the gown? You'll catch your death of cold on these floors—there's a draft in the halls."

"I don't care," Dominique murmured, refusing to lift her foot when Nancy knelt beside her. Nancy hurried to retrieve her mistress's jewels.

" 'Tis ridiculous to wear jewels, Nancy. Pray take them away."

"Nay," Nancy cajoled. "See how beautiful they'll make you feel."

Downstairs Dominique pushed through the conservatory doors to feel a warm rush of air. François Chastain's private jungle, a manmade forest of vines and exotic plants. Rain streamed across the skylights above her head and she was glad to be inside on such a day. Birds sang in their golden cages and she marveled at the beauty of a dreamy white orchid with a purple center. She stepped lightly down a brick walk to where flats of seedlings barred her way, a bank thick with purple-red flowers drawing her near.

"I'd be careful if I were you, madame. The nightshade of Africa is most deadly."

"Alexandre! I had no notion you were here. Forgive me, I'll leave."

"Don't go on my account. Pray stay a while. 'Tis all I ask." Dressed in black, Alexandre's face was lined; dark circles rimmed his eyes, an obvious loss of weight making him appear older. "I'm pleased to see you looking so well. You're more beautiful than I remember, if that is possible."

Dear God, don't let him touch her! Don't let him say something kind, take her hand or come another step closer! She felt helpless in his presence, as with a stranger. She looked down at her bare feet and thought how ridiculous she must look. "Thank you," she said finally, her voice soft as tears filled her eyes. She could not look into those warm brown pools of his sick eyes.

"That's all? You mean you're not going to call your husband *murderer?* Perhaps you don't know I killed our son?" he cried as he grasped her arm.

" 'Tis finished between us, Alexandre," she moaned. "You left my bed. You're no husband to me."

"What kind of woman are you?" He would not release her. "Don't you know what's happened here?"

"I know your father is dead and Jules Cocteau has escaped. My life is a shambles. Beyond that I care nothing."

"My son is dead!" he choked.

"My son, too," she replied. "Planted in my womb and nourished with my love and hope, all for naught."

He whirled from her. "And now you want the freedom you have sought so avidly?"

"Aye," she said, walking to the doors and pushing through. She made her way through the parlor to the grand staircase and began to climb, losing her footing and going down on her knees. She heard Alexandre calling to her from afar and kept going, climbing to the top of the stairs, and to her bed.

A few hours later, Dominique lethargically pulled on her clothes.

As Nancy entered the room, Dominique spoke without turning from the mirror.

"Have my mare saddled and fetch my warmest habit and fur cape. Tell no one where I've gone and don't come looking for me when I don't come home!"

The rain had subsided momentarily when Dominique guided her French-bred mare on the west forest path encircling the mountain. Something drove her to reach its crest, a place no woman had gone before, and in minutes she found the Indian trail that led upward.

"We can climb it, Jackie," Dominique coaxed the mare, leaning in her saddle and patting Jackie's neck. The mare went willingly where she was bid, hooves clattering over stone as the ascent began. The pine forest thinned where gnarled red cedars beckoned like maidens in distress, the rain returning in a drizzle as the climb became more hazardous. The granite was slippery and it was not long before the mare refused to move.

"This way, my lovely French lady," Dominique cooed. The view of Racemont was lost in a drifting haze and Dominique realized it was a ruinous undertaking. The mare was not made for climbing rock as slick as steel. Jackie pricked her ears at something on the wind. *Voices?* Dominique pulled her collar about her face, gripping the mare's mane and lifting her leg from the pommel.

"I'll go alone on foot," she said as she swung down and tied the mare to some bushes. "You stay here and I'll return by nightfall."

The vicious wind whipped her skirts, wrapping her cape about her face as she finally climbed the last few inches to the summit. She reached the rock's crown to find an obstruction barring the way. A stone wall of an ancient fortress circled the entire summit's rim.

"Damn!" Her voice was lost on the wind, her breath escaping in white clouds. Clinging to the stone wall, she tried to peer through the stones. Strange chanting reached her ears. Dear God, who lurked on the other side of the wall? Gathering her wits, she found an opening and groped her way through the narrow, jagged tunnel. In seconds she was on the other side. Her heart stopped. She counted twenty, fifty, one hundred figures . . . more? Men garbed in feathers, antlers and horns, or nothing at all, circled a blazing fire. Dominique's scalp tingled. She was on the brink of a discovery. Who these men were she didn't know, but she was bound to find out!

Sorry she had not worn sackcloth or veil, she listened as the men spoke in tongues, one, several, many! Hundreds of Indians—savages, heathens, she thought—kneeling, sitting, hunched together like toadstools in a mystical forest, countless faces around the roaring fire, the whole damnable Creek tribe for all she knew!

Suddenly she became aware of something. What would she do if they saw her? Alone and unarmed, outnumbered—and a white woman! Perhaps they were bloodthirsty killers, murderers who ate helpless females? Her ears pounded with uncertainty, her cape billowing in the tempestuous wind like a ship's sail in a mighty storm.

The chanting stopped, an awful hush more frightening than the savages themselves filling the air. Dominique stood motionless, her cloak drifting about her as she molded herself to the stones and prayed for invisibility. Then a savage screamed—a warcry—and she was running as fast as she could and screaming back through the hole in the wall. Suddenly light on the other side darkened as she caught her foot on a stone. She felt herself yanked backward. Four iron-strong hands grasped her legs as they swooped her up into their arms, her own waving wildly.

"Unhand me!" she shrieked, the drums so loud she couldn't hear her words. Two giants held her between them, their bald heads and scalplocks a sickening sight as they carried her back through the sacred place to which no woman had ventured before. "Put me down!" she wailed, as her hat rolled to the ground, releasing her hair to float around her waist.

A great moan went up in unison, her hair shining about her shoulders like muted gold. She stood like a fiery goddess before them, cape swept up into the glowing sky, face lit with firelight.

"Who is this female who dares to climb this mount?" an angry voice asked. "The gray egg is sacred, an ancient place of worship for peoples of many nations."

Impossible to understand the language, she absorbed the threat in the Indian's tone. She lifted her head and tossed her curls in a gesture of defiance, remembering Joan of Arc.

"A brave woman!" a deep voice shouted, first in Creek, then in other tongues. "Bring her to me!" A tall figure all in white came out of the smoke and Dominique wiped her eyes. Her heart fluttered. It was the man called Rising Moon! Did she have a chance?

The giants lifted her in the air between them again and carried her to Coosa. "Kill the woman and we have war before we're prepared. Coosa Tustennuggee takes responsibility for the woman's errors. Spare her life and give her to Coosa for his slave." He spoke in her behalf with knitted brows, a furious frown on his face as he pointed to her. She embraced a slab of stone and waited for the bloody blow. Men argued over her and she concentrated on the fire first, the flames licking a massive lid of stone placed there to prevent the flames from leaping skyward. Pondering the reason for the strange fireplace, she was not prepared when the giants pushed her down.

"No woman trods hallowed ground and lives!" a Choctaw chief said. "The Stone Mountain is the altar of the Great Spirit Himself, designed by Him for worship. Females are forbidden!"

Coosa smiled. "We do not worship Him this night. We come instead to talk of war, not a needless hopeless slaughter against the white eyes who outnumber us like the stars above our heads!" His voice rose like a great orator's, capturing his audience's full attention. "Who among us can say a single one of us could survive such a waste?" Coosa walked to the fire and stood beside Dominique, so close his foot touched her hand. She counted the beads on his moccasins, yellow and blue, the blue a second time as her eyes turned with the heat of the fiery furnace.

"You're not one of us, Coosa Tustennuggee!" an old voice accused. "It is well known the white eyes' blood flows in your veins!"

"Coosa Tustennuggee is Creek!" Coosa's tone was vehement. "One of you! A fearless warrior from the illustrious Wind Clan who doesn't deny his parentage and has proven himself to be for his mother's people first!" Coosa's eyes glinted in the firelight, his voice firm and strong like the puma's. The crowd argued, debated, as Coosa's eyes scanned their faces like an eagle's. Fighting an urge to touch the Creek's buckskins, Dominique succumbed, discovering the leggings were soft and warm on muscled legs, the feathered fringe proving a delight beneath her fingers.

The talk went on for a long time. "The woman trespassed on

holy ground! No Indian maiden is permitted here, no Creek, Cherokee, Catawbas or Choctaw woman! Not even of royal rank! You know the laws, Coosa Tustennuggee. The woman must suffer the consequences. Burn her and throw her off the mountain!''

Interpreting the angry shouts as her decree of death, Dominique's ears hummed. "If you kill the woman, it will be a needless shedding of blood!" Coosa argued, never leaving her side. "Are we barbarians? Must we give the Georgians reason to call us savage and heathen?"

The arguing raged on.

"Lift your head, woman!" Coosa finally roared. His big fist clasped her chin lightly and she fell back, glaring at him. "Lean on me if you must, woman, but show them you're not afraid," he said low. He yanked her head up by her hair, snarling like a rabid beast at her. "Women are nothing beneath a warrior's feet!" His voice was loud enough for all to hear. "Women are a needless burden upon Mother Earth, worthless, selfish creatures who must do as men command!" He gave her a good push and she fell down on her knees. Anger overtook her, a renewed strength surging through her as she picked herself up and faced him.

"Damn you, Coosa Moon!"

"Good!" He laughed. "Show them your rare and resplendent beauty!" He spoke through clenched teeth, pretending anger at her. Dominique hit at him as Coosa took her by the shoulders and forced her to stand alone. "Defy me the way you did that day on the trace, then smile and thank the chiefs for your pitiful life!" Stretching her neck, Dominique swirled her cape about her like a dragon's tongue, reaching for the hem of his jerkin.

"*Non!* You must stand alone and show your infinite gratitude to the great chiefs, then follow your lord to where you entered this sacred place."

Doing as she was told, she stood alone, a silly smile strangely effective as each ugly face turned into a red blur. Coosa marched her stoutly to the wall. She went with him meekly, turning her back on the countless eyes and expecting a piercing arrow through her heart any second. Reaching the wall, Coosa knelt to a hole and slid through first. Dominique died a thousand deaths then, thinking how she hated the Indian and planning her revenge.

"Quickly!" Coosa cried, reaching out dark hands for hers. Staring at his fingers, her mind was benumbed with fear. How did she know she could trust Coosa? Suppose Coosa had been chosen to kill her!

"Come!" Coosa said, peering up at her through the hole. Then he saw the fear in her eyes and pulled her through swiftly standing her up and holding her in his embrace for a short moment. "This day will pass," he assured her. "Coosa will not harm you." The wind came at her with a vengence then, tearing open her habit, and exposing her breasts. Coosa's gaze darted to where the fur lapels parted, his dark eyes searching hers, his paisley turban fighting the envious wind. He took her hand and pulled her down the face of the mountain while she pleaded with him to stop. "Nay, please, don't make me go down this way!"

She was so frightened she couldn't move, but Coosa dragged her to where huge boulders formed a cave.

"Please," she begged, shaking her head as his headdress whipped about his face, his hawklike eyes penetrating her to silence. "Please don't take me!" she pleaded.

"There are no serpents on the Great Spirit's holy altar, Domma-nique," he said. "Trust Coosa. Stay here until Coosa returns."

Dominique woke with a start, shivering as visions of vipers crawled through her mind. Unwinding her arms from her neck, she rubbed her cheek and opened her eyes wide. Peeking through the open rocks of her cave she saw a basin of stars above and a full moon lighting the sheer drop to the earth below. Coosa had promised to be back, but there was no sign of him. Who cared! If the Creek expected her to be his slave, he had another think coming! Once she told her tale to the authorities, the whole Indian nation would have to run for their lives. If Alexandre heard her story there would be bloodshed. Chastain men didn't take lightly to their women being manhandled by anyone! There would be reprisals, killings. She sucked in her breath, seeing little children suffering because of her vengefulness. She dare not speak of the incident. She would have to deal with Coosa herself. Aye, he'd saved her life, but she'd never called him lord! She had gotten up the mountain and she'd get down . . . somehow. Where were the red men and their horses? The rock was a monster and their mounts could be anywhere. *Jackie!* If the Indians found her mare the French beauty would be the prize of some fearsome warrior. Forcing herself out of the cave, she stood on the edge of nothingness, searching for a way down. Pebbles rolled when she moved her feet, tumbling into space. Her hands tingled at the incredible height. She was on the most dangerous side of the mountain, the rock's face. Coosa had turned her around somehow and she trembled at her plight, leaning against the rock cave to think. Deciding to crawl upward along the sheer face of the rock, she set about her task.

Within moments she found a rocky ledge between two boulders and stopped to rest. Closing her eyes, she pictured the Creek. Splendidly proportioned and taller than any of the Chastains, Coosa had been noble in his defense of her, resolute and ready for the fray. What if he hadn't been there? She could have been roasted alive, or worse! But she must hurry. She wasn't safe yet. She must steal away before dawn.

She saw the stunted tree and then the trail. The blue-gray mare neighed softly and Dominique's heart soared at the familiar sight. "Jackie, my sweet, did you think me gone forever?" She slid her hand over the beast's neck and Jackie whinnied her reply, lifting Dominique's cape with her nose. Dominique pulled her cape about her face to hide her breath, turning the mare and leading her from her granite cell. The descent took longer than expected, but then the moist sand caressed the mare's hooves and Jackie trembled with relief. Dominique mounted from a loose boulder, moving the mare in a brisk walk and leaning forward in her saddle. Deliverance was near and the forest smelled of rain and moss. Wet pine boughs slapped her face as Jackie picked her way along a narrow path between the mount and the lake. Dominique had just lowered her head to escape a limb when she was plucked from her saddle like a bag and dropped on the ground.

Jackie disappeared in a flurry of hooves and broken branches as two Creek warriors stood over their stunned prey. Dominique lifted an eyelid to look. The two bald and brazen braves, naked to the waist, and in buckskin leggings, moccasins, and quivers of arrows, caught her eye, a golden gorget about one's neck. The biggest one, who sported stretched ears that hung to his shoulders, poked her with a club; the other touched her hair and laughed.

She played dead, her arm and shoulder throbbing with a dull

ache. The one with the gorget rolled her over, twisting her
cloak about her neck and chuckling when she opened her eyes
and clamped them shut again. The biggest one had green
tattoos and thick lips and shook her like a rug, forcing her to sit
up with a sharp prod in the ribs.

"Coosa will get you for this!" she shrieked, pulled to her
feet with a yank. She held one arm and watched them as they
repeated her words, making the name *Coosa* sound different.

"Coosa's squaw!" one taunted, hurting her breast when he
jabbed with a thick finger.

"Aye, snake!" she hissed, slapping his hand away and
staring into his eyes. "You'd best remember my name is
Chastain!"

The one wearing the gorget motioned for her to go with him
into the woods and she refused with a shake of her head.

"You can't make me go!" she snarled. "Try, and I'll bite off
your finger!" Yanking her cloak about her, she threatened them
like a mad dog. Then one of them gave her a shove and took
her by the hair, dragging her to the stream. Her hair hid her
tears and she was glad, thinking of what horror would be next.
Would they take her in their turn, or would she be killed? They
knocked her to the ground and she crawled quickly to the
stream's low bank and pretended to be heaving, spying a sharp
rock and pulling it to her breast.

"Chastain woman!" They laughed. Gagging, she felt hands
stroking her hair and waited for the right moment. The Indians
laughed. When a large foot came to rest beside her face, she
decided it was the right time for her move. She brought the
stone down heavily on his toes.

"Woman!" she shrieked, laughing as the one with the
smashed toes danced on one foot. Her laughter faded into a
moan as the other one grasped her head and brought it sharply
against a tree and blackness engulfed her senses.

Dominique opened her eyes and saw a misty whiteness
shrouding the pines, waving treetops giving her a glimpse of
shimmering sky and waning starlight, the moon pale. She
breathed in the scent of wet pine and moist earth, cuddling
beneath a red woolen cloak and turning to the warmth of a fire.

"You slept well, she-wolf," a masculine voice said.

It was *him!* Coosa—back to haunt her. She heard the high-
pitched yelping of hounds in the distance.

"The hounds come for their lady," Coosa said. "Soon they will be here." Standing, he moved to put out the fire and break camp.

"Those were your men, weren't they?" she accused, throwing off his cloak and coming to her knees.

"You are in fine spirits!" He grinned, his deep voice and strange accent subtly wooing her, his cool manner inflaming her temper.

"Am I your prisoner?" she queried.

Coosa helped her up, his height overwhelming. She stepped back into his shadow. "Are you bound? Do leg irons encircle your feet and does rope smart your neck?" He lifted a shaggy brow and stared her down. "You're Coosa's slave to do with as I please. But I would have more than obedience from you." His eyes were black coals that swallowed up her haughty gaze. In their depths she saw more than she wished. The damnable savage was a man! His headdress gone, his hair was incredibly thick, like rich forest loam, and touched his shoulders. He wore the same buckskin jerkin and leggings she'd seen before, the manmade scratches beside his eyes silvery, oddly becoming in the morning light.

"I'm not any man's slave," she said evenly. "I'm not bound by your Indian laws and I'll not obey! I'm Mrs. Alexandre Chastain, and you'll not ever tell me what to do!" Looking at him made her weak. Turning on her heel, she headed in the direction of the bridle path that circled the mountain. Coosa mounted his pony and followed at an easy walk.

"The way to Racemont is long and there are copper-headed vipers about. A fine lady such as you should ride with her lord."

She clapped a hand to her mouth to still a cry, her eyes perusing the path. He jested with her. It was winter and serpents were in their holes.

"The lady would rather walk through snakes than ride with a two-legged one," she retorted. "I climbed your damnable mountain and I came down by myself. I know where I am. I can find my way home, thank you." She threw him a black look and swirled her cloak about her aching shoulder.

"Very well." He chuckled softly. "Alexandre told me you were not like other women." He walked his horse beside her. "Coosa sent his best braves to entrap a she-wolf and she did not keep them waiting." His laugh was deep and warm, the look in his eyes maddening as his hair wavered on the breeze. Dominique swept past him with her nose in the air, listening to the hounds in the distance. Alexandre was coming, and if not her husband, his brother Jacques or his slaves. What would her husband say when he saw her with the savage? No time to reason, she leaped to one side when she heard a rattle in a distant bush. "Coosa!" she screamed.

Coosa was at her side instantly, lifting her in his arms and seating her on his ornately carved saddle. A frown rippled his brow. "The name is Coosa Tustennuggee, madame. King of the Lower Creeks, *mico*, hunter, human, and man."

12

The baying rose on the morning air as Coosa led his steed out of the piney woods into a clearing whitened with frost. Dominique sat on the piebald stallion observing the man who led her mount. What a pity one so tall and exceedingly handsome was a heathen savage. She shrugged. The squaws could have him and good riddance.

Coosa raised a bronzed hand and his piebald halted. "Many hounds are coming, two white men with them." How did he know, Dominique wondered. Minutes passed, the thunder of hooves crossing the high shoales unmistakable. A great pack of howling beasts swarmed over the rise. Hounds of every description—bloods, otters, fox, wolf—barking and baying at the top of their lungs, breaking, bursting, panting, beating the brush for their mistress's scent, their voices thrilling to the ear.

"Music of the gods," Coosa said.

Dominique remembered her hound Macbeth then, with a little stab. Three horses crossed the ravine in the distance and Alexandre's stallion came into view. Jacques rode Togar with the gray mare in tow. Dominique concerned herself with the questions Alexandre would ask. The horses came closer, the yelp of the hounds reaching a high pitch.

"Greetings!" Jacques shouted, riding up to his son and

dismounting. Alexandre dismounted, too, never acknowledg-
ing his wife sitting on Coosa's mount. Hounds rolled in waves
around the horses, barking so loudly it was impossible to hear.

"Little sister, are you well?" Jacques asked.

"I am. How great is his vexation?" she asked softly. "Tell
me before 'tis too late."

Jacques smiled reassuringly. "You had us all in a fit,
madame. 'Tis a husband's right to be angry. His mood will
pass, given time."

She took Jacques's hand and allowed him to draw her down,
smoothing her muddied, rain-spotted habit and trying to hear
the conversation between Alexandre and Coosa. "What's he
telling your son?" she asked, unable to understand the rapidly
fired French between the Creek and the doctor.

"About the tragedy," Jacques advised. "Coosa didn't
know."

But there was more, she knew. Alexandre was informing the
Creek his wife was not well, changed mentally. Pulling herself
into her saddle, she wheeled Jackie about and called the
hounds. She gave Jackie her head and clattered off in a mad
gallop.

"The bone is broken above the wrist, madame." Alexandre's tone was agitated, his manner professional as he lay her
hand down and left the side of her bed to prepare a splint small
enough for a tiny wrist. "Where did you spend the night?" He
never looked her way. It was the first time he'd spoken to her
since her return from the mountain. She'd ridden all morning
trying to get the hurtful words he'd said to Coosa out of her
mind. It was late now, almost dark.

"On the ground," she replied casually, not wanting to argue.

"Was the Creek with you?" His tone was mannerly, as if he
were asking her to pass the salt at the dining table. He set the
bone, paying no heed to her white grimace, refusing her the
warmth of his soft brown eyes, his usual words of comfort.

"The savage found me and brought me home to you, if that
is what you want to know." She let out her breath slowly,
narrowing her lips as he wrapped her arm.

"You're fortunate, madame. Your fall could have been
fatal." He laid her arm in a linen sling and tied the cloth about
her neck. Relieved to hear he knew she'd fallen, she wondered
what Coosa had told him. Alexandre could be trying to catch

her in a falsehood. Why worry? She'd done no wrong, committed no crime, was guilty of no sin. Alexandre finished with
her arm, standing to gaze at her face, his eyes ablaze.

"You will not leave this hall again without my permission,
madame. And then only in the company of my brother or
myself, or slaves of my choosing. I've selected two young
bucks to accompany you when Jacques or myself cannot."

Had she heard rightly? Was he revoking her freedom of
movement? Eyeing him curiously, she noted his thin face and
hands. He seemed so weak beside the Creek. So very, very
weak. Closing her eyes, she asked forgiveness for the cruel
comparison.

"You're Mrs. Alexandre Chastain. I find I must remind you
of that fact." Turning to the windows, he stared at the
mountain. "I still care for you." He hung his head. "These
past months have been difficult for us all. We must start anew."

She looked hopeful, a smile tugging her lips, her heart
pounding as the dimple appeared beside her mouth. He loved
her. He loved her!

"We must be seen together . . . for appearance's sake."
He faced her. "We shall dine together and perhaps a walk in
the garden with Desiree now and then would be wise." His
hands shook and she believed him a stranger, feeling pity for
him and shrinking back on the pillows to grasp her throat. She
loved him, she knew that now. Loved him with all her heart and
soul, all her being.

"I expect nothing from you in the way of wifely duties," he
was saying. His voice broke and he turned away. "Children?
Not now, not for several years. I shan't trouble you on that
score, have no fear."

Didn't he know how brutal his words were, how merciless?
Did he loathe her, thirst for her blood? Looking at him, she was
unable to speak, wanting to call his name and beg him to come
to her, touch her, hold her, enfold her in his embrace. Instead,
he was cutting her off, severing their ties! It was several
minutes before she heard the door open and close, several
minutes before she knew what she must do.

The night was hell and Dominique woke with a throbbing
arm and head to match. Her hair clung to her wet face, and she
sobbed. Hours passed, and still she trembled. Little by little,
her brain began to work, her feminine wiles at play. It wasn't

Alexandre's fault. Had she ever told him she loved him? Gone to him and given him the wifely comfort and compassion he so sorely needed after the loss of their babe? Why did it hurt so much to lose his love? Surely she didn't expect her husband to come to her, get down on his knees after *she* had done him wrong! Recalling the nightmarish climax of the Jubilee, she wanted to die. She had endangered herself, their babe. Alexandre blamed her for Jules's abuse; François's death; the babe's loss.

But she couldn't leave her child without a mother. She didn't *need* Alexandre; she didn't need any man! He'd been the one who'd left her bed, not her! She'd been the one who'd been wronged. She tried to think, applying logic and meaning to the tangle, going over and over the chain of circumstances in her mind. If she left Alexandre, where would she go? The world was rather limited in the wilds of Georgia. Savannah lay only days away, Augusta and Charleston, too, but the real world was in the North—hundreds of miles away! Wiping her eyes, she thought of her beasts, the horses and hounds she professed to love. She couldn't leave them, couldn't give up her dream of breeding superior horses. What a fool she'd been! Wasting precious time. Precious, precious time!

The table was draped in its best linen, silver gleaming beside china of a Tuscan-rose pattern. Tall white candles burned brightly in crystal candelabra beside a Ming vase filled with blood-red amaryllis. "Is Missus Chastain joinin' you gentlemen fo' dinner?" Marie's bottom lip pouted.

"'Tis uncertain, Mère. You know Madame as well as I," Alexandre said.

"But yo' done told me da missus was comin' outta her room today, doctah! I been roastin' dem ducks all day, fixin' dem trimmin's dah way she likes 'em, applesauce cake 'n' all! Even set dah table dah way she taught me!"

"Serve my brother and me and send a tray to Madame's bedchamber," Alexandre instructed. "I'm off to Athens to attend a sick man."

"Athens, why so far?" Jacques asked in surprise.

"Mr. Drummond is a very important man, a politician who knows the governor and President Jefferson. Drummond's been ill a long time and has asked me to be his physician." He crumpled his napkin and signaled to Moses to pour him another glass of wine. Jacques studied his brother's face, noting how many glasses he had downed already.

"I'd ask a favor," Alexandre said to Jacques.

"Anything."

"My wife, I want you to—" As if thunderstruck, Alexandre looked up as Dominique swept through the doors into the room, dressed in a gown of cool lime silk with sleeves and decolletage bordered in silver braid. Her hair was partly up, with long curls falling to carress a bare shoulder. Emeralds sparkled at her earlobes. Her smile caused both men's blood to stir, big shoulders bumping together as they came to their feet.

"Delighted you could join us. Mère has prepared a feast in your honor." Jacques smiled and seated her.

"How very nice." Dominique's reply was demure, noting the look Alexandre gave Jacques.

"May I say how divinely seductive you look, madame?" Jacques grinned.

"Thank you, sir. A lady appreciates kind words, especially when they are so seldom heard."

" 'Tis the company you keep, madame." Jacques threw a pointed look Alexandre's way. "Some folks don't know what they have till they've lost it."

Alexandre slammed down his goblet and called for Marie. "Egads, Mère, either serve me or forget it altogether. I've a long journey ahead of me this day!"

Marie pushed through the swinging doors with a swoosh, girl slaves only steps behind. "Yo' is mighty on edge these days, Doctah Chastain. What's wrong, huh? Ain't yo' happy?"

Alexandre ignored his cook's bold inquiry, motioning to have his goblet refilled, watching his half-brother's every move toward his wife. "You needn't worry about me, Mère. You'll not have to contend with me once I finish this meal. I'll be gone the rest of the week. I expect you'll keep my house in the meantime."

Marie stopped where she stood, setting down her tray on the mahogany sideboard. "Yo' jus' go and have a fine time, doctah. Jacques 'n' me are goin' tah look after dis hall 'n' yo' darlin' sweet wife, too. We gonna keep dis place shinin' like a piece o' Spanish gold 'n' yo' brother is goin' tah watch after us colored folks."

Dominique swallowed a giggle, trying to spread a pat of

hard butter into a fluffy roll as big as a man's fist. Jacques offered his assistance and Alexandre glared.

"I'm aware my brother can handle the plantation and its workers. I presume I can rest easily since Madame will be confining herself to the hall . . . at least until her arm is mended." Giving Dominique a satisfied look, he believed her arm would prevent her from riding.

Dominique smiled beguilingly at Jacques. "Stay as long as necessary, doctor. Dear Jacques and Mère will look after me. If I'm bored I have two new companions, thanks to you. Pray tell me who the young bucks are?"

Jacques swallowed a mouthful of steaming rice and Dominique lifted her lashes to give Alexandre a look that would have melted a frozen pond.

"I trust you remember our talk, Madame." Alexandre rippled a brow and drank from his goblet. "You're not to leave these premises without permission from my brother. I trust I need not remind you again."

"You do not!" she said, finding his tone annoying, sorely tempted to throw her wine in his face. He tossed his napkin aside and stood to leave.

"I'll say good-bye now. Moses has my carriage ready."

"Your manservant can wait a moment more," Jacques advised, pushing out his chair. "I'll leave you along with your wife. 'Tis certain you'll want to say your farewells in private."

"My wife and I have nothing more to say to one another." Alexandre caught Jacques's sleeve and held him forcibly. "I'll be gone now."

Jacques looked at his sister-in-law and saw her raise a trembling chin. Alexandre exited by way of the kitchen and Jacques smiled widely, showing off a flawless smile.

"You have my permission to go wherever your heart desires, Madame Chastain. So long as I'm with you." Chuckling, he heaped his plate with second helpings of everything, moving to the head of the table and sitting beside his ravishing mistress.

In the days that followed Dominique acquainted herself with the new mares. There were two mulberry Andalusians from Spain, descendants of the Jerez stud, and two frothy-white Lipizzaners from Austria, chosen by Bonaparte himself. The horses adjusted beautifully to the Georgia climate and Dominique longed to share her enthusiasm and suggestions for their matings with her husband but he had not yet returned from

Athens. It was a bright clear morning when she stood watching
the mares at play. How magnificent they looked in the
breathtaking glow of the sunrise. Her thoughts were interrupted by fierce barking from the paddock as Jacques approached. "The sheepdogs from France, little sister." Jacques's face was lit with a smile. "I've been their keeper since
they arrived and they sense I'm near."

Dominique looked at Jacques quizzically.

"Chien Berger de la Brie, madame," he said. "French
sheepdogs, selected for their superior type by cousin Josephine
herself. Rare and unique dogs, my brother says, but who am I
to say? I know nothing of hounds."

"Take me to them at once!" Dominique said. Jacques led
her to the yard behind the stable where two dogs stood with
paws on a wooden gate. One was black, the other tawny with a
black muzzle and ears.

"Natural guards," Jacques said. "Yet intelligent enough to
know we're friends."

"They don't like me." Dominique eyed the barking beasts,
backing off from them.

"How could they not like you, little sister? I just told you
they're not stupid." He smiled and held out his crooked arm
through which she looped her arm. The male sheepdog was
tall, almost to Jacques's waist, easily mistaken for a wolfhound. The bitch colored smoky gold jumped up and licked her
on the chin. "You see!" Jacques laughed. "They love you."

"I must write the Bonapartes and thank them," Dominique
said. "Without Josephine I'd never have known such animals
existed." She hugged the dogs, assuring Jacques she was
pleased. "I can't wait to see the puppies! We shall have
dozens!"

"We have half a dozen now." Jacques grinned. "Felice has a
surprise for you. Come." Leading her inside the kennels, they
saw the boy Saul kneeling in a pen with Felice, the wolfhound.

"They're beautiful!" Dominique leaned over the fence to
admire the new litter. "Is there a promising dog?"

"Your husband's the houndsman, not I, madame," he said.
"You must ask him."

Making no reply, she wondered if she'd ever ask Alexandre
anything again; how could she approach a man who wanted
nothing to do with her?

"My brother requested I present you with a gift he meant to give you on Jubilee. May I do so now?"

Dominique stared in perplexity. "A gift from Alexandre?"

Jacques nodded, taking her arm and guiding her to a narrow cell at the back of the kennels where a mastiff bitch with rich apricot coloring stood and barked a greeting. Dominique wiped a tear from her eye. "Her name is not Juliet, but she dearly loves Romeo."

Dominique placed her face beside the bitch's black muzzle.

"She's been hidden away for a long time, little sister. Your husband didn't think it was the time to bring her out before."

"Poor darling," Dominique cooed, sliding her hands over the female's flanks and feeling a surge of love for her husband. "She'll come to the hall at once and sleep in my chamber with Romeo."

Jacques smiled. " 'Tis only fitting. The lady comes from the most prestigious kennel in England. Alexandre wanted the best for his wife."

"Thank him for me." Her heart wept for the man who'd thought enough of her to secure such a fine gift. She wavered between loving and hating him. Perhaps he'd stay in Athens with his important patient and never return to her bed? She told herself she didn't care, but she would die if he didn't come back.

Dominique primped and lounged in her bath longer than usual. Two giant mastiffs lay beside her as she sat in the tub, the mistress's good arm dangling to pet their heads in turn. Her injured arm was nearly mended now; aside from feeling stiff at times, it seldom bothered her.

"Do you miss having a man around?" Dominique asked Kish, the tall Ashanti girl who stood ready to assist her. Kish repeated the question slowly. "Aye, mistress. Moses my man."

Dominique dropped her sponge. "Moses is supposed to be teaching you English. I think I'd best have a talk with him."

Nancy laid out an apple-green habit with a red-fox bonnet for her mistress. "What will the doctor say when he finds out you've gone riding, Miss Nikki?"

"Who'll tell him?"

"Not I, Miss Nikki, but there are those who will."

"Meaning the Tory, Mrs. Yarborough, I suppose."

"One and the same. But if the Tory doesn't see you leave, she can't tell a thing! She's in the nursery watching your little darling ride that rockin' horse your father sent from Pennsylvania. I'll go and start a juicy conversation about Kish and Moses and that'll keep the old hen occupied while you make your getaway."

"Nay, don't tell the Tory about Kish and Moses. Talk, aye, but keep the lovers out of it."

"Whatever you say, Miss Nikki."

Dominique padded swiftly down the runners to the stairs, then slipped through the doors to the outside. Jacques waited patiently at the stable. "I'll ride part of the way with you, little sister. You don't know the boundaries of Chastain lands—'tis important you learn." Reaching inside his jacket, he withdrew a letter for her. " 'Tis from your husband."

Dominique quaked as her fingers tingled. "Read it, please," she said. " 'Tis not a letter of love, I am certain."

Jacques broke the seal, and removed a single sheet of folded paper. "Madame Chastain, My patient, Maxwell Drummond, has a bad case of the gout and begs my assistance longer. Considering the plantation does not need me back so soon, I've agreed to stay in Athens another week. Trusting your arm is mended and you and the child are well. Your husband, Alexandre Chastain."

"No love letter," Jacques said, bewildered. His brows creased. "No wonder you tremble at the mention of his name. Who would believe this message came from a loving husband?"

Dominique lifted her head and Jacques took hold of her shoulders. "Do you love my brother?" he asked in earnest.

"Aye, I do," she replied.

"Then Alexandre is a fool!" he exclaimed.

She saw Jacques differently then, his eyes green like hers, not the same deep green, but green nonetheless and filled with fire. She turned away. "My husband has his duties. I knew what they were when I married him. His patients come first."

Jacques led out the mare, Jacqueline, dismissing the grooms from the stable. "A woman is not complete without a man, little sister. 'Tis how we are made, for God's sake!" He momentarily bowed his head against his moroccan saddle, then stood to his full height.

"There's something troubling you. I wish to know what it is.

We're friends, are we not?" He looked quizzically at her. She turned around, musing that he was a man of character who had earned her respect. She couldn't ever use him to her advantage. Jacques spun her around.

"Does your husband know Jules is your daughter's sire?"

She gasped, peering into his eyes. He was clever, this half-breed Chastain who was still a slave. What a relief for someone to know! She dropped her head on her chest and closed her eyes in shame. "Aye, he knows."

Jacques raged. "It happened before you were wed?"

"My wedding night."

Releasing her gently, he picked up his quirt and slapped it against his thigh. "*Mon Dieu,* how?"

She recounted the bitter tale and wept as she spoke, tears spilling down her cheeks. "The bastard is Satan himself!" Jacques roared. "No wonder my brother suffers from self-inflicted pain!" Going to her, he lifted her chin with his hand, wiping away her tears with his sleeve. He turned away. "It's getting late, you'd best take your ride."

Green skirts flapped on the wind as the blue-gray mare took off in a run. Jackie covered the broad avenue of sand in no time, slipping through the iron gates as Jacques held them open.

Before long Dominique was following the bluff down to the river's edge. She heard a turkey gobble and glanced over her shoulder to see a piebald stallion trot down the side of the bank toward the mighty Chattahoochee.

"Dom-ma-nique!" Coosa shouted.

"Go back!" she screamed, not wanting to see the Indian and trying to outdistance him. Hooves drummed along the river's shores, the piebald taking up the chase. Coosa howled like a wolf and Dominique clung to her mare's neck. Jackie's sides heaved and Dominique's heart was in her throat as the Creek came alongside, his stallion's mane trimmed in black and white feathers, a golden crown atop the Creek's head.

"She-wolf!" he shouted.

"Go away!" Lashing out at him, she caught his face with her quirt, the hot sting of braided rawhide cutting into Coosa's cheek. The piebald came closer and Dominique felt herself being plucked from her saddle. "Damn you!" she cried, digging her nails into the Creek's bare chest. But he held her tight until coming to a thunderous halt beside the curving river. Dominique sat motionless with the Creek in the sun, waiting for Coosa to relax his hold. When he did she bit deep into his arm until she tasted blood.

"*Ayee!*" Coosa yelled, so enraged with pain he hit her solidly in the jaw. "Dom-ma-nique!" She slumped like a sack of grain in his arms and he observed his captive curiously. What charms the lady had when she was still. Narrow waist and bulging breasts beneath a fluff of foxtails. A creature designed by the gods. "Great Spirit, how you tempt me," Coosa whispered. "Thou hast sent me a she-wolf in the disguise of a woman!"

Dominique whined, moving against the smoothness of his bronzed chest, her mind a whirlpool of nothingness as she cuddled into his embrace. "Alexandre," she moaned, her eyes shut tight, her lips turned up in a smile that brought a dimple beside her mouth.

"Madame."

"Heathen bully!" she cried, opening her eyes to his tattooed face. She felt the Indian release his hold then, and she fell to the ground squarely on her newly mended arm. "Ohhh!" she howled. "Damn you!" she spat.

"Pray forgive me." Sliding down, Coosa attempted to help her up.

"Touch me and I'll scratch your eyes out, Coosa!"

Coosa's brows knitted as he spread his long, muscled legs and folded his arms across his chest. "Coosa only wanted to show you the river of his people. Nothing more."

"I doubt your father would approve of your attacking women," she said.

"Attacking?" Coosa rubbed his cheek thoughtfully, then his face became strong. "If you were Coosa's woman, I would never allow you from my side. I'd carry you with me everywhere, you would become my shadow, my joy, my most prized possession. There would be no attacking!"

"Surely you jest!" she said, her voice ringing with superiority. "I'm not your woman and I never shall be!"

"Ahh, one day you will be Coosa's woman," he said evenly. He called her *beloved woman* in Creek, standing so close she nearly swooned in his presence. "I will teach you Indian ways and tame you, she-wolf, unlock your heart so that we may dwell on Mother Earth as the Great Spirit's children . . . knowing Him and one another as one."

Touched by his tender words, she dared not show it. His black gaze was so captivating she felt powerless in his spell. She was enthralled by him, enchanted by his raw manliness and poetic speech. "I'm the wife of a white man, Coosa," she said, framing her words with care. She was afraid she'd inflict a deep wound. He was an Indian, but an educated one. She knew he'd been schooled by priests and sent abroad to study their doctrines. The King of the Lower Creeks was known to be a Christian, believing in the White Man's Bible.

"I'm no heathen, White Man's Wife!" Overpowering her, the Creek pinned her wrists to the ground on either side of her head. Twisting under his powerful body, she was afraid of him.

"Do you find me repulsive because my skin is red, or because my father's skin is black, madame?"

Shaking her head fearfully, Dominique was afraid to reply. She begged with her eyes as Coosa pressed his thumbs to her temples, slowly lowering his face to hers. "Coosa could take you now, but he will not, white woman!" His voice was laced with emotion, tense. "Remember this day, for you will crave Coosa in the end!"

That was the last straw! "*Crave you*! *Crave* you!" she shrieked, trying not to cry despite her aching arm. "I shall remember this day, Coosa Moon!" she sneered, spitting on the ground. "You're no different than your white brothers. All you braggards who hide your brains in your breeches. I'm a woman, damn you! Not a dog to be owned and used as best suits my master!" Coosa's eyes turned from black to copper, his nostrils flared, his bottom lip thrusting out. He forced her back on the ground, holding her hands securely in his. "Please!" she cried, "don't take me!"

"Coosa does not take what is not his, Dom-ma-nique." His voice was soft as he pressed his open mouth to the curve of her neck, moving his lips where her pulse leaped beneath translucent skin. She whimpered and he saw her jaw was blue from their struggle on the horse. "Coosa is sorry," he whispered, caressing her bruise with his lips and comforting her with Creek words. He fondled her ear and removed her bonnet, dipping into the depths of her hair and removing its pins. "Dom-ma-nique, Dom-ma-nique. How well you are made! I've never doubted you were a full-blooded woman, and one

day you will be Coosa's woman!" Then, ever so gently, he laid
her hands on her breasts and traced the curve of her lips with
one finger.

"Nay," she moaned, closing her eyes so she wouldn't have
to see the black scratches beside his eyes. Her heart fluttered in
her breast as his hair tickled her cheek, its texture incredibly
soft and warmed by the sun. His scent was clean and fresh like
the forest, her body tingling as he reached for his knife and
raised it.

"Please!"

"Do not worry." He chuckled as he carefully slit her sleeve.
His fingers felt the heat of her wrist and she moaned in pain.
Returning to his mount, he pulled a pouch from its trappings,
removing the contents of the bag and wrapping her arm in bear
grease and thick strips of buttery-soft hide. "You're almost
tame," he teased, bending low to kiss her hand and swoop her
up into his arms to gaze into her eyes. "I shall call you
Summer Eyes after this day." He placed her feet firmly on the
ground, shaking his head in amusement.

"Damn you Coosa!" she swore as he mounted his pony with
effortless grace and rode off. She used every bad word she
could remember and then she saw him circle and ride back.

"Meet Coosa where the buzzard roosts on Stone Mountain
in ten days' time, Summer Eyes." Flashing a smile, he handed
her her quirt.

"I'll meet you in Hades!"

Wheeling his horse, he rode back to feast his eyes on her.
"Tell Coosa where Hades is and he'll meet you there."
Dominique gasped when he dismounted and lifted her into her
saddle.

"Imbecile!" she said, cracking her mare's flanks with her
quirt and digging in her heel. The mare bolted into a wild
gallop and Coosa watched the woman's green skirts flying on
the wind, the shade of her habit blending with the piney
woods.

"Jules Cocteau has escaped from Savannah's jail," Alexandre said, watching the fog roll in from the Savannah river,
his mind on the falsehood he'd told his wife. *Oui,* part of what
he'd told her was true: he was with Maxwell Drummond, a
rising politician who had friends in Washington. But Max

wasn't sick, he was quite well. And they were in Savannah, not Athens, planning the capture of the madman Jules Cocteau.

" 'Tis no surprise, doctor. The jail walls couldn't hold a well-fed rat much less a cunning criminal.'' Maxwell Drummond lit his pipe and set his thumbs inside his blue frock coat's pockets. His red hair was aflame in the glow of a roaring fire. "What do you wish me to do now, Doctor Chastain?"

"Up the bounty, Max. I want Cocteau alive. Be certain you make that clear." Alexandre's face was taut, as Drummond dictated a letter to his secretary alerting the men on his payroll of the new reward, ordering two copies of the letter sent by separate routes to make doubly certain one found its way.

"What of Catharine Ross?" Alexandre queried.

"You've not seen her since we've come to Savannah?"

"*Non*! I have no reason to see the woman. Cat has no use for me, nor I her."

"The woman's under surveillance. 'Tis my belief that Jules Cocteau will contact her soon."

"And my father's estate? Does Cat know the provisions father left for her?"

"Aye, she does. Mrs. Ross wasted no time instructing her lawyers to institute a breach of promise suit. She says she has letters, documents, jewels . . . we have no proof that she's telling the truth."

"Then get proof, and quickly!" Alexandre's tone was controlled but bitter as he rang the bellpull for Moses.

"Good as done, doctor. As for the money you offered her, Mrs. Ross says she won't settle for the cash set aside in your father's will. The lady wants more, much more."

"What, for pity's sake?"

"Racemont plantation. She wants it all."

"Greedy, isn't she? But Cat doesn't concern me now, as you well know."

"I know your top priority is Jules Cocteau, doctor. Your instructions are being carried out to the letter, I assure you."

"Good." Alexandre returned to the window to stare out at the fog, missing his wife, seeing her face in the mist.

"I'll notify you when we have the culprit." Drummond laughed. "My need for a physician will be dire."

Ruthe entered the library at Chastain House with a tray bearing a bottle of Madeira and crystal stemware as Moses

helped Drummond into his fur-trimmed greatcoat. Alexandre
bid Drummond good-bye.

"I live for my revenge, Maxwell."

"You shall have it, doctor." Drummond left and Alexandre
poured himself a drink, speaking quietly to Ruthe.

"My wife must never know I've been to Savannah, do you
understand, Ruthe?"

"Aye, doctor." Ruthe curtsied. "You can count on me."

" 'Tis good I can, Ruthe. Without you and your husband I
could not accomplish what I've set out to do."

" 'Tis our wish as well to see that scum behind bars,
doctor."

Alexandre's face changed. "Jules shall know untold agonies
before I'm finished with him."

Moses saw something in his master's eyes that made him
worry. "I must remind you of your schedule, doctor. If you
wish to return home in four days' time, we must leave now."

"*Home?*" Alexandre repeated, looking confused. Moses
gazed in dismay at Ruthe, the servant's eyes conveying their
mutual concern for their beloved master. "You're overtired,
doctor. Perhaps another night in Savannah would be wise?"

"*Non*! My wife and my brother are together and I don't trust
them." Alexandre downed another drink and thought of
Dominique. She'd haunted his every thought since he'd left
Racemont. 'Twas hell having a beautiful wife like his. But did
he have her? Was she really his? His heart pounded as jealousy in the guise of men's faces gripped him: Jules . . .
Jacques . . . Coosa. Suppose the Creek had touched her,
made love to her? The thought nearly drove him over the brink
and he ran his hands through his hair.

Must he lock her away, build a wall around his hall? His
mind was unclear for want of sleep, he told himself. Perhaps if
he got her with child again. Men would leave her alone if she
were pregnant. Then he remembered the horrors of the Jubilee,
his having to take his unborn babe's life! But perhaps it would
work this time. Perhaps keeping her in a family way was his
only hope of holding her.

"You were in Athens and not Savannah, do you deny it?"

"I do! I was in Athens at the house of my patient, Max
Drummond. Didn't you receive my letter?"

"I also received this." Dominique handed Alexandre a sheet

of paper scrawled with a message. "I found it on my bureau this morning."

"Who wrote this rot?" Alexandre tossed the paper aside. "Tell me who wrote it and I'll have them thrashed."

Dominique smiled, knowing he would never thrash anyone. "You weren't with Cat in Savannah?"

"Certainly not. 'Tis a bald-faced lie. Someone's playing a cruel prank on us." His frown was deep and he eyed her arm, going to where she lay on her bed and sitting beside her. "May I see your arm, please?"

"What for?" Her reply was indignant.

"For the same reason you questioned my presence in Athens."

"My arm is mended, thank you." She withdrew her arm beneath the quilts. "Jacques set it as good as you."

"Set it? 'Twas nearly mended when I left for Athens. Why would Jacques have to set it unless you broke it again?"

"I fell. You know I'm prone to accidents."

"I do." Laying back the quilts, he lifted the sleeve of her blue satin nightdress. "Where did you fall?"

"The front steps," she lied. "They were slippery with dew one morning."

"You'll have to be more careful if you expect the limb to return to normalcy."

"I shall." She tried not to cry out as he applied pressure to her wrist. He laid her arm down and went to the fireplace and poked the fire.

"Mrs. Yarborough tells me you went riding with my brother while I was away." His voice was low, his tone casual.

"What else did your spy tell you, I wonder?"

"Only that you returned in a sorry state with Jacques hot on your heels." His mouth hardened. "You broke your arm when you were with him, didn't you?"

"What does it matter who was with me? I broke it, that's all. Believe what you like."

"I would like to believe my wife is faithful." Crossing the room in long strides, he stood over her. She observed the pained look on his face, the hurt in his eyes. Reaching down, he twisted the bodice of her gown and yanked her from the bed. "Tell me, my dear wife, I wish to hear it myself from those honey-sweet lips. Did the black bastard please you?" He waved his fist, then ripped her gown from her breasts, his long fingers groping for her neck. "Tell me!" he demanded, "or I'll choke the truth from you!"

"Doctor!" Moses shouted as he broke into the room, trying to secure his master's arms from behind. The black servant gritted his teeth and used all his strength to break Alexandre's strangle-hold. Dominique fell back on the pillows and gasped for breath. "Speak to me, madame," Moses begged. "Tell me you're not hurt."

"Take me home, my good man," Alexandre said, staggering across the room to the door. "Take me out of this wretched city and back to Racemont."

"You must forgive him, madame," Moses urged. "The doctor is not well."

Dominique held back a sob and watched as Moses lead her husband from her chamber. Alexandre had tried to kill her, *wanted* to kill her! Rolling into the quilts, she felt cold all over, visions of Jules's attack and the horrible loss of her babe pressing in on her. Dear God in heaven, was she going mad? Mrs. Yarborough's words echoed in the recesses of her mind and she felt nausea overtaking her. It was *her* fault the babe had died, *her* fault François was dead! Trembling with the truth, she told herself she didn't deserve to live, not when she'd caused so much unhappiness to others. Getting out of bed, she trembled uncontrollably while she bathed and dressed herself, the cool silk of fresh undergarments and her wet hair causing her to shiver all the more. She saw herself in a coffin. She rubbed her neck where Alexandre had left his mark. He wanted her dead and she'd oblige him. Life wasn't worth living the way things were. She wasn't happy, Alexandre wasn't happy, no one needed her, not even the child. Slipping into a warm habit of black wool with matching tricorn, she pulled on her Spanish boots. Before she could complete her dressing, the door opened.

"Where do you think you're going?" Dressed in gray breeches and black boots, Alexandre wore no shirt. His hair hung loosely about his face.

"Away," she said shakily, walking to the armoire to search for her gloves.

"Leave this hall, madame, and don't bother to come back."

"As you wish," she returned in a whisper. "My father will come for my daughter."

"*Our* daughter, madame. Remember that when you send for her."

She wanted to scream and tell him the child was not his, to tell him she was sorry for losing his son. She said nothing; words were useless now. Desiree would be safe in his care and it wouldn't matter anyway once she was dead. Nothing would matter then. Closing the armoire, she attempted to walk past him when he caught her arm and swung her around to face him.

"You're certain you want this?"

"Aye." Removing his hand from her, she walked briskly to the door.

"Go then, and quickly. You're free, as of this moment!"

She held onto the wall, making her way to the staircase, gripping the balustrade and biting back hurtful tears as she ran quickly to the foyer. Jacques was coming in the door.

"Little sister, what's wrong? Did he strike you?" Jacques's eyes were filled with fury.

"Nay." She smiled, noting Jacques raise his eyes to the top of the stairs where Alexandre stood watching. Dominique wanted to thank Jacques for his kindness to her, and to tell him good-bye. She saw the dark worried faces of the house slaves watching from the kitchen door, but her only thought was to mount her horse and ride as far as she could go.

It was nearly dark when Jackie's hooves tore through sand on the banks of the Yellow River. Her rider rode in a daze; her cheeks were streaked with tears, her eyes blinded by the hopelessness of her life. Deep melancholia rode with her, convincing her she should die and set herself free. Alexandre would be happy if she were dead; everyone would be happy. The gray mare turned onto the Indian trail that led to the tail of the granite mountain. The air had turned cool as the horse and rider disappeared into the piney woods. Ten days had passed since Coosa Tustennuggee had asked her to meet him on the mountain. She could see the Creek's face and hear his voice, reasoning she'd see the Indian one last time before she left the earth.

Dominique left Jackie to graze on young grass before beginning her ascent up the mountain alone. She didn't have to wait long for the Creek *mico*. Coosa Tustennuggee was waiting where the cedars clung to the earth, where the buzzard had his roost. She was halfway up the mountain when she saw his familiar smile. Dressed in buckskins and furs, the tall Creek laughed aloud as his face lit with happiness and he ran to take her hand.

"Coosa is overjoyed to see you again, Dom-ma-nique." Her name was a supplication on his lips, his fiery gaze warming her like a blaze on a cold winter's night. She held her face rigid, looking past him and refusing to see what was written in those liquid black eyes. "Your family is well?" he queried, offering his arm as they climbed the mount together.

"Aye."

He took her hand when they reached the summit, pulling her through the opening in the stone wall and showing her to a pallet of furs he'd prepared before the ancient stone altar.

"I can't believe you're here." He added fuel to the inferno that raged beneath the altar, tongues of orange and yellow and blue that licked cold bark and pinecones. Dominique moved closer, her thoughts caught up in the fire's intensity, wondering if she would burn in such a fire once she'd taken her life. 'Twas wrong to involve the Creek in her misery, but she needed someone to talk to. The savage wouldn't understand, but he had been a friend. A good friend.

"I shouldn't have come." She hung her head.

"My heart pounds because of it." Coosa came to stand beside her and she reached up and touched his face to make certain he was real. Placing the tip of one finger in the cleft of his chin, she discovered it fit perfectly.

"Ahh." He moaned pleasantly. "You've found where the Great Spirit marked Coosa for his destiny."

"You believe such things?"

"*Oui*, Indians believe life is a circle."

"I've reached the end then."

"*Non!*" He laughed. "You're not even halfway round."

"Why are you called Rising Moon?"

"Because I joined Mother Earth when the night luminary rose anew." He looked down into her eyes with the moon and stars on his shoulder. "Leave your life with Alexandre, Dom-ma-nique. Continue on your course and ride with Coosa evermore." His voice was earnest and her heart was touched.

"Pray say no more." She stiffened as he lifted her off her feet and cradled her in his arms, sensing her need for love. "You are sad, Summer Eyes. I know not why. Coosa will help. Ride with me to where the earth meets the sky, to the high country where the mountains are rimmed with smoke. Tennessee has hills and valleys unknown to the white eyes. My mother's people would make you welcome, you'll see. You would be their sister and their daughter and Coosa's beloved. You would never be alone." He spoke in bursts of enthusiasm, and she became drunk with her mood and the scent of him. "Your comeliness is beyond measure, Dom-ma-nique." He carried her to the pallet of furs and laid her down gently like a bird with a broken wing. She imagined herself his woman for a fleeting moment, thinking it ironic to be lying in the arms of a heathen and trusting him more than her civilized husband, the husband she loved.

"I love Alexandre, Coosa."

Coosa frowned. "That does not matter, Dom-ma-nique. Nothing matters but our destiny. The fact that we were meant to spend the rest of our days together. To lie together in the darkness and the light, to wake to the dawn and watch the sun set behind the treetops. You're a woman who needs the outdoors and adventure." She held her breath as he drew her against his splendid body on the furs. The mountain was lighter now and his golden gorget caught a moonbeam, his lashes brushing her cheek. "Lie with Coosa," he entreated. "Begin your new life."

" 'Tis too late for us, Coosa." She breathed in the odor of leather and furs and he lifted his head to the light. She saw the patterned scratches on his cheeks, felt compelled to sample the incredible softness of his hair. Her fingers traced the line of his jaw to the corner of his mouth.

Perplexed by her newfound tenderness, Coosa smiled. " 'Tis never too late, Summer Eyes, so long as we both draw breath." She could not tell him she did not mean to draw breath much longer. She trembled as he took the ribbon from her hair and kissed her mouth the way a spring breeze caresses a newborn leaf. "Our gods made us to be together, Dom-ma-nique. You must believe."

"I believe nothing, *in* nothing, Coosa. The world is wicked and the people in it are evil. I've brought nothing but unhappiness to everyone I meet. Even you, dear friend. You could have died because of me."

"You did nothing to Coosa! I would die willingly to give you life!" His lips met hers in a kiss so sweet she could not pull away. He drew her closer, calling her beloved in Creek. "You have seen a baby horse born, have you not? A tiny flower kissed by a dewdrop? What of the leaves in autumn and the virgin snow of winter? Our gods remind us often they care for us. Why should we be different? What greater gift can we give one another than our love, Dom-ma-nique? The love we hold deep inside and have given no other, the love that will make us strong enough to face the greatest challenge of our lives. Coosa pledges eternal faithfulness to you, beloved woman. He asks for nothing in return."

"I can pledge nothing, I am nothing. I am better off dead."

"*Non!* You are woman—able to bring forth life. Coosa cannot have children by himself! Coosa does not want children without his beloved woman!" He held her close and she felt his sheathed knife against her leg. She deftly removed it with her fingers. He was a man, no different than the rest, she told herself. Perhaps if they'd met sooner, in another time, another life . . . ? With the blade in position, she ducked beneath Coosa's arm and deliberately rolled over the weapon.

"Dom-ma-nique!" he cried, picking her up in his arms and seeing what she had done. Removing the blade, he called to his god and then to hers, talking pitifully in French and Creek. he bawled like a boy, howling like a wolf and panting to kiss her paling face. The wound seeped blood and he left her long enough to find a small pebble and close the gap in her chest, pressing the stone hard until the bleeding stopped. He held her in his arms, rocking her until the moon rose above the buzzards' roost, embracing her until the sun rose and lit the mountain, then fell again. He could find no life in the body of his beloved on the second day. It was near noon when he laid her to rest on the pallet of furs and knelt before the altar of the Indian's god.

Coosa prayed and then howled like a wolf to the sky, the sound of his yelps echoing again and again as he picked up his obsidian knife to stab himself over and over in the chest and arms to proclaim his love.

13

———————◆———————

"Sober him up or lose your happy home!" Jacques roared at Moses, Alexandre's manservant, as he rushed down the back stairs to the kitchen. He'd tried discussing Dominique with his brother but it was useless. Alexandre had emptied several bottles since the mistress left the house. God only knew what else he'd taken. Jacques had pitied Alexandre for the last time, he told himself. His pity had turned to disgust.

"Brew a pot of coffee, Mère. I want the doctor fit when I return!"

Marie frowned. The master needed more than coffee to her way of thinking. "What if yo' don' find dat chile, Mr. Jacques?"

Jacques squeezed Marie's arm affectionately, pushing through the kitchen doors to the outside. "I'll find her, Mère, don't worry." His black stallion, Togar, waited in the cold morning air. "Release the hounds!" he shouted to his men. "We ride for the mountain!" Togar galloped through the courtyard at breakneck speed followed by fifty men on horseback. "Spread out!" Jacques cried, standing in his stirrups. "Meet me at the mountain!" His anger increased with each hoofbeat. He'd find his sister-in-law and when he did he'd talk some sense into her. She must leave his brother and go to

Savannah. He had some money saved, not a fortune by any
means, but enough to take care of her for a decent period of
time. Surely his father had left him money, though the will had
yet to be probated. Clenching his fists on the reins he recalled
Dominique's face the day before, the despair in her eyes. He
knew now Alexandre had harmed her, and vowed his brother
would never touch her again. Not if he wished to live!

Jacques lay low in his saddle as his stallion glided over a
deep ravine, Togar's hooves touching granite where Stone
Mountain hunched like a great gray whale above the forest.
Feeling nothing but contempt for his brother now, Jacques
couldn't understand why Alexandre had allowed drink to
control his life. Alexandre bore a great burden, *oui*, but there
was no excuse for hurting a woman. None!

Dominique's breathing was weak but she would live. Coosa
held her in his arms and shielded her from the wind. He had
believed her dead for some time before he'd discovered the
pulse in her neck. Then he'd cried aloud to the gods, so fierce a
cry the buzzards had left their roost. He'd washed her wound
with the rainwater collected in the pitted granite, applying
salve made from roots he always carried in his pouch,
wrapping Dominique tightly in furs and keeping her warm by
lying beside her on the pelts.

It was morning now, and the pelts were damp. Coosa
clenched his teeth in pain, covering the wounds on his chest
with draped pelts of wolf and puma. Jacques found his son
holding his sister-in-law in his arms. He saw in a flash that his
son loved his brother's wife.

"You must give her to me, Coosa, my son. Her husband is a
physician and will treat her wound properly." Jacques chose
his words with care, seeing the possessive eyes of his son.
When Coosa made no answer, Jacques ordered his men to
subdue the Creek.

"She's mine!" Coosa cried like a wolf. Several men
approached to restrain him. "You cannot have her!" he
growled. "You won't have her!"

A stretcher designed of poles and pelts bore Dominique
down the mountain in haste.

"You must never see her again, my son. Promise me you
will obey me in this."

"I cannot, father," Coosa replied, his arms and legs held by five men who strained to keep him still.

"Tie him up and guard him till the sun disappears behind the mountain," Jacques told his men. "Until the darkness covers the gray egg."

Alexandre met the horsemen on foot as they approached the south gates of Racemont. Hounds barked and bayed when they saw their master.

"What's wrong with her?" Alexandre asked. His face was sober as he regarded his wife pale and still on the stretcher, Jacques riding at her side. "Is she dead?"

Jacques dismounted and attempted to calm his brother. "There's nothing you can do here. We must get her to her bed."

"God forgive me!" Alexandre cried when he lifted the furs that covered her and saw her wound. Jacques waved the stretcher bearers on their way and Alexandre ran to catch up with them. "Who did this to her?" he asked the slaves.

"She did it to herself," Jacques said. " 'Tis thanks to my son she lives."

"Coosa was with her?" Alexandre's eyes blazed when he heard the Indian's name.

"Praise God someone was with her," Jacques said. "Had Coosa not been with her, she would be dead now." Wheeling his stallion, Jacques rode off in a mean gallop.

" 'Tis a puncture and deep, but by the grace of God no vital organ was harmed. Infection is the worry now. We must cool her down." Alexandre gave Mrs. Yarborough instructions to wash his wife's wound, then watching her closely to make certain the wound didn't bleed.

Jacques could watch no longer, leaving the master's chambers by way of the gallery to lean heavily against the cool walls of the mansion and breathe deeply. He pulled his fleecy coat about his neck and slid down to rest his bones. He was speculating on the relationship of his mistress and his son when he fell asleep. He was awakened hours later by Marie's voice below, the first rays of day breaking on the horizon. He reached the bottom of the steps in time to see two Creek braves parading their horses, a slain bear across one mount's back.

"You red men get outta here 'n' clean dat animal yo'self, yo' hear! Ain't no women here knows how tah skin a bear!''

Jacques went to the braves and queried the Indians in their mother tongue. He discovered the slain bear had been sent by his son; a gift of good will. Jacques instructed the braves to skin and quarter the animal far from the house and deliver the meat to the kitchen.

"No mention of this to the doctor, Mère. He has enough on his mind with his wife." Jacques went to the kitchen to strip to the waist and wash.

"Yo' mean I don' have tah cook no bear stew, Mr. Jacques?" Marie stirred a massive pot and pursed her lips. "Ain't none o' mah business, but what happened to dat chile on dat mountain anyhow? I hears she tried tah do herself in when she was wit dat boy o' yours?"

Jacques plucked a clean linen from a rack beside the door and went outside to lift a wooden bucket of rainwater over his head. Marie followed, waiting patiently for answers and watching Jacques dry himself. "Coosa's no boy, Mère. My son's a man to be reckoned with now." He shrugged into a shirt. "Madame's had a freak accident and Coosa found her, 'tis all."

Marie followed Jacques into the kitchen, her lips pursed. "Ain't dat sweet chile lucky tah have dat red man aroun' when she needs help? My oh my, I wish ole Mère gets so lucky! *Ouiii!*"

Jacques shook his head and looked at Marie, thinking he'd never understand women. Picking up his clothes he bent low to go out the door, slamming it so hard it reverberated through the room.

Every morning thereafter the King of the Lower Creeks sent gifts to the mistress of Racemont. Wild turkeys the first day, quails the second, wild geese and ducks the third, all alive and in woven baskets. Then came the deer and antelope skins, furs from wildcats and black mountain lion. The seventh day the *mico* himself arrived outfitted in a robe of lynx that draped over his stallion's flanks. Two proud hunters rode behind their leader, the carcass of a bull elk laying across one of their pony's backs.

"Dah missus ain't havin no callers, Mr. Coosa!" Marie pushed away a woven basket with two small parakeets inside. "Dah master ain't sposed tah know yo' sendin' all these gif's,"

Marie whispered in the cool morning air and tried to warn Coosa and his friends away. Alexandre opened the front door and stepped outside.

"What's going on out there, Marie—what's all that racket? Who's there?"

"Ain't no one here, doctor!" Marie called. Then Coosa dismounted and swirled his robe about his shoulders, walking to the twin stairways to confront Alexandre.

"Coosa Tustennuggee, what are you doing here? What do you want?" Alexandre demanded as Marie retreated to the safety of her kitchen, slamming the door behind her and sending for Moses.

"Coosa has come to see Dom-ma-nique," Coosa replied politely. "Coosa can wait no more."

Alexandre's face reddened as he came down the steps, his hands clenched into fists at his sides. "You can't see her," he said low. "Heed my warning well, Coosa, King of the Creeks. If you so much as look at Madame Chastain again I'll have you hunted down and hanged! Is that clear?"

Marie looked out the kitchen window and saw Coosa step forward, glaring threateningly at Alexandre as the wind tossed the flap of his paisley turban about his handsome visage. The basket of little birds swung gently from his hand. "*Non,* it isn't clear, Alexandre. I'm an Indian, remember, ignorant of civilized ways. Pray explain your meaning to me."

Alexandre gritted his teeth. "An Indian of your description made an attempt on my wife's life some days past when she went riding by herself. The name Chastain is respected in these parts. The Georgians could do wonders with such information." Alexandre smiled vengefully. " 'Tis not my wish to see your village burned or your mother ravaged, but . . ."

Coosa didn't wait for his uncle to finish, seeing blood and striking a deadly blow that sent the doctor reeling back against the stairs, then to the granite setes. Alexandre lay still and Coosa stepped over him, climbing the steps with his furs trailing behind him.

"Coosa!" Jacques called, riding up on horseback in time to see Alexandre downed. "What are you about?" Dismounting, Jacques helped Alexandre to his feet, watching as the doctor wiped his bleeding lip with the back of his hand.

"Get your half-breed son off Chastain lands or by Jehovah I'll kill him!" Alexandre cried, eyeing Coosa above him at the

front portal. Moses opened the door and Coosa thrust the
basket of birds into the black man's hand.

"Tell your mistress Coosa Tustennuggee was here! Tell her
Coosa will return!"

"You will keep silent about the red man's visit and you will
dispose of the birds." Alexandre gave Moses orders and the
manservant stared at his master's bleeding lip and puffy eye,
confused by the scene he'd just witnessed. "But what shall I do
with the creatures, doctor?"

"Release them, man! Must I do your thinking for you?"
Alexandre went down the hall and climbed the grand staircase,
leaving Moses to ponder on the matter. Sharing an incurable
romantic's nature, Moses thought the brightly colored birds
unusual indeed, knowing the Creek meant them for his
mistress. Lifting the woven basket to the light, he saw the birds
fly about fearfully.

"Don't be afraid, little ones," he whispered. "I'll do as my
master bids and you shall be free." Smiling, Moses went to the
conservatory and released the parakeets, confident he'd done
the right thing.

Spring came late that year. March was unseasonably cold
and April was wet with fierce storms that uprooted trees and
destroyed crops. May came at last and the gardens of
Racemont bloomed in glorious splendor. The sky was an
unbelievable blue the morning Dominique was carried outside
in her huge peacock chair and set down amid budding
magnolias. Alexandre dismissed the servants and stood looking at his wife.

"How does it feel to be up and about?"

She sought to evade his gaze, uncomfortable in his presence.
"I don't need your help, doctor." She pulled herself away as
she thought about how he'd aged, his face gray with dark
circles beneath his eyes from lack of sleep. He frowned
dejectedly, hurt by her snub.

"Why did you do it?"

A chill rippled down her spine then, hearing the Creek's
voice calling her in his odd fashion. "May I go in now,
doctor?" She turned away from him and he took her hands in
his, turning her chin and making her look into his eyes.

"I've been blind to your needs," he said compliantly.

"Savannah and Charleston are beautiful this time of year, Paris or Philadelphia if you prefer. I can arrange . . ."

She felt his hungry gaze sweep over her in a frenzy, over her longer hair, her eyes still dim from lying abed so long. She was dressed in white, her high-necked gown of Indian gauze hiding the bright pink scar that would forever mar their relations. "Nay," she said in earnest, wanting to touch his cheek, but holding herself from it. "I'll stay."

His face was lit from within and he smiled for the first time in weeks. "My love, my love . . ." Falling on his knees, he bowed his head on her lap. "I worship you." Arms wrapped about her waist, he wept into her skirts. "I need you so much, so much. Forgive me if you can, *chérie*. I'll change, I promise. Things will be different between us, believe me."

She closed her eyes and soothed his wet cheek with the palm of her hand. "Forget the past, Alexandre. It will destroy us if you let it. 'Tis I who ask you to forgive me. You needed me and I was so lost in my own private hell I was unaware of yours. I share the burden you bear over the death of our son; we'll share it together." His eyes filled with tears and he looked up into her eyes, pressing her fingers to his lips. "Our son is dead," she whispered. "All our tears and anguish and blame cannot bring him back." Her hands were wet with his tears. "We must be strong for Desiree. She is our daughter."

Thus did Dominique resume her normal activities. The mistress could be found any hour of the day with her horses or her hounds. She acquainted herself with each animal personally, learning names and habits, characteristics and individual needs. There were innumerable slaves at her disposal, grooms, strappers, stableboys, tack cleaners, kennel girls, all patiently instructed by herself in the care and management of top-class horses and hounds.

"'Tis not possible to breed a jumper," Dominique advised Jacques one early morning. She was supervising the dressage of a lovely jet-black Arab on the flat.

"Togar has natural ability," Jacques insisted, staring appreciatively as Dominique held a straw hat near her skirts of palest peach, her small waist cinched in green that matched her eyes.

"I have seen you and your stallion together, Jacques. You have a rapport that's rare between horse and rider. 'Tis something I admire greatly."

"You and I had the same rapport once, little sister."

She changed the subject. "Pray tell me of your son, Jacques. Is Coosa well?"

"We don't speak of the Creek at Racemont," Jacques replied, following her along the path to the house.

"Have you heard from him?" she persisted, picking up her stride.

"*Oui*, little sister, only two nights past . . . he came to say *adieu*."

She gasped, stopping in her tracks. "Did he leave any message for me?" she whispered.

Jacques frowned. "The King of the Creeks has sought to see you many times over, little sister. Coosa camped nearby to keep abreast of news of your health and sent gifts of good will to you. His runners have come daily for weeks with messages."

Her heart fluttered. "No one told me. Dear Jacques, I must see him before he leaves, you must arrange it!"

Jacques shook his head, wishing to be dispassionate yet caught up in the emotions of loyalty, blood, and personal need. "I don't recommend it, madame."

" 'Tis not for you to recommend nor advise against," she retorted gently. "Sometimes you presume too much, my friend. 'Tis my wish to apologize to your son, nothing more. I owe him a great debt of gratitude."

"Seeing him again could prove dangerous to you both. Listen to me, little sister, and heed my warning, please."

"Pray help me," she said, pleading with her eyes. "I did a despicable thing involving him the way I did. I wish to give him my thanks. I owe the man my life."

Jacques relented. "Ride with the hounds in the early morn. The one you seek will find you, have no fear."

"How will I escape the eyes of the boys my husband chose to watch me?"

Jacques smiled. "Being the excellent horsewoman you are, I have no doubt you'll manage. I leave you now to send a message to my son."

"Bless you," she said sweetly, wanting to kiss him. The dimple appeared beside her mouth, elating him. "I shall be forever grateful, dear Jacques." Before they parted, she asked one more question she could not restrain. "Would you have told me he was going away had I not asked?"

"I think not, Madame Chastain." He bowed low, touching the red clay with his hat and standing proud before her. She saw something in his eyes that reminded her of Coosa, thinking him virile in his cream shirt and planter's hat held over his heart. "Is that all, madame?" he asked.

"Aye," she replied. His heart was curiously heavy as he turned to go.

"This need to ride is a passion I'll never understand, *chérie*. But then I've never understood you, have I? Your father warned me I'd have to take second place to a horse once we married. I see now he meant it."

"Pray ride to the hounds with me, Alexandre. 'Tis my favorite thing in the world and I'd be happier with you at my side. 'Tis my wish to show you how well Jackie jumps." She pleaded with her eyes, her health plainly restored.

"You know I must stay and supervise the building of the new hospital, *chérie*. We'll go riding another time, as soon as the structure is under roof, I give my word."

She lifted her face to his, radiant and pouting as he placed a light kiss on her lips. Undeniably distracted by her appearance, he stared after her, watching her caress her mount's nose and smooth its mane. Outfitted in the softest of silk velvets, she wore a riding dress of cream molded tightly to her curves, the habit's masculine cut discreetly revealing the valley between her full breasts. She wore her hair pulled back in a stylish chignon beneath a three-cornered hat, its creamy plumes astir on the breeze. "You look much too fetching to be riding to the hounds, my love. If it weren't for my dedication to this project I'd carry you off posthaste to our chambers." He helped her to the mounting block and gave her a boost into her saddle. "Remember, my strong-willed wife, no foolishness. Ride no farther than the fallen timber this side of the rock and back. My boys and the master of the hounds will follow so I'll have no need to worry, eh?" He frowned, unconvinced she heard.

"Pray keep your boys and houndmaster here, Alexandre. If a lady can't ride with her husband, she would rather ride alone."

"The boys go, madame," he said between gritted teeth. "They've waited a long time for this. Pray don't disappoint them." Handing up her quirt, he slapped her mount on the rump and waved good-bye. "See you at supper! And wear that dress!"

Dominique smiled her prettiest at the blacks who waited timidly for her to take the lead, each two hundred pounds or more and badly scarred by the pox. Jackie cantered around the drive and Dominique called to the slaves. "Have you ridden to the hounds before?" The boys shook their heads, smiling shyly. Alexandre had chosen them with care, she thought, but their steeds were of lesser quality than hers. They were nags of plantation vintage, no match for either the French siren Jacqueline or the lady of the hounds.

"Come on, then," Dominique said, motioning with her quirt. They rode down the broad avenue of sand under a canopy of interlacing limbs. Alexandre followed on his peppered stallion for a ways, then heading off alone for the village.

"*Adieu*!" he called, watching his wife ride like a woman possessed. Once Alexandre was out of sight, Dominique spurred her horse into a canter, wilefully devising a way to outride and outmaneuver the men who followed her. She'd wait for the right moment and be rid of them, she mused. Smiling mischievously, she gave the mare her head and moved into a mettlesome gallop, taking off like a silver bullet for the mountain.

Dogs and horses raced across the green fields of Racemont, past fallen timber and pine woods, fern-covered banks, and sandy river bottom, high shoales strewn with granite outcroppings and red stretches of Georgia clay. Before long it was time to make her move. Dominique leaned forward in her saddle and applied her quirt on Jackie's hind, until they disappeared over a ridge sweeping into a forest of silvery hardwoods. Stifling a giggle with a creamy pigskin glove, the lady of the hounds sat motionless in her saddle, hidden by a sweetgum tree, waiting for the riders she knew would eventually come. So they did, fat Matthew up front with fatter Mark trailing behind, their nags frothy and wheezing, the old houndmaster's mulish-looking gelding bringing up the rear followed by canine novices too tired to bay. When she was certain it was safe, Dominique came out of hiding and turned away from the hounds, exploring the length of the ridge until she found the Indian trail leading into the forest. Where the path would take her, she didn't know.

They entered a lovely glade by way of a creek that rushed headlong over rock and sand. Slim sycamores bowed, inviting them to stay, wood violet, trillium, and leatherleaf smiling amid bloodroot and mayflowers. " 'Tis as good a place as any to wait," Dominique told Jackie, dismounting with a sigh of self-satisfaction. She doubted the Creek would find her and stretched her legs while Jackie took a cool drink from the stream. Seeing trillium growing in profusion, she walked upstream and stripped off her gloves. She dropped to her knees in deep grass, feeling the moist earth through her velvet habit and sitting down on a rock to gather a bouquet. Then Jackie lifted her head and snorted.

A piebald stallion appeared like a mirage between two trees on the opposite side of the branch, his creamy head and mane decorated in feathers and silver trappings, pawing the earth as his rider sat boldly and unflinchingly. A crown of gold caught the sun's rays filtering through the trees. The rider's chest was hung with a breastplate of golden eagle feathers, his long lean legs hanging free. Dominique clutched her flowers to her bosom and came to her feet slowly, knowing the Creek was too much for her, knowing she couldn't trust herself with him. Turning on her heel, she slid down a fern-covered bank and ran to her mare.

"Hold, Jackie," she whispered, hands trembling. The mare pranced uneasily as she swung onto its back, then wheeled toward an opening in the forest. Her chest ached and her fingers clutched the reins as her mount pushed through the branches. Then the piebald was behind her. Her stomach twisted in a cramp. Beaten on the flanks with her quirt, the beast left the water in a fantastic leap, climbing a bank thick with cane and tearing through the woods. *Run for your life, Dom-ma-nique,* a voice whispered inside her head. *You dare not see the King of the Creeks again!*

Out in the open again, Jackie raced along a clay ridge like a silver streak in the sun. Hooves drummed behind her, the spotted pony gaining steadily until the Creek came alongside. Dominique's face paled. Suddenly she was clinging to the Indian's neck and the piebald came to a skidding stop beneath a dead oak.

"Lady of the hounds." Coosa jumped down, pulling Dominique with him. Their hearts raced in concert and she tried to find her voice. "How did you find me?"

"Coosa is a hunter." His face was proud. "A she-wolf is not difficult to trail when one knows her habits."

Too weak to argue, she held fast to his arm, gazing into his tormented black eyes. Green eyes pleaded for quarter and she wavered slightly, straightening her habit and stepping back to wipe her nose on her sleeve.

"I must find my horse." Blinded by trepidation, she wandered aimlessly and sank her boot into a hole, falling headlong. "Ohhh!" she wailed. " 'Tis your fault, Coosa!"

Coosa laughed, utterly bemused, then frowned. "Forgive me, my lady." Swooping her up into his arms, he held her in an unyielding embrace.

"You're going away?" she asked.

"You came to ask me that, Summer Eyes?" She nodded and he seemed amused, lifting her onto his horse and vaulting up behind her, spurring the pony into a gallop. "I have been reflecting on the English word *love*," he said in her ear. " 'Tis written in your holy book that love never gives up but is always patient and kind, never jealous, conceited, or proud." He rode to the glade where he'd first seen her, dismounted by the stream, and drew her down to lead her to a carpet of white flowers. He spread his red cloak and lay her down, releasing her hair from its pins. "Love is here, Dom-ma-nique." Searching her eyes for truth, he entreated, "Pray do not cheat it."

She was helpless in his spell, enchanted by the face she'd once feared. His looks were divine now, his skin gold-hued like the most precious of metals, his voice soothing like the warm wind. His lips titillated hers in a gentling kiss.

"I came to ask your forgiveness for what I did that night on the mountain, to thank you for saving my life, to tell you good-bye, Coosa."

Making no reply, he laid open her dress and kissed the still-pink scar that marked her breast, covering its trembling tip with his mouth and moaning. "Say *oui* to love, Dom-ma-nique."

"I cannot, I dare not. I belong to Alexandre." Her reply was faint and he frowned. "What you ask is forbidden."

"I ask for your love, Summer Eyes. You belong to Coosa!" She felt the heat of his breath on her belly as he hastily cast aside her skirts.

"Love! You don't know the meaning of the word! You're

nothing but a savage, Coosa! Another ruthless, rutting savage,
like your white brothers!''

"Coosa is no savage!" he growled. He held her wrists and
pulled her into his embrace. "You leave me no peace, she-
wolf! Your summer eyes haunt me and your courage has won
my heart! Your golden hair brushes my cheek in slumber and I
see your face everywhere I look! Alexandre doesn't know how
to appreciate such a woman."

"Let me go," she pleaded, tears welling in her eyes as she
tried to hold him off.

"You must accept fate, Dom-ma-nique. Accept this love we
have found together."

She trembled as he ingeniously stripped off her clothes and
drew her down with him, covering her with his hard body. Too
enamored to breathe, she closed her eyes and trembled. "Nay,
you mustn't, Alexandre will see you hang!"

"Summer Eyes," he moaned, kissing her face and pressing
his strength hard into her thighs. She whispered his name
against his breast-plate and then it slipped to one side, enough
for her to see his scars.

"Coosa!" she gasped. "Dearest, dearest, Coosa!" Covering
his chest with kisses, she poured out the love she'd held
within. "Coosa, dearest, my love, my love." Oh, so tenderly
they kissed then, their tongues meeting for the first time,
tasting, entwining, their bodies struggling to be one. Coosa
covered her body with kisses, whispering Creek words of love.

"Summer Eyes," he cried. "Please accept Coosa's love."
They lay together until she ceased to tremble, exploring each
other's bodies and touching, tasting. "Forgive me for looking," Coosa said shyly, laying on one side and gazing freely.
"You are wonderfully made." Taunting her with his lips, she
lay helpless in his arms, his tongue entering and leaving her
mouth, his fingers stroking the silken tips of her breasts, all the
while rocking gently over her. "Come to Coosa," he en-
couraged, his lips pressed between her breasts. She whispered
his name and sank into an ever-deepening languor. She was
misty-eyed and awed in his presence, swept by his dizzying
charm. Praying to God for forgiveness, she wept because she
wanted him so much. Coosa responded by closing her eyes
with kisses and opening her thighs. He took her the way the
rain takes the parched earth, filling her with his love until the
chills of their passion spread through her blood. She called his

name and held tight to his mane, riding with him on a beam of light until they heard the cry of the eagle and soared above the trees, their moment of rapture climaxed by a thrust that reeled her into a cloudless sky.

Water rushed over sand and pebbles and they lay bound together, arms entwined, too content to move. Coosa swept back her golden tresses lying moist against her cheeks.

"Now you must come with Coosa to the high mountains, Summer Eyes. For Coosa has tamed you and made you his woman."

For a moment she couldn't answer. She watched a trout dart behind a rocky isle and looked up at the Indian from the peaceful cover of his embrace. How complete she felt, how totally, blissfully happy. Dear God, if only the solace and contentment she felt could be truly hers . . . "I cannot, Coosa."

"Cannot! 'Tis a word Indians don't understand!" He wrapped her tighter in his arms, kissing her face. The morning drifted into afternoon. Soon the light slanted through the trees, a canopy of leaves casting shadows across the lovers where they lay in a bed of lilies quilted in fern. The treetops touched the clouds and the call of a cardinal, followed by a hunter's horn, made her sit up.

"I must go!"

"*Non!*" Coosa pressed a kiss atop her head, laying her back on the flowers once more. "Ride with Coosa to his lodge in the Smokies now, this day! Stay with Coosa evermore!"

"I cannot, Coosa. You've made me exceedingly happy this day, but 'tis over now." She smiled, the dimple appearing once more. "I must return to my real world now."

"Real world?"

"Aye, my love." She placed her finger in the dimple in his chin, answering him with a tear in her eye. "Racemont, Coosa, the world of the Chastains."

Coosa's brows locked. "Is Coosa's world so false?"

" 'Tis not my world," she explained. "I'm a married woman with a child and a husband. You are—"

"A savage?" He curled his lip. "Or does *heathen, redskin,* or *bastard* best suit your needs?"

"Nay!" she cried apologetically. "You're none of those things to me! You are *mico*, chief, warrier, brave, honest and true. You are the kindest, noblest man I've ever known, Coosa, dearest. Never again will I call an Indian savage or heathen. For you are wise, well bred, and strong, knowing God better than me, better than most." She lay her face against his dark muscled leg as he stood over her. "Forgive me, but we cannot meet again."

"We can! We shall!" Drawing her up, he bent to kiss her face. "Gather up your child and leave Chastain lands now! He will never appreciate a spirited woman like you."

" 'Tis not as simple as that, Coosa. Try to understand, I implore you. There can be no life for us. No happiness beyond this place, this moment!"

A dreadful silence fell between them and she studied the trillium, each flower, each leaf, each whorl. "Coosa will never give you up! Love is patient and never fails, love is eternal!" Cupping her face in his hands, his tears fell on her cheeks. "Coosa comprehends your English word now! Coosa possesses love and gives love to you!"

"Oh, my darling Coosa." She fell helplessly into his arms then, reveling in the warmth of his love, yet tormented by it as well.

"Coosa will wait until the sun sinks behind the gray egg, until the sun rises again and again! Leave Alexandre and your reality and never look back, Summer Eyes! We shall spend love together!" His kiss was so intense she met his tongue with hers in unspoken desire. He engulfed her in his arms as passion consumed them, their hearts beating wildly as they ached for one another. "We shall abide together, Summer Eyes. Say *oui*, or I'll never let you go."

"*Oui!*" she cried, too vulnerable to utter the truth. She said nothing more for his kisses, at last assuming a carefree air. "Go and fetch my mount so I may join the hounds." She laughed. Watching him in awe, she saw him swing effortlessly onto his mount and ride in search of her horse. The water was cold when she waded in and washed herself off, struggling with her habit as she did with her emotions. Leaving Coosa would be the most difficult thing she would ever do, she knew, but leaving Alexandre would prove far worse.

"Fly on the wings of the wind and return before dawn, Summer Eyes." Coosa grinned, returning her mare and presenting her with a sprig of trillium. She slipped the delicate lily inside her bodice and pulled her hand from his at last, looking up into his black eyes and forcing herself not to weep.

"Good-bye, Coosa," she said at last. "Good-bye, my love." Coosa smiled broadly, helping her to her mount and making certain she was comfortable before letting her go. Then he waved and watched her make her way through the woods and back to the Indian trail, then disappear into the fading light.

Jacques was waiting at the mounting block before the twin stairways. "I've been worried beyond measure, little sister. 'Tis nearly dark. Where have you been?" Helping her dismount, his gaze swept over her crumpled habit. She climbed the stairs without a word, her legs shaking, her hand on his arm. Something was wrong, she sensed it. Marie stood on the gallery above her, her big checkered apron pressed to reddened eyes, the children of the house slaves hovering behind her.

"What's wrong, what's happened?"

"Your husband had an accident, missus."

Dominique's mind reeled. Was this her punishment? "Alexandre, is he . . . ?" Jacques slid a comforting hand over hers and led her inside the house away from the curious eyes that watched.

"Not dead, but he may yet die." She suddenly felt ill and caught Jacques's arm. Jacques held her up. "He's been experimenting with berries." Jacques's voice seemed far away. "Poison berries. A strange plant from some primitive jungle in the islands." They climbed the stairs together, reaching the master chambers where Mrs. Yarborough stood behind the netting draped on Alexandre's bed. Marie sobbed beside the door. Then Dominique saw her husband's face, pale and still, so gaunt he looked dead. Fighting the waves of insensibility that threatened her, she sank to the floor in a swoon.

"Get the smelling salts!" Jacques ordered, lifting his sister-in-law onto a chaise longue beside the fire. "My lady, can you hear me?"

Dominique felt Jacques's touch and smiled, closing her eyes against all that was outside. "Coosa," she moaned. "Coosa . . . Coosa."

"Breathe deeply, little sister," Jacques said loudly. "Open your eyes." Moses returned with smelling salts and held them to his mistress's nose. "Your husband is not dead, madame, he's alive."

"If he dies, his blood'll be on yur hands!" Mrs. Yarborough's tone was cruel.

"You have a vile and viperous tongue, woman!" Jacques snarled at Mrs. Yarborough with ire in his eyes. "Be gone from these chambers now, for if my brother dies you shall surely know the meaning of vengeance!" Mrs. Yarborough cringed, slithering from the chamber followed by Mère and Moses. "The old biddy fancies herself my brother's mother. She's jealous of you." Jacques laid his hand on Dominique's hair where she knelt beside her husband, lifting her to her feet. "You must forget her, she's old."

"I'm leaving this house, Jacques," she said despairingly. "I can't live here any longer."

"I'll not let you go." He held her hands.

"You can't stop me. Don't try." She broke away and went to the bedpost for support. "I thought I could see it out, but I know now I can't. This place holds nothing for me. I should have left long ago."

"If you leave your husband he'll surely die. Do you want that?" She tried to block out his words, going to the armoire and throwing open its doors to pull out fresh clothing. Jacques turned her around. "Is that what you want, madame? Do you want Alexandre dead?" Jacques's dark eyes flashed and for a fleeting moment she saw Coosa.

"If I stay, 'tis I who will die." Her eyes clung to his and the air was charged between them. "Pray leave me now, I have to change."

Jacques strode to the door, his fingers resting on the silver doorknob. "I'll leave, madame, but I'll not allow you to destroy all I hold dear. Mark my words well." The door closed with a note of finality.

Sitting on the bed beside her husband, she touched his forehead.

"Forgive me, Alexandre, I've tried to love you, truly I have." She pressed a kiss to his brow, then went to the door to summon Nancy and Kish. "Dress the child and pack her bag for a long journey. Hurry!" Pouring water in the washbowl, she freshened herself, warning her servants to keep silent, swearing them to secrecy and giving Kish a message to deliver. Dressing in a sensible habit of cotton cord, green to blend with the trees, Dominique donned a cape of heavy green satin threaded with silver, her hair fixed in place by a silver net. Nancy helped her mistress into kidskin boots and spoke low.

"Will you be wanting a bag for yourself, Miss Nikki?"

"Nay. Be a good girl and tell Mocha to meet me at the stable with the child. I go to prepare the horses." When Nancy was gone, Dominique went to the bed to tell her husband good-bye. "God love you and keep you well, Alexandre." Her voice broke and she kissed his cold lips, rushing from the room and down the halls.

Running swiftly to the stable, she was surprised to find Jacques waiting for her at the door. The look he gave her sent chills through her body. Walking past him she schooled her face to calmness and called for a groom.

"There is no one here but ourselves, little sister."

She studied his eyes, knowing why he'd come. "No matter, I know how to saddle a horse."

"Your mare is spent," he said firmly, grasping her arm and holding her fast. "Travel-weary like you. Pray return to the hall and rest."

"Don't tell me what to do!" she cried. "There are other horses. I'll take Ramir."

"You have no need of a mount, madame. You're going nowhere!"

Staring at him incredulously, she defied him with a glare. "You don't tell me what to do! I'm riding away from this place and if you don't unhand me I'll scream."

"Do you think I'm not aware of where you are going?" Taking her by the wrists, he held her in his grip. "Do you really believe me so ignorant that I don't know you mean to run off with my son?"

Her mouth agape, she was powerless to move. Jacques's eyes were filled with vehemence. "Your child's in her bed, madame, and I've informed your servants their mistress has decided to delay her trip indefinitely."

She slapped him across the face so hard she thought she'd broken her hand. Jacques's eyes blazed with anger. "You try my patience, madame," he said stonily. "If you were my wife . . ."

"*Your* wife?" she cried, so high the horses all turned their heads to look at her. " 'Tis lunacy I hear! Does it run in the family?" Twisting from his grip like a vixen, she pulled a horsewhip from the wall and raised it.

"You may whip me," he said smoothly, "for I'm nothing but a lowly slave. But I'll not let you go!" He felt the sting of leather as the whip sliced painfully through his gauze shirt and laid open his dark skin on his shoulder. "*Mon Dieu!*" Blindly, he leaped to still the source of his agony, forcing her hand over her head and twisting the whip from her trembling fingers.

"I hate you, I hate you, I hate you!" she screamed, beating him in the chest with her fist and clawing his face until she lost her strength and fell to the dirt on her knees.

"If you're through with your tirade, I'll try reason. Don't ever ask me to turn my back on what I cherish most, my family and my son." He hesitated, studying her bowed head. "Think what your leaving would do to Alexandre. Even now his men comb the earth for the beast who assaulted you in this very building. And the poor soul doesn't know the worst of it, does he? Go with Coosa and Alexandre would hunt my son like vermin and see him dead. Murdered—and perhaps other innocents with him? I know what white men can do to those whose skin is a different color."

"Nay!" she cried, looking up at him.

"My son has been chosen by the five tribes to go on a mission of peace. 'Tis a great honor for the Muskhogean peoples. Coosa makes his mother and father justly proud." Jacques raised her up and forced her to look at him as he pleaded passionately with her. "If you go to Coosa now, he'll leave his people and serve them no more. I know my son has sworn an oath to you. 'Tis my duty to interfere before 'tis too late." His words found their mark and she sobbed in defeat, lamenting her situation with bursts of uncontrolled words. "Coosa . . . didn't . . . tell . . . me . . ."

"I thought not." Jacques's breath ruffled her gathered hair.

"I can't . . . live . . . without . . . him . . ." she wailed, her body rigid against his.

"*Oui*, little sister, you can. Believe me, you can." Holding her closer to comfort her, he felt the wild beat of her heart, her tears wetting his shirt and skin. "You'll live and Coosa will live. You're both young."

14

Dominique listened to the morning call of a dove, the mournful hooting of an owl. Thunder growled as light streamed through the closed shutters, a breeze stirring the drapes. Was Coosa waiting? Unable to sleep, she turned over in her bed, her eyes wide. Coosa would hate her after today. Perhaps his hatred would be so great he'd come for her and carry her off? If only he would. Sleep, she must sleep.

The next day when Alexandre came out of his fever, Dominique was at his side. "*Chérie*." His voice was weak and he lifted a trembling hand to touch his wife's tear-streaked face. "You've come back to me."

Relieved because of his smile, Dominique clasped his hand and kissed it as Jacques entered the room.

"You gave us a good fright this time, my brother. What in blazes did you take?"

Alexandre laid his arm across his brow. "I remember now. The giant you purchased in Charleston gave me some black berries from his country; he said they were magic. Indeed they were. I dreamed things I've never dreamed before. What a headache!"

"Serves you right," Jacques admonished. "Must you sample every pod, berry, and root unfamiliar to you? Poisons

221

are dangerous, as you've told me many times. Next thing I know, you'll be eating toadstools."

Alexandre ignored his half-brother and smiled at his wife. "Are you angry as well, *chérie?* For if you are, I can find some toadstools."

"Don't joke about death," she said. "The slaves need you, the plantation needs you, the South needs doctors."

If only she needed him, he thought. He attempted to sit but blackness engulfed his vision, his limbs in a tremor. Jacques rushed to his brother's side, trying to still his shaking. Alexandre's teeth chattered. "Take care of her, Jacques. See that she wants for nothing. I'm ill, so very ill . . ."

Jacques feared for his brother's life. He watched the doctor slip back into unnatural sleep.

"Will he recover?" Dominique asked anxiously, covering her husband with a downy quilt.

"God knows. I pray he'll be himself soon."

And so he was. The doctor regained his strength slowly but steadily and although he was confined to his bed for months, his wife was constantly at his side. She had become a devoted wife and ran the plantation as well as any man, with Jacques's help. Stronger than ever physically, she worked daily with the horses, riding the fields or visiting the slave village and caring for the sick. She loved the hounds, second to the horses, and it was not unusual to see the mistress of Racemont walking about the grounds at any hour of day or night with her dogs, on the gallery with Oliver the owl, or staring absentmindedly at the stone mountain that dominated the landscape. Madame had suffered the loss of a great love, the slaves whispered. But it was Ruthe who noticed her mistress had lost considerable weight, bringing it to the attention of her master's brother.

Jacques found Dominique alone in the kennels one rainy morning, leaning over a polished pine rail that enclosed the pens. Dressed in what she called "beasty clothes," a brown dress with a patched wrap-around apron, she looked a classic beauty.

"Good-looking pups," Jacques remarked, eyeing the litter of half-grown wolfhounds, then his mistress's face.

"Aye. I wish Alexandre would tell me which one to keep."

"You must make the decision, little sister. My brother is not well enough to decide such things. There have been many requests for pups from Savannah and Philadelphia, New York and Boston, too, as you know. You must choose now."

" 'Tis not fair," she moaned, her lips pouting as he cupped her dainty chin in one hand. She looked into his black eyes and thought of Coosa.

"Your face is the face of the lovelorn, madame. Your eyes have lost their sparkle, your cheeks paler than I've ever seen. I'm worried about you. You've been working too hard and not getting enough sleep."

She looked up at him and frowned.

"See what I mean? When was the last time you smiled, eh?"

Spinning away, she felt his penetrating gaze on her back. "I'll choose a pup now. That one!" She pointed to a big grizzled dog, with sad eyes and the head of a bear, in the corner. She rubbed her hands together. "Would you like to assist me in choosing the best Berger de Brie?"

"*Oui,* but before we pick your French sheepdog, I'd like to request the pleasure of your company at dinner this evening. Alexandre will be joining us for the first time in months and Mère has prepared a feast to end all feasts."

"I have medicine to distribute to the horses and the barn needs whitewashing . . ."

Jacques caught her arm before she could go. "Coosa is well," he said evenly. Her green eyes stung and she searched the depths of his dark ones, seeing in them a reflection of her own anguish.

"You heard from him?"

"This morning. A runner came with a message."

Her heart thumped wildly, the scar on her chest aching with each beat. "Where is he, when will he return?"

"My son will be gone longer than at first anticipated. Many moons perhaps. I cannot say where he is. There are those who would disrupt the peace between the Indian nations." He reached inside his short-fitted jacket and drew out a small packet enfolded in white linen. "He asked me to give you this."

Dominique looked bemused, afraid to touch the bundle. "Go on." Jacques smiled. " 'Tis not a viper." Clutching the parcel to her breast for a moment, she then unwrapped it excitedly, finding a tiny but well-worn leather-bound Bible inside. She looked at Jacques and he shrugged. She opened the worn pages and spied a dried sprig of trillium in I Corinthians.

*Love is patient and kind, not jealous or conceited or proud, not
ill-mannered or selfish or irritable. Love does not keep a
record of wrongs, love is not happy with evil but is happy with
the truth. Love never gives up, its faith hope and patience
never failing. Love is eternal.*

She wiped a tear from her eye, using the soft linen from the
packet and smiling so exquisitely Jacques saw a summer's day.
"Jacques, dear Jacques. Bless you! I can live again!" The pups
barked, the hounds baying together, Jacques chasing after her
as she ran out the door and into a sudden downpour.

"Where are you bound?"

"I must ride!" she returned in a happy voice.

" 'Tis raining cows and sheep!"

"Is it?" She laughed, looking up into the dark roiling sky
overhead. She watched the rain come down in her face, opened
her mouth, and tasted it. Jacques shook his head, mystified
about what his mistress could have read in the good book that
made her so happy.

Two moons came and went, shining like a golden omen in
the skies overhead, giving Dominique new faith and a greater
understanding of love. Love was Coosa Tustennuggee, the
gentlest most unforgetable man she'd ever known.

It rained every day for weeks and when the heat of the
summer finally reached its zenith, flying insects plagued the
land. Fever was everywhere and no one escaped the burning
sickness. Early one morning, a young Creek runner came with
an urgent plea for help. The village of the Lower Creeks had
many people sick and dying. Women, children, young and old,
were felled. So many died there were few alive to care for the
sick.

"How many days do you guess the Creek was in coming?"
Alexandre asked Jacques.

"Perhaps two? I must go to my people. My Creek brother
tells me my wife is very sick."

"I'll ride with you," Alexandre said. "There's need for a
physician."

"But the plantation; your wife?"

Alexandre placed his arm about Jacques's neck. "I leave
Racemont in my wife's able care. She's proved she can handle
it as well as we can. Our people like her and trust her. Mère
will take care of the house, Mrs. Yarborough the child. Moses

will be here, too." He ran upstairs to pack his things and found his wife had already done it for him. "I need only my doctor's bag and some shirts, *chérie*." He drew her close and kissed her brow, too troubled to recognize her lack of response. " 'Tis your chance to take over my kingdom, madame. I know you can do it." His hand slipped from hers and she watched him walk to the door and down the hall, running to the stairs like a lad going out to play. Rushing to the windows, she saw Jacques ride up with the horses, and framed a silent prayer for her men's safe return.

Two days later the Creek runner died. Dominique had brought the Indian into the house and put him in her husband's bed. The Creek reminded her of Coosa and she soon found herself witness to his death. "Pray give him a decent burial," she told Moses. "Treat him gently." With Kish's help, Dominique had the Creek wrapped in clean linen, and then placed his body in a newly built pine box. "I pray this isn't the beginning of the end," she remarked to Moses as she watched the pine box carried down the stairs.

"What do you mean, madame?"

"The plague, Moses."

"There are many plagues, madame."

"You're right." She thought then of the yellow fever epidemic of '93. She'd been a child when her father had sent her mother and her to their summer home in the Pennsylvania mountains. Her father had nearly died that year, working with the sick until he had collapsed and had been ferried back to Germantown in a wagon.

"I've never seen the plague," Moses remarked. "I understand 'tis hell on earth."

Two days' ride away, in the village of the Lower Creeks, Alexandre and his brother discovered what hell on earth really was. The stench of death filled their nostrils and the village air at night, despite the cool evening wind. The sons of François Chastain slept like the death they sought to cure amid the sick and dying and there was no way to treat the burning fever, as it was called. Alexandre knew of no cure and could only make his patients comfortable. If they died he saw to their decent burial. By the time the harvest moon rose bronze and fiery in the autumn sky, the Creek village of five hundred souls had been reduced to less than fifty, and the Princess Summer Sun was dead.

Back at Racemont, sunshine streamed through the lights of the conservatory roof. Dominique felt Coosa's love as she watched the Carolina parakeets sit side by side on a limb above her head.

"Missus, come quick!" Kish screamed. "Bad trouble in the village! The conjure doctor says 'tis our punishment for doin' evil!"

"Bring my mare at once, a horse for you as well," Dominique instructed Moses. "The children must stay here in the house," she told Kish. "Don't let them out of your sight." Speaking slowly and distinctly so there would be no misunderstanding or panic, Dominique prepared for the worst.

The conjure doctor growled in a thick accent and met Dominique and her husband's manservant when they arrived in the village. Dominique's hackles were up. "Remove this witch doctor from my sight or I'll have him tarred and feathered and run off Chastain lands." She raised her quirt threateningly, but he clung to Jackie's reins, chanting in his mother tongue. "Unhand my horse, you black devil!" Dominique shrieked, bringing the crop down on his hand. The slave howled and retreated finally, cursing Dominique to everlasting torment.

"What did he say?" Dominique queried Moses as they walked to the cabin of the slavedriver.

"He blessed you, madame."

"Good and proper, too." She laughed. Inside the slavedriver's cabin they found his wife and child down with the fever. "How long have they been like this?" Dominique asked. "One day," came the reply. Dominique gave instructions to round up the women to nurse the sick, then sent word to the house that the mistress would not be returning until the fever was over. "Tell Mère to put food in a wagon once a day for the village and you'll do the driving," she told Moses. "No one from the house is to come near the village, understand?"

"Aye, madame. I'll fetch Kish to help you."

"Nay!" she warned. "Kish is to stay in the house with the children." She set about making the slavedriver's wife and child comfortable, telling them they were under quarantine. "Leave this cabin and I'll have you skinned and hung up to feed the birds!" Shaking her small fist in the slavedriver's face, she tried to make him understand.

* * *

" 'Tis a damnable epidemic!" she told Kish angrily. "What are you doing here? I told Moses to keep you in the house with the children."

"Mocha and Mère are there," Kish said innocently.

"And Mrs. Yarborough?" Dominique queried.

"Here!" Mrs. Yarborough snorted, standing behind Kish in the open door. "The only qualified person on the premises when it comes to sickness." The servantwoman faced her mistress. "You can go back to the hall now, madame."

"You'll take orders from me or high-tail it down the road, missus!" Dominique said through gritted teeth. "And not in the direction of the hall." She spoke quietly, not wanting the child she was tending to be upset. "Now then, little one," she said sweetly. "I'm off to see to the other sick ones in the village. I'll return to see you before dark." Hugging the child, she noted there was no change in the child's expression as she removed a rag from the tot's head. "Start at the opposite end of the village and work this way, Mrs. Yarborough. With any luck, we should meet on the morrow."

Mrs. Yarborough nodded. "You mean in a week, don't you? You don't know what you're in to this time." The statement proved true. Work on the plantation had to be curtailed as the village was closed off. Still, the fever spread like ink through linen. Matthew and Mark were kept busy building coffins. On the fifth day, Alexandre returned home, searching for his wife and finding her in his physician's cabin.

"*Chérie*, are you awake?"

Dominique rubbed her eyes and looked up, tears wetting her cheeks as she whispered her husband's name. "Alexandre, thank God, you're back."

"I'd never have left had I known this would happen." He drew her into his arms, noting how unhealthy she looked, pushing back her tangled curls and seeing her eyes rimmed in red.

"Examine Kish," she said. "Tell me she's not going to die like the others, please."

Alexandre knelt beside the young black woman and quickly observed she was in serious condition. Lifting her lids to look into her eyes, he shook his head.

"God, nay!" Dominique cried. "Not Kish! She's so young. What will her baby do without a mother?" Alexandre took his

wife and led her outside, walking away from the stench of
death.

"I'm not certain what this fever is. 'Tis a new variety to me,
a fast and sure killer. How long has it been since you slept,
chérie?"

She sank into his arms and he carried her inside his cabin,
laying her down on his cot and covering her with his coat. It
was not until a low and perfect harvest moon shone through the
windows that the mistress of Racemont slept in her own bed.
Ten horror-filled days had passed since she'd ridden to the
village to help her people. She opened her eyes and saw Mrs.
Yarborough and pulled the covers over her head.

"Your wife's awake, doctor," Mrs. Yarborough announced.
Alexandre came into the chamber accompanied by six giant
hounds. Two of them jumped on the bed with their mistress.

"Not on top of her!" Alexandre scolded them. Dominique
dodged a long wet tongue, smiling as a French sheepdog
settled on her feet. "They're happy you're well, *chérie*. And
so am I."

"Kish?" Dominique asked.

"Buried in the garden under the big magnolia. I don't think
she suffered."

Dominique sobbed softly, covering her face with her hands.
"How many more?"

"Nearly a hundred. We were fortunate; it could have been
worse."

"Fortunate! Dear God, who is left alive?"

"We are *chérie*. The Creeks didn't fare as well. They lost
their best braves and most of their women and children.
There's barely a handful left. The fever was devastating to the
Lower Creeks. I know nothing of numbers in other villages,
but in all they must have been reduced to less than a hundred."

"Dear God," she murmured, thinking of Coosa, praying he
was well and untouched by the fever. "What is it, do you
know?"

"I don't know. I only know it was the worst I've seen in my
life. Jacques is with his people. His wife died, you know."

"Summer Sun is dead?"

"*Oui*. But enough talk of death, *chérie*. I have a surprise for
you, something you're not going to believe."

His elation barely penetrated her grief-stricken thoughts as she reflected on Jacques and his poor people, the Creeks, who she considered family.

"Did you hear me, *chérie?*" Alexandre reached for her hand across a hound's back. "You're traveling to Virginia to the President's house."

Dominique screwed up her face. "What?"

"You've been invited to take part in a happy occasion. Read this and tell me that you're not excited." Handing her a letter, she opened it and read quickly.

"It's from Philadelphia, from cousin Jenny. She's getting married and wants me to be her maid of honor. She's marrying the social secretary to Thomas Jefferson, the President of the United States. Father will be there!"

"Exactly what I've been trying to tell you." He chuckled. "You'll be leaving as soon as you're well enough to travel. The wedding is in December. I've sent word to Captain Cooper to keep the *New Hope* in readiness. I'll accompany you to Chastain House in Savannah."

"But I don't want to go to Virginia, Nancy. My place is here with my family. The plantation needs me. Aye, 'tis exciting to think about, but it's too far to go for just a ceremony." Dominique groaned and complained to her maid as she finished her bath, all the while thinking of Coosa.

" 'Tis more than that, Miss Nikki. You'll be a guest in the house of the President of the American people. Your father will be there, too. 'Tis quite an honor for all of you!"

"Jefferson's just another man." Dominique sighed. "No different than all the rest, 'tis certain. It isn't as though I'll be meeting the Creator."

"Think of the thrill of it, Miss Nikki. That fine house on that hill and all those beautiful ladies wearin' gowns from the finest couturiers. You'll be the grandest of all, of course."

"I wish you could go in my place, Nancy. I can't make it across my room yet."

"You'll be walking soon," Alexandre said, pushing aside the Chinese screen that guarded his wife's privacy. He checked her pulse and heartbeat and pressed an ear to her breast. "You must take care for a while yet, but I believe I can safely set a departure date before the month is out." He smiled. "Needless to say, there will be no Jubilee this year."

Dominique looked at him, Jules Cocteau's ugly face flashing

across her mind, the horror of her first Jubilee so vivid she stiffened in terror. "How long has it been since I've seen my father?" she asked. "And why aren't you coming with me?"

"Our daughter will be four soon, *chérie*." Alexandre squeezed her hand gently. "I can't go on a trip like that. 'Tis regretful, too. I'd dearly love a sea voyage and holiday as well, after the hell we've been through of late." His eyes consumed her. "I'll be riding with you to Savannah to take care of some unfinished business there."

When Dominique's convalescence was over, she was bundled in woollens and furs and lifted aboard a coach-and-six bound for Savannah against her will.

"I beg you to let me stay! I don't want to go to Savannah or Virginia. The trip will surely make me worse." Alexandre tucked a blanket about her legs and set pillows behind her back. "If I must go, pray allow me to take my daughter with me. I don't want to leave Desiree here."

"We've agreed the best place for the child is here," Alexandre said tersely. "You need to get away, but you would get no rest with a child of Desiree's energies."

"I don't want to leave her, Alexandre! 'Tis against all my motherly instincts!" Tears filled her eyes and she wiped them with a gloved hand, still weak from her bout with the killing fever.

"Have a safe journey and return soon!" Jacques called as the coach lunged forward and the horses moved out, trotting handsomely around the circular drive of Racemont. Dominique watched the faces she loved disappear and, wiping her wet lashes, thought how distant Jacques had become.

"Jacques mourns for his squaw," Alexandre said. "Now that he's free to marry one of his own kind, perhaps he'll start a family." Alexandre sat beside her and the coach picked up speed.

"What do you mean?" Dominique asked, removing her gray-fox bonnet.

"He can marry a slave like himself, of course." Alexandre settled into his seat and Dominique sat stunned, unable to reply. Was this the man she'd married, the gentle man she'd once known?

"Do you have someone in mind?" she asked boldly.

"No one. I'm not one to match my slaves like my hounds, you know that. I'd like to see Jacques happy. One day we'll be sharing all this." He looked out the windows of the coach, pointing to the vast lands lying emerald and golden among the fringe of thick trees. Surprised he would mention such a private matter as his brother or what they owned, she could not help but wonder. Alexandre had not confided in her of late, especially about family finances.

"When will you make Jacques a free man?"

Openly irritated, he gave her a black look and laid his head back to let out a long sigh. Then, after a long silence, he begrudgingly replied, " 'Tis something I have to think about a good while more. We shall see." Patting her head like a dog's, he attempted to appease her, but she was not satisfied.

They were in bed together in Chastain House when she asked herself when she'd ceased loving him. Dominique studied the sea of freckles on her husband's back, the way his hair waved behind his ears. Had she ever loved him? The questions seemed fanthomless. There was a void inside her, an unsatisfied longing that wouldn't give her peace. She yearned for love, craved it, ached for Coosa's arms, his lips, his body . . . She didn't know where the Creek king was, didn't even know if he was alive.

Tears clouded her vision as Alexandre woke. She'd come to know something of his habits even though she didn't understand him. How could a man who loved mankind and creation change so? Had she been fooled into believing her husband was something he was not? Had death and despair and drink turned a good man into a stranger? She turned over in the bed, recalling Jacques's sad face and feeling compassion for him. She couldn't forget his eyes the day they'd parted . . . they reminded her of Coosa.

Alexandre rolled into her and she knew what he wanted. Her eyes were open, but she didn't react, her limbs growing rigid and tense as he lifted the hair on her back and laid it over her shoulder. "Pray don't touch me tonight," she whispered. He pulled her to his body roughly and held her tight.

"I have a need, *chérie*. One I can't contain." Slipping over her, he forced his knee between her thighs and she turned her face away, pushing him with all her strength.

"What is it, wife? Are you ill?"

"Pray don't call me *wife*!" she snapped.

"What would you have me call you?" He grinned. "Wife is what you are to me."

She closed her eyes and longed to hear Coosa calling her Summer Eyes, wishing she were in bed with the Creek instead. Alexandre's cold lips covered hers and as she twisted away, her nails clawed his back like a mad cat's.

"Don't touch me, please, leave me be!"

She saw the hurt in his eyes mixed with anger and humiliation, feeling sorry for what she'd said. Alexandre rolled away and sat on the side of the bed for a while, breathing deeply. Then he got up to cross the room and she heard him pouring a drink and gulping it down, then dressing himself. She pulled a pillow over her head and waited for the slam of the door until it came.

It was daylight when an angry and embittered Alexandre met with Maxwell Drummond's men in a small room behind a tavern overlooking the river in Savannah.

"Your man was sighted two days past, doctor, in town in bold daylight. Now he seems to have disappeared."

"You ask me to believe in magic?" Alexandre fumed. "Are you all incompetent?" He surveyed Drummond's men through eyes burning from lack of sleep and a night of drinking. His nerves were frayed. "Five men in a city the size of Savannah and you can't round up one criminal, one filthy beast?"

"That's just it, sir." One young man attempted to placate the doctor. "Savannah's no longer small. I dare say the city's changed since you were here last. There are hundreds of places a man can hide: houses and cottages and buildings. The waterfront alone is a monstrous beehive."

"Enough! I don't pay for excuses. If I had the time I'd find the devil myself! Are you watching his mistress's house?"

"Every day, doctor. The woman senses something, too. She's outwitted us more than once, leaving the house undetected."

Alexandre bent down to face the man. "A mere woman more cunning than a professional manhunter!"

The man, also a student of law, leaned back in his chair to avoid the doctor's berating. "A woman, true, but clever and cunning."

Alexandre threw up his hands. "I can't waste time listening to this rot. Catharine Ross is a woman who is known by everyone in this town. Put more men on her house, if need be! I'm paying for it! Now, I have other things to attend to here. When did Maxwell leave for the North?''

"Mr. Drummond sailed a fortnight ago. He should be in Richmond about now."

Alexandre pulled a leather pouch filled with gold coins from his coat pocket, tossing it onto the table. "I'll return in five days, gentlemen. Best you have news of the devil by then or consider yourselves unemployed!''

It was three days before the *New Hope* sailed for Virginia when Dominique decided to call on Mrs. Ross. It was partly thanks to Cat she was alive, after Jules Cocteau's vicious attack the day of Jubilee. Dominique had reminded herself of the debt she owed Cat many times. Now that she was in Savannah, she must go to Cat and thank her in person.

Alexandre had not returned from wherever he'd gone early that morning and she could be back from Cat's before he discovered her gone. With Ruthe's help, Dominique dressed modestly in a coatdress of wine-colored wool with bonnet and muff to match. She walked to the bright blue house on the square and lifted the knocker. Cat herself answered the door.

"Dominique, what in the world are you doing in Savannah? Have you left your husband?''

"I'm sailing for Virginia in three days and wished to call on you before I left. Alexandre's in town on business."

"Oh?" Cat made a face, her full figure poured into a bright yellow-and-black-striped coat, her dark curls crowned by a hat of the same fabric plumed in black feathers, and her violet eyes were transfixed on the square behind her caller.

"May I come in? 'Tis cold out today."

Cat seemed preoccupied with the square, smiling oddly. "Of course. I was expecting someone else and I thought I might see him."

"A gentleman caller, I should have known." Dominique smiled. "Forgive me, I can come back when I return to Savannah."

"Nay, come in now."

"You're well?" Dominique lay her muff down on the table in the hall beneath a gilded mirror, rubbing her hands together nervously.

Cat left to peer through the drapes, her back to Dominique.

"I'm fine, honey." Cat stood on tiptoe, her face pressed to the glass.

"I've come at an inopportune time. I'll come again, Cat." Dominique was turning to leave when Cat stopped her.

"Don't leave . . . not just yet, honey. Did you say you're leaving Georgia?"

Thoroughly puzzled, Dominique deduced Cat was trying to keep her from going out into the street. "In three days' time. My cousin's marrying the President's secretary. I'm going to her wedding at Monticello."

"The President of the United States?"

"Aye, Thomas Jefferson's home in Virginia."

"But it's winter up there. There'll be snow and miserable cold. Is Alexandre going with you?"

"Nay."

Cat rolled her eyes. "You're not going by yourself?"

"My maid will accompany me to Richmond and we'll be met by friends of my husband's there."

"Friends?"

Dominique nodded. "How is your arm, Cat?"

"The same, thanks to the butcher you call husband." Cat's eyes grew large and Dominique was sorry she'd asked. That seemed to put an end to it. She was shown to the door and hurried out into the street where Cat watched a carriage roll by, something in her face making Dominique aware of the carriage holding someone Cat knew, perhaps her gentleman caller . . . ? "Good-bye, honey, stop by again when you get back to Savannah. I was just on my way to the market."

Before Dominique could thank Cat for what she'd done for her the day of Jubilee, she found herself alone on the square. She caught the carriage that had passed the house rounding the corner, her trained eyes admiring two magnificently proportioned Welsh cobs with unusually long coats and tails. Horses she'd not soon forget.

After parting company with the manhunters, Alexandre found himself overly in need of a drink. Drummond's men were incompetent to say the least, and Jules Cocteau was still on the loose. Thinking on the wife who had rejected him the night before, he decided to take his miserable self to the nearest tavern. Five shots of rum later, he sat staring into a crackling fire in the tavern's fireplace and considered his marriage. He'd wanted Dominique more than anything once, but now that he owned her legally, he wasn't certain if she belonged to him or to someone else. Trying to reason, he decided their marriage was a sham, a play they acted out daily for the sake of others. He saw her face the day of Jubilee when he'd presented her with the mare from France, believing he'd seen love in her eyes. Or had he read her falsely? Perhaps he'd mistaken love for gratitude. She'd been with child, and women always acted differently when they were pregnant.

He struck a fist against the oaken table and ordered another shot, downing it and sighting the *New Hope*'s sails. His wife would be gone for God only knew how long soon and he wanted her before she left. Fancying himself with her, he felt her silken skin and heard her moans of ecstasy as he took her, her arms wrapped tightly about his neck as he sunk deep inside her wondrous beauty. How many men had touched her the way he had? How many had she touched back? Wretchedly sick with the thought, he cursed the woman he loved, knocking the glass across the table and onto the floor. What a fool he'd been to trust her. His tired and confused mind painted pictures of Jacques and her together; Mrs. Yarborough's words echoed in his brain. *"The two of them rode together all day, your half-brother of a slave and the wife you hold so dear, her habit ruined when she returned home. Ruined!"* What must it take for him to see the truth? How many more men would come knocking at his door? She'd been with the King of the Creeks as well. They'd surely spent the night together on the mountain! Laying his head in his hands, he wept. A moment later he regained his senses and stood up to leave the place quickly.

It was raining outside, a cold rain that pelted the cobblestones as ice. Alexandre pulled the collar of his greatcoat up on his neck and walked down the narrow steps to the Savannah River, his mind shoving up the evidence against the wife who'd betrayed him, cuckolded him, denied him!

Dominique lay trembling in her bed, unable to sleep. Finally, she got up and slipped into a honey-hued cashmere robe, tying its silken cords about her waist. Alexandre hadn't returned for dinner and the supper hour had come and gone hours ago. 'Twas nearly two in the morning, the church bells having tolled twice, when she looked out into the street. Rain beat hard against the windows and she wondered where her husband was on such a night. Half afraid to believe her eyes

she saw a man crossing the square in front of the house, his
black tricorn pulled over his face, and recognized the brown
greatcoat as Alexandre's. He was walking strangely, as if he'd
been drinking.

The key turned in the lock and the door opened with a bang.
"I'm home, wife!"

Pulling off the robe hurriedly, Dominique jumped into bed
and feigned sleep, hearing loud and fearsome footfalls up the
steps. Her bedchamber door was flung back with a terrible
bang. "I call you wife because you are mine, madame!
Tarnished, *oui*, but mine nonetheless!"

She held her breath and waited as he came to her bed and
yanked the covers from her shaking body, forcing herself to be
still while deciding how best to deal with a drunken sot.

"Alexandre, pray let me sleep."

"Never!" he roared. "You're going to get up and entertain
me before you go away. 'Tis a good thing you're leaving, eh?
Perhaps in Virginia the bastardly blacks and Indians will leave
you be. Those who seek to take away what's mine!" He sat
beside her and snatched the pillow from her face, the smell of
liquor so strong she wished to knock him off the bed.

"Let me be, please, Alexandre."

"Let me be, Alexandre," he mocked. "I'm your husband,
madame. 'Tis my legal right to do with you as I please, use you
however I desire." He laughed. "I claim that right now!"

Drawing herself back against the pillows, she prepared
herself for a battle, trembling uncontrollably. "Rights! What
right have you to treat me like one of your hounds?"

"I treat my hounds better than most men treat their wives."
He sneered, trying to keep his eyes on her. "I'm through
playing the good husband. Tired of turning the other cheek
while other men take their share." He pulled her up roughly.
"From now on I take mine first, when I feel the need!"

Oh, how she hated him! Coming up on the bed like a cobra,
she slapped him hard across the face. She saw blood in his eyes
as he brought a hand to his burning cheek and she leaped out of
the bed. Before she could reach the door, he caught her gown
and ripped it down her back.

"*Mon Dieu*! No wonder the competition is so keen!" He
grinned, his eyes near closed. "Your beauty blinds me,
madame."

"You've insulted me for the last time. I believe you've lost your mind." She stepped out of her gown and was attempting to gather it up from the floor when he grabbed her and held her against him, striving to enter her where they stood. "Damn you!" she swore, biting him in the lip when he kissed her. Giving her a good push, he cursed her in French, his temper hot. She was trying to dodge him when he picked her up and threw her, kicking, over his shoulder, whirling her around until the room went upside down and they fell backward onto the bed. The bed collapsed beneath them with a terrible crash.

"What's going on up there?" Ruthe called from downstairs.

Alexandre held his hand over his wife's mouth. "My wife is teaching me how to ride. Go back to sleep, Ruthe. Your master has the mistress well in hand."

"Rogue, wife-beater, madman!" Dominique shrieked when her mouth was free. He pulled her from the debris by her legs, Dominique all the while hanging onto the bedclothes as he dragged her beneath him. His rum-drenched tongue twisted deep between her lips as he held her down and they rolled together over the blue Persian rug toward the fire. Her struggling against his kisses, grunts, and murmering was for naught. "I don't know you!" she wailed.

" 'Tis your husband, for a change," he rasped. "How do I compare to the beast and the black bastard, eh? To his half-breed red son-of-a-bitch?"

Gripped by a desire to kill him, she dug her nails into his back until he howled for her to stop and released her. His face was twisted with rage, his hands holding hers while he kissed her body, so clumsily she could have wept for them both. Paying no heed to her cries of protest, he proceeded to take her against her will. An act of ownership that was over quickly. Dominique sobbed into the pillows as he rolled off and left her alone at last.

"I thought a woman likes to be dominated. I'm sorry." He closed the door behind him and she didn't see him again until the bells of Savannah rang clear in the cold damp air, the night as black as ink when he returned to kiss her cheek. She turned away.

"I'll miss you," he said.

" 'Tis you who sends me away. Remember that when I don't return."

He thought her childish and chuckled at her threat. "You'll return, *chérie*. I don't easily part with something I value as highly as you. I'm sending Ruthe with you. My friend and lawyer, Max Drummond, will see to your safety once you're on Virginia soil. Max is an adviser to the President and serves me well."

"Surely your lawyer will bed me as well?" she jeered, pushing him away and wrapping the covers around her, sitting on a chair before the fire. "If I find myself with child from this, I'll throw myself overboard. I want no child from a drunken brute."

"Even that won't be possible where you're going, *chérie*. Believe me when I say you'll be watched every minute you're out of my sight. Drummond will hire an army if necessary to make certain you don't roam." His eyes adored her and he drew her up to join him before the hot ashes of a dying fire. "I know you, my love. You're wild like the Spanish horses on Georgia's golden isles. A priceless commodity in any man's eyes. That's why I fell in love with you, you know—your wildness is part of your charms." He frowned. "Nevertheless, you're mine legally, and I'll have any man killed who tries to take you from me!" He fondled a full and ripe breast and bent to kiss its delicious tip, but she pulled away. "Think about it, *chérie*. You'll have ample time for thinking on this journey. Don't play me the fool for I know more than you think." His eyes laughed and searched hers as she looked up at him in disbelief. "Surprised? I told you once no man would have you the way I have and I meant it. Now I've taken measures to make certain!"

Jules Cocteau picked up the wine-colored muff Dominique had left on the hall table of Cat's house. Sniffing the soft material, Jules caressed it with his fingers. Then he saw his face in the mirror, the ugly gray scar that ran from his cheek to his lip, the mark he would have to live with for the rest of his life. All because of one Chastain savage and another Chastain who refused to stitch his face!

"The lady of the hounds was here, was she? What a pity I missed her."

Cat felt the cutting edge of his remark, the white flash of jealousy. She thought of sharing Jules with another woman, a young and beautiful woman she could never be again. "Why's she so important to you, honey? Nikki's a married woman with a child." Jules's ears pricked.

Child? "You told me she lost the weakling's brat."

"The child she had in the North, honey, before she came to Georgia."

Jules's mouth lifted in a smirk. "A boy?"

"A girl. Desiree is her name. She lost her son because of you." Cat twisted the words like a knife.

"Filthy little alley cat!" Taking Cat by the throat with one hand, Jules shook her until her eyes rolled. "One day I'll kill you, puss, shake the life from your fat little tail and toss you to the sharks!" His laugh was low and guttural. "The sea's cold this time of year, puss, cold and gray and deep!" Releasing his fingers on her throat, he pushed Cat into a chair and chuckled, a soft hissing sound like a snake slithering away in dry grass. "Now tell me everything she said, from the beginning!"

Two days later, Alexandre and his wife stood on the deck of the *New Hope*. "Have a safe journey. Give your father my best. I'll meet you here on your return. Max will take good care of you, you can trust him." Kissing her cheek, he whispered in her ear. "Say you love me even though you don't mean it, *chérie*. Captain Cooper and the servants are watching."

"I've never loved you," she said chillingly. "You killed everything between us last night. Do you think I will forget how you called me whore and abused me just like the man you pretend to hate, took me against my will? Now you have the audacity to ask for my love. I hate you with all my heart!" she lied. Pulling away, she walked briskly across the deck, her scarlet black-lined cape blowing skyward.

"Forgive me for last night," he said softly, following her, "I had too much rum. God knows I love you. Can't you find a decent word to say in my behalf?"

Shaking her head, she held back tears of regret for having so cruelly hurt him, wanting to hold him in her arms and tell him she was sorry.

"I almost forgot." Reaching into his coat, he retrieved a slim red-velvet box and handed it to her with a smile that made her realize she couldn't be angry with him for long. "Open it, I want to see it on you." She looked at him incredulously, her lower lip trembling, knowing well she'd softened.

"I can't accept your gift, Alexandre. Pray take it back."

He opened the box for her, watching the sparkle in her eyes

as they caught sight of six perfectly matched emeralds hung on a string of black velvet. "They match your eyes," he said. "Tell me you love me a little."

"Please take them back. I can't accept gifts from you. I have no right . . ." Unable to say more, she felt resigned to keeping the gems.

"I can tell by your expression that you love them, *chérie*. 'Tis time to part now." He took her hand and kissed it, bowing before her and backing away.

"Good-bye, Alexandre," she breathed. "Take care of the children. I shall write."

"So shall I. *Adieu*, my love."

15

The journey overland from Richmond was long and grueling. Winter had set in and the road to Monticello was nearly impassable in places. Deep ruts, swirling mud, and fallen trees made the going painfully slow. The rain turned to snow, whipping across the soaked horses' manes as the coach-and-six driven by Max Drummond's men rolled northward.

"I've never been so cold, mistress." Ruthe tucked a beaver robe about Dominique's skirts and feet. Dominique never moved, her eyes fixed on the iced glass of the coach's window and the mountains in the distance white with snow. "Just one more hill and we'll be there, mistress. I saw a sign that said Monticello." Ruthe scraped the ice from her window with her fingernails. "'Tis lucky we made it before the storm." Dominique breathed deeply. She hadn't been feeling well since she'd left Savannah. Cooped up in tight places made her ill and she hadn't had a decent night's sleep in weeks. Ruthe insisted it was nothing but motion-sickness, but Dominique knew better. "I can't wait to see your father," Ruthe said eagerly.

There would be scores of questions then, Dominique thought. Her father would want to know everything about Georgia and Alexandre and his family and Desiree. The horses began their climb up the winding road to the Jefferson plantation, a road in excellent repair, speeding them on their way. Dominique pressed her nose to the frosty pane, observing the roads and roundabouts of remarkable design, joined at select places by bridle paths and walks. She thought of riding to meet Coosa. She turned his little Bible over in her gloved hands; a sweet memory of the Creek made tears sting her eyes. Her life had taken several complicated turns since their encounter in the glade. She recalled Alexandre's cruel accusations in Savannah, then shook her head to dispel the memory.

Faceless men rode alongside the coach on horseback, heads wrapped in woolen scarves and furs, blankets around their shoulders, strangers all. She was a prisoner with no hope of escape, a rich man's wife forced into exile. Snow rode the back of the wind, spitting flakes that swirled and landed silently on the frozen earth, turning the Virginia landscape into a mountainous fairyland. A small burial ground came into view, the names *Martha and Jane Jefferson* plain to see. Dominique whispered prayers for her host, Thomas Jefferson, author of the Declaration of Independence, a widower who had also lost a child.

The coach plowed through the open gates of Monticello, a plantation of breathtaking beauty beneath snow-filled skies. The unfinished house was a marvel of workmanship, the elevation on which it sat the perfect spot for the great house that meant "little mountain" in Italian.

Dominique sat up and stretched as if awakening from a dream. The house inspired her, its brick walls, dome, and arched windows capturing her imagination. Servants ran out to meet the coach, and the front door was open wide beyond white columns.

Dominique followed the housekeeper past a great Philadelphia clock to a back staircase that climbed to the second floor. A hot fire roared in the fireplace and Dominique warmed herself before it, her cheeks itching as she turned around to lift her skirts and thaw her frozen backside.

"Not too much too soon, Mrs. Chastain," the housekeeper warned. "You must rub the circulation back into your limbs, then a tepid bath will do the trick." The housekeeper told Dominique the President's daughter was away visiting a sick relative in a nearby village and Dominique and her party were the first to arrive. Jenny and Elton Winburn had been delayed in Washington by bad weather and it was conceivable it would be days before they arrived. The President and Jenny's betrothed were in the capital until the week was out and Mr. Drummond had sent word he'd be arriving in time for the nuptials, or ten days hence.

Dominique leaned back in a copper tub set upon a fur rug and tingled with the heat. She and Ruthe had been given two small rooms side by side and the servant busied herself unpacking the trunks.

"If my question seems odd, please be patient for I've a reason for asking, Ruthe. Does your loyalty lie with the master or myself?"

"With you as always, ma'am. Your father gave me and my man employment when we needed a roof over our heads and we promised we'd take care of you for him. I respect the doctor as your husband, but I knew you first."

Dominique slid deeper into the tub, soaping herself with a sponge lathered with English lavender. "You know well of my love of horses, Ruthe."

Ruthe grimaced, gripping the four-poster. "Aye, how could I forget? My Thomas blames himself for what happened Jubilee day."

"I'm sorry for that, Ruthe. I meant to bring no harm to anyone, least of all my babe. I'd rather have died than lose him the way I did."

"Pray don't speak of it, Miss Nikki."

" 'Tis those men!" Dominique frowned unpleasantly. "Those confounded thieves and vagrants my husband paid good money to Drummond to guard me. Have you seen them?"

"Aye, ma'am, a sad lot, if you ask me."

"That's exactly what I mean. Why on earth are they here?"

"We're in Indian territory, the way the housekeeper tells it— the Virginians the doctor hired are to be on the lookout for heathens."

Dominique laughed. "Where do you think they are now? Drummond's men, I mean?"

"Holed up in the servant's quarters out back, I'd say, wishing they had a bottle or two on such a cold night as this."

"And we shall provide them with one." Dominique stood up in the tub. " 'Tis my intention to explore the paths of Monticello. Our hostess assures me I can have my pick of the

President's mounts." Her eyes sparkled. "There's an Andalusian from Spain, Ruthe! I've always wanted to ride one!"

Ruthe looked at her mistress, aware she couldn't resist the
irresistible. "What do you want me to do, ma'am?"

"Lay out my habit from Paris, the gray with the black cloak
and military collar."

Ruthe giggled, delighted her mistress was herself again, her
face aglow with a newfound game of chance. Then Ruthe's
heavy brows met in worry. "How can two women delude four
men, ma'am? Surely two watch the house while the others
rest."

"Perhaps." Dominique wrapped herself in a warm blanket.
"Send six bottles of our best wine to them with my compli-
ments, assuring the low-lifes your mistress sleeps soundly in
her guest room. Tell them to relax and warm themselves before
the roaring fire on such a cold night. They deserve a reward for
riding all the way from Richmond!"

"You don't mean to ride in this weather, surely, ma'am—'tis
snowing."

"I do."

"Then best you be off before the stuff reaches your fancy
mount's hocks and the paths are lost in darkness. If you're
going, be gone now." Ruthe winked. "Leave the men to me. I
know a trick or two."

"Thank you, Ruthe." Throwing her arms about her servant,
Dominique hugged her, then stepped into her gray habit lined
in black fox. It felt wonderful to be clean again, and dressed
decently after so many days on the road. Dominique spun
around before the mirror beside her bed. "I shall return before
the moon sets. 'Tis a promise."

Leaving the house stealthily, Dominique followed young
house slaves to the stables where she mounted a magnificent
stallion from Seville named Zapata, a true pleasure horse that
showed years of schooling. The horse snorted as Dominique
patted his neck and enjoyed an exhilarating gallop around the
hill. They stopped to enjoy a view of the valley below, a
glistening river of ice and a ribbony road curving for miles
across white fields. The moon outlined a row of silver-frosted
mulberry trees. Dominique fancied the trees a sentinel protect-
ing her from Drummond's awful men and the snowflakes
misplaced flower petals from heaven as the night took on an
ethereal glow. The snowfall was endless and Dominique

looked skyward, watching flakes drop on her face and stick to
her lashes. If only Rising Moon waited for her in the wood.
How marvelous it would be to guide her mount to where he
waited, horses and riders disappearing into the gray and blue
night, silently. Zapata weaved among the trees and then a bird
took flight and a branch snapped as she noticed fresh hoofprints
in the virgin snow. A tiny chill crossed her scalp. She breathed
cautiously, gathering her cloak about her and making certain its
hood covered her face. Surely the brash Virginians hadn't
followed?

Breaking into a gallop, the big horse pressed on through the
darkening wood. A rush of air lifted the rider's hood, exposing
her face as her heart pounded anxiously in her chest. They'd
covered some distance, yet the prints wound ever onward
through the trees. A ghost horse? Dominique's courage
mounted. Nay, 'twas flesh and blood, a filthy intruder on her
privacy, and she'd just as soon give him a piece of her mind!
No child was she to be spied upon! "Who's there?" she called
out bravely. "Come out and show yourself if you're a man!"

The wood grew darker, but the moon befriended her, illumi-
nating the ermine path. Hooves of another horse crunched
snow and Zapata laid back his ears, every sinew and nerve
tense as the gentle monster came to a graceful halt. They were
in a narrow place where oaks rubbed branches with elms,
creaking mysteriously in the frosted air. A snowy owl with
golden eyes looked down and blinked on the night riders, then
took wing with a screech that dumped snow to the earth.
Zapata balked, rearing and lifting Dominique into the air. The
powerful steed pawed the snow and bared his teeth as he
snorted in fear. The other horse was a stallion! Why didn't it
come into view? All was still and then branches snapped as a
snow-covered horseman came through the falling flakes,
treading the path with care. The rider was clad in red, his dark
head adorned simply in garlands of snow, his face hidden in the
darkness. His horse was pale with a long silvery mane that
glistened with ice in the light of the moon. A multicolored
mantel hung to his knees. 'Twas a dream, Dominique told
herself; in a moment she'd awaken and the fantasy would be
gone. No manner of miracle could bring Coosa Tustennuggee
to the hills of Virginia; never on God's earth could they be
reunited this night!

Believe, her feminine reasoning entreated. Accept what men cannot! Closing her eyes, she wished the rider to be Coosa so much her flesh tingled. Then fate took her in her care, utilizing her imagination at will. The earth was warm, not cold, the wind whispering words of love in her ear; the path she rode was ermine and the mulberry trees were sentries. The moon came out from behind the trees and lit the way for the horses of white. Truly the night was blessed.

"Our gods planned well!" The rider dismounted, his long cloak unfurling from a great height, his long black hair tucked about his shoulders. He came toward her, silently and steadily through the falling snow, his face still in shadow until revealed by moonlight.

"Coosa!" Dominique stared at the high cheekbones, looking down at her man as he raised his hands to her, his cloak slipping over buckskin and furs as he helped her down from her horse. "My love," she gasped, "is it really you?" Snowflakes lit on their hair like butterflies as Coosa kissed her, gripping her waist and holding her fast. Clinging to him, she laughed until she cried, whispering his name as if she'd lost her mind in a vision that would soon disappear. Coosa laughed, too, caressing her nose and cheeks with his lips, stroking her hair and whispering prayers of gratitude to their gods.

"I have known loneliness and despair without you."

"And I!" she cried, holding him tight. He saw tears flowing down her cheeks and took her hands in his, warming them with his breath and kissing them tenderly.

"Feel the clip of my heart and never speak of parting again, Summer Eyes." He placed one of her fingers in the cleft of his chin and held it there.

Dominique closed her eyes. "It can't be happening. Tell me where I am so I may believe 'tis truly you, Coosa."

"We are in a land called Virginia, atop a mount that rises gently from a valley, a green sloping place called Monticello." Wrapping her inside his cloak, he went on. "Mother Earth sleeps peacefully at our feet for the Great Spirit has covered her lovingly with a blanket of purest white. The trees are silver and shimmer in the moonlight, touching their hands to make a song for us." He kissed her palms and then her face. "Your skin is the color of the rising mist that shrouds the South's mount of stone, your eyes verdant like the pine woods of Georgia, your mouth pink and sweet like wild honeysuckle."

Dominique sighed, relishing each word, thrilling to the musical tones of his voice.

"The woman I see is called Dom-ma-nique by her kind, richly garbed in the color of the Indian's holy mount, her tresses spun gold against a black night."

Dominique kissed his cheek.

"The woman has the courage of the timberwolf and the cunning of the puma, yet she is gentle like the dewy-eyed fawn when shown understanding."

" 'Tis a dream!" she cried. " 'Tis impossible! You are a mirage, I know it!" Then she rememberd Drummond's men and made a face.

"Why do you look that way?" he asked.

"We may not be alone," she whispered, holding tight to his sleeve. "My husband hired men to watch me since we last talked. They may be here, with us!" Her face showed fright and she drew him close, devouring his splendid strength and the comfort she derived from his embrace. Coosa's lips curled.

"My warriors watch the wood as well. Do you think the *mico* would journey so far from his homeland alone?"

"You don't understand, Coosa. These men are paid to watch me—they have nothing to do but follow me wherever I go."

Coosa smelled her hair, nuzzling his face into it and moaning deeply. "You're the same, Summer Eyes?" He slid his tawny hand swiftly downward over her belly and frowned. "You don't carry our child?"

She felt guilty then, and looked up into his moonlit eyes, thoroughly enchanted by him. Oh, how she'd missed him, the sound of his voice, his tender touch, his regal air. The King of the Creeks was only a snowflake away, his body pressing eagerly into hers, the undeniable swell of his manliness inviting her to sin. She shook her head. "Nay, Coosa."

"One day, perhaps?" He smiled. "With the merciful blessing of our gods. Now we must rejoice with the thrill of our happenstance, transport our thanks to the heavens above!"

They laughed together, drinking in the perfection of the night, stretching to touch the iced limbs. Dominique slid over the length of Coosa's hard body, resting her boots on his, parting her lips to receive his kiss.

"So long, Summer Eyes. Six moons!"

"Aye," she breathed. She, too, had counted six moons. Her eyes glistened as he unhooked the front of her habit.

"Coosa has burned with fire in his dreams. Grown weary with the wait and dejection!" Tears wet his bronzed cheeks as he bent low to kiss the scar that marked the crest of her breast.

Dominique looked up at him, reveling in their felicitous meeting. He explained that he'd been sent by the five tribes of the Southeast to speak to the President, made _Hopayuki_ because he was a combination warrior and prophet to his people.

"Coosa asks you to stand by his side evermore, Summer Eyes. To be his wife," he said into her hair.

"Oh, yes, but how? There is no way!"

"There is, Dom-ma-nique. You will see."

"Alexandre will never set me free, Coosa. I'm his legal property." Falling against the flanks of her horse, she wept bitter tears.

"Coosa will free you," he promised, pulling her from her misery and kissing away her tears. "We were made to be together."

"How?" she asked. "I cannot believe the impossible! Make me no false promises, Coosa. I still don't believe you're here."

He cried out in frustration to the stars. Pulling his hunting knife from its sheath, he cut his finger, red blood wetting the snow. Dominique gasped, recalling the night on the mountain of stone when she'd tried to take her life. "I bleed warm blood. No dream blood is warm! Touch my blood, prove to yourself Coosa is real!" He held her gloved hand and let blood trickle onto it. She stared at its splattered mark on her hand.

"You're impossible, Coosa—I believe, I believe!"

"Indians believe all things are possible." He chuckled, wrapping her in his arms with gentleness. "We Creeks fear only the Great Spirit. Your husband is but a man. If he won't release you, there are other ways." He cleaned his knife in the snow and returned it to his sheath in one sweep.

"You would not hurt Alexandre, would you? Promise me you would never take his life, Coosa. Promise."

His face constricted and he touched her cheeks with his fingers to calm her. "I can make no such promise, Summer Eyes. Coosa is sorry." His expression was soft, his hand pushing back the wet curls that fell across her forehead.

Gazing into his eyes, she imagined a bloody scene with her husband and Coosa. Would she be the instrument that would somehow destroy the two men she loved? Indians were capable of anything, she knew, and Coosa was a trained warrior. Alexandre could die!

Coosa frowned. "What are you thinking? You accept Coosa as a breathing soul, do you not? Tell me why you came here, Summer Eyes?"

"I'm here for a white man's ceremony. A wedding between my cousin and the President's secretary."

"I have met Thomas," Coosa said plainly, walking with her through the darkened wood. "I have been in these parts for more than two moons now. Talking with Thomas in Washington."

"Thomas?"

"*Oui*, that is his name. A very busy man, your president. Newly appointed to this land's highest office and already encountering problems with Indian territories. Thomas tells me he's making preparations to send two men to the Northwest. I seem to recall something about a wedding as well. Two people from Pennsylvania or Virginia, I believe. Some important people from the South as well," His eyes twinkled, his lips forming a wide grin. "A Mr. Drummond of Athens, Georgia, and a Mrs. Alexandre Chastain from a place called Racemont. Wife of an important doctor from Philadelphia, or thereabouts."

"Coosa! You knew I was coming, you knew all the time!"

His chuckle warmed her bones. "*Oui*, I did. Thomas invited me to his little mount to hunt and wait out the days for his coming. I and my warriors have camped out these past few nights, eagerly awaiting the lady of the hounds." Smiling, he took her in his arms and kissed the snow from her face, noting that she trembled from the cold. "You must return to the hall at once. Coosa will wait for you here when the sun falls behind those hills." Pointing to a chain of blue peaks, he lifted her into her saddle, slapping Zapata on the rump before Dominique could say good-bye.

A cock crowed and Dominique leaped out of bed, then slipped into a cardinal-red habit with matching capelet and bonnet of fox. Dressed, she ran to pull on her boots and went to the door to open it with care. No one was about and she heard nothing but the tick-tocking of the Philadelphia clock downstairs. She crept down the back stairs and out the side door.

Once at the stable, she sighed in relief to be in the company of horses, even though they eyed her suspiciously. There was no sign of the dreaded men her husband had hired. She awoke the stableboy, ordering a lovely Virginia-bred mare with white stockings and blaze to be saddled at once.

The morning air was frosted and the ride around the little mount's summit was both pleasurable and invigorating. The sun had begun to rise when she entered the woods, bathing the snow in gold and pink. Reining in her mare, Dominique sought to find the place where Coosa's blood had spotted the snow, then tethered her mare and began her search in earnest. They'd stood there, she told herself; no, there! Strange—she could find no sign of their footpirnts as she followed the curving path. Rounding a bend, she stood erect to ease her back, and spotted a rider on the track some fifty feet away. What if the rider was one of the Virginians and he saw her? Turning to run, she was too late as the rider came after her, his horse so close she could feel its hot breath on her back.

"Whoa!" the rider yelled, bringing his horse under control just as Dominique threw herself into a snowbank to escape ironshod hooves.

"Damn!" she swore. "Isn't it enough that you spy on me? Must you trample me to death as well?" Wiping the white stuff from her face, Dominique never stopped to look at the man who offered his hand. "Stupid, clumsy fool! Didn't you see me? 'Tis good that we finally meet." Looking curiously at the man's attire, she saw he was dressed in a fine knee-length redingote of brown frieze, a shorter jacket of pale buff, and close-fitting breeches of biscuit whipcord. His ascot hung with silver chains to hold his bottle-green cloak across his shoulders. A tricorn covered on brow, the other brow showing carrot-red and arched in a frown.

"Blast, miss, if you're through with your tirade, I'll ask you what the hell you were doing on my trail?"

"Your trail?" His tone chafed her, her ears stinging with the cold. She brushed snow from her habit, the heat of her frenzy warming her cheeks. Her bonnet slid from her hair.

"Mine and yours, of course. Forgive me, please."

"Be gone before I say something unbecoming to a lady and tell your employer he shall hear from me!" Turning on her heel, she marched off toward her horse.

"Wait, allow me to explain, will you?"

"Follow me again and I'll see you lose your scalp!"

Mounting her mare, she swore beneath her breath and rode off, shaking snow from the trees.

"I'd like a crack at the lady meself, lads. Between her looks and her wild streak, she'd drive a man clean out of his head!"

"Wouldn't we all like to get a piece of Miss High-'n'-mighty, eh? Drummond ain't come yet—why don't we?"

"Drummond would skin us alive, he would. We're runnin' a risk as 'tis. Ain't one of us watchin' the big house to make sure she stays put."

" 'Tis just about time them ladies and gents wake up in their big houses. Ain't no one come or gone this mornin'. I bin up since six!"

George Limpton had had all he could stand from his men. Drummond hadn't returned from Washington and George was in charge. He looked through the glass in the door of the servants' quarters and wiped sleep from his eyes. "I was told the young lady has a mind of her own and's mad for horses. But as far as I know, the lady's never left the house."

"Unless she's slipped out and back in without us seein'," one sleepy-eyed young man commented.

"Maybe I'm worryin' too soon, eh? The lady's just arrived, ain't she?"

"What if she sneaked out last night whilst we all was drinkin'?" Turbin squinted his small blue eyes. "If she did, we missed a good piece of fun, I'd say." Turbin laughed, tilting his head back and running a hand between his legs.

"I'll have no more talk like that, Turbin! Drummond put me in charge while he's gone, and I'm livin' up to my word. I want none of ye lookin' sideways at the lady, do ya hear?" George Limpton glared at Turbin until Turbin looked away. "The woman's fine, too fine for the lot of us. I want no trouble, now or later. If ya give me some, I'll make ya sorry, I swear!" Limpton's wide body blocked the morning light and his men settled down, all but Turbin. Limpton was sorry he'd taken on the brutish sailor from Richmond. But Turbin was down on his luck and he always felt sorry for a man in a predicament. Cursing himself for hiring him, he went to talk to the new man, the islander with the strange smirk who'd kept to himself from the minute he'd hired on at Richmond's docks. Drummond had instructed Limpton to hire as many able-bodied men as he needed to guard an important lady traveling to the President's house in the hills of Virginia. It was not a difficult assignment. All they had to do was make certain the lady met with no one and if they spotted anyone suspicious, they were to take the party in hand and hold him prisoner until they could be dealt with by the authorities. Limpton had worked for Drummond before, finding fugitives from justice, and the rewards were well worth the effort.

"What name do you go by, friend?" Limpton asked the dark bearded man who sat in the corner with his hat over his face. The islander pushed his hat back and smiled.

"Jacques."

"Jacques 'tis then," Limpton said. "You're not from Richmond, are ya?"

"*Non.*"

"Ya sound like a Frenchie, sir. New ta these parts, are ya?"

Jules Cocteau wanted to kick Limpton out the door into the snow, but he held his temper.

"*Oui,*" he muttered, pulling his tricorn over his face.

Dominique sat very still while Ruthe wound her long topaz hair round her head, holding it with Spanish combs and black ribbons. The two women had spent the day preparing for this moment. Now, all they had to do was get Dominique past her bodyguards.

"There's a man at every door, mistress—Drummond's men they are. Best we forget about your ride."

Dominique frowned, slipped into a black woolen riding dress with matching cape, its front and hood bordered in gray fox. "You jest, Ruthe. 'Tis a fact of life I ride daily, you know that."

"Aye, mistress, but can't you forego sitting a horse for once? You're bound to get caught if you leave the house."

Dominique stared at her blood-spotted gray gloves, then went to get her black ones and stuffed the grays beneath her pillow. "I'll not get caught if you do as we planned, Ruthe. We're dealing with brawn, not intelligence, here."

"As you wish, mistress." Ruth curtsied and descended the stairs to the west wing, letting herself out to approach the man who guarded the door.

"Did my mistress come this way, sir?"

Turbin eyed Ruthe up and down, scratching his chin. "Nay, no one's left the house, I can attest ta that."

Ruthe threw her hands over her mouth and wailed frantically. "Dear God, where can she be? You must help me find her or I'll have to report you to Mr. Drummond."

"No need fer that, woman! I'll help ye find your mistress." Turbin's mind raced. So the bird had flown her cage? Well, she hadn't gotten past him, so she was probably still in the house. Following Ruthe, he went back into the house and down the hall to the stairs. When they were out of sight, Dominique stepped out from under the stairs and ran out the door, racing across the dark roundabout to the stables. By the time Turbin realized he'd been duped, she'd be riding hard for the woods to meet Coosa. She'd delayed leaving the house until well past twilight. It was dark now and her heart drummed with the horse's hooves, wondering if Drummond's men followed. Once inside the woods, she dismounted, leading the Andalusian to where the horse wouldn't be seen. Time dragged by and she thought she'd freeze in the cold. Then she heard the sound of hooves and her pulse leaped, anxious to find herself in Coosa's arms. A horse appeared beyond the bend and stopped. Then she heard footfalls on the snow and ran to meet Coosa, a joyful smile on her lips, her eyes sparkling with excitement. In a moment they would touch and kiss, embrace. Rounding the bend she ran into him and a chill rippled up her spine, spreading in shivers across her shoulders and over her scalp. She screamed at the face leering in the starlight, a face she didn't know, unshaven and alive with lust.

"Don't be scared, yellow bird. I'm one of Drummond's men sent to find ya. Your woman told me where ya was. Come here ta me, I won't hurt ye." Dominique shivered as he opened his arms as if to catch her. She turned and fled as fast as she could, cold fright catching in her throat and choking her. The path was lost and she didn't know which way to go. Stumbling and running together, she knew the man would catch her. She wanted to scream for Coosa, but could make no sound.

"Come 'ere!" Turbin called angrily, caught fast by a bush that snagged his clothes and beard and refused to let him go. "Judas!" he cursed. "Wait up, I only wanna fondle ye a bit!"

Gasping for breath, Dominique plunged blindly into the cover of the wood, holding her skirts and dodging branches that scratched her face and drew blood, yanking hair from her head as she went. A terrible pain in her side made her stop and lean against a giant tree, holding her breath to listen for her follower. Nothing but the pounding of her heart met her ears. She badly wanted to scream to Coosa, but dared not. Shaking with the terrible cold, she realized her hands and legs were numb. Suddenly two long arms came out from behind the tree and a big hand clapped over her mouth, pushing her swiftly into the snow. Her face was freezing and for one frightening moment she was back at Racemont on the stone floor under Jules Cocteau. Blackness swirled around her and she tried vainly to fight, her hands held behind her back until her strength was sapped by fear. She fell limply to the wet snow, the cold seeping into her throat and wrists and heart, a deep icy pool dragging her down.

Coosa dropped his scarlet cloak over Dominique's form and waited like a warrior of old, knife clenched between his teeth, eyes ablaze. Two Creek braves, faces tattooed with birds and fish, crouched motionless behind the *mico*, two more across the path, their poison-tipped darts in place, cane blowguns pointed at the man's heart as he lumbered up the path.

"Mrs. Chastain, darlin'!" Turbin called sweetly, holding his hands between his legs to soothe his mounting lust. "Don't hide from me, ma'am. I'm a man you'll like, I tell ye." Cursing to himself, Turbin stepped forward cautiously, suspicious of the sudden silence. "Come on, lady, I know you're hidin' here abouts. Come out and get acquainted."

Stepping back into the shadows and away from Dominique's still form, Coosa watched Turbin as he squinted in the darkness, gawking hard at the sight of a red cloak spread over the snow.

"I see ye now." Turbin laughed. "Waitin' fer me, eh?" Mouth salivating, Turbin crept closer in the snow and reached down to lift the Creek's woolen mantle. One swift blow rendered the Virginian senseless, followed by four clean strokes of a hunting knife. Skillfully disfiguring Turbin's head, Coosa clucked like a pheasant hen and his braves finished the grisly task as the *mico* went to lift Dominique into his arms and carry her swiftly to her horse. Then, pulling himself up, he rode with her into the protection of the night.

Later Dominique opened her eyes to Coosa's face illuminated by firelight. Whispering his name, she drew him down by the fringe of his jerkin, locking her arms behind his neck. "Coosa, Coosa." A roof of skins from which smoke rose to the stars was propped against some trees. The air smelled sweetly of burning hickory and apple, a fire hissing with life. Coosa rubbed her hands and feet, then removed her soaked clothes and boots. She lay still as deft fingers peeled off her wet stockings and opened her sopping habit, replacing the cold clothes with warm furs of soft beaver.

"You are safe here in my hunting lodge," Coosa said. " 'Tis newly built and not in the mountains of Tennessee, but prepared with you in mind."

"I'm so cold, Coosa!" Teeth chattering, she was ravaged by chills, a sudden pain cramping her neck and shoulders.

"You are hurt?" Coosa asked ruefully. She shook her head and tried to pull herself up, falling back into his arms as he pressed a kiss to the base of her neck and swept his lips upward over her face. "Coosa will make you well, Summer Eyes, care for you because you belong to him. You have belonged to him from the beginning."

Smiling, she looked at him in awe, wondering how a man who looked so frightening could be so kind. Did he have another side like other men she'd known, a side that might repulse her if she saw it? "You're in danger being with me, Coosa. Even now we could be observed by Alexandre's men."

Coosa thought her as charming as a child who spied a black cloud. "Perhaps." He flashed a grin. "We must lie low and pull the furs high. The night has many eyes."

"If you don't care about my husband's men, I do! If they found us together I would never see my daughter again!"

"We are alone, Summer Eyes. My braves watch the wood for danger. There is none." His smile was satisfying, but she knew the real danger lay in succumbing to him.

"I must go back, Coosa. Give me my clothes, please."

He reached for her clothes and tossed them to a far spot near the door where she could not reach.

"Why did you do that?"

Coosa's eyes twinkled in the flickering light and she shook her head. "Nay, we cannot!"

Pulling the robes of beaver over her head, she felt him lay down beside her and remove her furs. His lips parted hers and twisted artfully over them, his tongue playfully catching hers and sending chills all the way to her toes. "Pray let me go, Coosa."

"*Non*," came the sweet reply. He found the drawstring of her fragile chemise, praising his god for creating her for him, murmuring prayers of gratitude into her hair and trailing kisses from the loops of her gold earrings to her pounding heart. "Coosa will never let you go, Summer Eyes. There is no other world for you, no other life." His hand cupped her breast as if it were a flower and he tasted its sweetness with his tongue. "You must believe, Summer Eyes, you must believe."

" 'Tis madness you speak, Coosa. I cannot believe! I cannot!"

Frowning, he took the combs from her hair and untied its ribbons, releasing the thick golden bounty until it cascaded over her shoulders onto the lynx that carpeted the floor. In awe of her delicate beauty, he touched the white skin.

"Coosa will lead the way, Summer Eyes. Don't worry."

"Coosa," she sobbed, returning his kisses with fervor, their bodies now in harmony. The night was magic and took on a scarlet hue as they made love. "My love, my love," she moaned, falling into his arms and weeping with joy, the radiance of their love so beautiful she couldn't bear more. He held her close and she took him deep within and drew him into her arms until they were one, fulfilling the plan of their gods.

Later, Coosa's head lay on Dominique's breasts as she toyed with his hair, the scent of skins and burning wood creating a tranquility and peace she'd known only with the Creek. "Coosa, Coosa," she whispered, enjoying the sound of his name. "Do you sleep, my love?"

Pressing a tender kiss to the scar on her left breast, the *mico* studied it. "Why did you do this?"

The act now seemed beyond reason to her. Yet she tried to explain. "Because I believed my life empty, finished, hopeless. Now, because of you, my life is just beginning."

Coosa's face grew dark. "You must leave Alexandre, Domma-nique. With him you have half a life. With Coosa, your life will be whole. I accept you for who you are . . . your love of the woods . . . your riding . . ."

"Help me, my love. You must help me come to you!" Grasping his hair, she drew his face to hers, her forlorn expression hidden in the eclipse of his hair. "I cannot accomplish it alone. Alexandre is wise and set on keeping me at any cost."

Coosa's scowl was black. "We shall walk on Mother Earth together. If Alexandre won't release you, I will have to take you from him." He shrugged, rising. "Trees are endless in this land, mountains rising forever. Coosa will carry you to the farthest place, where white men do not go!"

"Alexandre has the means to find us, Coosa, the men to search us out. He's warned me and I know he'd stop at nothing to keep me. He'd follow us to the ends of the earth, if necessary."

"Let him come! Coosa Tustennuggee is no coward. The *mico* of the Lower Creeks would die gladly for you now!"

She saw a spark of the savage erupting in him, chilling her to the bone. "But I don't want you dead, Coosa! I don't want anyone dead, don't you see? I could not live with a murderer. You mustn't spill any man's blood because of me. Never!" She closed her eyes against the tears. "Dear God, I'd end it now, rather than live with the threat of you and Alexandre killing each other." She looked up into his face. " 'Tis hopeless, my love, don't you see?"

Pulling his obsidian knife from its sheath, Coosa growled back at her. "Hopeless? Where is your faith, woman? In the book your God inspired, King David had his woman's husband killed. Do you think Indians are different? It is not unusual for the wife of the murdered man to accept the murderer as her husband."

"Nay, you mustn't think such things!"

"Why not? If the wife doesn't accept her husband's murderer, the man would be permitted to prepare for his death. Coosa's execution would be made swift with arrows because he is *mico*."

"God!" she cried. " 'Tis madness, barbaric! How could I be happy if you were dead, Coosa? I'd die, too!" Wrapping him in her arms, she wept softly as he kissed her hair.

"Five tribes await word from my mouth, Summer Eyes. The mission I must carry out will be long but meaningful in the end. Pray wait for Coosa in Georgia and he will join you on the gray egg when the mountain blooms with yellow flowers." His mouth touched hers and her breasts grew hard beneath his touch. She knew nothing would stand in his way.

"My life is yours," she whispered, knowing she must spend the rest of her days without him. She would return to Racemont and never see him again.

"Summer Eyes." He fingered the gold loops in her ears,

caressing the base of her neck with his lips. "Perhaps you will be carrying my child when next we meet?" His grin was proud, his dark eyes dancing in the firelight. Pray God she hadn't conceived by him. Alexandre would kill her! Trembling with her thoughts, she knew she would be happy if she carried Coosa's babe. If she couldn't have a king, perhaps she could have a part of him. Tears stung her eyes and Coosa stroked her hair, pressing kisses to her breasts.

"Why do you cry? Coosa will not be cruel to you. I shall build you a lodge of cedars high on a mount so we may be close to the gods . . . a place where we can walk and talk together . . . where we can be together always." Her eyes never left his face, storing away its features for later reference. "I will care for you, Summer Eyes," he continued. "Feed and clothe you." He kissed her again. "We shall ride together and lie together and Coosa will give you all he possesses and more!"

Oh, how she wished to be part of him again, drawing him near and placing her fingers to his lips. "Pray say no more, Coosa. Bring me my horse and place me on it. I've been gone too long."

He heard a strain in her voice and saw languor in her eyes. "*Oui,* go back now to the big house and rest. Meet me on the morrow on the path, when the moon takes it place above the mulberry trees."

Dominique did not see Coosa again after that. Every breath was a painful reminder of the Creek, his face everywhere, even in her sleep! Longing for the *mico*'s touch, she dreamed of him day and night, whispered his name, cried out in her sleep for him. In her misery, she thought he tapped at her window; she jumped at the sound of a bird, the whispering wind, the howl of the wolf. Unable to bear the thought of going on without Coosa, she wished to God that she carried his child.

The days passed slowly and she kept to her room. It was nearly a fortnight later when Elton Winburn and Jenny arrived from Pennsylvania.

"You don't look well, my girl. Are you with child?"

Dominique heard her father but made no reply. She pulled back the heavy winter drapes in the library of Jefferson's house, wondering if Coosa still camped in the wood. It was the first night of her father's arrival and Jenny had retired early, exhausted from the long trip from Philadelphia. Elton stood behind his daughter and thought about her severe head injury years before, wondering if she still suffered its ill effects.

" 'Tis possible. I'm a married woman, you know."

"Aye, you are, but take care. You shouldn't become pregnant so soon after you miscarried." Smiling warmly, the father took his daughter's hand in his. "You're so young, my girl. There's time for children." They walked to the settee and sat down before a silver tray that held steaming chocolate and biscuits. "Tell me, is Alexandre good to you?"

Dominique heard Coosa telling her he'd be good to her and she smiled. "My husband gives me everything, father." She patted his hand and went to stand alone before the fire.

"What is everything, Nikki? Pray tell this old man."

"Horses and hounds, fine jewels, great houses, clothes fit for a queen." She shrugged. "I'm tired, father. I want to sleep."

"Ruthe tells me you sleep overmuch. It sounds like—"

"What, father?"

"Melancholia, my dear. Now, I want to know what's troubling you, my daughter." His voice was kind and she couldn't look at him as she leaned against the mantel, trying not to weep. "Nikki, my girl, what is it?" Going to her, he took her in his arms and listened to her quiet sobbing. "Is it Alexandre? I can't believe it is, but then I'm just a stupid old man. Your husband's human, so he's capable of anything, isn't he?" He talked to himself and asked questions, his tone concerned. "Has he hurt you, mistreated you, manhandled you? Dear God, girl, you can trust me, you're my blood and you can't do wrong in my eyes. What is it? Tell me before I . . ." His voice broke and he found himself near tears, unable to face his daughter's sullenness. They went and sat together on the settee, Dominique's head in her father's lap.

" 'Tis all so complicated, father. You could never understand." Her tears soaked into the black wool of his breeches as she stared at the silver tea service.

"Try me, dammit. Aye, I'm old, but a man as well as your father. I've seen life at its filthy worst, my girl, most of it deadly painful, rotten, and hopeless." He wiped her eyes with his big white linen handkerchief. "Don't look at me that way, daughter. I'm not too slow of wit or narrow of mind to understand life." He smiled, pulling her close and thinking she was as great a beauty as he remembered.

" 'Tis all so strange, father. Like a horrible dream." She watched the firelight paint images on the silver teapot, seeing Jules Cocteau on her wedding night and reliving the agony of the birth of the child that followed, the long trek to Georgia and the first time she'd seen Coosa Tustennugge on the trace. She'd told her father everything by the time the dawn pressed boldly against the night sky. Elton jumped to his feet and lit a fresh candle.

"Bastard, dirty, filthy guttersnipe! And to think I trusted him!" Dominique trembled at her father's language, the curses hurled beneath his breath as she curled into the hard sofa. The fire had been reduced to ashes and the house was cold.

"Please, father, don't blame Coosa. He's good like you, God-fearing and kind."

Elton spat into the ashes. "I curse the beast who took you against your will!" he growled. "If I could catch Jules Cocteau, I'd see him swing from the tallest tree!" Elton's face was near purple and his eyes were filled with rage. "To think he sired that cherub of a child! My precious granddaughter!"

"I'm sorry I told you," Dominique wailed. " 'Tis too much for you to bear." She embraced the settee and wept quietly into it.

"My dearest daughter. Thank God you're alive to tell the tale! I raised you up to be loved and cherished, not manhandled by a parasite! Had I once suspected such a thing I'd have locked you in your room and thrown away the key!" Inflamed with anger over his daughter's abuse, the elderly physician finally understood how one man could kill another and never feel remorse. "And to think the demon is still loose! No wonder poor Alexandre is not right. I for one would have gone mad by now!" Dominique couldn't stop sobbing and Elton laid his head on hers. "The hour is late and I'm so weary now I fear my brain's incapable of reason. But I do know this much. You must never see the Indian again."

Dominique sobbed even more.

"God will forgive you for your sins and time is with you. You must salvage your marriage, Nikki. Marriage is sacred, and none is without its problems. If you want it to work, it will, 'tis that simple! In the meantime, should you find yourself with child, you must convince Alexandre it's his. With the Indian's bloodlines, 'tis entirely conceivable you could get away with it. Lastly, you can always come home to me. There is still Winwood.''

The silence engulfed them both.

16

Thomas Jefferson and his daughter, Martha Jefferson Randolph, arrived at last from Washington and Charlottesville together with Anthony Adams, the President's social secretary and Dominique's cousin Jenny's betrothed. Monticello hummed with preparations for the wedding.

Time flowed like a river and Dominique saw the moon rise and hang suspended in a cold winter's sky, a constant reminder of her beloved Coosa. Pray God he didn't wait for her . . . didn't hate her too much. In her loneliness for Coosa, Dominique rode every horse in Monticello's stables, rising early every morning and riding until noon, or until she could endure the cold no longer. When she wasn't riding she would sleep, taking the sedatives her father had prescribed for her. On the eve of the wedding Jenny came to her cousin's bedchamber and Dominique reluctantly got out of bed to let the bride-to-be in.

"Forgive me, Jenny, I was asleep. Father gave me sleeping powders." Dominique crossed the room shakily, nearly collapsing before she reached her bed.

"How thin you are," Jenny remarked. "We've not seen one another in over four years and we've scarcely talked because you're always riding or sleeping. Tell me, Nikki dear, what's wrong?" Jenny was fair and fresh, young and alive with the excitement of marrying for the first time. She wore her hair in braided loops, her face scrubbed clean until it shone, her dress of pink silk and lace framing her quiet beauty.

" 'Tis the air here, cousin. I can't seem to get enough sleep."

"We're all worried about you. Pray tell me true, are you with child?"

Dominique knew she didn't carry Alexandre's child. But if she was pregnant by Coosa, now would be the time to speak of it. " 'Tis entirely possible. I've not felt well in weeks. My husband wants another son."

"Then I'm happy for you, dearest, and that explains why you spend so much time abed. Pray you feel well enough to join us tonight—the last night before I become Mrs. Anthony Adams and leave for Charleston." Dominique was about to beg off when Jenny said, "Mr. Drummond has just arrived and expresses a keen desire to meet you. And you haven't spoken two sentences to my Anthony. He thinks you don't approve of him."

Dominique observed a pout on her cousin's lips, her eyes glinting in the candlelight. "For your betrothed I shall rise and dress, Jenny, dear. But you must find Ruthe and send her to me at once. I fear I can't handle all this hair alone."

" 'Tis no wonder," Jenny fussed. "Mrs. Randolph says you haven't eaten enough to keep a parrot alive and all this sleeping is bound to make you weak. I want you to come downstairs so I can show you off, but don't get up if you think you'll be too ill to attend the wedding service on the morrow." Whirling about the room, Jenny's full skirts were a blur of pink before Dominique's eyes.

"Do you love Anthony, Jenny?"

Standing like a ballerina, Jenny held her arms about her neck and closed her eyes. "Very much indeed. Anthony's very sweet and terribly clever."

Dominique recalled her own wedding day, the fear she'd felt, the chilling night that followed. "Pray stay in love, dearest Jenny. Stay in love evermore." A tear broke from her lashes, trailing down her cheek.

."You're crying, dear." Jenny went to touch her cousin's forehead with her palm. "You feel feverish to me. Has your father looked in on you recently?"

Dominique smiled. "Father looks in on me regularly." In

truth, her head ached and chills swept over her body, every bone aching as if she'd been beaten with a hammer. " 'Tis this mountain clime, so cold and damp." She pushed herself off the bed gently. "Go now and be with your love every second you can. I'll dress and come downstairs presently."

"Perhaps you shouldn't, Nikki. I'm worried about you. I'd rather you stayed in bed until morning. 'Tis dreadfully important to me for you to stand by my side when I take my vows!"

Dominique felt the dull throb of pain in her neck and shoulders. "I'm fine. Send Ruthe to me, please."

"Right away, cousin."

When Jenny left, Dominique took her time with her bath, not dressing until she heard the sound of music downstairs. Ruthe had pulled her mistress's hair back into a cascade of long curls and caught them atop her head with bows of rich brown velvet. She helped Dominique into a tight-fitting gown of hushed peach satin with a deep-cut square neckline sewn with golden threads and draped with a capelet of brown squirrel.

"You look pale to me, mistress. Perhaps some rouge?"

Dominique shook her head and it hurt; she was unable to rid herself of the chills that racked her body and found it difficult to stand when her father came into her room.

"Your cousin was correct, dearest." Elton's tone was concerned. He had just received a distressing report from Jenny and Mrs. Randolph about his daughter's health. "You're feverish, truly."

"Because I bathed in heated water before the fire, father. You would be hot, too."

Elton wasn't satisfied and stood studying his daughter, observing her finery. "You look like a fairy-tale princess, my beautiful girl, but then you always did." Smiling, he took her arm and walked with her to the door. "Take care you don't outshine the bride."

The parlor was an elegant room in the form of a semioctagon, separated from the great hall by glass doors. Dominique held tightly to her father's arm and stepped lightly across the cherry parquet bordered in beechwood. Martha Jefferson Randolph was busy playing her piano when all eyes turned and fell on the stately blond beauty from Georgia. When the music stopped, a man in the latest evening dress strode across the room. His frilled shirt and neck-cloth of white lawn framed a face that Dominique felt an instant aversion to.

"Mrs. Chastain, Alexandre's wife, 'tis indeed my pleasure to meet you at last." The tall Englishman was dressed in sapphire blue and ivory, his coppery hair tied back to expose side whiskers of a brighter hue. "Maxwell Drummond of Athens and Washington at your service, ma'am." Dominique extended her hand.

Dominique drew back her hand as Drummond's lips brushed lightly against her fingers, and she wiped her hand hard on her gown's skirts when he looked up. This was Alexandre's friend and patient from Athens, the man Alexandre had hired to *watch* her. Taking her father's arm, she moved past Drummond to the safety of a comfortable chair. If she swooned, the floor wouldn't be so far down. The music began again and all was hushed for the musicale. The housekeeper playing the harp was accompanied by a string quartet of unusual accomplishment. When the music was over, President Jefferson joined them, entering into a conversation with Elton about the composer. Drummond strolled across the room to stand by Dominique, staring for a while, then bending down to speak.

"Pray forgive me for staring, my dear lady, 'tis just that I've rarely seen a woman of such utter perfection before. I find myself dazed from simply looking."

Saying nothing, she stood to leave, then faltered and walked slowly to the windows to gaze up at the rising moon.

"Might I bring you something, ma'am? A drink of wine perhaps? We'll be spending time together from now on. I'm your guardian while you're at Monticello, did you know? I regret I wasn't here when you arrived, but politics took me to Washington first. Had I known you were here, I'd have returned sooner. Alexandre's told me much about you. I wonder if you'd do me the honor of riding with me before breakfast? I'll see to it no one follows us."

It was as if Drummond didn't exist then, for Dominique hadn't heard a word. Something had drawn her eyes to the gilt clock on the mantel as it chimed eight times, filling her ears with the pleasant sound. Viewing the room through two large French pier mirrors, she watched Jenny arrange a score on the music stand for Mrs. Randolph, the fire burning brightly behind a Hepplewhite screen. Drummond was still talking, but she didn't hear him. The lanterns in the room had dimmed, the candles fighting wildly for their lives. A cold draft swept across her upper arms and then she saw in the mirrors the doors open wide. Dear God, could it be?

A splendid man dressed in native and European attire stood between the doors, in Dominique's eyes the most vital and magnificent man the Creator had ever formed. Coosa Tustennuggee's magnetism drew her, the red plumage of his headdress a signal between them on the frosted air. His golden crown signifying his nobility, the King of the Creeks was no less than spectacular as he entered the parlor in bleached doeskins and milk-white stock that highlighted the dark cast of his skin, an ebony cape lined in peacock feathers swirling around him like a sea of emerald eyes.

"Coosa, my friend!" President Jefferson strode across the room and shook Coosa's hand. "Delighted you could come, *mico*. Look at you! You must meet my guests."

Coosa's eyes searched the room quickly, coming to rest on the only face he wished to see, his sharp gaze an invisible ray of heat that scorched Dominique's flesh. The string quartet took up playing, a mixture of brisk stiff notes no one seemed to hear. Dominique heard the voice of Coosa, its melodiousness bringing her to attention, her chest aching as her shaking hands came to her mouth and she coughed.

"Are you ill, ma'am?" Drummond held her arm and she looked at him. "You gave me a fright just then. What's wrong? Did the red devil frighten you?"

Had Drummond said something? Dominique's head filled with a high-pitched whir like the howling of the wind, making her uncertain of where she was. She coughed again, losing her balance and nearly falling into Drummond's arms.

"Dear lady, we'd best get you to your chambers at once!"

"Nay, pray help me to a chair, sir."

Coosa watched from across the room with sharpened sight, observing Drummond and his every move. The lanterns glowed, the light setting the Creek apart from everyone else, his proud aplomb commanding all eyes to look at his natural splendor. A crowd gathered around, the great pier mirrors reflecting the intricate beadwork on his white doeskins. He spoke hastily with the President about a mission, and bargained generously for the Andalusian stallion. Drummond watched, too, his keen hearing uncovering some secret plan between the Creek *mico* and the President that included Alexandre Chastain's wife. Jefferson nodded approvingly. "You wish to speak to the lady now?" Coosa made no reply, his expression one of suppressed longing. Jefferson set his chin, glancing knowingly at Dominique, and excused himself to join his other guests. Drummond came to attention, preparing himself for the *mico* who strode majestically toward them. Coosa bowed low before Dominique, his hand over his heart.

"Lady of the hounds."

"The lady is not well, chief. I suggest you go back to your people." Drummond's tone was threatening, but Dominique heard nothing. Sitting in quiet reverence, her chest throbbed with a pain that wouldn't cease and her green eyes were gray with fever. "Must I say it again, chief? You're not welcome here."

A muscle became rigid high on Coosa's cheek, his brows directing a black glare at Drummond. Sinking to the parquet floor on bended knee, the King of the Lower Creeks knelt before the woman he adored. "Summer Eyes, Coosa has come for you, to take you away." He took her hot hand in his and drew its fingers to his lips, speaking gravely. "The Englishman speaks truth, you're not well."

Attempting to smile, yet unwilling to change her mind about him, Dominique's arms ached for the Creek king's arms to encircle her, every fiber of her tortured body burning from a heightening fever. "How splendid you look, Coosa." She tried to sound bright, realizing it pained her to breathe. "Pray help me to the terrace."

Coosa looked inquisitively at Drummond.

"The lady is ill. Her husband put her in my charge and I say you'll leave this house at once."

Dominique shook her head, anxious to get Coosa outside. "Pray help me to the door, Coosa, I'm in need of air." Giving Drummond a black look, Coosa helped his love across the room, her hand clutching his steady and able arm. Drummond followed several paces behind and Elton met them in the entrance hall, barring the way to the outside.

"Doctor Winburn, sir, the lady's father." Elton stepped back, overwhelmed by the Creek's height, costume, and exceptional looks, Coosa's face alone overpowering, something inside the doctor rebelling against the difference between them.

"Coosa Tustennuggee, your servant, sir." Coosa bowed and

flashed a smile, gazing down at Dominique and squeezing her hand, his glittering midnight eyes holding hers.

"Pray let me speak to Coosa alone," Dominique said softly. "I can breathe better outdoors." Elton frowned and she smiled at him. "Please, father, I'm overheated from the closeness of the parlor and the excitement of the festivities." She attempted a reassuring look. "I'm fine, now that Coosa is here." Her unmitigated charm won them all when she smiled. "Pray fetch my cape, Mr. Drummond."

"Your wish is my command, dear lady." Drummond glared at Coosa, doing as his client's wife bid.

"Your daughter is more precious to me than anything on earth, doctor." Coosa's expression was completely earnest. "I'd have you know that now." The Creek held out his heavy hand and Elton shook it, studying the tall Indian he believed to be sincere and wishing to God he could do something to stop his daughter.

"And to me, chief. Nikki's my only child and in her husband's absence I must remind you she's valued highly by all who love her."

Coosa's face was staid. "A wise man would perceive so, doctor. Your message is clear."

Drummond returned with the capelet and laid it over Dominique's shoulders, gazing up at the Creek and scrutinizing Coosa's garb: his pale leggings and breeches hugged long muscular legs, the European cut of his jacket and the watered silk of his French shirt were chained with gold and hung with silver gorgets. So this was the King of the Creeks, the *mico* to red men in the South, the half-breed savage Alexandre considered a threat! What in blazes was the red bastard doing in Virginia? A rendezvous with Alexandre's wife, perhaps? Drummond harbored an old hatred for Indians that far exceeded Alexandre's hatred for Jules Cocteau. Coosa would now feel the heat of that hate.

The frosty night air made Dominique's breathing less labored and she held tight to Coosa's arm while he fastened the frogs of her capelet, pulling the furry hood about her face. Coosa's eyes were sad, his pain seeming to seep into her bones with the icy wind as he whispered his name for her. "Summer Eyes." The words were a caress as he encircled her waist and guided her on the walk that overlooked the snow-clad valley below. The mulberry trees creaked and Dominique gasped for breath, her hand tugging at Coosa's sleeve.

"Don't walk so fast, Coosa, I can't keep up."

"I'll carry you." Sweeping her up into his arms, he held her masterfully, cupping her face in his hand and looking possessively at her. "Coosa watched the white moon disappear from the sky and the flaming sun take its place and fall again, watched another cold moon rise, another and another. Still my lady did not come." His voice was pitiful yet pointed, cutting to the very core of her. She buried her face in the delicate plush of his doeskin jacket, dampening his white stock with tears and catching her breath as she wound her arms about his neck.

"I, too, watched the moon rise, seeing the one who bears its name and dying in its light for want of him. I love you, Coosa. I fear I shall die without you, but we must part." Her tears fell and he covered her trembling lips with his, hiding his face in her hair and holding her in a wild embrace as his stride increased.

"Why didn't you come to me?"

"Because there is no life in this world for us," she choked. "Our sins are many . . . 'tis ended now."

"*Non!* Coosa's love grows stronger with each rising moon! We cannot change our calling!" His voice broke. "I cannot live unless I can have your love! Return love!" He held her close, weeping and walking as she looked up into the sky and sensed her death. The wind swirled around them, snow dusting her hair and chilling her flesh. She wondered if she'd ever be warm again, growing colder and colder with each step he took. She'd been unworthy of the Creek king, her fight for their happiness now finished.

"Leave me this night, my love," she entreated. "Go on your mission and forget we ever met." The bows slipped from her hair, her curls falling limply across his chest, like wheat in the wind.

"I'll never leave you! We belong together! You belong to me!" His gaze was fixed on the vast darkened whiteness of the land, sharp as an eagle's as he searched the shadows. "I'm taking you away with me now. We'll ride to the high country when you're stronger, to the land where the Cherokee and wolf roam free. There you'll be Coosa's woman and be united with him evermore."

"Nay!" she whispered.

"*Oui*! Be still now, you no longer have a say in it. We ride into the night."

"I cannot!" she cried. "God knows I want to, but I cannot! If you love me you'll take me back . . . please." Her tears came, then she caught the sounds of horses. Four Creek horseman clad in long fur robes armed with bows and arrows rode out of the wood leading two horses, one purest white like the snowy landscape, the other piebald and prancing. Both horses were draped in bright blankets, heads plumed in red feathers, saddled and bridled in the silver trappings of the Spanish. Dominique lifted her head and eyed the Creek braves, knowing well she could never withstand a fierce night ride.

"I cannot, Coosa. Drummond and his men will follow us!"

Coosa smiled contemptuously, calling her his beloved woman. "You worry needlessly, Summer Eyes. You must trust Coosa." He was about to lift her onto the Andalusian's saddle when the doors of Monticello opened and Jefferson himself rushed out, Doctor Winburn at his side, Drummond and Anthony Adams behind him. Drummond was armed and Dominique's blood cooled; she turned breathless as the dark braves drew. arrows from their beaded quivers and notched them to their bows.

"Coosa, my friend!" Jefferson ran ahead of the other men. "My horse is yours as agreed, great chief of the Creeks, but don't take the woman. She's not well." Jefferson approached with his hand outstretched and spoke in a conciliatory way. "You're not thinking, mighty *mico*! Pray hear me out now and don't do this thing."

"This doesn't concern you, Thomas. Leave us!" Coosa held Dominique to his chest protectively, her arms wrapped about his powerful neck, her face against his. Jefferson moved slowly, the heavy snowfall a white sheet between them.

"You're wrong, Coosa Tustennuggee. The lady is my guest and under my protection so long as she's on my land. Mrs. Chastain is very much my concern and I intend to see that she doesn't leave here this night."

"There's no use talking to him, sir! He's not a man! He hasn't the brains of a dog!" Drummond pushed forward, leveling two flintlocks at the Creek's legs. Coosa's nostrils flared as he lowered Dominique to the snowy earth, pushing her behind him. "Take the woman and I'll spill your father's black blood where you stand, heathen! I vow it!" Drummond shouted to the sky. Dominique's eyes filled with terror, and she managed to pull herself up by Coosa's jacket fringe to run between the men.

"Kill Coosa and kill me, too!" she cried. Her hood fell back, her golden hair quickly covered with snow. "Don't let them do this, father . . . please . . . please . . ." No sooner had her voice died than she slumped to the ground. Coosa went to her, Elton plowing through the snow before Drummond's pistols as the Creek horsemen spread out in an arc around them.

"My girl's hot with fever, Coosa. She's sick and she'll die if we don't get her inside! Help her, man, the poor woman can't speak for herself!" Weighing the situation quickly, Coosa cautiously lifted Dominique into his arms, his heart heavy. Elton saw the effect of his words and kept talking. "You don't want her to die on your account, do you? It would be no credit to you or the Creek people if she did. Her husband and I would hunt you down and see you punished for her murder!" Elton edged his way toward the Creek and reached out for Dominique's hand. "Feel her skin, man! She's burning up even in this weather! 'Tis vital we get her to bed! If we don't do something quickly she'll die! Are you so blinded by passion that you can't see that?"

Coosa touched Dominique's cheek and she opened her eyes as he removed a golden loop from her ear and pressed it into his hand.

"Send this to me and I shall come to meet you on the gray egg." Coosa closed his fingers over the cold metal and Drummond lowered his flintlocks, having seen and heard what had passed between the lovers.

"I'll not leave until you say she's past danger, father." Anthony Adams and Drummond took Dominique from the Creek and hurried through the snow to the house as Coosa ran to his horse. The *mico* took two heavy chunks of gold from his saddlebags and gave them to Elton.

"For her care, father."

Elton looked at the weighty gold, his mouth agape. "I can't take this from you, Coosa. The girl's my daughter. Besides, we have no need of gold."

Coosa pushed the gold into Elton's hands. "Your daughter was born to ride at my side, doctor. The gold is for Dom-ma-nique's keeping until that time comes."

Before Elton could protest, the Indian ran to his waiting companions and mounted his piebald stallion, riding into the night, snow covering his tracks so completely the doctor was left to wonder if the Indians had ever truly been there.

Jenny Winburn was married quietly to Anthony Adams on Christmas day. Dominique Chastain took no part in the ceremony. Her condition had worsened during the night and the young marrieds stayed at Monticello to be near in her time of need.

"I should've shot the red bastard when I had the chance!" Drummond's face twisted into an ugly mask as he stood in the passageway outside Dominique's bedchamber.

"Why blame the Creek for my daughter's illness, sir? She was feverish before he came here." Elton tried to appease the man Alexandre had chosen to guard his daughter, but it was no easy task. Drummond paced back and forth in the south passage of the second floor.

"Quite a coincidence, wouldn't you agree, doctor? Your daughter and the Indian here at Monticello together."

"What do you mean, sir?" Elton's tone was angry.

"I mean your son-in-law hired me to see that his wife had no visitors while she was in Virginia. 'Tis true Alexandre was thinking of Jules Cocteau, but he was aware of the Creek's attraction to Mrs. Chastain as well."

"Are you insinuating that my daughter and Coosa are lovers, sir?"

"You saw them. She gave him her earring."

"Aye, I saw. 'Twas an act of friendship and nothing more. The man's her husband's nephew."

"A man would have to be blind not to see the look the heathen gave her. There's more to this than you think, doctor."

"You're making a mountain out of a molehill, Drummond."

"Perhaps. But if your daughter dies, I'll see the Indian suffers for it!" Dominique moaned inside her room and Drummond's brow creased in a frown as he clenched his fists. "God's blood, can't you do something for her?"

"We're doing everything humanly possible. Pneumonia is a deadly disease. Thank the Lord she's young and in good health, otherwise . . ."

"But the windows in her room are open! 'Tis madness if you ask me!"

"She needs fresh air, sir. The fire's lit and she's bundled up. I'm a physician and I know what I'm doing. Calm down. She's my flesh and blood. Don't you think I'll do my best for her?"

Drummond wanted to shout at the elderly physician, certain he would lie to protect his beloved daughter. He bent low to look out the low-set windows to see if the Creek *mico* still kept his lonely vigil outside. The snow hid the trees, but he could see the Indians on their horses, all of them still there.

"He's still out there, the red devil. Sitting atop his fancy horse like a bloody statue. If he doesn't go away soon, I'm going out there and make certain he leaves!" Drummond cursed beneath his breath, leaving the window to pace the floor.

Elton went to have a look at the Indians, warming the frosted panes with the palm of his hand. "Coosa's her friend, I tell you. He wants to make certain my daughter's out of danger before he leaves for the West."

"Well, he's getting on my nerves and I don't like it."

"The man has feelings like you and me. He loves her in his own way."

Drummond sneered. "Rubbish! What does a red savage know of love? 'Tis an English word and no red man understands it. Indians know nothing but murder and killing. Devils, every one!" Returning to the window, Drummond rested his elbows on the sill and watched Coosa.

"Coosa's not like other Indians—my daughter says he's kind and good. No savage."

"Ha!" Drummond laughed. "He's a savage all right. Look at him. He's been sitting out there in the same spot for two days and he hasn't frozen to death yet. Tell me what white man could endure such weather?"

Drummond was right. Coosa Tustennuggee didn't feel the cold bite of the central Virginia winter. The *mico* of the Lower Creeks hadn't taken his eyes off the window in which a single candle burned. He whispered prayers for Dom-ma-nique, for the woman his heart beat for. If his beloved woman died, he would die. For death was a natural thing to Indians. In death they would find one another and walk in the elevations with their gods. In death they would listen to the four winds and sit in the corridors of the thunder and lightning. In death they would watch the noble eagle as it wheeled over the gray egg. In death they would ride astride winged steeds and gallop over the white clouds to view the setting sun . . . the rising moon.

Ah, but Coosa enjoyed the feel of the red clay beneath his feet too much, enjoyed the sand in his moccasins. His heart pounded like thunder over the mountains as he dreamed of the future. Dom-ma-nique would live and they would be reunited on the gray egg in Georgia. He would show her the rainbow that rose over the rock mountain after a storm and he would ride with her to the hills where great packs of elk, deer, and bison grazed in the Smokies. Together they would lie in a field of yellow daisies, together they would be joined when the leaves fell from the trees. Smiling with his thoughts, he imagined Dom-ma-nique's mouth pressed to his, hearing the gentle rain on the roof of his lodge while they slept on rich furs.

"She will not die!" Coosa cried out in Creek, raising a blood-curdling cry that set the hounds in the kennels howling. The Creek king's braves moved at once to his side. "Coosa Tustennuggee wills the woman to live!" he yelled. He would give her his strength and send it on wings of love and she would know she must live for him!

The new year brought snow that engulfed Monticello, wrapping the house in a cocoon of white enveloping its walks and terraces, its pavilions and gardens. The icy wind blew like an unseen demon, howling victoriously and dominating the land, even the graveyard and its crosses of stone. Fires groaned in the intense arctic cold, warm gray smoke curling from four chimneys as if the house wished all the world to know there was still life inside.

Thomas Jefferson left Monticello to return to the young nation's capital, leaving the ailing Dominique in the care of her able father. Chills continued to rack the young woman's body and a hard dry cough, high fever, and phlegm in the lungs made it harder and harder for her to breathe.

"It has been ten days, doctor, and your daughter's no better in my eyes." Drummond crashed a fist against the wall outside Dominique's room, burning with the uncertainty of his rich client's wife's life.

"She'll soon reach the crisis, sir. Pray what did Alexandre say in his letter to you?" Elton's face was prematurely wrinkled and drawn, the pressure of his girl's condition and the exhaustion of constant care taking its toll. Drummond pulled a folded letter from his jacket, fingering it nervously.

"Alexandre knows nothing of her illness, of course. He wants her home as quickly as possible. Read it yourself."

Elton sank despondently into a chair outside his daughter's bedchamber and mopped his brow. The letter was dated nearly a month before and he read between its lines. "Aye, he wants her back now. The fool realizes his mistake in sending her away." He rubbed his eyes with a fist and read on. "He's purchased a new mare for her, another Arab." Elton looked up from the written word, glancing out the window to see a vision of Dominique atop El 'Ramir the day he gave the Arab to her. "She's quite a horsewoman, did you know?"

"I've heard, doctor." Drummond crumpled Alexandre's letter in his fist. If only he were not employed by Chastain . . . if only he and the good doctor had never met. A male cardinal flew to the glass window and chirped urgently.

"The poor bird seems to have lost his mate, Mr. Drummond. I believe my son-in-law will find himself in a similar position soon." Elton's eye caught Drummond's and held. "And you, sir, what will you do now? Jules Cocteau seems to have disappeared. The madman could be on the island of Martinique by now."

"Nothing has changed, doctor. Although, I must admit, the Creek was a surprise. 'Tis quite a turn of events. One even Alexandre didn't expect, I'd wager."

"I'm sorry for Alexandre, truly I am. In truth my daughter has her heart set on that Creek king out there in the cold. You may as well know it and accept it as I have."

Drummond gritted his teeth and rubbed his red sideburns with his fingers. "I'd see the heathen dead first. I speak for myself and not Alexandre now."

"In heaven's name why, sir? What has the Indian done to you?" Elton pressed a forefinger hard against pursed lips.

"He's trying to take your daughter for himself, doctor, isn't that enough? Where's your sense of decency? The man's a bloody half-breed!"

"Your reasoning's off, sir. Are you as feverish as my girl in there? What we need in this world is brotherly love and understanding, not ignorance and bigotry!"

Drummond regained his composure, watching the gentle snowfall outside the window and picturing the fair-haired beauty in her peach satin gown and fur capelet, snowflakes caught in the gold threads of her hair, his mind's eye mischieviously granting him a view of Dominique with Coosa. The thought made him seethe!

"The Creek's days are numbered! I, and others like me, won't stand by and allow an Indian to bed a white woman! Heathens like Coosa Tustennuggee are standing in the way of our great country's progress and they must be done away with! Indian territories offer untold prosperity for all of us. Can't you see it, doctor? This land of ours free of every color of man but white! There's conflict ahead, I'll not deny it, but there's no place for savages in our Christian world."

Elton's stomach turned sour, conflicting emotions warring within him. "I wouldn't want to live in that world, sir! Now, if you'll excuse me, I have to go back to my patient."

Drummond thought on the long carriage ride back to Richmond, the long sea voyage alone with Dominique, the starry nights with no Indians about. He smiled confidently. "You don't know me, doctor. When you do, you'll learn I don't back down from any man. On the trip back to Georgia, I plan to talk some sense into your daughter. In time she'll forget about the heathen. Then, after her divorce, who knows what the new year will bring?" Drummond shrugged, smiling as he thought of the colonists who'd kill a red man for a single piece of gold, even less.

By then, Elton had decided he preferred the half-breed savage, with all his feathers and gold, to the well-bred English barrister his son-in-law called friend.

The hours that followed proved to be the worst for Dominique, the night crucial. It was early evening when Ruthe stood back from the white muslin–draped bed and shook her head.

"She's no better, doctor. My mistress can't last the night if she can't get her breath."

Elton sent the servant out of the room with instructions to keep everyone in the house downstairs. Slipping his hand gently behind his daughter's neck, he raised her head slightly, speaking firmly. "Nikki, you must breathe!"

Dominique made no move, her face pale as the fine snow pelting the windowpanes relentlessly and settling into their corners. The fever had worsened and the doctor stuffed pillows beneath her back, quickly checking her vital signs. Finding no heartbeat, the elder doctor panicked, calling on God for help. Ruthe came into the room and Elton demanded her immediate assistance. "Help me get her to the window, woman! Hurry!" Ruthe quickly helped the doctor lift her mistress from the bed, stepping back in horror when she saw how terrible the patient looked.

"Dear God, she's dead!" Ruthe wailed, hugging herself and breaking into sobs and screams.

"Fetch me the Creek, damn you!"

Drummond came running and was shocked by what he saw. "Holy Jesus, she's dead!"

"She's not dead, but she will be, dammit. Fetch me the Creek and be quick about it!"

Wasting no time with the woman who meant money in his pocket only if she was returned to Alexandre Chastain in one piece, Drummond flew down the stairs to the entrance hall, sighting the Indian's horse outside the door. Coosa sat motionless atop his piebald, his hair and doeskins covered in white like some ancient of ancients, the saddled Andalusian at his side. Drummond thought it a lowly task calling on the Creek for help, swallowing his pride before he spoke. "You, there, Creek! The doctor wants you now!"

Galloping his horse to where Drummond stood in the doorway, Coosa dismounted in one leap, his ebony cape a threatening cloud behind him as he broke through the door and ran up the stairs, bounding them by fours and reaching the second floor. Ruthe stood huddled in the passageway weeping, wailing louder when she saw the Creek. Coosa's heart fell like a great stone over a grave as he reached his love's door and gasped, grasping the door frame with both hands in a surge of weakness, his face aghast with disbelief.

"Breathe!" Elton held his daughter's face in the open window, her body limp as the drapes beside her. Fine snow blew against her hot cheeks and the windowsill. "Breathe, Nikki!" Elton shouted despondently, falling on his knees with her, exhausted and sobbing miserably. The doctor saw Coosa and sobbed pathetically. "She's gone, Coosa. Our Nikki's gone."

Coosa's composure snapped and he rushed to the window to snatch Dominique into his arms, crushing her to his chest and whispering deeply from the depths of his throat in Creek. "Coosa is here, Summer Eyes!" He called her beloved woman and cried fervently. "You will not die!" His lips pressed against her lids and temples, his ear brushing across her mouth. Then he tore her gown loose, searching for the beat of her heart.

"Do you hear it?" Elton said, coming to his feet. "Tell me, for I cannot!" Grabbing hold of the Indian's arm, Elton tightened his viselike grip. "Tell me, damn you!"

Coosa wasted no time with a reply, breathing air into Dominique's lungs for what seemed an eternity, cradling her in his arms and pledging his undying love and devotion, his face ashen and fear-ridden. Then her chest rose. Dominique gasped for breath and Coosa continued breathing air into her lungs, forcing her to fight for life, giving her his strength and his love.

"Coosa," she breathed, regaining color and opening her eyes to see the man she loved. "Rising Moon." The Creek's name was only a murmur, but enough to make the mighty *mico* weep, his tears of joy sinking into the tangled mass of his beloved's hair.

It would be a fortnight before Coosa Tustennuggee would descend the little mountain called Monticello on his way north. The Creek king would spend most of every day alone with Dominique, much to Drummond's displeasure. At times the Indian simply sat on the floor and watched Dominique while she slept. Other times he'd sit holding her hand, neither of them saying a word. Elton knew the Indian was the best medicine he could give his convalescing daughter and he welcomed the Creek with all the affection of a loving father, believing the tall dark man from the South had in truth saved his girl's life, wishing to God he could tell Coosa so. Slowly, but surely, Dominique regained her strength and soon she lay gazing into the bronzed Creek's eyes, musing on the irony of their situation. There was a red savage in her bedchamber! She laughed, having been warned by her father that Drummond didn't like the Creek, yet content that the young man she loved was no illiterate red man, but a well-bred gentleman who kissed a lady's hand in the European style and spoke many tongues.

Poor Elton understood none of it, that story so painfully unfolded on his arrival of how his daughter had been ravaged and nearly killed by a man still loose and unpunished, and now his daughter in love with a Creek king. Why, in God's name, had the young doctor he'd loved as a son changed so? And which man had sired his grandchild, Desiree? Why did men stand around like a pack of dogs waiting to get to his girl? Dear Nikki had been cursed with beauty, the elderly physician surmised. He'd watched the buckskin-clad Indian stride into her bedchamber with a polished Spanish guitar in one hand and observed the profound joy spilling from his daughter's sea-green eyes at the sight of him, laughter filling the house when the two were together. Who was he to say if the Creek was right for her? Who, in truth, knew why God had put men on earth with different colors of skin? His girl needed someone strong and masterful and wise . . . a man who would tame and gentle her both. Frowning deeply at the mysteries of the world, Elton scratched his gray whiskers and shook his head. But the chief of a tribe of southern red men for a son-in-law? Holy God, how the world had changed!

" 'Tis a gift I shall treasure forever, Coosa." Dominique smiled, stroking the satin-smooth wood of the guitar inlaid with gold and silver, her face radiant. "How did you come by it?"

Coosa admired the upturned mouth of the woman who lay propped up in her sickbed, smiling warmly over her and thinking the musical instrument he'd given her a small and valueless thing, wishing he could give her the rainbow that framed the gray egg after a rain, the thunder of Toccoa Falls, the North star, or the rising moon. "A Seminole chief from the Floridas traded with me. The guitar came from Barcelona, fashioned for a fine lady of the court, so I was told. 'Tis yours now, Summer Eyes."

Listening to the endearing note in his deep voice, she smiled apologetically. "I regret I don't know how to play it."

Coosa sat beside her on her bed, making them both grow warm inside. "The Spanish guitar requires proper positioning on your left knee." His hand on her knee, although her legs were covered by satin quilts, was like a spark to tinder. She threw back her head on the satin and lace pillows, her tresses once again lustrous, her robe of peacock blue open to reveal the curve of one white firm breast. " 'Tis the placing of the hands that matters," Coosa said, forcing himself to concentrate on the lesson. "One must pluck the strings so . . ." Taking her hand in his, he held it as if it were a rose. Dominique thought his gentleness incredible, the impact of his touch so powerfully erotic she closed her eyes. "The right hand in particular," Coosa continued, responding like an atuned lover as he brought her fingers to his lips. Dominique sank deeper into the pillows whispering his name, drawing him closer to slide her hand around his neck, her longing arousing him.

"Coosa would carry you out of this house now if he could, ride with you on wings of love to his lodge in the mountains." He set the guitar aside and pressed a tender kiss to her lips. "But I have learned great patience from my mother's people." His expression was like a starved wolf's. Her eyes were inviting, her fingers gentle as they explored the high bones of his cheeks. She smiled when she saw he wore her golden loop in one ear. "Coosa pledges fidelity to you, Dom-ma-nique, striving toward permanence in our meeting and longing for a love that is greater than the two of us, love that will endure any difficulty."

Choking back tears she watched as he buried his face in her lap, his voice muffled by the bedclothes. "I pray to our gods you will never return to Alexandre again, Summer Eyes. My heart is heavy dreading it."

Caressing his head, she wrapped her arms about him. "You forget my child is in Georgia, Coosa. 'Tis my only reason for returning, you must believe that."

Coosa lifted his head and stared at her face a long time, speaking low. "We shall meet on the mountain where the buzzard makes his roost when the yellow flowers bloom. When the leaves fall." His hand laid on her belly and his eyes sparkled in the candle's glow, her fingers tracing the weaving of the beads on his buckskins. "I pray you carry our son. Coosa rides beyond the blue mountains now, west of the city of your birth." He took a lock of her hair and brought his face down to kiss it, then separated her lips in a good-bye kiss that sent shivers to her toes. "You belong to Coosa." He grinned.

A tear streaked her cheek and she wiped it away. "I belong to Coosa. Send me the golden loop I gave you when you return to Georgia and I'll come to you on the mountain. I promise it."

"Go back for your daughter!" he said with enthusiasm. "Coosa Tustennuggee goes to serve his people and afterward, he makes clouds of dust for the South!"

She laughed. Oh, how she loved him, wishing they could be off together atop his stallion, his strong arms wrapped about her waist, his hungry mouth against her neck. How many moons until they would meet again? she wondered. Sighing, she knew she'd count every one, closing her eyes as Coosa squeezed her hands and she sent him away. "Go now, brave *mico* of the Creeks. Finish your mission and return to me." Standing tall, Coosa walked slowly to the door, so quietly she didn't hear a single footfall. When he was gone, she was suddenly very cold.

Coosa bid Elton a fond farewell and left the Spanish stallion behind for Dominique. The doctor didn't like watching the Creek king go, sensing the approach of some danger. Attempting to dispel the worrisome thoughts from his mind, Elton stood on the north boundaries of Monticello and enjoyed the view. Drummond joined him, silently eyeing the five Creek horsemen disappearing into the bare winter trees over the glare of the clean white windswept lawns of the plantation that were nearly blinding. The air stung after several minutes' exposure, the sky turning black and forbidding. A howling wind grew stronger by the hour. Elton shivered, pulling the lapels of his greatcoat up on his neck.

"There goes a fine man." The doctor sighed. "Thanks to him, my girl lives."

"He'll never reach the mountains to the west, the red bastard!" Drummond growled. The harsh words echoed past Elton's ears and he spun round to face the Englishman his son-in-law had hired to protect his daughter.

"What say you, sir? What do you mean he'll not reach the mountains?"

Drummond's look was more chilling than the wind. "I mean I've sent an armed posse for the red bastards. They wait in the valley below, even now." Kicking the hard crust of snow, the wind caught Drummond's hair, parting it like the pages of a book. "One of my men was found scalped and brutally murdered by your Indian friends while the *mico* shared your daughter's bedchamber, doctor. Do you think I'd let her cold-blooded lover escape?"

"Watch your tongue, sir!" Elton's vexation was stirred deeply by the insult and he wished to God he were younger so he could lay low this Englishman.

"I had no trouble finding men who enjoy a good hunt in bad weather," Drummond laughed. " 'Twill be better sport than four-legged game."

Elton stared in disbelief, unable to accept the implication of Drummond's words. Nay, not after what they'd all been through, not after he'd come to know and respect the man his daughter called Rising Moon! Going to face the red-haired Englishman, he suddenly knew why he'd never liked the man. He was insufferably arrogant. But he was old and experience had taught him that nothing was gained by a display of anger. Then he saw the noble king of the Creeks riding through a snowstorm and ambushed by Drummond's murderers, caught in a crossfire as lead cut into his strong young body!

"God, no! The Indian will be killed!"

"You should have thought of that when your daughter placed herself in her precarious position, doctor. However, with the Indian out of the way, I see no reason why Alexandre need know the facts of her . . . indiscretion." Drummond turned. "There's a snowstorm coming, doctor. Feel it? Best you be off for Philadelphia before it reaches the mountains. Alexandre's wife and I leave tonight for the coast."

17

---●———

Jules Cocteau waited outside Jefferson's house as Drummond
had instructed, freezing in the darkness of early morning. It
was below zero and Jules cursed the English lawyer to hell and
back. What a bumbling fool Drummond was, Jules thought, a
man so smitten by his client's beautiful wife he'd failed to
recognize one of his own men. Jules laughed, wondering what
the arrogant Englishman was doing inside the house and what
was taking him so long. Drummond had instructed Jules and
two other men to ready the coach-and-six for travel because
Drummond was moving to the village to await word from the
rest of his ruffians on the outcome of the "welcoming party"
he'd arranged for Coosa Tustennuggee and his braves. Some of
his men on horseback rode ahead to open a trail for the
barouche. Drummond had planned well—for an Englishman,
Jules mused. President Jefferson and his household had left for
Washington or the village due to the threat of an impending
snowstorm and the newlyweds had long ago traveled south on
their honeymoon. No one was left in the house but Elton
Winburn, his daughter, and a servantwoman. All Drummond
had to do now was take Dominique off to the nearest inn and
wait for the snow to close the roads. A thought that made Jules
seethe with envy.

Torchlight lit the drive where Jules sat atop a coach-and-six.
He imagined Elton Winburn trying to stop Drummond from
removing his daughter from the house, raising a ruckus and
threatening Drummond with the law. What law? Jules laughed,
rubbing his bearded face in the icy wind. There were no
lawmen in the snowy mountains of Virginia. The horses
snorted and pranced, anxious to be off in the new snow that
was still soft enough for a coach's wheels to roll downhill
easily . . . if Drummond hurried. Then Jules heard voices
and thought of going to the door to see what he could, thinking
better of it when he realized he might be recognized. Finally,
the front doors opened and Drummond came through with
Nikki in his arms. She thrashed her legs and clutched
something that looked like a guitar. Drummond was holding
her close, much too close, saying things to her that Jules could
only guess at. He stiffened when he saw that Nikki's hands
were bound and something was tied across her mouth to keep
her from screaming. Drummond lifted Nikki into the coach and
gave Jules and the other men the signal to be off.

"Bastard!" Jules cursed, shaking out the reins and preparing
to endure each jolting step the horses took down the winding
road to the village. Jules rode in the freezing cold atop the
coach while Nikki and Drummond sat inside. Drummond
silently congratulated himself for having gotten away without a
scene between himself and the woman's high-minded father.
Stroking his thick red moustache, the Englishman eyed the
woman seated opposite, complimenting himself on a job well
done. Elton Winburn and the servant woman were still asleep
at Monticello and he was on his way with a woman he planned
to make his own. He'd wrapped her tightly in woolens and furs
over her pewter-colored traveling dress trimmed and caped in
fox with plump tails that trailed beguilingly over one bosom
and coiled on the floor of the moving coach. As pretty a sight
as any man ever saw.

"Forgive me, Dominique. 'Twas the only way I could get
you out of the house without waking your father and your
maid. I'm sorry to say your father doesn't like me. But that
doesn't matter now. You won't be needing him or your maid on
this trip. I'll take care of you from now on, my dearest. You'll
see."

The coach had begun its descent down the little mountain
and Dominique struggled against the strip of bedding Drum-

mond had tied tightly across her mouth. A blast of icy wind blew snow into the big barouche through the ill-fitting door and the coach rocked back and forth on the rough roads. The team of six, harnessed in red leather and bells, struggled together through drifting snow, Jules's angry whip cracking over the giant beasts's heads. Drummond patted Dominique's bound hands. " 'Tis as cold as a she-wolf's tits, eh?"

Dominique muttered something, closing her eyes and leaning against the cold wall of the barouche. Shivering with cold, anger, and uncertainty, she worried about what her father would think when he found her gone. Drummond hadn't even granted her the courtesy of leaving a note. Her insides cramped with the terrible crack of the whip. She couldn't stand anyone abusing horses and was trying to convey the fact with her eyes when a sudden jolt made her lean against Drummond. She had disliked her husband's choice of a lawyer; now she despised him with passion. Her fingers caressed the polished wood of the guitar sleeping peacefully against her skirts, finding solace in the gift Coosa had given her. She could hear the Creek's voice whispering his parting words, still feel his kiss on her lips, seeing the tall dark man she loved crossing the blue mountains on horseback, his steed's red plumes astir in the falling snow.

When she opened her eyes again she saw faint streaks of dawn behind black velvet hills. She shivered with the cold as the coach lurched and she was hurled into Drummond's legs. Bone struck bone and her curses approached screams as Drummond's hands caught her and held her head against his chest and she felt something stir in his lap.

"Forgive me, please. I'm a man and your loveliness overwhelms me."

Grateful for the dark, she saw his face, the shape of his long puffy lips and white teeth. She felt his breath on her skin, his hands on her arms, her waist, around her back, and she struggled to push him away as she managed to ungag her mouth.

"Damn you!" Her voice was shaky.

"The lady has found her tongue."

"My husband will see you hang for this!" Struggling to free herself, she was surprised when he untied her hands and returned to his seat. She considered striking him, pulling out his hair!

"You're angry and I don't blame you. Might you be warmer and more comfortable if we sat together? Can't you allow yourself the heat of my body?"

Her reply was a deathly look into the dark. Aye, she was freezing, still ill from her bout with pneumonia, if the truth be known. Every bone in her body ached and now the ride in the coach had worsened her condition. Too sick to fear him, her breath came in little pants, her throat constricting as her stomach pitched and rolled with the bumpy ride.

"Stop the coach, please." Unable to contain her misery another second, she bent over, trying not to be sick all over herself. Drummond moved beside her, touching her neck . . . fingering her hair.

"Motion sickness. I was afraid of this. Can't say your husband didn't warn me." Opening the coach's door, Drummond shouted into the arctic blast, "Stop the coach, driver! Madame is ill!"

Jules Cocteau reined in the six magnificent grays and hurled oaths to the wind as the barouche braked and careened into a snowbank, nearly turning over on its side. Dominique landed on the floor with her Spanish guitar, furs and hatboxes behind her head. She gulped in freezing air and Drummond pulled her out into the frosty night, stepping blindly into snow so deep they were nearly immersed.

"Take your hands away, you imbecile!" Dominique choked and pushed, floundering as if she was drowning in the cold snow.

"Be still, can't you? I'm trying to help you, dammit!" Drummond managed to help her to her feet as Jules looked down from above. "Can't you be nice to me?"

"Leave me here," she said, trying not to retch in front of him like a sick dog.

"All right, you may have your way!" No sooner had Drummond spoken when Dominique sank into the snow. "God's blood, woman, how long do you think you'd last on such a night? You're as stubborn as your husband said you were! Worse!"

"I am!" she said, struggling against him as he brushed the snow from her face. Slowly, they made their way back to the coach.

"I was told you have a hatred of wheels, but I didn't take it seriously. I see now it's true."

"Coosa . . ." Dominique murmured, dipping her hands into snow and touching it to her lips. "You didn't—"

"Don't ask me about your red lover, madame!" Drummond's tone was laconic as he tossed her furs onto the coach's seat in disgust and kicked the guitar to one side. "You saw him leave. 'Tis I who help you now. Not him!" Drummond drew her into his arms and held her one second too long for Jules Cocteau. Having seen and heard all he could take, Jules dropped like a stone from the top of the coach and knocked Drummond into the snow. Dominique screamed, unsure of what was happening, unable to see the man who had downed Drummond.

"You!" Drummond recognized Jules, but too late. Jules held Drummond's face in the snow until Drummond stopped struggling, his neck clearly broken. Dominique felt an old fear grip her as she watched Drummond's murderer come to his feet. Sick and frightened together, she was about to run when she realized it was no use. It was dark but she could see the beard, long and untrimmed, the same beard she'd seen in Pennsylvania and Georgia. Dear God, it couldn't be!

"Nikki." Jules came toward her as two of the horsemen who had been riding ahead approached them. She screamed to them.

"Help me, please, this man's wanted by the law!"

Jules laughed, taking her arm and lifting her into the coach as one of the men jumped down beside him and the other sat atop his horse awaiting orders. "The lady is · distraught, gentlemen. You're in my employ now and we'll be going to Hog's Head Inn as originally planned. Don't worry about the lady—certain she'll feel differently about me in the morning." Jules's laugh piqued Dominique's sickness and she drew herself into a ball in the corner of the coach. "What's wrong, Nikki? No thanks for ridding you of that fool your husband so foolishly hired to protect you?"

"You're not going to leave Drummond here?"

"Why not? He'll be frozen in an hour or two and someone will find him by spring." His laugh was as wild and devilish as she remembered. " 'Tis good to see you, Nikki. We have much to discuss—our betrothal and eventual marriage once you're free from that weakling you call husband, for one thing. Don't worry, sweet Nikki, Alexandre will be dead soon, you have my word on it."

* * *

The moon hung naked in an ominous sky, clouds scudding low, as Elton Winburn's mind filled with thoughts of his beloved daughter. He'd discovered too late his girl had been abducted from Jefferson's house in the dead of night. "Let her be safe and warm," he prayed. "Let Coosa reach the heights of the mountains and hide him from the evil eyes of his enemies." Elton called on God to send a storm, a snowstorm of such strength it would blind the murderous party who followed the braves and turn them back toward warm fires. The physician's lips were raw from the wind and he wrapped his scarf around his face. He thought of praying for Drummond's death or a miracle to bring Dominique and her Indian together. God only knew what Drummond had in mind for his beautiful girl and only God could help her and Coosa.

George Limpton wound the scraggly checkered scarf his wife had knitted for him around his leathered neck, wishing to God he was home in bed with her. Anywhere but out in a Virginia snowstorm in the morning cold. He swore, his hands and feet past feeling, his beard stiffened by the ice. The wind had turned killer and set itself on finishing him off before it was over. Aye, George was a believer in good and evil and tonight Satan surely rode the wind. 'Twas the devil's work he was about to do.

" 'Tis Lucifer's night, gents! What say we turn back before the evil deed is done?"

No answer came from Drummond's men riding at Limpton's side, their horses breathless and blinded by snow. Who could hear a human voice above the howling wind? And where was the moon? Lost like the oath Limpton muttered as he tried in vain to wriggle his toes in frozen leather. All would be better in the light, George told himself. Even cold-blooded Indian killings were better in the light of day. The thought of murder grew in his brain and became a malignant tumor, his head pounding with guilt. The most serious of sins, he told himself, but there was no escaping it now. He'd sworn on the good book to kill the heathens, then drank in revelry in the servants' quarters of Monticello. Jefferson's house was a day past now. Sure, he'd protested that the Indians had done no wrong, but he'd been put down. Jeered at, called yellow, and his protestations drowned in the heckling and laughter and curses of drunken men. Jules Cocteau had placed gold in his hands and told him the gold was his to keep. The Creek king would never be missed, Cocteau had insisted. Drummond had hired them to slay the savages from Georgia and had insisted that they were nothing but a blight upon the land. But George couldn't kill a man for pay, he knew that now. Too late, too late!

The rider in the lead lifted his arm in the air and the horses stopped in deep snow, lifting their tired heads and listening to the keening wind. Why were they stopping? Limpton wondered, half asleep in his saddle and shaking out the sting in his freezing fingers. Were the Indians so close the time of decision was upon him? Jack Shord wheeled his big chestnut gelding alongside Limpton, snow falling like a blanket on the two men.

"The good Lord's with us, George. Look at it come down!" Shord was right. The heavy snowfall and howling downwinds made it possible for them to butcher the Indians before they knew what had hit them. Death would be painless, merciful, unless some miracle prevented George from having to kill . . . George was so cold his brain didn't function.

"Let it be done, Satan!" he growled. The horses moved forward slowly into the foothills of the blue-wreathed mountains, past rock slides that had left huge boulders in the road. Shord jutted his arm into the air and the horses halted, ears forward, nostrils flaring. George smelled smoke, wood burning! Shord lifted his chin, motioning for George to come closer. They'd form a circle and move in cautiously, entrapping the Indians and allowing no one to escape. George tried to envision Shord's plan in his mind, but his thoughts were too sluggish. The Indians' camp was dead ahead, that much he remembered. The game had been sighted and it was too late to run. Every man would fire when ordered and make each shot count. There were ten of Drummond's men and only five savages. George felt the need to go behind a tree but there wasn't time. His stomach ached as his bowels burned. If he were lucky he wouldn't have to kill anyone by himself, realizing the Creek king would be dead before he took his scalp. George didn't know how to scalp, but Shord and the others would be watching and they'd vowed to kill him if he fled. Dismounting, George stepped painfully into deep snow, his feet sending agony shooting through his legs to his thighs. Smoke filled the air and Shord swore about his frozen hands and the damnable dark. The snow came down harder and harder as the wind became so strong it threatened to blow the horses away.

"They'll never know what hit 'em in this." Shord chuckled, his form lost in the snow as George considered shooting his companion in the back. George wanted to run but he could barely walk and there was no exit now. Then a hand grabbed his scarf and pulled it so tight he nearly died where he stood. "There, through those trees, in the quarry. See the smoke? Don't miss, George—I'll be behind you when we go in and clean up," Shord whispered. The Indians' horses came into view, as well as several crude shelters built of saplings and pine boughs that looked inviting and warm. Smoke curled upward in a sweet perfume. Then came the crack of nine rifles and George thought he'd be deaf forever as trees and branches scattered and splintered, horses screamed and fell dead. George watched the Indians' lean-to blow to bits, Drummond's men growling like starving jackals after fresh meat. Blood spattered the virgin snow and young bronzed men lay lifeless atop one another, one moving until Shord stepped forward and shot him in the head. Shord yanked George along by his scarf, leading him to the blood-stained earth.

"Find the chief and scalp him, George."

George Limpton couldn't move, his mouth agape as he watched blood ooze from a brave's mouth, trickling onto white snow. "God help me, I can't!"

"You yella son of a bitch! I shoulda known ya couldn't do it! Which one is he? Show me, damn you!" Shord pushed the dead Indians apart with his foot, eyes wild like a rabid beast.

"I dunno!" George choked. "God, help me, I dunno!"

"Find him and take his scalp! I'm goin' for his horse!"

One of the men kicked Coosa in the jaw, rolling the Indian *mico* over to spit in his face. "One less heathen, good riddance!"

George watched as Coosa's long fingers moved, his hand falling back to clutch a single golden ring in his ear. Snow covered the Indian's face and George froze. Coosa's eyes opened and looked up at the man who stood over him. Frowning, Coosa blinked his soft black eyes, gasping for breath and trying to speak.

"Forgive me, chief. God knows I'm weak, but I ain't no

Indian killer." Bleeding profusely from a wound in his chest, Coosa looked at George in a daze, not realizing he'd been shot.

"Summer Eyes . . ." Coosa whispered.

George struggled to clear his head, the gold earring in the Creek king's ear giving him an idea. Smiling, George pulled his knife from his belt and bent over Coosa, knowing he must act swiftly if he was ever going to get away alive. Coosa blinked snowflakes from his lashes and saw George's knife come unsheathed, rise over his head. "God forgive me," George whispered, his knife stripping away flesh from an Indian's flesh. Swallowing hard, George wiped his knife clean in the snow and wrapped the bloody thing in his scarf, then stacked Indian bodies like fresh-cut trees in his backyard.

"The Creek king's dead!" Jack Shord uttered proudly. A respite for Jules, yet tainted with uncertainty and doubt.

"You saw?" Jules stared into the flames that licked whole trunks of trees in the Hog's Head Inn's cavernous fireplace. Shord walked hesitantly across the room, uncomfortable with this eerie Frenchmen who'd taken Drummond's place. Tossing a checkered scarf onto the polished surface of a claw-footed table in the center of the room, Shord smiled.

"I did as Drummond instructed—here's your proof!"

Jules wheeled from the intense heat of the fire, eyes spotting the blood-stained scarf on the table. "What's this? I see no proof!"

Shord swallowed, seeing a glint of something in Cocteau's eye that frightened him. " 'Tis a blizzard out there, sir. I don't know how any of us got back alive. The men are near froze and saddle weary ta boot. Some lost forever."

Cocteau didn't care about the men, going slowly to the table with his eyes burning into George Limpton's scarf. "His scalplock?" he asked.

Shord rattled out the truth them. "That fool Limpton turned coward on me, sir. I didn't know till we was ridin' back he never scalped the red heathen . . ."

Jules's hair caught the light of the flames as he stood with his back to the hot blaze and grabbed the scarf to tear it apart like a starving bear. "What's this, some trick you thought would fool me? You said the red heathen was dead, and yet you give no proof."

Shord's short legs grew weak and he stepped back, afraid the truth wouldn't be good enough for the man who'd taken Drummond's place. "As dead as any Indian can be, Mr. Cocteau, sir. Froze stiff by now, I'll wager."

Cocteau's curiosity flared anew as he unraveled the scarf fully, discovering a piece of dried flesh as hard as leather, blackened with blood. "What have we here, the filthy dog's liver?"

Shord let out a weak laugh, but Cocteau wasn't amused. Before Shord could reply, Cocteau went to the fire to examine the piece Drummond had paid for in advance. "*Mon Dieu!* 'Tis a man's ear!" Jules bellowed. "And hung with a golden loop."

"That's just it, sir." Shord tripped forward. " 'Tis more than a bloody ear. Look closely at the golden hoop that hangs from it. See the initials carved inside."

Jules pulled the golden earring from what was once a man's flesh, examining it with care and casting the bloody flesh into the fire. The initials *D.C.*! Sickened by such irrefutable evidence that Nikki had been with the Indian who'd scarred his face, Jules bowed his head between outstretched arms and watched the ear consumed by hungry flames, inhaling the sour burning odor with joy.

"Where's the man who brought me this prize?"

"Lost, sir. Lost in the blue mountains this very night. Fifty miles back, I'd say. Frozen by now."

"How do I know the Creek king is indeed dead? Do you expect me to take this ear for proof?"

"He's dead, sir. I was there and we sneaked up on 'em like we planned. Jumped the lot of 'em in a snowstorm the likes a which I've never seen in these parts afore. All five of 'em dead, sir. Put a bullet through each and every one of their dirty heads meself afore I left." Shord was lying now, his expression firm, well aware his life was at stake with this crazy Frenchman.

Drummond's voice was expressionless. "The stallion?"

"Stabled with our horses, sir, but not liking it much. The Indian ponies are wild like the Indian was. Don't understand English, ya see. May have ta move 'em afore the night is out if he don't settle down."

"See the beast isn't injured," Jules said. "I mean to collect dearly for him." Jules squeezed the golden loop tightly in his hand, turning from the heat and motioning for Shord to leave. When Shord was gone, he thought about Dominique and the

Creek king. She'd given Coosa a keepsake, had she? He wondered if an Indian could live with a bullet in his head, reasoning no man could survive the arctic blasts and subzero temperatures of a Virginia blizzard. The Indian was dead and his hired killer with him. Better than he'd hoped for. Turning, he whispered into the fire that hissed and crackled back at him. "Burn in Hades, o chief of the Creeks. I've seen the last of you. Alexandre is next!"

The wind howled like demons, scraping under the eaves of the Hog's Head Inn, banging shutters and whistling around thick walls and casements, screaming at those who had escaped its deadly breath. Dominique woke with a start, leaping out of bed and wrapping herself in a robe of sheared beaver. She'd heard a horse screaming . . . or was it the wind? Rushing to the window, she pulled back heavy drapes and held them against her heated flesh, shivering as a draft moved her hair. Snow blew over the stone sill of the window, spilling onto her feet like fine powder as men shouted and ran to corner a frightened horse. It was difficult to see in the gray and white of the storm, snow spitting as the beast reared and kicked, its neigh so shrill it sent cold chills across her shoulders. Lantern light showed off the stallion's fine trappings, the sight of a familiar mark on the beast setting her heart racing. Dominique's brain formed images of Rising Moon, rubbing her eyes open wide to see that the horse was gone.

A shutter slammed shut and she jumped, the fire in her room sending wild shadows dancing as a key turned in her door. Jules Cocteau stood in the shadows, his bearded face hidden. "You refused my invitation to dine, madame. The journey to the sea will be long and trying and you'll need nourishment to survive." Jules closed the door and locked it behind him, stuffing the key into his pocket. Smiling, he came toward her slowly, as if amused by something. Dominique knew someone else might think him handsome, dressed impeccably in toast-colored Scottish wool over suede, his white woven shirt set off by a silver chain that hung across his chest. Sliding his hand inside his moleskin waistcoat he laughed softly.

"Where is Coosa Tustennuggee? What have you done with him? I demand to know!" Her voice was smaller than she liked, meek even, but clearly accusing.

Jules laughed, so tickled he bent over and allowed the

pleasure of her concern to rush through his body. "You ask *me* where your red-skinned lover is?" Going to the fire, he stepped up on the raised hearth, chuckling merrily. He failed to notice her fall against the snowy sill. " 'Tis a foolish question, Nikki. How would I know the whereabouts of your husband's bastard nephew on a night like this? He's probably rutting around for some squaw to keep him warm, if you want my guess. 'Tis a cold night out there, in case you've forgotten, cold enough to freeze a man till spring." His laugh lessened in ferocity this time and he looked up to see her falter, and he rushed quickly to her side. "Dearest Nikki . . ."

"Dear God, what have you done with him?" she murmured, the room spinning around as he caught her in his arms. She saw his eyes and knew the truth, reeling instinctively and cringing intensely. "Pray tell me I'm wrong. Tell me you haven't harmed him."

Jules's loins ached, his hands trembling at his sides as the thought of having her for his bride thrilled his body. Dominique read the truth in his eyes and choked back a scream.

"It *was* his horse I saw! Coosa's horse!"

Catching her in his arms, Jules muffled her screams with one hand and dragged her to the bed, where he hovered over her. His heavy palm crushed her lips and he spoke clearly into her face. "A case of mistaken identity, Nikki. 'Tis understandable on such a night as this. You forget we're in a village and there are many horses coming into the inn's stables because of the storm." Removing his hand, he allowed her to draw breath, seeing horror in her bright green eyes. "Scream again and I shall have to use other methods to calm you, sweet Nikki. My ways are new to you I know, but you must learn to obey me if you wish to live."

Turning from him, she cried into the bed's furs and shook her head, unable to believe that this had truly come to pass. Her tears were hot on her cheeks and she felt his body moving slightly.

"I've treated you badly, I know, but I'll make it up to you when we're married." His beard brushed her face and she lashed out at him, beating his face with her hands and cutting his lip with her ring. "You bitch!" Incensed, Jules jumped up, his voice changing from benevolent to galled. "You needn't pretend with me, Mrs. Chastain! I know about you and your Indian king riding off together, *sleeping* together! You're nothing but an adultress, madame, an unfaithful wife! Pity poor Alexandre." He laughed. "Pity the poor little boy whose mama died. Poor little fellow needed a mother so his father sent him to live with me. Sent him to take my mother's love from me!" Jules's eyes were wild with hate and Dominique pulled back on the bed, until he attacked her like a wild animal and held her down, pressing her hands to his chest. "We won't have to put up with Alexandre much longer, my love. I've waited a long time to get even with Alexandre Chastain and I mean to make him suffer before he dies!" His voice changed and he petted her hair, stroking her face and chin. "I knew you were going to be my bride when I saw you on your wedding day. You knew it, too, didn't you?"

Dominique saw the madness in his eyes and nodded, painfully aware that a false move and Jules would be on her like a rabid dog. Her screams were stayed in her throat and her heart pounded a warning as his voice changed again.

"How could you let that son of a heathen bitch touch you? *You,* the betrothed of Jules Cocteau!" His voice was a snarl beneath his breath and then he was calm again. "Were you so desperate for a man you'd lie down with a filthy cur? Or did Alexandre cut you off?"

Knowing well that what she did may mean her end, Dominique couldn't hold herself and spit in his face. "Coosa is a man! You're the filthy cur!"

Slapping her so hard she thought her jaw had come unhinged, she saw bright lights filling her head as the back of his hand sent her sprawling.

"I'll make you sorry for that!" Jules growled low and vengefully in his throat, his hot breath misting the air between them. He shook her to make sure she understood. "Drummond's men have your mongrel lover, Nikki, do you hear me?"

Her jaw slack, Dominique opened her eyes and looked up at him.

"Drummond's men work for me now, and they'll do anything I say. Your red king will die a bit slower because of what you just did. Bit by bit!"

"Nay, please, please, I'll do anything . . . anything . . ." Breathing in little pants, she whimpered and pleaded with her eyes.

"From this moment on you shall welcome me into your bed

like your red lover, do you understand?" He smiled, his words seemingly coming from afar. Dominique choked back a sob and nodded. "Good." Jules released her hands, removing his waistcoat and smiling. "I enjoy taking a woman by force, but perhaps I can learn to enjoy lying back and allowing you to take me. There are many things you can do to pleasure me, Nikki dearest, things you've never dreamed of!" His voice changed again. "Just remember I'm not soft like your weakling husband. I'll not stand for disrespect!" She lay trembling while Jules untied the sash of her claret-red gown and laid it open to gaze upon her swelling breasts, golden in the firelight. "Few men have seen such beauty in their lifetime, eh? How many men have there been after me, I wonder? Tell me now, or I'll thrash the living daylight out of you!"

She was shaking uncontrollably now, and her flesh rose as he stroked the curve of one breast. Ill and filled with suffering, she closed her eyes and heard Jules remove his boots, then toss his clothes on a chair. When he touched her again, she flinched and saw how powerfully he was built, his chest and shoulders covered with hair. She stiffened when he bent and slid atop her. "Move, the way you would for Coosa Tustennuggee," he commanded, rocking over her and drawing her legs apart. She couldn't look as he entered her, a thrust so sudden and burning it drove away her breath. Struggling for air beneath him, she prayed to God for Coosa's life.

"Don't hurt him, I beg you. Do as you wish with me, but don't hurt Coosa."

Amused by her entreaty, Jules laughed thoroughly, throwing back his head and driving himself to the fullest until he cried out in ecstasy. Dominique almost retched, but then she imagined herself in a verdant wood atop El'Ramir, lost in the cool pine woods of Georgia, far from the winter's cold.

Winburn praised God when he saw a horse coming toward him in the snowfall. Before he led his horse to the crossroads, Elton believed he was lost, having given up hope of ever being seen alive again. He'd ridden miles in the snow and the cruel wind slapped his horse's belly and made the trees crack under its bitter lash. Closing his eyes, he bowed his head in thankfulness, straining his eyes in the fury of the blizzard to see a man come closer on his steed.

"Can you hear me?" Elton called, his voice barely audible

in the keen wind. The man appeared to be frozen to his mount, but Elton saw him shake his head in confirmation. "Thank God, thank God!" Dismounting, Elton fought the wind to reach the stranger, handing up a flask of brandy and introducing himself. "Dr. Winburn from Monticello way!" he shouted. "Have you seen any Indians about?"

George Limpton took a long swig of brandy and then another, never bothering to wipe his frozen lips. "Massacred," he mumbled.

"Merciful God, that can't be!" Elton's strength left him, and he leaned against Limpton's horse.

"One may still live," Limpton muttered. "The king."

"Dear God, take me there quickly, sir!" Elton returned to his horse and prayed he wouldn't be too late. If he could summon the strength to ride to Coosa's aid, he knew he could save the red man. He didn't know how he knew it, but he sensed there was hope. Plodding behind Limpton's exhausted beast, Elton's horse fell into step. Higher and higher into the foothills of the Blue Ridge Mountains they went, until they halted beside the large boulders of a stone quarry where they were protected from the howling wind.

" 'Tis not far, doctor. We've no time to waste!" George Limpton led the way past a heavy rockfall into the quarry. Elton saw the bodies of men cold and lifeless on the quarry's floor. Limpton stopped before a pile of debris and fallen trees to uncover more half-clothed Indians. Murdered where they'd slept, the young braves were stacked like so many rocks cast aside by stone cutters, their bright feathers astir on the wind. "He's under the others, doctor. I wrapped the king up myself and piled the others on top of him to keep him warm. Look!" Limpton tried to run, but couldn't because of his frozen feet, falling and crawling to the mass of bodies. "He's alive, I tell ya, I didn't touch a hair on his head! The king's hurt bad, but I'm sure he's alive!"

Neither of the men realized the sun had begun to shine, the wind's bite lessening as the sky changed into a royal blue. Elton's eyes were veiled in tears, seeing blood on the snow, the stranger with him pulling the dead Indians by arms and legs to one side. Looking away from the eyes of the dead, Elton saw Limpton uncover a body wrapped in blankets and furs. *Coosa!*

"Dear Jesus, I believe you're a saint, man! 'Tis a miracle you've performed!" Together, they pulled back the blankets from Coosa's body, the furs that had helped keep the Indian chief from freezing to death. "We must get him to warm quarters immediately, but where?"

Limpton pointed to the waiting horse of one of Coosa's slain braves. "Tie him to the pony and follow me, doc. I saw an old cabin aways back! 'Tis our only hope!"

The cabin was only a shack, but it had a fireplace and four walls, a roof, and a door. When George got the fire going, the hot flames melted the wet snow from the logs and the sparse heat warmed the building enough to save everyone from a freezing death. Elton sat beside his patient of three days and dozed against the warm stones of the fireplace while George rubbed his feet and talked to himself. Coosa hadn't moved or spoken, his chest still torn and black where a lead ball had entered and been removed. The Indian *mico*'s body was hot with fever.

"All for naught," George muttered, looking at his discolored feet that would never feel the same. Coosa's long lashes fluttered open and he looked around like a captured animal in strange surroundings, eyeing the sagging timbers of the roof, the insect-riddled walls, and blackened stones of the fireplace.

"Dom-ma-nique."

Elton jolted upright and rubbed his eyes, smiling broadly when he saw the Creek awake. George crawled hesitantly to join them on the blankets and furs. "Welcome back," George said. Coosa attempted to lift his head, but Elton stopped him with a forceful hand. "You mustn't move, my son. You've been injured seriously and sewed inside and out by me. 'Tis this man who brought me to you."

Coosa looked at George, his hands sliding upward to touch the deep wound in his chest.

"If it hadn't been for the freezing weather you'd be meeting the Great Spirit by now, Coosa, my son."

Coosa's mind was fogged with fever and wild dreams, and he stared at the men's faces for a long time.

"The intense cold slowed down your flow of blood, Coosa, preventing you from bleeding to death," Elton said.

"Summer Eyes . . ." Coosa moaned.

"On her way to Savannah by now, I expect, my son." Elton lifted Coosa's head and placed a rolled blanket behind it. "May our gods protect her."

18

———————◆———————

Angry winds blew in from the sea carrying torrential rains and gray fog that enshrouded the ship's deck, pounding Jules Cocteau's barque against the shore of the Savannah River.

" 'Tis a gale, Mr. Cocteau! I'll find ye and yer woman a coach!" Jules's man shouted from the slanting decks of the barque, his voice almost lost in the howl of a winter storm. Jules made his way down the slick gangplank to the docks, dragging Dominique toward a waiting coach. He held a yellow oilskin over her head for protection against the cold rain that lashed them.

The coach was icy as rain streamed in over the door. Dominique shivered in the darkness, hating the feel of wheels as much as the rocking barque. Her clothes were soaked to her skin. Jules removed the oilskin and pushed it to the floor. "A spring storm. Not unusual for these parts. 'Tis good to be ashore, eh?"

Dominique made no reply to her captor as Jules covered her hands with one of his. "Your skin feels like ice, Nikki dearest."

Casting him a disdainful look, she pulled free and leaned into the wet coach's door, peering without at the rolling Savannah fog. Concentrating on the sound of the coach's wheels splashing through water and turning into Bay Street, she thought she heard the beloved name, *Coosa . . . Coosa . . . Coosa,* as the wheels she hated rolled over cobblestones in the fog that closed about them like the jaws of death. Chills ran through her blood and her teeth chattered as she wondered where Alexandre was, all the while trying to think of a way to escape the madman who'd abducted her. The coachman shouted at the horses and cracked his whip over his mighty beasts' heads. "Hah, hah, hah!"

Jules leaned forward, straining his eyes to see where they were. The coach had reached the high bluff of the city, rolling past large buildings over deep water and swirling sand. Sinew, muscle, and wheels worked in unison as the coach skirted fallen trees and airborne limbs; the storm was wreaking havoc on the entire coastline.

"'Tis a bloody day to come back, eh? 'Tis too bad your weakling husband didn't meet us." Jules laughed and then became perturbed with Dominique's silence, catching her arm and turning her around roughly to face him. "You'd best prepare yourself for his end, dearest Nikki."

Pushing his hand from her arm with disgust, Dominique gave Jules an odious look, her hatred for him apparent in her green eyes. "Your end is near, I can feel it," she said spitefully, glaring until her eyes watered with revenge. She fell back against the leather seat to hide her misery in the shadows of dawn.

"'Tis your lover's end you sense!" Jules rubbed his hand across his beard. "Do you think I've forgotten what the red bastard did to me? Every time I look in a glass I see him! And your weakling husband's rotting corpse for not stitching me up!" Raising one brow, Jules took a lock of her damp hair in his fingers. "'Tis a pity I didn't reveal the truth to you in Virginia," he mocked. "How I beat Drummond's face in and left him for the wolves. How I saved you from that scum of a half-breed Indian!" He smiled in the darkness and she saw the gleam in his eyes. "Perhaps the good doctor will reward me for my services? Give me the fat purse he's holding for Drummond?"

"Where is Coosa?" Dominique asked pitifully, fearing Jules's reply. "Tell me or I'll leap from this coach!"

"In Hades!" Jules exclaimed.

Dominique clung to the roof with her hands, kicking Jules

until he ripped her skirt from her waist. Then the coach struck a rut and Jules lost his seat, crashing against the door. Dominique screamed as she began to tumble. Mud and sand swirled over her and Jules yelled for the coach to stop. Dominique lay in a crumpled heap, her clothes torn and one leg twisted beneath her. Rain came down in sheets and Jules came running to her side.

"Nikki! Nikki, dearest . . ."

"You said you'd let him live . . . said you'd be done with me," she whispered.

Picking her up in his arms, Jules shielded her face from the rain, pulling his sodden cloak around them. She was unable to fight him now, her face and hand bloodied where she'd landed on the street, her side aching where Jules held her tight.

"I'll never be done with you, dearest Nikki. You know that, dearest." Kissing her brow, he carried her toward the coach that had turned around in the next square. The driver jumped down to help him and Dominique's heart nearly stopped when Jules said:

"Take us to Chastain House and be quick about it!" Once the vicinity of the house was determined, the coach was on its way with Jules and Dominique inside. " 'Twas a foolish move," Jules said to Dominique. "Now your husband will have to patch up your face. I wonder if he's home."

"He'll kill you," she said. "And I shall help him!"

Jules laughed. "I can't wait, Nikki, my love. Your husband couldn't kill a fly, and you know it."

"You said Coosa would go free if I bent to your will!" she sobbed.

"Ah, what pleasure it was, too." Jules laughed, recalling the way he had taught her to make love to him during those long nights in the Hog's Head Inn when the weather prevented man and beast from travel.

"I'll see you dead, if it's the last thing I do!" she promised. "I will repay you for all that time in the inn, in Richmond, aboard your barque. Oh, God, I wish I were dead."

Grabbing her by the throat, he shook her until her head banged against the door, the pressure of his thumb making it difficult for her to breathe. "Don't forget I can still have Alexandre killed," he threatened. "Tortured and torn limb from limb if need be!" Releasing her, he kissed her wet, bruised mouth and slid his hands over her torn and wet garments, clasping her close and whispering in her ear. "Feel what you do to me, Nikki! All of it is yours to do with as you please, my love. I'm ready!"

Aware that she held her husband's fate in her hands, she took Jules's hand and held it to one breast, then lifting it slowly to her lips. "You must have patience with me," she said huskily. "Now that Coosa is gone, I'll need a lover."

The look in his eyes was like a child's and she thought him almost human then. He caressed her breast and then she felt his hot breath on the curve of her neck. He pushed aside her hair, his tongue flicking inside her ear, his desire pressing into the base of her spine as she turned from him. "You *do* care for me, don't you, Nikki?"

Turning, she swept her arms around his neck and pressed her lips to his neck below one ear, biting deep into the tendons and muscles, her even teeth clenching and twisting as if she were a feline gone mad, giving a vicious bite that sent him howling in excruciating pain.

"Bitch!" Jules's jarring blow landed her on the floor where he kicked her back, pushing her down with his feet until her tears ran on the coach's filthy matting.

"Touch me again and I'll kill you!" she said weakly. " 'Tis a promise I shall keep!"

Still in pain from her bite, Jules muttered and kicked her again, slipping his hand inside his frock-coat pocket and dropping her golden earring onto the floor with her. "Before you do, know that I had your Indian lover murdered." His tone was malicious and then he laughed. " 'Tis true, he's dead. Cut down in Virginia with the rest of his heathen bunch, slaughtered and butchered like the swine they were!" Tightening his breeches, he smoothed out his dampened greatcoat and held her down on the floor with his boots. Dominique heard the words echo with the sound of the wheels as her ear touched the floor. *Dead! Slaughtered! Butchered!*

After a long silence, she fingered the hoop to see if it was truly hers, her stomach knotting as a terrible coldness swept her body. Coosa was dead and she didn't want to live. She must kill Jules Cocteau before he killed again. Before he killed Alexandre!

The yard of Chastain House was ruined in the flood, and pink buds from camelia trees floated past Dominique's shoes as Jules led her down the walk. The light of swinging lanterns

penetrated the drifting fog as Ruthe's husband, Thomas, came
from the house.

"Who's there? Who comes?"

" 'Tis I, Thomas," Dominique shouted. Jules held the
oilskin over their heads and pulled her along by her injured
arm. "Mr. Drummond is with me," she said as she had been
told.

"Welcome, mistress!" Thomas said excitedly. "So good to
have you home. The doctor will be so pleased!" Thomas
looked anxiously at the coach. "Where's my Ruthe, mistress?"

"Aboard ship," Dominique lied, having been coached by
Jules earlier. "She's waiting there until someone comes for
her."

"May I go and fetch her?" Thomas asked.

"Aye, Thomas, just as soon as you tell me where the doctor
is."

"Off to Sea Island plantation to care for a poor body hurt in
the storm, mistress. Took Mrs. Yarborough and the houseboy
in the coach-and-six. Left before dawn and won't be back till
the morrow."

"And what of the servants? Do you say there is no one here
but yourself?"

"Aye. The good doctor weren't expectin' ya yet, ya see. We
been waiting for word from Captain Cooper every day, but
none came."

Jules chuckled to himself, seeing that he had arrived at a
perfect time. Let the manservant go to the ship for his wife and
find the *New Hope* nowhere in port. He'd return, of course, but
Jules wouldn't be there . . . and neither would Alexandre's
wife.

Once Thomas was gone, Jules leaned Dominique against a
black marble table in the hallway. "The good doctor's away on
a mission of mercy," Jules jeered, repeating his words slowly a
second time to make certain she'd understood. "I suggest you
get into some dry clothes and crawl into bed, dearest. You look
a bit peaked, for the wife of the rich Dr. Chastain." Kissing
her, he noticed her lips were cold. "I'll wake you when I
return."

Dragging her upstairs, Jules pushed her inside her room and
locked the door behind him. She leaned against the door and
listened to his footsteps on the stairs, the slam of the front door
as he left. But had he indeed gone? She heard the ticking of the

parlor clock, the rain beating agianst the shutters and the wind pounding the trees about the house. *Pang . . . pang . . . pang*. The sound called up visions of Coosa shot and bleeding on the snow, his blood draining from his body to leave him cold and still. "Don't let him be dead," she prayed. Her hands were so cold they were numb and she stood still while lightning lit the room and thunder shook the tabby house to its foundations. The room was as lovely as she remembered. The bed was draped in peach silk with gray splashes over white organdy, the first flowers of spring were collected in a clear vase on the nightstand, and a gray velvet quilt appliqued with white horses caught her eye. As she unbuttoned her dress, a jagged pain crept across her lower back and rendered her helpless, staggering forward as she shrugged off her soaked clothes and fell into bed.

Dominique woke to a shutter banging and the incessant sound of rain beating against the house. Thunder cracked, the mighty storm still ravaging Savannah. Pulling the velvet quilt to her breasts, she fingered the golden hoop on her ear and recalled in a flash that Coosa was dead. But was he? Something wouldn't allow her to believe it or she, too, would have stopped breathing. She had examined the hoop in the light and knew it was the same one she'd given Coosa in Virginia, yet she still could not accept Coosa's death as fact.

She went to the window. The house was not high; an idea came to her and she seized it as her last chance. She climbed out the window and grabbed hold of the limbs of the old magnolia tree. When she landed on the earth, it was wet and cold like everything she'd touched of late. But there was no time to reflect. Jules would be returning soon and she had to get away . . . to find a horse.

Catharine Ross's house looked vacant in the rain and fog as Dominique hammered the brass doorknocker again and again. She hovered on the stoop in an old riding dress of brown cotton, trembling and holding a black cloak with one hand. Jules had probably already been to Cat's house and had taken the woman off with him. Where could she find help? Where? Then she remembered that Cat kept her own horse and buggy behind her house. She slipped through the closed gate that led to Cat's garden and hurried past ruined rosebushes to a sandy drive. A small carriage house revealed a fancy lady's English buggy and two horses in their stalls. A white mare stepped

aside when Dominique came close to look it over. Next to her
was a stallion, wide-eyed and eager to work. The stallion
neighed and kicked against loose boards behind him. He
looked too wild to ride bareback, and Dominique could see no
saddles or riding tack of any kind. Thunder crashed again and
again and the rain came down in a torrent. Dominique felt a
splatter atop her head and moved aside to escape it, then
another splatter on her hair. She couldn't go far in an open
buggy, she reasoned, despising the thought of wheels beneath
her feet again. Another drop of rain hit her head and she stood
back and held out her hand. The splash that came was red.
Horror gripped her. Blood was on her hand, her skirts, and
hair! Chills gripped her as she looked up into the rafters. Her
unbelieving eyes took in the sight of stockinged feet that
dangled, gray and white skirts and lace petticoats, lavender
ruffles, and a long bloodied purple sash. The wind caught the
door and swung it back with a bang, light filtering across the
hanging women, their slit throats still dripping. Screams filled
the air and the stallion kicked down his stall, bursting his pen
and escaping through the open door. Dominique's head spun,
and then her insides heaved as she bent to retch. A sharp pain
in her head presaged darkness.

Jules Cocteau looked at her a long while where she lay at his
feet. Stupid female, why hadn't she stayed in bed and awaited
his return? Oh, well, she was still breathing; the blow hadn't
broken her skin. Women were such trouble to a man. In truth
he hated women. All women. Hated them for their vile mouths
and lying ways. All women lied, he'd concluded, having
watched his own mother lavish her affection on Alexandre
Chastain while vowing her love for Jules. His mother had
never really loved him or she wouldn't have taken in Alexandre
for her own. His mother was dead now and he was glad. Glad
he wouldn't have to look at her face and listen to her ask about
Alexandre. Wouldn't ever have to hear her voice again!

Finding a length of rope, he bound Dominique's hands and
feet, the sight of her long legs exciting him as ever. He'd have
to wait, he told himself, twisting one hand in her hair and
dragging her across the sandy floor to the buggy. He heaved her
into the buggy and pushed her beneath its seat, covering her
with a heavy carpet.

His first thought was of the barque and then he decided it
would be too risky. The barque would be the first place

Alexandre would look. His mind raced: what place would be safe? He knew the riverfront well, having hidden there many times since his arrival in Savannah. There was an old warehouse where no one ever went. *Oui*, it would be perfect!

Having hitched the white mare to the cariole, Jules whipped her out into the storm. Sheets of cold rain drenched the earth, high winds racking the seaboard as the eye of the tropical storm moved upward toward the Carolinas. A roof was torn from the cottage across the square, limbs scattered helter-skelter in the flooding streets. Fog rolled in from the sea and the mare had difficulty keeping on the beaten path. The buggy crossed Drayton Street where a pack of soaked and muddied dogs leaped out at the horse. The mare reared on hind legs, dancing in the pouring rain, her flesh atremble. Dominique's eyes flickered open. A neighing horse had awakened her, stirred her beneath the heavy rug. Jules swore and she drew in her breath, listening to the snap of his whip as he brought the mare under control. Then Dominique heard a strange voice when a man came out of his cottage and accosted Jules.

"Pray help me, sir. A tree fell on my house and my son is injured and bleeding!"

"Out of my way, man!" Jules flung back, snapping his whip threateningly over the man's head.

"I implore you, sir, my boy could die! Please stop your horse and help!" In desperation, the man grabbed the mare's head and held her.

"What do I care what happened to you? I've business of my own at the river!" Jules snapped his whip and Dominique moaned, rolling her head from beneath the carpet, crying out weakly for help. "Help . . ."

"Did I hear a woman's voice?" the man asked Jules, his face twisting in the icy downpour. "I'd swear I heard a woman's voice calling for help."

"You're hearing things!" Jules said, cracking his whip around the stranger's shoulders, slicing through his shirt. One more crack sent the mare into a mad gallop.

"*Help*!" Dominique wailed as the cariole splashed through water on its mad roll toward the river.

"Scream all you like now," Jules jeered, once they were beyond earshot of the man on the street. He kicked her with his boot. "We're going for a Sunday drive, sweet Nikki. Don't give me any trouble unless you wish to end up in the rafters with Cat and her darky slut!"

Attempting to free herself, Dominique twisted her hands as the heavy twine bit into her wrists and ankles. No one could hear her screams in the storm and Jules would surely kill her as he'd murdered Cat and her maid.

The buggy turned down Bay Street where warehouses rose from the foot of the bluff in the distance, tall buildings made of stones from ships' ballast. The mare slowed her pace, picking her way over slippery stones and beginning her descent down the hill to the riverfront. Jules fingered the reins nervously as they approached Commerce Row, a place where all manner of goods were sold. A black cat darted in front of the mare and Jules cursed all cats as the buggy swerved. Buildings devoted to cotton and slave trade lined the narrow street, warehouses and countinghouses alike. The wheels rolled down a wooden ramp built to carry wagons and carts to the water and Dominique craned her neck to see tall masts of ships peeking over rooftops. Jules swore and reined in the mare.

"Here's where you get out, sweet Nikki." Jules said. Dominique's heart sank as Jules rolled back the carpet to smile down at her. It was still day, although it was as dark as night. The buggy was sitting in the shadows of the bluff and the only things Dominique could see were kegs of rum stacked against a stone wall.

"What are you going to do to me?" she whispered.

"You shall soon find out!" Jules cried. He pulled her to her feet and out of the buggy, dragging her along behind him. "'Tis a high dry place I've chosen for the wife of my dear friend, Dr. Chastain. 'Tis nothing you can't get used to." He laughed. "You'll like the company, I guarantee it." Jules thought it thoroughly amusing for the wife of the rich Alexandre Chastain to end up on the rat-infested riverfront of Savannah. He stopped to get a firm grip on her, then heaved her over one shoulder. Dominique trembled, watching the light disappear as they entered a black tunnel beneath a cast-iron archway that connected the warehouses. Jules felt his way along a wall and set her down in a doorway. "You'll have friends here," Jules said as he opened a huge oaken door that creaked on rusty hinges. Rats squeaked and scattered and Dominique cringed. The warehouse was cold and damp, its air smelling of vermin. Cotton was piled to the rafters, baled and ready for shipping to England.

"Please don't leave me here, Jules."

"Don't worry, sweet Nikki. The wife of Dr. Chastain will be on a higher level." With a grunt, he lifted her and began to climb shaky stairs.

"I could help you get away," Dominique said haltingly. "You could take your barque and return to Martinique. No one knows you killed those women."

"True," Jules replied as they reached the top of the stairs. "No one will ever know so long as you're here." Light fingered through a slatted door that faced the river, two windows shuttered on either side. They were two stories up and the air was better, smelling of sawdust and pine. Her eyes became accustomed to the dark and she saw the outline of boxes stacked to the roof. She eyed them with a sickening dread, now afraid her worst fears might be confirmed. The boxes were coffins, pine boxes for the dead.

"You wouldn't leave me here?" Her voice broke and Jules sat her down on a pile of dusty burlap bags, then went to the door to let in more light.

"We'll be together awhile longer, dearest." He looked for a suitable place for her, knowing the pine boxes had been brought over from the British Isles for the Creek epidemic, to bury the filthy red heathens. Dominique panted, forcing herself to remain calm, envisioning Alexandre looking for her, and what he might find. Would she starve, or be eaten by rats?

"If you don't kill me, Alexandre would give you anything you want." Her voie was frightened, desperate, barely audible over the driving rain and wind outside.

"I wouldn't be foolish enough to kill the golden calf." Jules chuckled. "*Non,* sweet, you're the woman who is going to make me wealthy."

She began to cry with relief, then shivered again as renewed fear washed over her. Jules came to her side, staring down at her.

"Why do you weep? Save your tears, sweet Nikki. We can enjoy each other's company for now. Make the best of being caught alone together in a storm." He reached out and stroked her hair, admiring her lovely face in the fading light. "I couldn't ever kill anything as beautiful as you, my dearest."

He caressed her with the length of his body and his breathing became deeper.

"What have I done to make you hate me?" she asked innocently, attempting to allay him now. Jules touched her face with his hands, sliding his thumbs over the high bones of her cheeks.

"You're his wife!" he snarled. "Do you think I could allow him to have you . . . to enjoy you . . . to live happily ever after?" She saw madness flare in his eyes and her blood slowed.

"I won't be his wife much longer." She shrugged, tossing her gold mane and forcing herself to look into his eyes.

"What?"

"I'm going back home to Pennsylvania. I should never have left."

Jules stared, circling her where she sat atop the burlap heap, then smiled, laughing softly. " 'Twas there I first had you, remember?"

She tried not to let him see the terror in her eyes. "How could I forget?"

He ran his fingers down the bridge of her nose to its tip, traced the outline of her lips ever so slowly. "You're afraid, aren't you?"

"I'm cold," she said softly.

He opened the front of her habit and marveled at her treasures, his eyes wild as he caressed the curving column of her neck. "I've not been north since that night."

"We could go back together. On horseback there would be little chance of being seen."

He laughed heartily, rising to pace the floor, thinking he'd caught her. "Do you take me for a fool?" he roared. "I've heard tales of your adventures on fleet-footed beasts! Think you'd get me on a horse and wear me down, eh? I'll do my riding indoors, thank you. And you'll be my steed!" Ripping her habit from her slim waist, he dipped his hands inside to feel her warmth, her loveliness, filling each hand with a trembling peach-crested mound. Moaning, he kissed her lips and moved behind her to slide his mouth down her back. She closed her eyes and shivered.

"Forgive me, for I can't please you in return," she said softly.

"Whoring Chastain slut!" he swore to himself as he

knocked her to the floor. "Do you think me such a fool to believe your lies!"

"Please," she sobbed, "I'm hurt, I think my leg is broken."

Quickly, Jules went to undo her ropes, her feet first, and then her hands, bending to lift her when she propelled herself into him, driving her feet against his chest and knocking him backward. She had rolled off the sacks and into the shadows by the time he came to his feet. She crawled on her hands and knees to the stairs and hid behind the coffins, dust rising in her nostrils as she held back a sneeze. Jules stood to come toward her, and she leaned against a stack of pine boxes, waiting, her hands ready. The time was right. When Jules came close Dominique toppled the coffins and hurried to the stairs. Jules swore, breathing heavily, and followed on her heels. When Dominique ran for the door and found it latched at the top, she pounded against the door with her fists. "Help me! Please help me!"

Then Jules was behind her. He clapped one hand over her mouth and ripped her dress down her back with the other. Spinning her around, he gave her a swipe with his hand, pressing her to the door and twisting his mouth over hers. Dominique felt the bulge of his manhood throbbing against her and felt sick to her stomach.

"I'll kill you!" she spat into his face when his mouth lifted from hers. She raked his face with her nails and Jules struck her so hard she sank down onto the floor. Then he picked her up and sprawled her over a bale of cotton where he ravaged her, again and again.

She heard the sound of long nails being driven home from the darkness of the pine box. Her spine arched against the hard surface of unyielding wood, but she was unable to reach out, kick, move. She screamed until no sound came from her mouth, but it did no good. She felt the smooth planes of the wooden lid that covered her face, panicked, and beat her hands against the sides of the box until she heard laughter.

"Save your strength for me, sweet Nikki," Jules whispered, his face pressed against the coffin's lid. "I'll be back to have you again tonight, have no fear."

Nay! she screamed mutely. She'd die before he returned.

" 'Tis up to your husband to save you now, Madame Chastain. Pray he doesn't come too late." His devilish laugh accompanied his footsteps as he moved down the stairs, leaving her to the dark that slowly faded into unconsciousness.

Alexandre had returned from Sea Island plantation. The roads had been washed away in places and he'd not slept in twenty-four hours. His clothes were soaked through when he met his servant, Thomas, in the street outside Chastain House. The servant helped the doctor carry in his things and related a story about his mistress returning home and then disappearing.

"You're telling me my wife came back with Drummond yesterday and now they're both gone?"

"That's it, doctor. I went off to get Ruthe, my wife, but she wasn't there because the *New Hope* never docked."

Alexandre hung his sodden cloak before a roaring fire and rubbed his hands together, then poured himself a drink. "What did Drummond say to you?"

"Nothing, that's just it. The mistress did all the talking now that I think on it. The man said nothing."

"Drummond has flame-red hair. Did you see that much?"

"No, sir, he was holding an oilskin over his head. I never saw his face or heard his voice."

Alexandre told himself there was no cause for alarm. His wife had probably gone to Cat's house, having visited the woman before the *New Hope* sailed. "How long has my wife been gone?"

Thomas shrugged. "Can't tell ya, doctor, sir. She weren't here when I returned."

Alexandre ran up the stairs to the master chambers to have a look, finding Dominique's torn and wet clothes on the floor, the bed slept in. He was racing down the steps to call for a horse when Moses came into the house, clearly excited.

"Murdered, doctor. Mrs. Ross and her girl were found hanging from the rafters like hens in the marketplace, their throats cut from ear to ear, blood everywhere!" Moses went with his master into the parlor where they both downed a drink and he related what he'd discovered at Cat's house. "I broke into the house and found blood everywhere, doctor. They had apparently struggled and rolled down the stairs, I'd say. The murderer must have done the evil deed in the bedchamber for the bed was soaked with blood. The worst mess I've ever seen—pearls and blood, pearls and blood."

"My wife was gone when you returned?" Alexandre asked Thomas again.

"Aye, doctor. There was no sign of them."

"Then Drummond's with her, wherever she is . . ." Alexandre held his face in his hands.

"Why not rest, doctor? Your wife has no doubt wandered off to visit with friends. Women are like that. They like to be with other women. I'll contact the authorities at once and see if Mr. Drummond can be found. We'll find her, master."

"I'll go with you," Alexandre said, reaching for his wet cloak where it hung before the fire. As he did so, Mrs. Yarborough knocked and entered, walking briskly to her employer's side.

"For ye, doctor. The boy says 'tis terrible important. Won't leave till he gets his piece of silver. A matter of life and death, says he."

Alexandre perused a sealed letter with his eyes, then ripped it open with trembling hands and reading it. "Where is the person who delivered this?" he demanded, standing to take Mrs. Yarborough's arm.

"In the kitchen, doctor. I wouldn't let 'im in your fine parlor with muddied boots."

Alexandre pushed the letter into Moses's hand and swept past Mrs. Yarborough. The manservant skimmed the letter addressed to Alexandre Chastain. *"I have your wife. She will be returned after I receive one hundred thousand pieces of gold delivered to the barque Merchant. You have twenty-four hours to comply."* The signature was that of Jules Cocteau. Moses went to find his master who was in the library behind closed doors.

"The devil has her." Alexandre stood behind his desk, his voice wavering as he withdrew paper and pen. "I might have guessed Jules was behind this. 'Twas he who murdered those women."

"What did the messenger tell you?" Moses asked.

"He was accosted by a man bearing Jules's resemblance late last night. He was just a boy. The lad had been waiting for me to return from Sea Island all night. He'd been instructed to deliver the letter to me and no one else. Jules promised him a reward."

"Then why didn't we go with him? He could lead us to Jules, couldn't he?"

Alexandre shook his head, scrawling a letter to Myron Smith, the young lawyer who'd handled his father's estate in Savannah. "Not likely. He doesn't know where Jules is now."

"May I ask what you're doing, doctor?"

"I'm making arrangements for my assets to be changed into gold—there's no time to waste. My wife's in the hands of a madman." Alexandre was pushing himself up by the arms of his leather chair when Mrs. Yarborough burst into the room.

"Excuse me, doctor, but there's a man here who needs your medical assistance at once!"

"Show him in," Alexandre said. Mrs. Yarborough stood back as a man dressed in old clothes stepped inside the room, his face set in seams of gloom.

" 'Tis my son, doctor. I've had a hard time tracking you down. A tree fell on my house and my boy's leg's broke clean through. He's lost a lot of blood."

"I regret I have troubles of my own, monsieur. Forgive me, but I can't help your son. You'll have to find another doctor."

"But there's not another man of medicine in all Savannah, sir! You must come, my boy's in bad pain and he'll die if you don't help him!" Seeing he was getting nowhere with Alexandre, the man turned to Mrs. Yarborough. "Tell him to come with me, won't you ma'am? Is there no one in all of Savannah who'll help a poor person? Has the whole world gone mad?"

Alexandre's conscience spoke to him, his eyelids fluttering as he remembered he was a doctor under oath, a healer of the sick and helpless. An innocent needed him and there could be no priority for revenge.

"I asked a gentleman in a fine buggy for help and got the sting of his whip for it," the poor man mumbled. "I used to believe you could tell a gentleman by the way he dressed, but no more. The man said he had things to do at the river, he did. But why would a man go to the river with a lady wrapped up in a carpet, I ask you?"

"What did you say?" Alexandre spun around, his eyes ablaze. "What did you say about a woman?"

The poor man's jaw fell to his chest, his eyes fearful that he may have offended the doctor he needed to save his son's life. "Nothing, doctor. Didn't mean no disrespect. 'Twas a stranger to me, a Frenchie like yourself. Dressed like a gentleman with a cloak and hat and in a fine buggy. Do you know why such a gentleman would wrap his lady in a carpet and make her ride on the floor of his buggy?"

Alexandre took the man by the arm and led him to the fire, setting him down in a comfortable chair and giving him a drink. "What did this gentleman look like . . . his face, did he wear a beard? What time of day was it? Did you see the woman?"

Downing the drink, the man thought. "Yesterday, doctor. About noon, I'd say, during the big storm."

"What did the woman say—did you see her face?"

"Aye, sir." The man was befuddled, trying hard to recall details which he hoped would lead to rewards. "She was a beauty, I did see that! Gold hair, long, as I recall, and a lovely face. It was raining buckets, you know, and she was crying, but I saw her face, I did. She cried out more than once, too."

"What did the man say?"

"Said he couldn't help me. Cursed me and gave me his whip around the neck. Swore and said he was off to the river and had no time, said he cared less for my trouble. 'Twas a Frenchie, like I told you."

Alexandre's blood ran cold and his limbs trembled. Visions of his wife in Jules's hands swept through his mind, an image so horrible he couldn't stand it.

"Will you be coming to help my boy now, doctor?"

Alexandre went for his black bag and cloak, helping the man from his chair. "Gather as many men as you can and ride for the river, Moses. I'll join you as soon as I've helped the boy."

Wheels rumbled over cobblestones, and a driver cursing the fog woke Dominique with a start. Her heart beat wildly, her back aching as she tried to remember where she was. Her mind responded slowly and she heard water slapping against a wharf, a ship's bell clanging in the distance. She was cold and her brain struggled to remember, dampness seeping into her bones from the cold wood she lay upon. The past days fell into place and she recalled the storm, Cat's body dangling from the rafters, Jules Cocteau! She moaned and found that her mouth was bound.

Rain drove into the shuttered windows of the warehouse where she lay imprisoned, soaking the stone walls and roof. Sucking in her breath, she felt pains stab her womb, creeping

slowly down her thighs to her legs. She'd known pain before
like this. She was losing a babe. Trying not to cry, she
reminded herself that tears were a waste of precious energy.
She blinked into the darkness, her eyes searching for light.
How long had Jules been gone? Was he coming back for her?
Who could save her? No one knew where she was. How long
would it take to die, how long . . . how long?

She tried to turn, then tried to draw up her legs. Her feet
were freezing and her toes were numb with pain. The wind
howling outside reminded her of climbing the mountain. The
wind had been with her then, too. She thought of God and
Coosa and wondered if there was truly a hereafter. A tear ran
down her cheek. If only Coosa were there, he could help her,
but Coosa was dead. Nay, she cried inwardly, she didn't believe
the Creek was dead, she'd never believe it. Coosa was alive!

Screaming into the wad of cotton Jules had stuffed inside her
mouth, she told herself not to go to pieces. Her worst fear was
now realized. She had dreamed of dying inside a box countless
times and her father had begged her to tell him her dream but
she never had. How could a child tell her father of a nightmare
so frightening it made her lie awake all night for fear of
dreaming it again? She'd dreamed of dying all her life, away at
school, even after she married Alexandre. Locked inside a box
and rolling over stones to her grave, wheels beneath her,
turning wheels . . . turning wheels, always turning!

Rodents' feet scampered over the lid of her coffin and she
envisioned the tiny eyes and long tails over her face. Rats! Rats
everywhere, squeaking! She began to whimper low in her
throat, shivers engulfing her as she realized she must be close
to death. Alexandre would find her missing and come looking
for her. But Alexandre was away and Thomas couldn't even
tell her husband where she was. She heard Jules's parting
words over and over in her mind. Jules could return any minute
and then he'd open her coffin and let her out. She wept,
thinking of her father and mother and the blue mountains of
Virginia. Coosa coming toward her in the snow. She thought of
Alexandre and their child . . . Jules's child! Jules had set out
to wreck her life and now he'd won, he'd won! He'd ravaged
her, taken her against her will, beaten her, made her do things
that made her burn with shame. God forgive her, she'd rather
die and never see the sun again than have Jules touch her again.
She prayed she would die.

* * *

Alexandre's horse threaded through dense fog above Savannah's bluff. He'd covered Bay Street from one end to the other looking for some sign of life. Anything that might lead him to Jules Cocteau and his wife. The driving rain and fog made the going difficult, blinding the way. God help him, his wife could be anywhere, in a warehouse, outbuilding, tunnel, shed! How in Hades could he find her on a night like this? The river was lost in the fog though it was nearly daylight.

Urging his horse westward, he leaned into the rain and realized he was going in circles. He turned his horse inland, thinking of Racemont and warm weather, wishing he were in bed with his wife in front of a warm fire . . . holding her close and telling her of his love. He saw a light from a lantern and wheeled his horse to have a look. The light was below in an alleyway, between the bluff and Factors Walk, down the steep ramp to the cotton warehouses. The first sign of life he'd seen may mean something. It was worth a look. His horse turned down the ramp, plodding its way to the street below where a door swung open and slammed shut.

Dominique's heart sank. Jules had come back for her . . . come back to kill her! Footfalls approached up the stairs . . . closer and closer. She heard a knock on her coffin.

"Anyone home?" Jules called.

Dominique quaked where she lay, wishing she'd died in the last hours of torment. She heard the sound of tools striking the floor and started. A metal bar pried open the lid of her box while she shuddered with fear, the scrape of wood against iron . . .

"I've come back to see if you missed me." Jules chuckled, thinking of taking her again and having the supreme satisfaction of murdering her during the act. It was light now and he could see the fear leaping from her eyes. Green eyes, as green as the hills of his Madiana, the plantation Alexandre had so generously given his father. *Given*? What had a Castain ever given a Cocteau? His father, Baudoin, had earned every penny he'd received from the wealthy François Chastain. All the Chastains' gold could never repay Jules for the childhood he'd spent hating Alexandre, the boy who could do no wrong.

"I see you're still breathing, Madame Chastain," Jules said, removing Dominique's gag and twisting one arm to pull her from the box. She didn't speak for fear of arousing him, then whimpered softly and tried to stand, the pain in her stomach causing her to fall back. "What's wrong?" Jules asked as he pulled her along behind him. She tried to stay afoot, wondering where he was taking her and smelling liquor on his breath, thinking of wheels over cobblestones and graves in the fog and cold rain. "Perhaps I can warm you up before we go, eh?" Pushing her against the coffins, his mouth came down on one exposed breast. "We have time, time to waste, dearest Nikki."

"Please," she begged, "kill me, but don't . . ."

"No one can accuse me of letting a woman go to waste." Jules smiled. "I came back because I wanted you, Nikki. I want you now!" Giving her a hard push, she fell against a stack of pine boxes, knocking them apart. "You have nothing to lose. See what I have for you." As he unbuttoned his breeches, his mouth slid down her neck.

"My child . . . my husband . . ."

"Your husband's not here and your child be damned."

She was trying to tell him she was losing another babe when he struck her in the jaw and she saw red and black blend into white.

"I want to tell him how it felt to take you!" Jules rasped. "I want him to see how it feels when I take you in front of him. Make him listen to your moans and hear you begging for more!"

Dominique was lost in a swoon as he stripped off her clothes and pushed himself into her, raising her legs and pounding as fast as he could until the door opened downstairs, screeching on its hinges.

"Anyone here?" Alexandre called. Dominique moaned, coming to, seeing Jules rocking over her. She screamed, and Jules pulled back, shrinking as he picked up an iron bar. Alexandre walked across the floor below them. "Dominique, Dominique Chastain!" Jules stood in the shadows, the iron bar raised over his head in wait as Alexandre climbed the stairs. "Dominique . . ." Alexandre called as he approached the top of the stairs. Jules struck out and missed Alexandre's head by an inch, the bar striking his shoulder and then skidding across the floor. Alexandre winced, the pain of the blow stunning him. Dominique screamed again and again as Alexandre shook his head and Jules grabbed the doctor from behind, tearing his dripping oilskin to take him by the throat. Alexandre gasped, then brought up his arms to break the devil's hold. Jules's madness made him capable of incredible physical strength. His eyes gleamed in the light like a wild animals, his beard and scarred face twisting into a fiendish smile. Dominique drew back into the shadows, looking for something to hit Jules with as Alexandre crossed his arms and broke Jules's stranglehold. Alexandre whirled around and Jules knocked him back, Jules's fist catching Alexandre on the jaw. Alexandre crawled on his hands and knees and reached for the iron crowbar. Jules kicked the tool from Alexandre's fingers.

"Fool!" Jules growled, coming at Alexandre and knocking him back with a swift kick to the ribs. Alexandre lay dazed and still as Jules picked up the bar to raise it over Alexandre's head. Dominique screamed and Alexandre rolled to one side, the bar missing his head by a breath. Coming to his knees, Alexandre crawled toward the door and Jules came at him, his face lit by a grin. Alexandre dove for Jules's legs, and the two men rolled against the door. It burst open. Dominique screamed as wind and rain blew into the room, blowing the door back with a crash against stone walls. Jules had Alexandre by the throat again and was easing him toward the open door. As if in a dream, Dominique saw Jules lose his balance and fall through the rain and fog to the street below. Dominique went down the stairs as fast as she could, although she was bleeding so much she could feel the moisture between her legs. Dust filled her nostrils as the door slammed agains the stone wall and the wind howled in the rafters. At the bottom of the stairs she slid to the floor, unable to get up and walk again. Then, helpless, she heard footfalls and knew Jules was coming to get her. She prepared to die.

"*Chérie!*" The voice was soft and thankful. The face of her husband was blurred at first, then she saw the pained expression on his face and wondered why she wasn't dead. "You're safe now, *chérie*. You lost the babe but you're alive and that's all that matters. You're all that ever mattered, my love." Alexandre wept and she longed to tell him how sorry she was for all the unhappiness she'd caused, wanting his forgiveness. "Rest, *chérie*, the past's forgotten and it's a new day." Bending to kiss her lips, he touched her hair with his fingers and held her gently in his arms. Then a door closed and she shut her eyes to the knowledge that she'd lost the Creek *mico*'s child and possibly her husband's love.

19

Alexandre sat beside his wife's bed absorbed in thought. He'd nearly lost her this time. She'd very nearly bled to death and was fortunate to be alive. Mrs. Yarborough yawned, patting her master's shoulder and shaking her head before she left the room. They'd taken turns nursing Dominique for days and now the crisis was past. Dominique had called the Creek king's name in her delirium and Alexandre couldn't forget. His wife had been with the heathen. Coosa and Drummond were dead; he'd been assured of their deaths after talking at length with Drummond's men. He'd never meant for Coosa to die, although Drummond had assured him he'd kill anyone who became a threat. He'd known Drummond hated Indians and was capable of murder. That was one of the reasons he'd hired the Englishman to find Jules Cocteau. Alexandre never dreamed he'd be sending his wife into the arms of his half-breed nephew when he put her on the *New Hope* bound for Virginia. Now his brother's bastard son was dead and he couldn't deny he was glad. *Glad!* His pale brows lowered at the truth. Coosa had wanted his wife because she was beautiful. Every man who'd ever laid eyes on Dominique had wanted her. Lusted after her! Coosa had never been his friend. No man would ever be his friend when it came to Dominique.

He'd not slept or eaten right in days, drugging himself to stay awake. His hands shook and his legs barely held him as he went to the window to look out over the rooftops of Savannah. Jules was out there somewhere, unless he'd sailed for Martinique with the fortune he'd paid in ransom for his wife. Satan would take care of Jules, but devils had a habit of prowling the earth and the next time Jules Cocteau surfaced Alexandre would be ready. He vowed it!

Dominique stirred and he went to cover her. It was spring outside but it felt like winter. The fire in the fireplace reminded him of the last time he'd lain with her in that very room. He'd been drinking and they'd argued, he'd pushed her to the floor and taken her before the fire. His lashes moistened, his face red with shame. He'd been cruel and inhuman and he was sorry, promising to make it up to her. It wasn't like him to force a woman and he didn't know why he'd done it. She'd carried his babe two months, he calculated; the child she'd lost had been his. Church bells rang and he vowed never to speak of Coosa's death. Perhaps his wife would never know. The Creek king's horse was still in Richmond and he'd instructed Drummond's men to return the beast to the Creek people in Georgia. He needed no reminder of his wife's infidelity. He decided then to risk getting his wife pregnant as soon as possible. A babe could be the means of bringing them back together. The idea satisfied him and he looked forward to returning to Racemont.

The forests were alive with color: pink azalea, lavender wisteria, white dogwood. Lush foliage bloomed everywhere after the long winter's rains. A creamy mare pranced daintily around the ring, her mane frothy in the warm April sun. A tiny tot sat on the mare before her mother and squealed with delight. "Faster, mama, make the horse go like the wind!"

Dominique laughed at her three-year-old daughter, Angelique. "Only spirits go like the wind, Angel. Spirits of the mighty Creek kings and warriors who have inhabited this land before white men ever heard of it. Who inhabit this land still." Dominique saw Coosa as he was in life then, tall, bronzed regal, his black eyes lit with love. Undying love. Tears stung her eyes and she kissed the gold top of her wee daughter's head, glancing at the mountain of stone. The gray egg brooding . . . waiting for her return. Shivers climbed her spine. She'd not climbed the mountain since she'd last been there with Coosa and she'd never climb it again now that he was dead. She placed the reins in her little girl's fist, thinking deeply of the past. How could someone be dead when he lived on in her heart, her mind, her soul? No night had passed without prayers for Coosa's safekeeping, without dreams of his kisses, his caresses, his sweet words of endearment. Aye, she'd lain with her husband countless times since she'd lost Coosa's babe, but each time she'd lain with Coosa.

Wicked, deceitful, wrong! Alexandre was her husband; he had given her a second chance, saved her life! Alexandre had been good to her and she loved him, of that there was no doubt. 'Twas a mannerly love, aye, love with no mountains or valleys, but love given honestly for love received. The love she felt for Coosa was different. Wild, untamed love, love filled with shooting stars and thunder, joyous and eternal.

"Please, can't we climb the mountain, mama?" Angel pointed to the huge granite bubble on the landscape.

"No! 'Tis forbidden, you know that!" Desiree rode up on her black pony, its hooves overturning earth as it galloped beside the white mare.

"She rides like an Indian!" Alexandre called from the rail from which he watched his ladies. Desiree rode astride like a man, her dark curls shot with gold threads braided into a long tail that was jostled as her pony tore through the orchard's gate and halted among pecan trees.

"A natural horsewoman!" Dominique called back. It was a pity they weren't close. Desiree could be a good riding companion, but the girl was on intimate terms with no one, spending most of her time with Mrs. Yarborough.

"I want Desiree to go to school in Philadelphia, Alexandre," Dominique said that night in the privacy of her bedchamber. She sat brushing her long topaz tresses before a dressing table skirted in shamrock-green silk. The gold-leafed mirror reflected her worried expression. Alexandre frowned from their bed, exhausted from a long day of surgery in his hospital in the slave's village. He couldn't sleep until his wife lay beside him. It had been that way since Jules had nearly taken her from him in Savannah. Now, Dominique was seldom from his sight. When she was, he had her bodyguards take over. He wasn't taking chances on losing her again. He'd kill any man who set hands on her or his darling daughter Angelique. He had no complaints. Dominique had matured,

settled down, become a good wife and mother as well as
serious breeder of horses and hounds. How proud he was of
her, he mused as he watched her dress her hair. She'd returned
to being mistress of Racemont in her stride. He watched her
arrange her hair over one shoulder, pushing the golden mass
atop her head. She was growing more beautiful by the day, he
thought as he eyed her black French wrapper over a gown of
palest yellow, caught beneath her breasts with black satin
ribbons, the thin fabric revealing a figure that could have
excited a man of any age. "Did you hear what I said?"
Dominique asked as she climbed into bed. Alexandre reached
out and took her hand, drawing it to the center of his chest to
feel the beat of his heart. She was with Coosa for a fleeting
moment, feeling the knife wounds the Creek had inflicted on
himself because of her. "I love you in yellow," Alexandre said
softly, his eyes closed.

"Did you kiss Angel good night?"

"*Oui.*" He moved beside her and pulled her into his arms.
"Do you think I'd forget my little Angel?" His lips found her
shoulder and she heard his breathing change. He was asleep
and she was relieved. She didn't want him to touch her tonight.
There was a full moon and she longed to ride in the moonlight.

The next morning Angel was not in her bed and Dominique
rushed downstairs to the kitchen. "Good mornin', missis."
The boy, Moses, was arranging a basket of flowers for the
breakfast table. He looked crisp and clean in his starched shirt
and striped breeches, a red bow at his neck.

"Good morning, darling. Have you seen Angel?"

"Gone ridin' with Miss Desiree in the dark," the slave boy
replied. "On Harmony." Harmony was Desiree's English
pony, a beast not yet schooled for tiny tots. Dominique turned
to gaze out the windows and saw the spirited pony gallop
across granite setes in the pink dawn. Desiree beat the animal
with her quirt, prompting Dominique to throw open the door to
run along the lower gallery.

"Desiree, stop that at once! Don't ever beat your horse!"

Desiree reined in her pony and jumped down amid a pack of
panting hounds. The girl released the dogs, too; no telling what
the beasts had been up to. Angel could have been injured
seriously, killed! Dominique tried to control her anger. Desiree
couldn't be trusted with Angel and Dominique lived in fear the
girl might harm her baby. It was a difficult situation. Domi-

nique didn't want Desiree to know she distrusted her. Desiree was wild and careless and hadn't had the benefits of mothering that Angel had had.

"Mama, mama!" Angel reached out her arms to Dominique, clinging to the mane of the still trotting pony. Dominique ran for her child through wet grass, still barefoot. "I was afraid, mama!" Dominique swooped the child into her arms. "Harmony goes too fast!" Dominique held the child to her breast and Desiree pushed past, running into the house and slamming the door behind her, tossing her quirt onto the kitchen table.

"I'll have my breakfast in my room, Mère," Desiree said curtly, pushing through the doors to the dining room.

"Miss Prissy done tole me she wants tah eat in her room again," Marie complained to Dominique as her mistress came through the door. Marie shook her wooden spoon and reached out to squeeze Angel's chubby legs. "That girl needs some manners!"

"I'll take a tray up to her, Marie. Keep Angel here till I return."

"I will, missus!" Mère laughed, delighted to have the tot to herself. "I keep dah little princess anytimes." Angel giggled and Mère swept the child into her arms, tugging at Angel's near-white curls caught up with ribbons. Dominique carried a tray painted with violets and rosebuds and holding a pink tulip in a vase and French china rimmed in silver. The breakfast consisted of fresh fruit, steaming sausage, and biscuits, scrambled eggs and grits topped with butter—things Desiree liked.

"You were rude to Mère this morning, Desiree. I want you to apologize to her. Mère loves you; we all do." Dominique stood in the doorway of her daughter's room, unable to decide where she'd gone wrong with the girl. "You'll be going to Germantown to live with your grandparents in the fall. There's a good school there, the same one I went to. You'll be leaving at summer's end."

Mrs. Yarborough directed her mistress to set the tray down on the bed and Dominique went deliberately to the opposite side of the room to set the tray down. "Please leave us alone, Mrs. Yarborough, and close the door behind you."

"I'll be back," the servant woman said to Desiree.

"I don't like flowers and you know it," Desiree said, flinging the tulip on her tray into the fireplace.

"How could any daughter of mine not like flowers? Flowers are—"

"Yours!" Desiree interjected. "Everything here is yours." Desiree stared her mother down, daring her to counter. "What do you want?"

"May I sit down?"

" 'Tis your house."

"This is your house, too, darling, everything—"

"Don't call me that! I'm not one of your black darlings." Desiree's eyes narrowed and Dominique was stunned. The girl hated her, her own flesh and blood. Dear God, how could it be?

"You look ill, mama. But then you're always sick, aren't you? You're never going to be well, are you? You were sick when my father married you and you've never been right since."

Dominique saw Jules in her daughter's eyes. *Jules is your father, not Alexandre!* she wanted to say. "Perhaps Savannah would be more to your liking, Desiree. 'Tis cold and damp in the winter, but your father and I could come to visit you often. You could live in our house there and—"

"Savannah's nothing but a pesthole for darkies and Indians and pigs! Send me there and I shall tell my father everything I know about you," Desiree threatened. "I dare you."

It was later than usual when Alexandre came to bed. He expected his wife to be asleep but a candle burned low beside the huge bed as Dominique fingered the Spanish guitar Coosa had given her in Virginia. The instrument had been returned to her by Jacques and it was the first time Alexandre had seen it.

"I didn't know you played the guitar." Alexandre cast his clothes to a chair, sliding under a satin coverlet with his wife.

"I don't," she said softly, blinking back tears. " 'Tis a thing of beauty to me, something I enjoy touching."

"Is something wrong, love?" He thought about horses and hounds, of Angel's French lessons and the troublesome Desiree.

"Nay." Caressing the guitar, Dominique returned it to the protection of a silk shawl and put it away in her armoire, then returned to bed. She couldn't tell Alexandre about Desiree. It was something she must work out between her and her daughter.

"I'm going to Charleston in the morning." Alexandre lifted the coverlet and slid one arm beneath her neck to draw her head to his chest. He nuzzled her hair, running one finger down her cheek. "Jacques will see to things here. No one's on the death list and Mrs. Yarborough will take whoever she needs from the house slaves to the hospital once a day. There are no pups to whelp and you needn't go near the stables unless you want to."

"You know I want to."

He kissed her nose, happy because he knew she couldn't stay away from the horses or dogs. She'd rather be with animals than with people and never missed a day without riding one of her horses.

"Alexandre." She pressed a finger to his lips so his reply couldn't come. "Why Charleston?"

"A building there interests me." He was no good at lying and hoped she'd believe him. The building he was going to see was the Charleston jail where Jules Cocteau had spent some time. He knew the mere mention of Jules's name would upset her for days, so he lied.

"I don't want you to go," she whispered. "Don't leave me."

"I'm not leaving you, my beautiful wife." He chuckled. " 'Tis time we were separated, though. I hear married people who see too much of one another get bored. I don't want that to happen to us."

"Please," she begged, cuddling close and pulling his arms around her, moving one hand to her breast. She loved him with all her heart then, afraid to tell him so.

"I'm sorely tempted." He covered her with the coverlet, tracing a fine line with his finger to her neck. She kissed his hand and listened to her heart warning she was only half alive without Coosa. "I'll miss you. 'Tis certain I'll not sleep without you beside me." He peeled off her gown of pale green and beheld her rare beauty. "I love you," he said, unable to bring himself to touch her again.

She whispered Coosa's name to herself and encircled Alexandre's neck with her arms, wanting to share the pleasures of holy wedlock with him.

"I love you," she said, her fingers locking behind his neck as he looked into her eyes.

"I wish I could believe that, chérie."

" 'Tis the truth," she murmured. "Truly 'tis. I have no reason to lie."

In another bedchamber the candles burned brightly. Desiree sat in her bed, legs drawn beneath her, her white cotton gown making her look far younger than her years. Twisting a lock of ebony hair in her fingers, she listened attentively to Mrs. Yarborough's exciting tales of the past.

"Jules Cocteau was your uncle's name. He knew your father as a brother, but your mother favored him more, if the truth be known." The woman winked at the girl she'd raised from a babe, setting the child's imagination spinning. Scenes of lust and adulterous love had been described to Desiree, wild encounters between her and mother and a dark-faced stranger from the islands.

"Tell me more, Yar."

" 'Twas the last Jubilee celebration ever held on this plantation—"

"I know about the Jubilee," Desiree snapped. "Get on with the part about my mother."

Mrs. Yarborough screwed up her face and unbuttoned her dress for bed, preparing to sleep in Desiree's room. "Your mother came up missing that day, your poor father off lookin' for 'er like he'd done so many times before when—"

"What?"

"He found her in the carriage house, her dog dead and your poor grandpa, too. Attacked by the islander Jules . . . or so she said. Violated, if ye believe that." She paused, watching for Desiree's reaction. " 'Twas their plan ta meet, the way I see it. The two of 'em alone while the rest of us was at the Jubilee. When your poor father caught her in the act, she cried rape!"

Desiree stared at the servant woman a long time. Yar wouldn't lie about something as serious as this. The servant woman had told her many times her mother had cheated on her father, but Desiree couldn't accept it as truth. "What's a whore, Yar?"

The woman frowned, expressing shock at the girl's language, but feeling a surge of pleasure rush through her as she nourished the girl's hatred for her mother. "I've heard the mistress called that. Let's just say your mother didn't want your father's child and managed ta lose it, the babe the doctor wanted more than his very breath." She shook her head sadly.

" 'Twas a big beautiful boy and nearly full term, too. I'll never forget the day."

Desiree's face registered surprise, the news of her mother's miscarriage new. "You mean she lost my little brother?"

"Killed 'im, I'd say, dear. First she made a cuckold of your father, and then she got rid of his babe. 'Tis the reason your father took ta drink and that's not all of it."

Desiree's eyes filled with tears, trying to think of a way to avenge her father. "She's been whoring around again, too." Desiree's unladylike language made Mrs. Yarborough let out a great gasp, as if a blade was stuck between her ribs. "She went out riding last night and I followed her to the mountain."

"God protect ye, child, what did ye see?"

Desiree smiled, hissing the words that followed. "Her with Uncle Jacques, the two of them meeting at the foot of the mountain."

"I knew it! Her and that half-breed slave have always had eyes for one another."

Desiree shivered with the truth about her mother. She didn't want to hurt her mother, but why not? Her mother didn't love her. She loved Angelique and the horses and slaves. "Uncle Jacques was a slave?"

"*Is* a slave, child! Now I know why your father's never given the darky bastard his papers all these years. She's the reason!"

"Now she's sending me away and you're allowing it!"

"What can I do? Your father says I have ta stay here and help care for the darkies. But don't you worry, I'll look after your mother, too."

"What do you mean, Yar?"

"Who else could take care of a madwoman and her brat? 'Tis high time the both of em fell ill, I'm thinkin'. It wouldn't surprise me if your mother and her darling Angel were ta come down with somethin', somethin' serious."

Desiree thought about what Mrs. Yarborough was saying, afraid of losing her mother, and uncertain that's what she meant. "Would they die?"

"Nay, 'tis best you're not here, don't ya see? When they're real sick, they'll go back north to be with your grandpa. When they're gone we can be together and they'll never interfere. All the horses will be yours and you can ride her blue mare and any stallion ye want."

Desiree smiled. Her mother never allowed her to ride her mare and the stallions were said to be too wild for her. If her mother and Angel were in Pennsylvania, she could ride to the hounds every day if she wanted.

Dominique saw Jacques in the kennels later that morning. She'd come to evaluate a litter of puppies. "We must talk," Jacques said, pretending interest in the hounds for the sake of the kennelboys who swept the stone floors behind them. "You made an old man of me last night. I didn't expect to see you when I went riding in the moonlight."

"Nor I you." Two boys came down an aisle raking pinestraw from the floor, another scrubbing the huge wood pallets the dogs slept on.

"Our meeting was not planned but we might have a difficult time proving it if Alexandre were told. A member of your family followed you when you went riding last night. The girl's pony was lathered when I returned Ramir to his stall."

Dominique had ridden to the mountain of stone and met Jacques there by chance. The girl would tell Alexandre and her husband would think the worst. "We have a new foal this morning," she said aloud. "Do you want to see him?"

"*Oui!*" Jacques guided her through the stall's gate, then ushered her down the wide aisles of the kennels. " 'Tis a relief to be out of that racket."

"Don't worry, Jacques. We've done nothing wrong. If Desiree goes to Alexandre, we'll just have to face it."

"Face the firing squad, you mean."

"It won't be that bad. Alexandre will listen to reason."

"Will he, little sister?"

"Why don't we go for a real ride when your husband goes to Charleston? I have some land to survey beyond the river. We can invite Desiree to ride along."

"That's a splendid idea. I can't wait to tell her."

Dominique was waiting when Jacques arrived at the stables. Desiree wasn't with her. When she'd explained that Desiree had refused to ride with the two of them, he gave her a leg up on Ramir and pulled himself onto his gray gelding. He thought her lovely in a cabbage-green riding suit cinched at the waist with a wide belt of hammered silver. A cool breeze caught the tendrils escaping about her temples, making her appear angelic.

After a while, they dismounted beside a frothing stream.

"I buried Coosa's mother in the shade of that black walnut up there." Jacques lifted her down.

" 'Tis a nice spot." She stepped toward the walnut and wanted to ask about Coosa but instead said nothing while she tethered her horse.

"I'll build a house here one day. There's a spring with plenty of sweet water."

She began to walk and he followed. "Why can't I accept his death?" she asked.

"Because he's alive and well and asks to be remembered to you."

She stopped where she stood in deep clover, her heart racing as her mind spun. "I knew it! Dear God, why haven't you told me?" she cried.

"For many reasons, little sister. Any of which involves my brother and your husband." She stared at him, eager for facts yet knowing the answers. "Tell me now, please."

"Your father found him with the help of a man named George. Coosa was alive and your father nursed my son back to health. Many moons passed and Coosa believed you were with Drummond. When Coosa was well again, your father made my son promise never to see you again because of Alexandre. Because of the children."

She let the truth sink in. She didn't blame her father; he was a physician and good and in truth he'd saved her much grief in making the Creek vow to stay away. "Where is Coosa now?"

"Always within reach, but out of sight. He watches over you, little sister. He rides where you ride, always vigilant and waiting like the mountain. My son has much patience."

Dear God, she wanted to see him, to touch him, to thrill to his wild embrace. She shivered. "He must go away, Jacques. You must tell him to go away!" Dominique watched as Jacques mounted his horse. "Where are you going? Don't leave me here alone!"

"You'll not be alone. I'll wait on the other side of the river."

Then she saw the white horse appear on the ridge, silhouetted against the black of hemlock. Her face twitched and her limbs quivered when she saw Rising Moon riding down the hill toward her. "Don't go!" she called to Jacques, running after him and falling. But Coosa's horse came swiftly, and she felt herself pulled into the air and then held beneath the Creek king's muscle-bound arm. They entered the wood as thunder rolled above the treetops. Coosa slid down from his mount with her in his arms and faced her, his uncommon face more splendid than she remembered. He was in his prime and completely healed from his wound. His dark alert eyes seemed to speak to her. "Summer Eyes."

"Coosa," she whispered. They embraced a long time, then he led her to a hidden place, the roar of water over stones lessening as they entered a cave.

"I tried to stay away," he said hoarsely, holding her in his arms and breathing in the scent of her hair. "You taught me about love and I find I cannot forget." She felt his tears on her skin and stroked his face, pushing back the thick black hair that framed the handsome features she loved so much.

"I knew you were alive!" she cried. "I've always known you were alive and I'd see you again. But father was right, Coosa. You must go away and never return."

His eyes communicated pain more intense than anything physical. She'd hurt him deeply and the agony was cutting into her, too, a sharp piercing as if a knife cut her flesh.

After voicing a deep moan, Coosa tightened his lips and turned away, speaking to the wall. "Coosa will return you to your horse. Coosa will not leave the land of his mother. He will stay."

Dominique took to her bed after that. The servants tended the house and Jacques saw to the animals, Mrs. Yarborough confiding to Desiree that her mother was going to be ill a very long time. Mrs. Yarborough came with a tray of food one morning, and the hounds in the room growled and barked at the sight of someone they didn't like. "Breakfast in bed while the good doctor's away, mistress. Told me himself ta serve ye while he was gone. Hot chocolate and applesauce cake, berries 'n' cream. Everything ye like. Marie cooked special all mornin' for ye. The least ye can do is eat for her." Romeo rolled his big brown eyes and lowered his massive graying head to his paws, his lower jaw trembling with a threatening growl. Angel squealed and ran past the dogs, swooshing against the servant's muslin skirts, with a bouquet of flowers for her mother. "Papa told me to give you these, mama. To say he loves you very much!" The child deposited the French lilacs and cherry blossoms on her mother's bed, then crawled up to kiss her mama.

"And English roses, mistress. The doctor said I was ta put white ones on your tray every mornin' with breakfast." Mrs Yarborough stood with her hands folded in front of her apron. "Is there anything else you'd be wantin'?" Dominique looked up at the woman she knew hated her, not understanding the sudden change in her behavior. "You may go," she managed.

"Did you see the present on old Romeo's neck, mama? Papa said you'd see it but you didn't, did you?"

Dominique looked at Romeo, a curled ball on the floor. A box was tied to his massive collar with silken cords, and a note was attached. Angel went to fetch the box and handed her mother the message, struggling with the mastiff to hold him still while she unfastened the box from his neck. "*Beloved wife. Forgive me for not saying good-bye. Your faithful husband, Alexandre.*" Dominique choked back a sob. "Open it, mama!" Half crying, half laughing, Dominique wiped her tears and hugged her little daughter.

"Open it for me, darling."

Angel pried open the box, her eyes wide with surprise when she spied a golden choker engraved with hounds chasing a fox. Rubies were fixed in each beast's eye and there was a clasp of seven emeralds. "Put it on, mama! I want to see it on your neck!" Dominique kissed Angel's rosy cheek and opened the choker's clasp. " 'Tis too beautiful for words, darling."

"I told papa you needed something to make you better."

"I feel better already, darling."

"It belonged to the queen of France, papa said. A lady related to me!"

"Josephine Bonaparte." Dominique touched the piece in awe. "The empress herself!" Dominique drank her chocolate and found it bitter, setting it aside with a frown and thinking her husband and his cousin terribly thoughtful to give her such a gift.

"When's papa coming back?"

"A week or so." Dominique swallowed the last of her chocolate, despite her distaste. Her stomach cramped and she tried not to let Angel know she was in pain.

"Now we can ride to the mountain, can't we?"

"Nay, we cannot. Papa doesn't want us on the mountain.

'Tis too dangerous for little girls. There are Indians and all manner of animals.'' Angel pouted and Dominique saw Alexandre in her eyes. Thinking of Coosa, she decided she didn't have long to live. There was something wrong with her and she knew it. She hadn't been a physician's daughter for nothing. She thanked God for allowing her to see Coosa one last time, but was concerned that he wouldn't go away. If she was dying, she wanted to know that Coosa and Alexandre wouldn't fight, knowing the best thing for all concerned was for Coosa to go far away. She couldn't die in peace knowing Coosa was out there waiting. Waiting for her.

"What's wrong, mama?"

"Nothing, darling. Run along and stay with Mère and Mocha in the kitchen. Mama will be down shortly.''

At the noon meal Dominique was surprised to learn from Jacques that her husband had gone to Athens on his return trip from Charleston. "He didn't tell me," she said. Dominique's mind whirred, as she set her teacup down and saw Jacques's face blur for a moment. "Are you ill?" Jacques's shaggy brows met. "You don't look well to me. You're color is off, I think. Pray you aren't coming down with something with the doctor gone."

"Yar will take care of her." Desiree pushed through the doors from the kitchen, carrying a plate of cold meats and bread and cheese. "The woman's a wonder when it comes to sickly people."

Jacques gave the girl a hard look, getting up to feel Dominique's forehead. " 'Tis not a fever. Thank the Lord, you're not hot."

"I'll go to my chamber. Please excuse me." Dominique got up to leave, but found she couldn't walk by herself. Jacques took her arm.

"Can you walk?"

"Aye, with your help."

"We'd best not take chances." Jacques swooped her into his arms. "Are you with child?" he asked quietly as he carried her up the stairs. She shook her head and he was somewhat relieved. "I insist you stay abed until your husband returns. I don't want to see you on your feet again until you're fit." Carrying her across her room, his hand brushed her cheek and she thought of Coosa. Suppose she died and never saw the Creek again? It would serve her right, she thought. She had sent him away. Jacques left the room and closed the door as she wept. Tears for the mess she'd made of everyone's life.

It was several days later when Dominique sat in the garden and watched the Percherons walked out for her approval. Jacques had insisted on carrying her down into the warm sun and Mrs. Yarborough had served breakfast from a mahogany table. "Sit there and take your time eatin'," the servant woman said kindly. "Gettin' it down is what's important."

Dominique smiled graciously and waved the servant away. She wasn't hungry and couldn't stand the sight of food, refusing to eat anything except Mère's chicken soup. The bright sun hurt her eyes as she watched Desiree canter about on Harmony, observing the child's natural horsemanship. The girl always seemed to be in command and she'd found it impossible to talk to Desiree. What did the future hold for a girl who refused to see the folly of her ways? A girl who believed the evil lies fed to her about her mother? Dominique sipped orange juice, wishing things could be different between her and her first-born. She felt another stab of pain in her stomach. She wished to ride with Desiree and show her the mountain. She'd always ridden with her father when she was little, but Desiree had made it known she didn't want to ride with her mother. How sad it made Dominique, realizing the world was changing and the children with it. How very sad for everyone.

Jacques came and gave her a wide grin, bringing Samson, the Percheron stallion, to see her. "Sam's sweet!" Angel cried out. Jacques swept the child up in his arms and sat her atop the great steed's back. "Take care," Dominique said, thinking Angel the most precious thing ever in her life at the moment. She thought she'd known the ultimate rewards of love until the babe had been laid in her arms. Angel had been heaven-sent, filling the void left by the loss of Coosa.

"Alexandre's favorites are the Percherons. We Chastains are from La Perche, you know. The Percheron's homeland southeast of Paris."

"Alexandre never told me."

"There are many things your husband never told you. Our grandfather kept a dozen stallions and more than sixty mares on his farm. Father took Alexandre and me there once. Ask Alexandre about it sometime." Jacques led the magnificent stallion around with Angel on his back and Dominique saw something of Ramir in Samson's eyes, recalling that Arabs had been introduced into the Percheron bloodlines many years past.

"How did the piebald stallion get back to Georgia?" she asked Jacques later, when they were alone.

"The steed was returned to my son's people by Alexandre. The horse is considered sacred and no one can ride him. Only Coosa," he whispered as he carried her back to her room and placed her in the bed, covering her with a satin quilt and filling her glass with fresh water from a decanter beside the bed. "Promise me you won't drink or eat anything not prepared by Mère or myself." Jacques's eyes were concerned and Dominique looked at him, puzzled. Mrs. Yarborough knocked on the door and walked in with a cup of tea. "Ye didn't finish your tea, mistress. I made a new cup for ye. 'Tis hot and you'd best drink it down now."

"Remember what I said," Jacques said.

"I promise," Dominique replied, instructing Mrs. Yarborough to set the brew on the side table and sending the woman away.

Later that night, Desiree and the servant had words. "You told me you were going to wait until I went away. I know you're giving her something and I want to know what 'tis."

Mrs. Yarborough continued braiding her hair. "I couldn't wait. I couldn't bear to see her turn this place into the ground. Her and that black slave of hers. You saw them together in the garden this morning. 'Tis my job to see to this place when the good doctor's away. He told me himself to take care of his wife and I'm doing just that."

"What did you give her? She couldn't even walk—Uncle Jacques had to carry her."

"Your father taught me about drugs, he did. I'm just dabblin', ye see. 'Tis nothin' strong enough to make her breathe her last just yet."

"You wouldn't do that!" she exclaimed.

"A course not. Ye shouldn't worry about such things."

"You said you'd wait till I went off to school."

"I didn't know then about your father's trip to Charleston, did I? 'Tis a perfect time for your mother to be laid up while the doctor's away, don't ye think? Who could diagnose her sickness but me, dear? 'Tis I who'll set her right."

Desiree still worried. Her mother could be worse by the time her father returned. Yar could even *kill* her. Nay, Yar wouldn't do that. The woman knew what she was doing, slowly. Why not enjoy herself while her father was away and her mother was abed? It was a perfect time to ride to the mountain. She could take Angel with her and they could climb it and be back before anyone missed them. They'd leave after midnight.

The many clocks in the house struck midnight and Dominique opened her eyes. Visions of the devil chasing her still darted through her mind from her one nightmare after another. Chills racked her thin frame. Pulling the covers to her chin, she wrapped her arms around herself, tucking the covers in and trying to remember what she had to do. Moonlight spilled through the green drapes in the shape of bells and she smelled roses and magnolia. Coosa was calling to her and she must go to him. Somehow she must get up and rise to the mountain to be with the man she loved.

The warm fur felt good against her skin as she wrapped herself in a gown of beige silk and black velvet cape with a hood of red fox. Her legs were unsteady and her feet touched the hair on a hound's back before she could step over him. She breathed in the fresh gallery air, trying desperately to clear her head. The moonlight flooded every rose and path in the garden, the drive, the courtyard. She could see all the way to the lake. A hound bayed and her favorite dog, Galliard, formed a growl in his throat, looking up from where he lay beside her bed. Loyal creatures, dogs, she thought, envisioning the daughter who hated her. The night was lovely and she wouldn't think of Desiree. Her gaze wandered to the lake where she saw a horse and rider beneath the moon. The horse was white, the rider cloacked in red. Coosa! A breeze stirred her hair and she stood staring at him from the balcony. Her pulse raced. Dare she go to him? Dare she go down to the garden and cross the path to the lake?

Coosa wheeled his mount and rode to meet her, her bare feet barely touching the wet grass on the path to the lake when Coosa reached down and swung her up before him. She had all she could do to sit up as they rode full tilt for the mountain. It was a long while before the Creek reined in his horse, steadying her as his white-maned beast danced in the moonlight. The Stone Mountain rose before them.

"I came to you because I couldn't sleep. Because I saw you from the gallery. Because we are friends." In truth she believed she would not be alive much longer. Coosa's gaze roamed over her, catching the curve of her breast, the pale skin stretched over the delicate bone of her face. His profile was silhouetted against the blues and grays of the mountain, his chest bronze and gleaming with golden gorgets, his upper arms circled with silver. "You have been ill?" he asked. "Nay." She smiled, leaning against his horse for support. "You look well." He looked magnificent, younger, stronger than ever, the warrior ready for battle, believing he'd received the blessing of his gods. He stepped down from his granite mound and touched her hair, the moon turning it to silver as her cape parted and exposed one long white leg. "My husband and I had a child together when I returned from Virginia," she said suddenly, thinking she must talk quickly of family and husband. "My little daughter is heaven and earth to me, something I could never live without." She felt his eyes burning through her cape, watching sparkling tears as they ran down her cheeks. "Dear God, must I go on?"

He laughed. "*Oui,* I enjoy hearing your voice."

"I came because I couldn't sleep, because your damnable moon woke me . . . because I . . .

"Because you're only half a woman without Coosa." He caught her legs and pulled her down with him to the soft earth, their warm cloaks beneath them. "Because you're part of Coosa and Coosa is part of you. You are my woman and we are children of God. Created in pairs and sent to this earth. But you were lost from me, Summer Eyes, we were lost from one another. Now that we are together, we must never be parted again. Coosa will never let you go—'tis foolish for you to think otherwise." He pressed her back and molded his body to hers, his lips to hers, his arms entwined with hers, all fitting perfectly. "You see!" He smiled. " 'Tis how our God planned it. One dying inside without the other."

"Coosa . . . oh, Coosa, my darling love." She accepted everything he said, her mind so numb and her body so weak she slumped in his arms, unable to speak.

"Coosa has you now, Summer Eyes. I've come to take you away where Alexandre cannot find us." She listened as best she could, realizing he was serious, prepared to give her anything and everything he had, his life if necessary, taking nothing in return. His hand drew hers to the indention in his flesh, the terrible scar that forever marred his chest, an ugly place where a white man's bullet had ripped into his exquisite body. "My darling!" she gasped.

"Drummond!" he snarled, clutching her hand and holding it to his pounding heart. "Your husband's friend." She wound her arms around his neck and interlocked her fingers in his hair, knowing he'd almost died because of her. She felt the silkiness of his hair and brought it to her lips. Coosa kissed her hands, front and back, held her fingers to his cheek. "You love Coosa?" he asked shyly, blinking back tears of joy at the sight of her.

"I love Coosa," she repeated, trembling before him, so weak from the poison invading her system that she could barely move. Coosa laid her back gently, kissing her body and awakening her senses with his tongue, his wild caresses bringing back the passion they had known.

"Beloved woman!" he cried in Creek.

Dominique could have died then, happily, accepting her fate willingly, gratefully, wholeheartedly, despite wifely duty, mortal sin, and everlasting damnation. She loved this man. Their love was beautiful and good, a unique gift from their gods, something to be treasured. Why not savor love before it was too late, before her end came?

"Wake up, Angel. You want to ride Harmony with me to the mountain of stone, don't you?"

Angelique opened her big amber eyes and looked at her sister. Desiree never came to her room. Now her big sister was standing beside her bed dressed in her smartest black habit from France and looking all the world like a grown-up lady.

"Here are your clothes, darling, the boots mama had made special for you, remember?"

Angel tried to keep her eyes open. Something was wrong. Desiree never called her *darling*. Desiree didn't like her. She must be dreaming.

"If you don't get up I'll ride to the mountain by myself and you'll never know what's on top. Stay in bed, lazy, see if I care!"

Angel sat up and rubbed her eyes. She wasn't dreaming: Desiree really wanted to take her to the mountain. "Can Aimee go?" Angel's big eyes were bright now. Aimee was the little white powderpuff of a dog from France who now sat up in bed, cocking her head to listen.

"Oh, all right, the flea-bitten thing won't make it to the mountain anyway. But no hounds, they bark too much."

"Thank you." Angel picked up her little dog and kissed it. "What will mama say? 'Tis forbidden to go to the mount."

"Don't worry, darling, mama's not feeling well and we don't want to wake her. Hurry, we must be gone before sun-up." Angel shrugged, allowing Desiree to help her dress, to give her a hand with her velvet habit and brown jacket and sit her down to push on her boots. They tiptoed past an assorted pile of hounds in the hallway, past their mother's door where shaggy beasts raised their heavy brows to have a look, twelve tails thumping as the girls slipped by. "Harmony's saddled and waiting out front," Desiree whispered. "Give me your hand." Desiree hurried with Angel down the dark staircase, saying nothing until they reached the front door and then raced into the night air.

"Mama will be angry when she finds out." Angel stuck out her lower lip like her mother did on occasion.

"Mama won't find out, Angel. Now come on."

The moon loomed above the trees and Angel felt better when she saw how bright it was out. She stood shivering in her boots while Desiree adjusted the leathers on her pony. "I'm frightened, Desiree, and cold."

"Don't be a sissy. I can ride as good as mama and you know it. Up you go. Hold tight to me and I'll do the rest."

The girls didn't see the kitchen door open and the boy Moses ran down the steps with Romeo. "Where are you two going?" the boy asked, shrugging into his white shirt.

"None of your business!" Desiree said in an ugly tone. "Go back inside and help Mère with breakfast."

"We're going to the mountain!" Angel said proudly, glad to see the boy she considered her friend. "Don't tell mama."

"I'm going, too!" Moses said. "I've never been and I'll protect you."

"We don't need you," Desiree hissed contemptuously. "You don't have a horse and you wouldn't know what to do with one if you did."

"I do, too!" the boy exclaimed. "Julie lets me ride her all the time!"

"Julie is a mule!" Desiree giggled, careful to keep her voice low. "Now go back and do your chores and don't tell anyone you saw us or you'll get it when I come back." Desiree pulled herself into the saddle and positioned her legs, then clicked to the pony who was eager to be off into the trees. Moses watched the pony disappear and then ran for the house. He'd show Desiree he could ride. He'd go and get Jacques and the two of them would ride to the mountain together.

20

Desiree and Angel crawled through the tunnel and hole in the wall at the summit of the mountain, then struggled to their feet. It wasn't the way they'd expected. Windy, cold, desolate, and barren, gray bleakness in the rising mist greeted them. The wind played with a dark coil on Desiree's cheek. "Follow me, Angel."

"I want my mama." Angel wept softly.

"Don't be a sissy. Let's have a look around, now that we're here. I know we can see our house if we look down." Yanking her little sister along, Desiree wouldn't admit she was a bit frightened, too. What if there were Indians about . . . wild beasts? And could she find her way down?

"I can't see anything," Angel sobbed.

Desiree talked sweetly. "If you don't cry, I'll go and look for Aimee."

"Aimee's lost!" Angel wailed.

"I'll find her if you'll stop your blubbering." Desiree thought about how they lost the little dog halfway to the mountain, how she refused to stop and pick Aimee up when she fell. What would her father say when he found out the little dog was lost? What would her mother do? She could see her mother's face. Moses surely had told on them by now. She

340

shivered and wished she'd never come. Her mother would accuse her of wanting to hurt Angel, her father going along with his wife as he'd always done when it came to his oldest daughter. She'd only wanted to climb the mountain because she knew her mother had done it. To *be* like her mother. She thrived on danger and disobedience, Yar had once told her. All because of the naughty things her mother had done. If being loved by men meant she had to be naughty like her mother, then she'd gladly do it. That was the only way she'd ever be loved.

"Look!" Angel pointed at the ancient stones in the center of the mountaintop. Desiree sucked in her breath. The altar of the gods! She'd heard about it from Jacques. Rocks piled atop rocks to form a crossroad for the Indian nations, their place of worship. " 'Tis only rocks to sit upon or under. Sit and rest yourself. I'll go back and look for Aimee." A breeze lifted her black curls and thunder rumbled as if God was moving furniture about in Heaven. "I'm afraid!" Angel shivered. "Don't leave me, please!"

"You want Aimee, don't you?"

Angel stuck out her lower lip and nodded.

"I'm going back a ways to look for her, but you must stay here. If a storm comes, climb under the rocks."

"Nay, don't leave me!" Angel begged. Just then something large moved on the other side of the rocks, standing tall like another rock, something like a cloak billowing in the wind. Angel screamed and Desiree grabbed her, diving under the rock altar. Desiree clamped her hand over Angel's mouth. "It's an Indian. Be still and don't breathe!"

"Ho, who goes there?" a deep voice called. Friendly-sounding, but who could be certain? "If you come out I'll cook you supper. I'll wager you've never eaten fresh meat from a stick before."

He's going to eat us! Desiree thought, having heard only some of the Indian's words. She knew Indians ate people, especially little children and old ladies, who were always boiled alive. She tried to cover Angel with her long narrow frame, pushing the small girl farther behind her. They'd hide all night, if necessary. The Indian couldn't see them in the dark, or could he? Didn't Indians have the eyes of wolves? The Indian came closer; she could hear the voice trying to charm her. "Come out, little ones. I'm not going to eat you, I promise. I'm going to feed you if you'll be good enough to join me. If you don't come out, I'll have to start my fire and smoke you out."

"We'll never come out!" Desiree called to him. She knew the Indian couldn't come in after her because he was too big. "You'll not eat me or my sister!"

"I've never eaten a human in my life!" Coosa Tustennuggee chuckled. "You mustn't believe the stories you hear about Indians." Smoke snaked its way between the rocks, filling the girls' noses after Coosa lit a fire and the wind nourished it. "You'd better come out now, or get roasted like my ducks."

Angel coughed and Desiree knew if they didn't come out from under the rocks they'd be burned alive. If they made a run for it they could get away . . .

"Got you!" Coosa was waiting and caught the girls by their hair and they screamed and scratched, kicking him in the shins and beating him with their fists. "Two more like your mother, I see." Coosa chuckled, holding the girls at arm's length so they couldn't reach him. "Coosa's not going to hurt you."

"Coosa?" Angel cried. "Coosa Tus . . . tus . . ."

"Rising Moon." The Indian's voice was gentle as he held the two struggling females by the backs of their slim necks.

"But you're dead, aren't you? I heard my father say so to a man. Some man shot you."

"Do I look dead?" Coosa frowned. "Coosa is very much alive. Coosa lives." Slowly the girls sank back and ceased their struggling. Angel reached out and touched the giant Indian's hand.

"My mother told me you were a spirit that inhabits this land."

"Your mother told you the truth. Coosa lives on this mountain. The sacred rock is his home." Desiree waited for a chance to run, to make her way down the mountain and find Moses. But she couldn't leave Angel behind. She'd brought her little sister to the mountain to give her a good scare, but she couldn't leave her alone with an Indian. Coosa might kill her. He seemed nice . . . in a way . . . but Yar had warned her never to trust a heathen. "How do we know you won't eat us?"

"You don't. Coosa has no reason to harm you. Come, join me before the fire." They went to sit with him, the tongues of the fire licking the rocks as it radiated warmth to them. Sparks shot into the night sky and Coosa turned on a spit two ducks he'd shot earlier. Then he wrapped the girls in a robe of young puma, noting they still shivered from fear. Afraid of children-eating savages, he reasoned. He knew well who they were and who'd been telling them untruths about him and his mother's people. Mrs. Yarborough and her wicked ways weren't new to him. His father had told him what went on in the halls of Racemont. He'd seen the girls when he'd watched from afar. All the Chastain females rode horses in the morning as if in an Indian ritual. The oldest girl reminded him of Dominique when he'd first seen her, the young woman's good looks and fiery spirit the same. The girl's dark eyes followed him as he moved about, watching, showing she was prepared to fight for her life. He went to his horse and reached into the saddlebag, pulling out a frightened little dog and setting it down. "Aimee!" Angel squealed, jumping up to gather the French dog into her arms.

" 'Tis a good name, Aimee. French, eh?''

"*Oui*, monsieur." Angel hugged her dog, no longer afraid of the Indian she'd heard her mother speak of so often, but still somewhat confused to see he was alive.

"I must get more wood, ladies. Look after the camp, will you? You're in charge, Desiree." Coosa turned and Desiree looked at Angel. He knew her name! How?

The storm was moving off to the west, freeing the mountain from the wind. Desiree spotted Coosa coming back with an armful of wood from the scraggly trees that clung to the mountain's side. Her knee burned where she'd skinned it when she'd crawled through the hole and she noticed it was bleeding. Coosa offered her a tin of salve from his jerkin.

"Indian medicine." He shrugged when she didn't take it.

Desiree covered her knee as best she could with the torn fabric of her breeches. Coosa came and knelt before her, uncovering her cut and applying the salve with one finger. Desiree was touched by his kindness, wrinkling her nose at the medicinal smell.

"You remind me of your mother." Coosa never looked at Desiree, going to the fire to see to his ducks.

"Me?" Angel asked.

"Your sister," Coosa said. "The woman who lives for adventure and fast horses."

He'd called her a woman and Desiree had thrilled to the comparison to her mother. "Do you know my mother?"

"Doesn't everyone in these parts know the lady of the hounds?"

And they talked deeper into the morning.

Jacques was not as kind as Coosa after he'd climbed the mountain and found the two girls with his son. "You two will be the death of me yet! You know 'tis forbidden to climb the mountain and still you did it. Why?"

"Because they wanted to see what was on top." Coosa chuckled.

Jacques frowned. "Do you want to tell their mother that when she finds out they're gone? The poor woman's sick now. When she finds out about this, she'll be worse."

"Take them home and say nothing," Coosa told his father, unwilling to tell Jacques the girls' mother slept peacefully on the other side of the mountain where Coosa had left her protected from the wind. "Perhaps you should take the little one to Savannah for safekeeping, until you've decided what to do about Mrs. Yarborough?"

"Perhaps I shall," Jacques said to his son out of earshot of the two girls. "I'll do what's best for her, you can count on it."

"I been prayin' you'd come back, doctor," Marie sobbed. "Things done got outta hand since you lef." Alexandre helped the graying Marie to a chair in the library, his hands shaking as he removed his dusty coat. He poured a brandy from a decanter and drank it down. He'd no sooner walked in the door when he learned Dominique was gone. "Tell me what happened, Mère, exactly as matters took place."

Marie lifted her apron and wiped her tear-streaked face, eyes reddened from days of crying. "Mistah Jacques done took dah babe, Angel, tah Savannah and den dah missus came up missin'."

Alexandre poured another drink, swallowing it down. "Go on, Mère, tell me the rest."

"Jacques done tole dah missus she gots ta stay in bed 'cause she's been sick since yo' lef, sick like a dog, Doctah Alex. Po' girl could hardly walk and get downstairs."

"Yet she went riding alone?"

Marie wailed. "I dunno, doctah, I just dunno."

Alexandre went to the door and yelled for Moses. "Have a fresh mount brought around front at once. Get some men together for a hunt. The hounds, too!" Moses ran down the hall to do his master's bidding, still dressed in traveling clothes. "When did Jacques leave with my daughter?" Alexandre poured himself yet another brandy, sliding the decanter across the polished surface of·his desk.

"Two days ago, doctah, two days since he tole me ta pack up dat little Angel's duds. Lef a message in dah drawer for yo'."

Alexandre pulled out the center drawer of his giant oaken desk, seeing his flintlock beside his journal and an envelope addressed to him atop the book. "*Alexandre, in your absence, and in the interest of your daughter Angelique's safety, I have taken it upon myself to remove the child from Racemont. I shall accompany the child to Savannah where I'll see her safely aboard the New Hope, bound for Philadelphia. Word has been sent to Doctor Winburn of her arrival. I've entrusted the position of overseer to the Nigerian, Zombu, until I return. Any questions you have should be addressed to Marie. Your brother, Jacques.*"

Zombu was a good man, Alexandre thought, trained for just such an emergency. "Did he take anyone with him, Mère?"

"Nancy," Marie sobbed. "I ain't never gonna see dat babe again."

"You'll see Angel again, Mère." Alexandre tossed the note into the drawer and rammed it shut. "Just as soon as I find my wife, I'll send for my daughter. They won't have time to get out of Savannah if I have any say in it." Why was there no mention of Dominique in Jacques's note? Had Jacques seen his wife before he'd left for Savannah? Surely Dominique had something to say about the child leaving? He reached inside his coat and retrieved a flask of whiskey, taking a long swig and speculating on whether his wife had sent the child away. What of Desiree, his other daughter—what did she have to say to all this? These and other questions would have to be resolved later, once he'd found his wife.

Alexandre wasn't accustomed to the big red stallion brought out for him, but there was no time for argument. The horse was a recent import, having been brought over from Ireland for breeding, a long-legged beast not used to the trails and woods of Racemont. Jacques had ridden the horse once, deciding the stallion should be kept for stud only. Once atop the stallion's back, Alexandre found himself riding over rough terrain in search of his wife. Flat shoales and sharp outcroppings of granite, wild underbrush, and pines so thick no eye could penetrate them glided by him. He guided his horse toward the mountain, the most obvious place to take up the search. Mère had told him Dominique had been missing for two days. Thank God Coosa Tustennuggee wasn't alive, or he'd have suspected that Creek king had something to do with his wife's absence.

The mountain loomed in the distance and his hands trembled on the reins. What if his wife were lying stranded somewhere, unable to call out or to be heard, subjected to the elements and all manner of wild beasts? He reached inside his pocket and withdrew his silver flask, draining it of its fiery liquid and tossing the flask over the horse's head onto the granite. The flask caught the sun's rays and rang like a shot when it struck solid rock, echoing again and again. The red stallion spooked, rearing and sending Alexandre sprawling to the ground. Stunned, the air knocked from his lungs, Alexandre gasped for breath, his chest heaving as he lay still and tried to right himself. He cursed when he heard the Irish stallion's hooves racing over the granite roots of the mountain toward the plantation. The next thing he heard was the music of his hounds barking, mixed with a distant ringing in his ears. Did he have a concussion? He could move his arms and his head and his shoulders, yet his legs wouldn't budge. Dear God, did he have a broken leg? *Non*, 'twas much worse.

Alexandre stared at the beams in the library of Racemont and held back a sob. He had stared at the blue sky a long time before the hounds had discovered him. Stared into the sky until it turned pink and gold and he'd realized his legs were paralyzed. Reaching out, he cleared the surface of his desk with one arm. The crystal decanter that Mère had filled that morning was already empty and he hurled it to the floor, shattering it in a hundred pieces. He prayed to God, asking for strength and promising anything if God would only return his wife to him. How could he go on without her? Run the plantation without her and Jacques? Perhaps Jacques had taken Angel to Savannah where Dominique had been waiting. The two of them had planned to run off together, that was it, and Dominique had instructed Jacques to take Angel along! His imagination ran like the red stallion who'd thrown him and he tried not to panic. He rested in the library where he'd requested to be placed when Zombu and his men had carried him back from the mountain. Mrs. Yarborough had seen to it that he'd been put close to his desk and the tray of liquors. Good old Yar, faithful to the end, he thought. The woman would be happy now, content with the prospect of caring for him for the rest of his life without his wife. He choked back a sob, planning to kill himself first.

Coosa studied Dominique's face, the fine-boned nose and artfully drawn mouth. The creamy whiteness of flawless skin carried a hint of color this morning. Wishing he could take her someplace where white men did not exist, he reflected on the recent past. He'd cared for Dominique more than a fortnight now, cooled her fever and kept her warm when severe chills had overtaken her. He'd carried her halfway down the mountain on the steepest side, to an ancient niche in the bosom of the gray egg. He'd moved Dominique more than once when the horses and hounds had come looking for her. Then, with the help of thunderstorms and a few Indian tricks, they'd found safety on the face of the living mountain. No white man knew of the secret place: a ledge with an overhang of rock and earth and ageless trees. Now he sat and fashioned shoes from the hide of an unborn fawn.

"What are you doing?" Dominique sat up and rubbed her eyes.

"Your feet were cold. Now they'll be warm."

She looked around, seeing she was sheltered by limbs, great blue sky, and gray granite. She felt the chill of the air in the niche and a breeze caught her hair.

"Angel? I remember something about Angel."

"Your daughter came here to the mountain with her sister. You were ill and I did not awaken you from your drugged sleep. My father came looking for the girls and we thought it best your Angel be removed from harm's way. Jacques rode with her to Savannah and from there Angel will travel with friends over the water to Philadelphia."

"Why? I don't understand."

"Things are not good in the halls of Racemont. The servant woman who is jealous of you was turning your daughter with the dark hair against you. But I believe all will be well now that Angelique is gone."

Dominique stared at him, her heart pounding at what he'd just said. "You sent my baby away?"

"For her own good. To protect her until you are well and—"

"And what? How dare you do such a thing, Coosa. Alexandre will be coming back and find her gone. Me gone! What will he think?"

"That you are gone," he replied. "Nothing to worry about."

"I must go home at once."

"You're not well enough to ride."

"I am!"

Coosa took her in his arms and held her. "Coosa will decide when you can ride."

"I must go, Coosa." She closed her eyes, leaning on him for support, feeling dizziness engulf her as her cheek touched his chest through his open jerkin, his golden gorget cooling her fevered head.

"Summer Eyes." His heavy hand caught her chin and lifted it, the deep green of her eyes meeting the black night of his.

" 'Tis a time past, Coosa. A time forever spent."

"Forever is in our hearts!" Coosa crushed her lips to his and she wanted to scream. God help her, she could not fight his great kindness, his strength. His tongue invaded her mouth, gently arousing her, and she wound her arms about his neck. He swept her into his arms and laid her back on pelts of puma. Coosa's hands trembled as they unfastened the front of her habit, mouthing Creek words of endearment and caressing the satin sheen of her breasts with his lips. "Come to Coosa," he rasped, his thick black mane flowing over her nakedness. Whining like a pup, she rolled her head from side to side, filled with the knowledge that he would have her no matter what she said. His lips covered her breasts, the excitement and anticipation chilling their flesh. His tongue tasted her breasts and her head fell back in surrender, their moans rising into the sun-streaked sky of endless blue. "Help me, please!" she sobbed, hating her weakness and vulnerability. "Please help me with my life." Certain she was doomed to everlasting torment in hell, she held the Creek so tightly that her nails brought blood to his bronzed flesh, enjoying every part of him, his scent and the taste of his skin. "Coosa, Coosa," she cried, her eyes filling with tears as she gave in to the release she desired so much, allowing the man she loved to take her and fit himself to her, filling her with the seed of life that made her his woman.

After they had rested quietly for some moments, she looked at him. "You must take me back."

"Never!" His muscles tensed against her body.

"You must!" She looked deep into his eyes, still dreamy from their lovemaking. "I can't live with you, Coosa. Pray listen to me and understand."

"Coosa has listened before and I understand. Coosa is not ignorant!" He touched his hand to her cheek. "Your husband's servant wants you dead. 'Tis you who doesn't understand."

"If Mrs. Yarborough was poisoning me, then Alexandre may be in danger."

"So be it! 'Twas he who hired the woman and brought her here!" Coosa pushed himself up and rolled up the blanket.

" 'Tis what I'd expect from someone uncivilized!" she flung back.

"Coosa is used to white woman's insults. We two are leaving these lands. 'Twas not a hasty decision, Dom-ma-nique. 'Tis with my father's recommendations and the knowledge that you could die if you stay in your husband's house."

"You and Jacques decided what would happen to me, too?"

"Why not?"

"You had no right!"

"Indians have no rights." He chuckled.

"If you remove me from this mount and don't allow me to ride home, I shall never forgive you."

Rolling up the fur robes and the blanket, Coosa secured them on his back and took her wrist. "We're leaving this place now. There's no time for forgiveness."

"Please, Coosa," she pleaded, her eyes filling with tears. "Don't take me from my people!"

"Your people will destroy you, if you let them! Your people have used you and hurt you, fed you poison and cut my young braves to pieces with their bullets!"

"My children did none of those things. My husband and children are not cruel."

He twisted her around and held her in an iron grip. "You love your people, then—you love Alexandre, too?"

"Aye," she said. "I love them in a way you can't understand."

"There's much Coosa doesn't understand. Then I'm just a dumb Indian, am I not?" Pulling her along to the end of the ledge, he crawled upward, dragging her with him. When they reached the horses, he swung her up into the saddle, thinking four-legged beasts were more faithful than women.

Jules Cocteau read the servant girl's letter again. "*A. Chastain injured in fall from horse, unable to leave his bed. Madame Chastain, daughter, and Jacques gone. Servants remain. Come in haste. L.*" It was the second letter he'd received from the mulatto wench, Lattice. The first concerned her having arrived at Racemont and taking the place of the Chastain family's laundress, who had died. Ironic, he should be kept abreast of things at the Chastain plantation by the daughter of a man he'd murdered in Savannah. He snickered, recalling meeting Lattice and her father on the waterfront in Savannah after he'd fallen from the warehouse door and broken his leg. Lattice had taken pity on him and talked her father into taking Jules home with them. The old man's first mistake. His second had been turning his back on Jules when Jules had a knife. Jules had killed the old man and told Lattice a sailor had robbed and then killer her father. The girl had believed him, of course. He'd always had a way with the ladies, evidenced by the way the girl had crawled into bed with him after her father's burial, an activity they had pursued for several months while the bone in Jules's leg healed. Jules had talked Lattice into traveling to Racemont and securing a job there with the promise of joining her later and making her his mistress. The girl had believed him, the gullible little fool, and now the wench was counting the seconds until Jules arrived at Racemont's gates.

Jules thought of the beauteous Nikki, blessing the unruly nag that had thrown Alexandre from its back. He could feel Nikki's warm sweet flesh as he invaded her, and he trembled at the thought of his mouth on hers. He'd have her as often as he liked when he arrived at Racemont. His manhood pulsated at the thought. Raising his eyes from the letter he rested his head on the imported yellow damask of his wing chair in the parlor of Madiana, the plantation François Chastain had given his father when he left the isle of Martinique. Once the finest manorhouse on the isle, its fields now were wasted, its slaves long gone, its halls in disrepair. The Africans had run off due to his harsh and cruel treatment, the overseer leaving soon afterward and taking all the horses. Jules had lost the rest of the money Alexandre had given him in ransom to gambling and wenching. Now, with Alexandre bedridden, he could return to Georgia sooner than expected. It would be a small thing to rid himself of a woman and her children, should the family cause problems. It was what he'd planned for years. He had a score to settle with Alexandre and the time had come.

He drained his silver goblet and sat forward in his chair. Alexandre had gotten the cream while he'd contented himself with the milk. Alexandre had lived in luxury while he'd lived in squalor. Cursing, he stood and kicked the empty bottles around his chair with his boot. Servants gone, horses gone, wenches gone—how in the devil would he while away the time until he sailed for Savannah? His eyes reddend with self-pity and the knowledge that the very rug he trod upon was no longer his. "Let them have it!" he bellowed. "Let them have Chastain's filthy hand-me-down house!" Pounding his goblet on the table, he called for another bottle, but none came. Just as well, he thought. He'd be lord and master of Racemont soon. "To the master of Racemont," he bellowed. Perhaps he'd allow Alexandre to watch him take his wife before he killed him. He could prop the poor fellow up on pillows and get twice the satisfaction seeing his face while he pleasured his delicious wife. He laughed, nearly falling over in his amusement. *Oui*, he'd allow Alexandre to live a bit longer. In return for all the knowledge he imparted about his plantation he'd give him the last thrill of his life. Ah, to be rich again, he thought. He'd do nothing but bed wenches and watch his seed multiply. He'd plant Nikki first, he thought. Such a sweet bed, too.

Coosa watched Dominique staring into the distance, the mountain of stone long gone from their sight. "I want my Angel," Dominique said, casting a glance at the man who lay on his side beside her inside a council house.

"Your child is in good hands. My father is with her. You trust him, don't you?"

"Do you think they've left Savannah yet?"

Coosa creased his brow, and shook his head.

" 'Tis my hope that the whites accept the Indians one day," she said. Coosa grunted, not looking at her, thinking about carrying her off to Georgia's great swamp if necessary. They could ride for the Alabamas or the western frontier. Sail south to the islands on the coast of Georgia. In his misery, he wished to read the things that spun in her lovely head. He didn't wish her to hate him for taking her away, yet he couldn't live without her love. Tears hurt the back of his black eyes as he rolled away. She was a she-wolf and untamable and he would let her go. Perhaps she would return on her own and they would be together in the end.

Dominique placed her hand on his shoulder, sliding her fingers down over the scarred pits on his chest as if she knew what he was thinking. She had been angry with him for not taking her home, but she couldn't be angry with Coosa for long. Leaning against him, she placed a kiss beside his ear, breathing in the wild scent of him. "You've been good to me, Coosa. I'm grateful for all you've done, I want you to know that."

Unable to reply, Coosa closed his eyes and thought on her words, allowing them to echo in his mind, keeping her kiss for future memories.

"I've been thinking about our fathers, Coosa. How my father saved you on a snowy night in Virginia, how yours helped me by taking my baby away from danger."

Mystified, Coosa said nothing. What was she about now?

" 'Tis a rare thing to save another man's life. You've done so and you would do so again, I know."

Baffled, Coosa wished to roll to her and draw her down on himself, remove her chemise, and show her how much he cared. He heard her sniff and imagined tears sparkling in her eyes. She was saying good-bye, he knew it!

"Whatever became of that awful man who took my father to where he found you, Coosa? George Limpton, wasn't that his name?"

Coosa shrugged, amazed she should bring George Limpton up at this time. "Another worthless white-eyes. One of Drummond's hired killers."

Confused, she thought she'd heard the Indian say he liked George Limpton. Hadn't Coosa said Limpton was a misguided soul who wasn't bad at heart? Shrugging, she concentrated on the present, determining to ride off as soon as she got the chance. "I'm concerned for my horse." She nuzzled Coosa's ear. "He's an Indian pony and not used to being ridden by a woman. It would make me happy if you would allow me to ride him more often, to accustom him to my weight and voice."

"He grazes on wild grasses beside the spring, on the path that joins the trail back to Savannah."

"Thank you, Coosa. I'm turned around. Are we east or north of Savannah?"

A pain stabbed the Indian *mico*'s heart then, and his reply was short as he grimaced. "Due east, Summer Eyes. Savannah lies as the arrow flies to the west." He reached out and caught her hand, holding it for a long moment. "Good night, Domma-nique."

She pulled her hand away and considered his tone. He seldom called her by her Christian name. "Sleep well, Coosa," she whispered, laying down beside him and waiting for slumber to overtake him. It was dark and she would get up and dress quickly in Indian garb, find her horse, and then ride hard for Savannah. Coosa breathed deeply and soon she was certain he slept. His body was warm and inviting and the night air was cold. She'd not have a saddle and would have to ride like a man. Stealing from her bed, she slipped into doeskins and the slippers Coosa had made for her, snatching the *mico*'s red cloak from a peg and throwing it around her shoulders.

It was later that Coosa heard the sound of his horse's hooves pounding the Georgia clay. He leaped from where he lay, running to the door of the council house and throwing aside the skins to look. A man came toward him in the dark, dressed like an Indian in buckskins and jerkin, his hair wild, his beard straggly, his white skin burned by wind and sun. "You have news?" Coosa asked eagerly.

"Aye, chief. She's headed Savannah way."

Coosa walked a ways with the man he considered his friend. "Ride out after her and see her horse doesn't step wrong. Take two of my braves and make certain she doesn't see. Send word back to me and don't leave her from your sight." Coosa bid George Limpton good-bye, anxious to be on his horse and riding back to Racemont.

Moses tried to make his master comfortable. It was no joy to be bedridden, imprisoned in one's own house and helpless. Removing the soiled bedclothes, the black man rubbed Alexandre's back with scented oil after bathing him, turning him with care and then making his bed with fresh linen. " 'Tis hot in this damnable house, Moses. Is there no air?"

"Of course, doctor. Plenty of air. You can have all you

want." Going to the tall arched windows, Moses opened them wide. It had rained all night and the cool fresh air that rushed into the room ruffled papers and disturbed drapes.

"My hounds' papers!" Alexandre frowned. "Don't let them get away, Moses!"

"Have no fear," Moses cried, gathering up pedigrees written with care on parchment. The dogs kept the doctor's mind occupied, Moses mused, and it was a blessing he had the beasts. Six wolfhounds lounged about the room: Galliard, King Lear, Romeo, the old mastiff, together with their ladies. Moses looked at the dogs, thinking they understood. The beasts wagged their tails at the servant who was responsible for them now.

"What was that racket I heard last night, Moses?"

"Your daughter, doctor. She and Mrs. Yarborough were celebrating, I believe."

"I doubt that, Moses. My daughter misses her mother, I sense it."

"Yes, doctor," Moses said.

"Trust no woman, Moses. Most are deceivers. Do we have any wine? Chilled wine?"

"Of course, doctor." Moses removed ice from a pitcher he'd gone to the ice house to fetch just an hour before, filled a bucket, then set the wine bottle into its icy depths. "I'll go now and have a word with Mère about your breakfast."

"I'm not hungry. Save yourself the trouble and let the dogs out for the night. Leave the bottle where I can reach it."

"What would you like for breakfast, doctor?"

"Nothing!" Alexandre's glare was threatening. "Leave the bottle and be on your way."

Shrugging, Moses filled a tray with empty bottles and a bowl of ice and was about to set them down when he caught his foot in the rug and the tray and its icy contents went flying. "*Mon Dieu!* 'Tis colder than Hades!"

"Forgive me, doctor." Moses mopped up his master's soaked bed and attended to the errant chunks of freezing ice. "Hades isn't cold." He chuckled, trying to make light of the situation, nervous and embarrassed for making his master uncomfortable.

"Dear Jehovah!" Alexandre gasped, mouth agape at his servant. He threw back the covers and slid his hand between his thighs.

"What is it, doctor?"

"I can feel the cold, Moses, don't you understand? I can feel it here on my legs!"

Raising his head heavenward, Moses whispered a prayer. "Praise the Lord, it's a miracle!"

"I want all the house servants removed to the village immediately, Moses. Have a wagon sent around and load it with provisions. A carriage with four of our best and fastest horses for Desiree and Mrs. Yarborough."

"What on earth for, doctor?"

"For peace of mind, my good man. Peace of mind!"

21

A severe thunderstorm illuminated the mountain of stone, the night sky black as horses drew a coach along the narrow trace below. Wheels groaned, shuddering on their axles, the route to Racemont more a river than a road. Jules cursed as he was hurled onto the upholstered seat opposite him, the coach's door thrown open as the coach skidded sideways off the road.

"Black bastard. I'll have your filthy hide for that!" Jules rubbed his bruised arm and yanked a bottle of rum from between his feet to pound it on the roof. "Get this thing back on the road and be quick about it!"

Six Arabs from Persia strained in the dark, the driver's clicking tongue and fluency in Persian urging the frightened beasts across slippery granite onto higher ground. The wheels of the coach turned and the coach rolled into a downpour so heavy all visibility was lost. The African driver ducked beneath a tattered blanket, more concerned with the target he made for lightning than the cruel treatment from Jules Cocteau. The horses and driver had been confiscated from Chastain House in Savannah. Hun, the coachman, had been purchased by Jacques and sent to Savannah to work at Chastain House.

Jules uncorked another bottle, allowing the liquid to drain down his throat, wiping his mouth disdainfully as he laid out his plan. His thoughts of Nikki warmed him more than the rum. How she'd welcome him into the house that would soon be his. Women were all alike. She'd welcome him all right. With open legs! His mind spun back to the hills of Virginia and how he'd had her. He fancied her then, her upturned mouth and pink lips, her firm full breasts, those long, luscious legs he longed to have wrapped around his back. She'd driven him mad with desire in the past months, his mouth watering as his lust stirred. He grasped himself. Soon he'd have her. Soon! He banged on the roof again with his bottle, bellowing for Hun to go faster. Faster!

It was past midnight when the coach drawn by the high-bred Arabs tore through the gates of Racemont. Hun gave the horses their heads and the coach thundered down the broad avenue of sand and around the circular drive to the courtyard.

"Return before daybreak!" Jules commanded, opening the door of the coach to jump down into water that swirled around his boots.

"But the horses, master?" Hun peered through steady rain beating against his weary team's trembling bodies.

"Do as you're told or wish you had, bastard! Go to the mountain and wait!" Slamming the door of the coach, Jules watched the wheels spin over the granite, the tired team driven by an angry whip. Jules yanked his wet cloak about him, then ran through the soaked grass to where a woman stood on the gallery, her lantern held high to signal him.

"Monsieur Cocteau?" The slave girl Lattice shook at Jules's approach, her gray cape and hood stolen from Dominique's armoire. Jules held his breath, for a single instant imagining she was Nikki. "*Oui*," he replied, hurrying through the needles of rain that stung his neck. "This way," she directed, turning down the long sleek gallery to a stairwell between the pillars. Jules knew where he was now; he'd climbed the stairs before. He followed Lattice upward, approaching the French doors. "Where are the servants?"

"Gone, monsieur." Lattice removed her dampened cape, eyeing Jules in the lantern's light. Tall and broad-shouldered, she thought him sinister, the glint in his eyes strangely attractive. She could not see his face clearly behind his heavy beard. She forced herself to look away.

"Alexandre and his manservant?" Jules asked, stealing a second glance at her.

"Asleep downstairs in the library. They live there together, now that the master's bedridden."

"The hounds? I've seen none, heard none."

"Locked in the kennels by the doctor's order. Every one."

Jules thought it too good to be true. No servants or beasts about. Why? he wondered. "The mistress of this hall. Dominique?"

"Madame has been gone for some time now. Didn't you receive my letters? 'Tis not known if she's living or dead."

Jules attempted to hide his disappointment at the confirmation of what the servant's letters had said. He changed the subject. "The black brother, Jacques, where is he?"

"As I said in my letter, Jacques is gone as well." Lattice smiled, catching Jules's eyes as they roamed downward to her bosom. "Jacques took the child, Angelique, to the North to Madame's family in Philadelphia. The other daughter has gone to the village with her English nanny."

"Excellent." Jules studied the girl's face, then the room illuminated by the lantern. There was the green-skirted dressing table, creamy lace curtains framing the windows, a silver comb and brush, a huge bed with a canopy of pink silk and covered with violet quilts. Nikki's chamber. *His* Nikki's! He smiled, breathing deeply, catching the scent of familiar perfume. Lattice watched, bemused, while Jules went to the bed and caressed its silken hangings, running his hands over the bed's little pillows and smelling them. She understood men's moods and strange appetites and noted a change in Jules's breathing. Then she saw a strange smirk on Jules's face and took a step back, chilled to the bone by his expression.

"You're not at all like her," Jules said, observing her thoroughly and stripping her clothes with his hot gaze. "You're well-seasoned, she is not."

"Monsieur Cocteau, I don't understand."

"I'll wager you've pleased others, men who've never had quality."

She wanted to slap his face, but she stood still, even when he grabbed her and kissed her deeply. "You're hurting me," she moaned. Jules spun her around and caught her by the neck, guiding her to the bed and pushing her down.

"Whoring wench!" he said cruelly, unbuckling his belt and undoing his breeches. Lattice pulled herself up, easing her way to the side of the bed, eyes wide with fear. Jules breathed like a mad dog, his desire for Nikki having taken its toll on him.

Only minutes later Jules came downstairs buttoning his trousers, and knocked on the library door. Moses showed Jules inside his master's room reluctantly, apprehensively, all the while thinking what he'd do if Jules made one false move. He'd heard a commotion upstairs before and alerted his master at once; he'd heard the horses and coach, too. They'd both known Jules was in the house. "The devil's back," Alexandre had remarked as they watched while Jules went to the gallery. They'd been waiting for Jules to come down the stairs, knock on the door. The enemy had a helper inside the house and they had known it was Lattice. But they didn't know the poor girl was dead.

"Show Satan in, my good man." Alexandre watched as Jules entered the room and walked to its center to eye the book-lined walls, plainly uncertain of what he'd do if Jules attacked him. Jules set a lantern on the table beside Alexandre's bed and looked down at him. Alexandre lay still in his heavily draped bed, his eyes closed in feigned sleep.

"Master, we have company," Moses said softly. Jules waited cautiously, waiting for servants of all sizes to leap out of the dark and take him, giant dogs called to attack, gun-fire . . . But only silence and the sound of rain beating against the windows filled the room.

"Wake him!" Jules commanded. "Or I shall have to kill him where he sleeps."

Moses found it difficult to hold his tongue as he shook his master vigorously. Alexandre moaned and stirred, controlling his rage with clenched fists beneath the sheets, his heart pounding with hatred. Satan had returned to take what was left of his earth, he told himself . . . the dark halls of Racemont. Have faith, he prayed. Good would overcome evil in the end. Alexandre opened his eyes with what seemed great effort. "Moses?" he asked in a weak voice.

"Monsieur Cocteau from the islands," Moses said, his eyes conveying other information. Jules pushed aside the bedding and gripped the mahogany neck of an ancient hound statue. Alexandre breathed like a dying man, his face ashen, his eyes sunken hollows, cheeks unshaven, covers drawn to his chin. "What do you want, Jules?" he managed.

"Racemont, of course!" was the reply. "I've had the rest. Your precious wife, your father's mistress, your servant." Jules laughed almost hysterically. "The place is no good to you now, is it? Anyone can see you're as good as dead."

Alexandre thought of the son he'd buried after the Jubilee, his wife's premature labor brought on by the devil who stood over him. "You'll have to kill me," Alexandre said low, the muscles in his throat burning.

"Help you out of your misery, you mean?" Jules chuckled.

"After a few answers."

"Why not. You have until the dawn. Ask away."

"The night of my wedding in Pennsylvania."

" 'Twas a night I shall never forget, thanks to you." Jules snickered. "What a fresh piece I had in your absence, doctor. 'Twas clever of me to arrange it, eh?"

Alexandre trembled, thinking he might explode if he couldn't throttle the devil. *Control*, he cautioned himself. "You mean you were the one who started the fire?"

"Exactly!" Jules was proud. "I set it as a means to have Nikki."

Alexandre cringed, closing his eyes to recall the tortured faces of the souls who'd died that night because of the lust of a madman. Sucking in his breath, his fingers ached to choke Jules, his own blood.

"You're angry, aren't you? I can see it in your eyes. Save your strength, doctor. What happened that night was only natural, a communion of need, you might say. You couldn't satisfy her, so I simply obliged. You should be thanking me. 'Tis I who broke her in for you. *Oui*, she kicked and screamed, but that's not unusual considering my size. Before I finished she was pleading for more."

Alexandre's eyes burned, the agony of Jules's words sapping his strength. How could he delay killing the devil another second? Jules was still talking, going on about how he'd taken Dominique the day of the Jubilee, explicit details of his filthy rutting. Alexandre chose to think of other things then. Jules lying in a pool of blood, Jules's rotting corpse eaten by carrion birds.

"Savannah, Jules, what happened there?"

"Ah, Savannah, the pesthole of Georgia." Jules laughed, enjoying his chronicle of events. "Your dear wife came looking for me and found me with Cat. Jealous wench, your

Nikki. She became furious and we argued. I told her I was going back to Martinique and she pleaded with me to take her with me. I told her I needed money before we could make the voyage and she suggested a ransom. All would have been well if you hadn't come along. Nikki and I were about to run away together when I fell and broke my leg.''

"So you did break some bones?" Alexandre chuckled.

The doors of the library opened slowly and Desiree looked inside. "Who's that man, papa?"

Pleasantly surprised, Jules eyed the young beauty who bore a strong resemblance to her mother. "What have we here? Another delectable Chastain?"

Desiree pranced to her father's bedside and past Jules. "Are you all right, papa?" She thought her father had taken a turn for the worse, his face deathlike. Alexandre returned his daughter's concerned gaze uneasily, aware her presence had complicated matters. "Why are you here, Desiree? Why aren't you in the village with Mrs. Yarborough?"

"Because I was worried about you, papa. Did you think I'd leave you here alone with mother gone?"

Jules took in the domestic scene bemusedly, uncertain as to what it meant, but interested in the young maiden. Already a beauty, the young Chastain lady's manner was refreshing to him. Dressed in rich brown, she was quite fetching with black curls and wild wisps of hair that danced about her face and neck. "What's your name, mademoiselle?"

"Desiree," she said. "I might ask you the same."

"Jules Cocteau of Martinique and Paris." Jules bowed, thinking her spirited and a fine replacement for her mother. "I'm an old friend of the family."

"Is that so, papa?"

Alexandre knew he must protect Desiree at any cost, trying to scheme a way to get her out of the house and safely away. "*Oui*, Desiree. Jules and I go back a long way. Please leave us now, my daughter."

Frowning undecidedly, Desiree lifted her skirts and moved to leave the room. "I'll be upstairs if you want me, papa. Good night."

Even devils have to relieve themselves, Alexandre discovered, and when Jules stepped outside, the doctor spoke quickly to Moses. "If my plan backfires, take Desiree and Mrs. Yarborough to Savannah." Moses nodded, thinking his master's plan had better work. He had none of his own. "See Myron Smith in Savannah," Alexandre said low. "He has the necessary papers to free you and my brother, Jacques."

"Bless you, doctor," Moses said with dampened eyes.

Alexandre sank back on the pillows to wait and Moses blinked rapidly to dispel the tears that clung to his lashes. What was taking Jules so long? Had he followed Desiree upstairs? Alexandre shuddered. Then the door opened and Jules herded Desiree into the room, her hands behind her back.

"Papa," she sniffed. Alexandre understood when he saw his daughter's eyes red from crying. Every muscle in his body tightened, his heart pumping blood at a frenzied rate to prepare him for what he must do. If Jules had touched the girl he'd make him suffer beyond belief, Alexandre promised. Gritting his teeth, he noted that the girl's dress was unruffled, her hair in place.

"Make him go away, papa, please."

"Your father can't help you because he's as good as dead." Jules laughed and Desiree broke free, running to her father's bedside, tears streaming down her cheeks. Moses clenched his fists and Alexandre silently conveyed a command with his eyes. *Not now, my friend, not yet!*

"Come, Miss Chastain," Moses said, offering Desiree his arm.

"The girl stays!" Jules roared. "You may go, old man, after you've brought me a bottle." Moses nodded and left the room while Jules eyed Desiree hungrily.

Moses closed the door behind him and leaned against its cool panels for support, eyes wide with indecision. What could he do to help the doctor and save the girl from the lustful devil, he wondered? Then Mrs. Yarborough stepped out of the shadows.

"Yar!" Moses gasped. "What are you doing here?"

"I came with Desiree," she said. "Take him his bottle and quickly. I've prepared him a good one." The servant woman winked gleefully.

"Holy God, woman, whose side are you on?"

"The doctor's, of course. Do as I say, this once!"

Having no better plan, Moses saw the smile on the old woman's wrinkled mouth. The bottle held red Madeira and Moses pressed it close to his heart. 'Twas more than wine if he knew the Tory witch, a female capable of murdering her own babe in its sleep.

"About time!" Jules growled as Moses slipped back into the library and presented Jules with the Madeira. Moses opened the bottle and poured a sparkling decanter full, handing Jules a glass with shaking hands. "Give it to your master," Jules said. Clamping his mouth shut, Moses did as directed, taking the decanter to Alexandre and pouring some of the wine into a pewter goblet. "Drink it!" Jules said fiercely.

Alexandre saw fear brimming in Moses's eyes as he took a small sip of the wine.

"All of it!" Jules said. "Every last drop!"

Moses held the cup for Alexandre while the doctor drank down the bitter stuff.

"Now we wait," Jules said, grabbing the decanter and sniffing its contents, setting the bottle down on the table in the center of the room with a bang. Moses stood motionless, fear gripping his pounding heart. Had he just poisoned his beloved master? And if he had, how could he stand idly by and wait for the poor man to die?

The minutes seemed to hang as if time had stopped and then there was lightning and a great crash of thunder, hard rain pelting the shutters as a coach-and-six made its way up the broad avenue of sand. Jules's eyes raked Desiree's form, his appetite for a woman unappeased.

"A coach approaches!" Moses yelled, drawing Jules's attention away from the young woman. Jules went to the windows with quickening breath, his aspirations for Chastain wealth having turned to lust. Racemont would be his in a matter of moments, and everything that went with it.

Hounds barked and howled together from the kennels. Jules cautiously turned his back on the occupants of the room to look into the darkness. A coach drew up outside the grand hall, its fine steeds' flesh atremble as it came to a halt before the main entrance.

"Your Arabs have arrived, Alexandre. In time for your burial."

Alexandre's brain had dulled, vaguely recalling correspondence from France concerning six black Arabs and a magnificent carriage for his wife, open so she could view the sky, a large compartment for hounds beneath its seats, and a door bearing the Chastain family crest. Fit for a queen, his solicitor in Paris had written him. Alas, the queen had fled from Camelot. "Dom . . . Dom . . ."

"Papa!" Desiree screamed, seeing that her father couldn't speak her mother's name. Alexandre felt his tongue grow thick, his pulse slowing as the poisoned wine took effect. Dear God, he was dying! In their effort to save him, the servants had poisoned him!

"Seems papa is dying." Jules snickered, standing over the weakening Alexandre to observe his breathing. "Such loyalty in a servant touches me."

" 'Twas meant for you!" Mrs. Yarborough screeched, bursting into the room when she heard the girl's cries.

"Oliver . . ." Alexandre murmured.

"Oliver? Who's that?"

"His pet owl," Moses replied.

"Pet owl?" Jules howled. "His bird is that dear to him? How can we deny him his last request? Fetch the bird for him quickly."

"I'll have to open the windows to let Oliver in, monsieur. May I have your permission?"

Jules smiled, pleased with the way the black man had asked his permission. "*Oui*. Never let it be said that Jules Cocteau denied a dying man his wish."

Moses went to the tall curving windows that soared from the floor to the ceiling and opened one, letting in the cool brisk air and rain. Daylight was late in coming and Jules followed Moses to have a look into the darkness. "I see no bird," he complained. Just then the sound of great flapping wings caught his ear and he covered his head with his hands, stepping back to see a bird of extraordinary size swoop through the windows and fly to Alexandre's bed, alighting atop a post.

The owl screeched and ruffled his drenched feathers, shaking out his dampened brown and white wings and blinking huge golden eyes, his sharp talons clamped to wood. Jules looked at the feathered creature of the night who winked back at him.

"Now that you have your owl, you can die in peace, Alexandre." Jules went around the bed to fall into Alexandre's leather chair. " 'Tis too much. 'Twas not his wife or his gold he wanted, but his fine feathered friend." Laughing so hard he wiped tears from his cheeks, Jules roared until he choked.

"The man who had everything ends up with his bird. How amusing!"

Alexandre watched Moses herd the women from the room. Jules laughed uproariously, his back to Alexandre, the doctor slipped from his bed and drew the flintlock from beneath his mattress. Jules sat rocking in his chair as Alexandre stood as best he could, the gun in his hand catching the candle's glow.

"Did you really think I'd let you walk into my house without a fight?" Alexandre was the one smiling now and Jules stopped laughing, his face drained of color. His eyes opened wide at the sight of the weapon. Alexandre snapped his fingers and a monstrous hound leaped through the windows, followed by another and another, gray hounds, tawnies, blacks, silvers, all crouching and circling the room at Alexandre's command.

"Sit, my friends, and meet our guest." Alexandre's voice was weak, yet in command. Galliard, King Lear, Hamlet, King Richard, and the two gold-colored sheepdogs from France took their places at their master's side, lips curled in distrust, their sharp white fangs bared. Galliard snapped and stood snarling at the head of the pack, hair abristle, and each dog stepped forward one step at a time, like wolves eyeing a tender spring lamb.

"They wish to avenge Macbeth," Alexandre said. "The hound you killed in the carriage house the day you ravaged my wife." Alexandre snapped his fingers and the dogs growled and barked, their huge heads cocked to one side, chests hung low, rib cages taut, ready for the attack. " 'Twas not the only thing that died that day because of you, you murderer!" Alexandre cried.

Jules moved and Galliard lunged forward. Alexandre snapped his fingers and the dog stood at bay. "I wouldn't do that again, if I were you, Jules. The dog's been trained to kill and he's eager to prove he's learned his lesson well. We knew you'd be back once your money ran out. We simply prepared."

"Don't let them bite me," Jules murmured.

"Not yet." Alexandre chuckled. Standing barefoot on the carpet, every muscle in the doctor's chest and arms had come alive. The bottom half of his body was clad in gray leggings. He'd suffered a long illness, and his eyes and face sagged from a severe loss of weight. He called and Moses appeared at the door, two more giant dogs padding into the room, Romeo and his mate. Romeo was old, but he growled just the same, and his mate's thunderous snarl was enough to make the hair stand up on Jules's thick neck. At the snap of Alexandre's fingers, two hounds crept forward on the floor, their jaws drooling to taste Jules's flesh. The door was open and a steady line of hounds slipped through the door, pacing lions entering the ring for the prey, heads down, shining eyes fixed on the man who trembled like a cornered rabbit. Twenty-seven dogs in all.

The door closed and the bolt slid home as Moses locked the library from outside. Jules brought his hand to his mouth as the windows slid closed from outside, the sound of boards nailed in place causing him to moan. "God's soul, *non!*"

Alexandre smiled, his laugh almost hearty. "I can laugh now. I didn't know you believed in God, Jules. Come now, don't tell me you're afraid of my fleabitten hounds? Not the stud of the West Indies? Stand up!"

Jules did as he was bid, pulling himself up by the bed hangings. "Alexandre, my cousin, surely you can't forget we were raised as brothers. My father loved you, my mother, too. Your father wanted us together from the beginning. Can't you remember that now?"

"My father died because of you!"

"You jest." Jules's eyes bulged. The hounds barked and growled, their noise deafening as they danced about on impatient pads.

"One false move and they'll have you for supper, Jules. I made certain they'd be hungry when you came calling. They're ravenous now!" Alexandre mocked.

"You're dying," Jules said. " 'Tis too late for you."

"You'd better pray to the prince of darkness I survive, cousin," Alexandre cried back. "If I fall my hounds will tear your flesh from limb to limb and you'll never leave this room alive." He leaned against the bed, his strength ebbing. He waved the pistol. "Now drop on your knees. Beg the way those poor women did before you ravaged and butchered them! Before I shoot your pride and joy and make you worthless as a man."

"You wouldn't, you can't!" Jules cried.

Alexandre laughed. "I'm a surgeon, Jules. Trained in Paris in the ancient art of castration."

"Please, I beg you!" Jules fell down on his knees and sobbed. "Don't do this horrible deed, cousin."

Alexandre's hand wavered as he realized he'd had enough.

He held tight to the bedpost, thinking he might die before he competely humiliated and took care of Jules. Trying to lift the weapon, he found his strength and senses fleeing him. The flintlock fell to the floor with a clang and the hounds went wild, unable to wait no longer. Leaping from their places onto the man who knelt in the center of the floor, they tore into his flesh before the bolt could be removed from the door.

Dominique rode home through the wind and the rain. Exhausted, half frozen with cold, she saw lights in the mansion in the distance flicker through the swirling storm. Lightning flashed and she cut a sharp path through a peach orchard, galloping her horse across vast stretches of water. Then hooves skidded to a halt in the granite courtyard. Dominique flung herself down to the ground and looked up at the great sprawling hall, a vision of the first time she'd seen Racemont flashing across her memory.

Having reached the twin stairways, she broke into a run and climbed the steps to the front portico, taking a deep breath before she went inside. The house smelled of dampness and medicine. Where were the hounds, the servants, the children?

Hurrying through the foyer to the parlor, she noted the empty space above the mantel where her portrait was missing. Alexandre had taken it down, she thought, her worry surging as she followed the dark corridor to the library and pushed open the door. The room was dark, save for the white bed hangings draped atop the huge carved bed she recognized as her husband's. Then she heard Olvier's beating wings and the owl hoot a greeting.

"Missus Chastian, you're home, praise dah Lord!"

Dominique's heart pounded, the sight of Marie kneeling beside her husband's bed alarming. "Mère, what's happened, where is everyone?"

Desiree came out of the shadows. "Mother, oh, mother, I'm so glad you're home."

Dominique looked at her daughter, something in her face making her throw her arms around the girl and hug her tight. "Desiree, my daughter, what's happened?"

"Oh, mother, I've been so wrong, so very wrong. Can you ever forgive me? I didn't know the truth . . . I believed Yar and I almost . . ."

"Aye, of course I forgive you, and you must forgive me. Now, where is your father?"

"He fell from that wild Irish stallion and that horrible man from the islands came here and tried to kill him—"

"Dear God, nay. Where is he? Is your father . . ."

"He's been poisoned, ma'am," Mrs. Yarborough said as she left the room. "Ye can blame me for it, too."

"Poisoned!"

" 'Tis a long story, little sister. Alexandre fell, but he's going to be all right, I believe. Then Jules came here . . . but that's all over, too. The whole tale can wait for later. Alexandre needs you now." Jacques smiled as he left the room and Dominique attempted to piece the fragmented news together as she went to her husband's bed to sit beside him. He was pale and she barely recognized him, he'd lost so much weight.

"Chérie, is it really you?"

Shivering at the sound of her husband's voice, Dominique knew she loved him still, seeing him tall and tan that first day in Georgia, his creamy shirt billowing in the wind as he surveyed the trace to Racemont. How old he looked now. His face was lined and there was a deep furrow between his brows. His red-gold hair was streaked with silver. Had she ever known the man she'd married, loved him as he had loved her? The way she loved Coosa?

" 'Tis I, your wife. I've come home." She ran her fingers over his face, holding her cheek to his chest and pressing her lips to his heart.

"God knows I've missed you." He touched her hair with his hand, never looking at her, his voice pained and weak as she patted his hand.

"How are you? Mrs. Yarborough said you were poisoned."

"She gave me something to save me—she never meant me to die." He smiled. "The poor woman nearly did me in. Never fear. Your husband will be alive a while longer."

"Thank God." She couldn't ask for more. His words had reached the depths of her heart and she knew she'd hurt him for the last time. His eyes opened and the flames that had once burned there were out, flames of adoration and devotion, hot fires of love.

"Why did you leave me? Where have you been?"

She couldn't tell him she'd been with Coosa. The Indian was

dead in his mind and dead he'd stay for now. "I went off, 'tis all. I rode to Savannah to be alone, to sort things out."

"With Jacques?"

"Nay, not your brother, Alexandre. By myself . . . for reflection."

"What have you done to us, to yourself?" He studied her eyes, searching for the truth.

"I've made mistakes. But I love you, Alexandre. I think I always have. It took me a long time to realize that."

He smiled as if he were truly pleased. "Our daughter, Angel?"

"In Pennsylvania with her grandfather. Safe in Germantown until you're well enough to see her."

"Desiree?"

"Here in the house, concerned for you. She acted like she was glad to see me."

"She was. She's had a bad time of it, too."

She wanted to comfort him in any way she could, bringing her arms about his neck and trying to sound gay. "I'm back now. I've finally had my fill of roaming. I want to take care of you and my girls, my family of horses and hounds."

"*Non,*" he said low. "You were never meant for that. I should never have brought you to Georgia. I know that now. Alas, 'twas a lesson learned too late." He took her hand and brought it to his lips. "I want you to go back up north and take Desiree with you, *chérie*, back to Pennsylvania with our little Angel. Leave Racemont and make a new life for yourself. 'Tis what I want. 'Tis what must be."

"Nay, I want to be with you! I belong here, 'tis my home now!"

"Perhaps one day Racemont will be your home, but until then I want you to go home. To your home in Pennsylvania. Promise me you'll go and stay with Angel. Promise me."

She would have promised him anything then. The love she held for Coosa . . . her life . . . anything to make up for the unhappiness she'd caused him. "I promise, my husband. When you're well, I'll go away."

Dozens of pale blue butterflies, the color of the uppermost heavens, fluttered around the perfumed white roses Dominique cut from the rose garden. Twelve months had come and gone since the mistress of Racemont had returned home. Spring storms had caused the Yellow River to overflow its banks and Merino sheep grazed alongside well-bred horses. Young foals romped at their mothers' sides in green fields that stretched all the way to the mountain. They lifted their heads as a fine French chariot, drawn by four black Arabs, turned into the circular drive of the southern plantation.

"Your carriage, little sister." Jacques held his arm for Dominique. Dressed in a black traveling dress, her cape lined in green silk to match her eyes, Jacques thought his sister-in-law the most uniquely beautiful woman he had ever known.

"Dear Jacques, you know well I hate wheels."

"*Oui.*" He chuckled, waving the carriage on and raising his eyes to signal someone she could not see. Dominique held tightly to Jacques's arm, watching the ornate carriage rumble by, piled high with her trunks, the Spanish guitar, the precious jewels her husband had given her, her female mastiff, and a puppy from the two sheepdogs from France.

"I don't want to go, Jacques. Yet I know I must."

"Alexandre wants it this way." Jacques patted her hand. She was thinner now, having lost weight taking care of Alexandre and nursing him back to health. She had looked after the house and reconciled with Desiree and Mrs. Yarborough. Coosa Tustennuggee had stayed away until the time was right, aware that Alexandre had nearly died and was on the long road back to recovery. The days had passed for everyone, as time does. Aye, there were nights of loneliness and longing, guilt and tears. Dominique was not the same spoiled, foolish young woman Alexandre Chastain had brought to Georgia, but a wise and kind woman everyone had come to love.

And so time had flowed like a river. Alexandre had taken Desiree off to France to live with relatives and attend a young ladies' school in Paris. Mrs. Yarborough had been given passage back to England and Jacques and Moses had obtained their freedom from slavery. Dominique tried not to look at the sad faces of the friends who surrounded her, the eyes of loyal servants, horses, and hounds, all looking on with shining, moist eyes.

"These halls will never be the same without you, little sister. You know you'll always be welcome here."

"Aye, I know. Take care of the animals for me—I know you will, dearest Jacques. I'll be back one day."

"I shall keep the place in readiness for you and your

daughters' return." Jacques turned his face away so she couldn't see the tears that reddened his eyes. Then Dominique heard the thunder of horses and looked up to see a handsome dark-skinned man sitting atop a white stallion, his fine bronzed body arrayed in buckskin, and a paisley turban. His black and white egret feathers stirred on the wind.

"Coosa." She gasped so softly no one heard but Jacques, her summer eyes conveying the words she dare not speak aloud. The Creek king threw back his scarlet mantel and dismounted in a clean leap, coming to her with outstretched arms.

"Dom-ma-nique." Coosa motioned for George Limpton to bring up the Andalusian, harnessed in black leather and Spanish silver. Red and white feathers billowed in the wind from the beast's plaited forelock. "Good-bye, father," Coosa said in Creek to Jacques. Jacques took his son's hand and brought it to his heart, embracing Coosa, then watching as the Creek lifted Dominique into her saddle.

"Where to?" Jacques queried, watching his son swing up onto his steed. Coosa guided his pony forward and looked back at the woman he had sworn he would spend the rest of his days with. "To the great Smokies and north. To Pennsylvania to reunite the mother with her child."

"Where to then, Coosa Tustennuggee?"

"To wherever the gods take me, father." Coosa smiled. "Wherever love is."

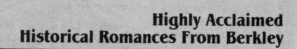